The Master Mechanic

The Master Mechanic

I. G. BROAT

ATHENEUM
New York 1979

Library of Congress Cataloging in Publication Data

Broat, I. G.
  The master mechanic.

  I. Title.
PZ4.B86342Mas 1979 [PR6052.R457] 823'.9'14 78-14518
  ISBN 0-689-10935-0

Designed by Harry Ford
Composition by Connecticut Printers Incorporated, Hartford, Connecticut
Printed and bound by American Book–Stratford Press,
Saddle Brook, New Jersey
First American Edition

*To Alfred Salkin and Anthony Salkin, without whose
knowledge and experience, generously imparted,
this book would have remained unwritten.*

*And always
to my wife, Linda, for her patience.*

The Master Mechanic

Steubenville, 1968

She had the sweetest, tightest little ass he'd seen in a long time. He watched the honey-blonde move around the near-empty restaurant before she came across to hand him a menu. "Just coffee," he said, not reaching out to take it.

She hesitated. "You're not eating?" she said.

"No."

She was under strict orders not to serve people who came in off the street and messed up the table linen for the price of a cup of coffee. "We're serving only meals, sir." She spoke as politely as she could. "There's a cafeteria across the street where you can get a cup of coffee."

Somehow this man was different from the local trash. His eyes bored into hers knowingly, as if he could read her mind. A flush of embarrassment began on her face. "I don't like cafeterias," he said softly. He clearly had no intention of moving.

She glanced around. It was a quiet time of day and she hadn't seen the boss for about an hour. Perhaps the guy would drink his coffee and go before Luigi turned up. Then she noticed the ten-dollar bill that appeared miraculously, as if from nowhere. Suddenly it was in her hand.

"Just coffee," he said. "You can keep the change."

In the Veneto a ten-spot tip was an occasion for celebration. "Yes, sir." She wheeled away smartly, knowing what she intended to do—if Luigi came in she'd make out a check for the cheapest platter in the house. She returned with a hot pot of coffee and fussed around the table a little. She gave him her best smile. "The pasta is very good here, sir. Won't you try a little?"

"No, thank you. Are you a local girl, Laura?" As she leaned across him, he read the name off the badge pinned to her ample left breast.

"Yes, sir. I've lived in Steubenville all my life. You here on business?"

"Sort of."

For an old guy he had enormous charm. He was well into his fifties, but he had the bearing of a young man. The skin on his aquiline features was clear, and only a small wrinkling about the mouth gave any indication of age. A strange mark across his forehead, transparently whiter than the surrounding pink flesh, marred his appearance. The blue eyes were attractive, though, and kind of made up for it. *His hair gave him away—guys didn't slick their hair down these days.* But it was his hands that took her attention. They were the most beautiful male hands she'd ever seen, with long, expressive fingers and carefully manicured nails.

Laura's attention was distracted by the arrival of a couple. She seated them, ordered their food, and returned to her station to sort cutlery while she waited for the order. She stole a glance at the old guy, who appeared preoccupied, looking through the window at people passing by in the street outside. She'd known at first sight he wasn't from this town, or anywhere around. He was dressed with a quiet, conservative elegance she hadn't seen before. *She'd be willing to bet the ten-spot his suit was custom-made, maybe even the silk shirt.* Probably he was one of those rich businessmen from Shaker Heights, over in Cleveland. She'd had a thing about Cleveland ever since she met Elliot K. Branner when she was helping out at the Union Bank dinner. He had class, too. At first she'd been an uncertain partner in that surreptitious weekend when Elliot's wife was cruising the West Indies. Then she'd surrendered herself to the luxury of his distinctive, echoing Cleveland mansion, reveling in the sensation of drawing her bath water from gold-plated faucets. Elliot had called her twice since, but she'd never gone back. Somehow she couldn't reconcile her ambitions to surrendering her body to a middle-aged man. *Even so, she had to admit she got a kick out of getting laid by the occasional good-looking transient who took her fancy. If Floyd ever found out, he'd kill her for certain.* She was really looking forward to marrying Floyd. They'd been saving hard to get a home together so she could give up slinging hash in this guinea dinery.

The couple's order arrived and she busied herself serving them. When she turned around, the interesting old guy looked as if he was ready to go. She walked over. "Is there anything else I can get you, sir?"

"No, that's it." He got to his feet.

"Maybe you'll look in another time. We have some swell food. Tuesdays and Fridays are pasta specials."

"I'll be leaving town in a few minutes."

"Next time you're in Steubenville, then."

"There won't be a next time, Laura." Behind his smile was a haunting sadness that did something to her insides. *Funny, an old man like that.*

"Oh, you can't be sure." She laughed.

"Yeah, I'm sure."

She paused, uncertain how to reply. She took the easy way out, as usual. "Well, have a nice evening, sir," she said lamely.

"Thank you."

As he turned, a crazy, irrational thought took hold of her. *Just once more she wanted to see those beautiful hands so that later, when she had nothing better to do, she could dream they were attached to Floyd. And instead of the calloused, hard skin and split fingernails that habitually explored her, she could imagine those artistic fingers leisurely caressing the mounds and crevices of her soft flesh.* Again a thrill started deep in the pit of her stomach, and she gave a small shiver. ". . . Sir."

"Yes?" He turned back.

4

"I—I suppose you're here on business at the Mill?" The words spilled out. How foolish they must have sounded.

"No. Nothing to do with the Mill."

"Would you mind telling me—I know I shouldn't ask—what sort of work you're in?"

For a moment he was expressionless, then the haunting smile slowly crept back across his face. "It's a long time since anyone asked me that question. No, I don't mind telling you, Laura." Strange, he'd almost forgotten himself what he was. It had been so long since he'd practiced his art.

She waited, her flush deepening. He took a long time to reply and seemed to search within himself for the words.

"I'm a mechanic," he said quietly. He turned and was gone.

For a moment she stood, staring at the closed door. *Just another nut, after all. The world was full of them. Jeez, working in this place you met them all.* She dismissed the man from her mind when an irritable voice behind her called for service.

Tony Vitale walked a little faster, feeling the chill of the Ohio October evening through his clothes. He'd become accustomed to warmer climes. He reached the barrier where the railroad crossed now-quiet Market Street and, slowly and deliberately, stepped out into the middle of the tracks. He stood, staring up and down the line, straining his vision along the empty ribbon stretching away in each direction. Then, from far away, perhaps from beyond the valley, came the baleful echo of a train's howl, and the familiar sound, buried deep in his subconscious, triggered off his memory, instantaneously transporting him back to his youth. To the times when he'd stood in this same spot, gazing up and down the tracks, wondering what magic was to be found where they went, to the mysterious outside world. The world outside Steubenville.

Then the horn changed its note, and he realized with a start that an automobile, waiting to cross the tracks was honking at him. He moved over and, as the car went past, bouncing across the lines, the driver lowered his window just long enough to shout, "Goddamn idiot," before roaring off.

He turned and began walking back. He should have known that returning here wouldn't help solve his dilemma. And now that he *was* here, he couldn't imagine what it was he'd expected to find.

The way the town had changed after all these years? That didn't interest him.

The inspiration of his youth? He must be turning into an old fool if that was what he sought.

To escape his fate? He was committed. Totally and irrevocably—there was no way out. To hope he could break with them was nothing but an unrealizable dream. They owned him body and soul. There was nowhere to run, nowhere to hide.

Nowhere in the whole wide world.

The rented Continental stood alone in the near-empty parking lot of the shopping plaza. He got in, fired up the engine, and turned the heat on full blast. Now his mind, too, was in Cleveland—Hopkins Airport, where the outfit's Learjet waited to transport him to Nevada.

Get the hell out of this jerk mill town.

The road before him curved away into the remnants of the setting sun, shafting red through ragged clouds on the horizon. He stole a glance in the rearview mirror as the lights of Steubenville disappeared around the bend behind him. Forever. He allowed himself a small, sad smile. Perhaps it had been necessary for him to return so that he could be reborn.

Into bondage.

BOOK ONE Steubenville

CHAPTER ONE

It was Saturday. The last working day of the week. Perhaps the last day he would work for a long time to come. A cold panic clutched at Bruno Vitale's heart and he cursed himself for being a fool.

"Good morning, Bruno."

"Good morning, Signor Boccardi. Please, allow me." He moved quickly to take the keys from his employer's hand and unlocked the door of the barber shop, then stood aside respectfully to allow Vincenzo Boccardi to enter first.

"Have you been waiting long, Bruno? You look cold. Am I late this morning?"

"No, Signor Boccardi, you're not late. I'm maybe a little early myself." Bruno busied himself immediately drawing the shop blinds.

"How is it we're back to *Signor* Boccardi? I been Vincenzo the last six months, at least."

"I think a person should show respect for his employer—the one who provides a roof over his head and food in the mouths of his children." Bruno said it quickly, and was sorry as soon as the words were out of his mouth. They sounded too patronizing. His hands were shaking slightly as he tied on his apron.

"If you insist'a calling me *Signor* Boccardi, I call you *Signor* Vitale. Our customers gonna think they walk into some classy department store by mistake."

"I'm sorry, I didn' mean to sound so formal." Bruno glanced at Vincenzo to see if he was displeased. He didn't observe the slight smile on the other's face as he turned away.

A week ago he'd given up his job at the Wheeling Steel Mill, the job that had fed him, his wife, Maria, and their two growing sons for the nine years of their new life in America. He'd given it up because he longed to become a barber again, just as he'd always been back in Salerno. Hardly a moment of those nine years in the dust and sweat of the Wheeling Mill had gone by when he hadn't longed to be back practicing his art in a cool, mirrored barber shop, its air scented with soap and shampoo amid the musk of male pretentiousness. For he was an artist with scissors, razor, and comb, of that he was certain. He'd sorely missed the small joys of the working day, the swapping of tidbits of gossip with customers. During those nine years, one of his few extravagances had been his fortnightly visit to Vincenzo Boccardi's barber shop on Adam Street. He could hardly believe his ears when Vincenzo had told him chair number three would be vacant.

"You offering me the job?" Bruno had asked incredulously.

"Well, must be a thousand times you tell me how you give your eye teeth to get outa that mill into a barber shop."

"I mean it."

"Here'sa chance. I need an experience barber."

"I doan know how to thank you."

"Course, if you get the job permanent depend on a week's trial. You appreciate, Bruno, we discuss your days as a barber in Salerno many times, but I never see you work."

"Of course. You won't be disappointed."

Bruno couldn't believe his luck. There must have been a dozen ex-barbers in Steubenville, many with no job of any sort, who'd have considered themselves blessed by the Virgin Maria had they been offered chair number three. In the exhilaration of the moment, he'd given his notice at the Mill. And just as soon regretted his actions, when he realized he'd burned his bridges. He worked out his notice with increasing anxiety. He'd become so accustomed to the line-up of sullen-eyed, patient immigrants awaiting work at the Mill employment office that they had, long ago, become part of the dust-laden landscape. Now, as his own employment there neared its end, he examined the line each morning with morbid interest, wondering which of these fortunate individuals would be stepping into his shoes.

Today he'd know his fate. Saturday evening ended his week of probation, and the barber shop owner would give his decision. He steeled himself to work through the day. It was moments like this when he doubted the wisdom of their traumatic move to the New World. Here in the cold winters of this far-off Ohio valley he'd suffered and aged as he had never suffered back in Italy. Somehow the abject poverty of his origins had been natural and bearable. Back home there had always been a few days' work to be found for someone as industrious as he, regardless of how bad things got. There was always the sun to provide light and warmth. There was almost always food to eat—some cheese, a little pasta, a few olives, and a glass of wine could be had for next to nothing. Here, more was expected of a man.

Bruno wasn't to know that Vincenzo Boccardi had made his decision earlier in the week, when he'd perceived the joy Bruno took in his work. Vincenzo was himself a family man, unremarkably among Italian families the father of eight children, and well aware of the terrifying responsibility of providing for hungry mouths in a desperate 1936. He saw no point in prolonging Bruno's agony until the end of the day.

"Bruno, we talk before the rest arrive. You wish to know what I have decide—if you stay or go."

"Yes, sir." Bruno stood at attention by his chair, bracing himself. He offered up a small, silent prayer. The lines that had appeared on his face in the years at the Mill deepened. Nowadays he had the demeanor of a man ten years older than his forty-five years.

"I'm satisfy with your work—I want you know that. You're a first-class barber,

10

just like you say. I been watching your cup and I see by your tips they're happy with the service." A flood of relief came over Bruno. It had been a calculated risk, throwing a few extra dimes into his cup each day. Hardly worth the loss of Bruno's trust. "Also important, you learn to speak the language. Some of our people, they wanna spend their lives making dumb-talk. Things changing around here—the old days are gone."

"I insist we speak English at home, for the sake of the children," Bruno said dutifully. "Does that mean I have the job?"

"Yes."

"I don't know how to thank you . . ." The lump in his throat prevented him from completing the sentence. He made an expansive gesture, holding out his hands to Vincenzo in supplication.

Vincenzo turned away, tears welling up in involuntary sympathy. "We Italians are too emotional," he said gruffly. "We gotta learn to behave more like men in this America."

Tony and Mokey Vitale set out on the mile-long walk along the dirt road home from school.

"They following?" Tony asked. He left it to his younger brother to look back over his shoulder.

"Nah, there's no sign of them." Mokey's legs pumped rapidly to enable him to keep pace with the long stride of the taller figure beside him. "Maybe they won't bother," he suggested archly.

"They'll bother," Tony said grimly. His gaze swept across the road ahead. "Keep your eyes peeled."

Tony was sixteen, an inch or two taller than average, with a bearing graceful beyond his years. It was already evident that he was to grow into a good-looking young man. As the elder son he continually justified being the apple of his father's eye. In Antonio Vitale were vested all the sublimations, the virtues and disappointments of the transposition of their family life to America, the compensations for trials and tribulations that dogged the otherwise unexceptional life of Bruno Vitale. It was a heavy burden for someone so young, but Tony was already demonstrating an admirable sense of responsibility, and his load was made lighter by the deep affection and enormous respect he held for his father.

Momo Vitale, known as Mokey, was one year younger. Just as an excess of fortune's good looks and refinements had been bestowed upon his brother, Mokey had been short-changed by his maker so that he was endowed with a grossness of Roman features. His bulky head and short arms and legs, attenuated to a long, thick body, were to maintain their disproportion throughout adolescence into his adult life. There was no compensation by way of mental ability, and his mind, in a way, matched his body; he was a misshapen entity, the very completeness of which held its own animal attraction. Just as he was physically out of proportion, his attitudes developed in such a way as to be always aggressively out of step with others. With the confidence of youth he, too, carried his burdens lightly. He also shared Tony's great respect for their father, although it was doubtful if he was capable of the depth of Tony's affection.

11

Both boys had worn a clean white collar every day of their school lives. Each morning their clothes, however threadbare, were brushed and neatly pressed by their mother, the fastidious Maria Vitale.

"You keeping watch?" Tony's words came as a sharp rebuke.

"Yeah, I'm looking out." Mokey stole a glance over his shoulder. "I ain't afraid of 'em," he said defiantly. "I can lick anyone in my class."

"I told you before, try using your head for a change. You keep fighting with everyone, you're gonna get the shit knocked outa you one of these days."

"I like fighting."

"You're a dope."

Tony's blue eyes betrayed his wariness as he strode along. There were lots of places where the Polaks could be lurking, in the shrubs and trees that lined the road ahead.

"I still dunno why they got so mad," Mokey complained, his breath coming in short, sharp bursts now. "We wasn't doing a thing—honest."

"It ain't me you gotta convince, it's them. Two guys find you in a book closet with their sister, they got a right to be suspicious."

"It was her idea, not mine," Mokey retorted. "That Inchka, she's nuts."

"Just what you imagine she had in mind? A little book reading in the dark?" Mokey made no reply. "Cause nothing happened, don't mean it wasn't going to."

"You got me wrong. It was nothing like that."

"Oh, yeah?"

"She wanted to tell me she's in love with me. Only she couldn't say it out in the daylight, where I could see her face."

It was stupid enough to be plausible. Mokey's guile hadn't yet developed to such a degree of refinement, Tony reasoned. He also knew the exception could be where girls were concerned—this was an area where Mokey's burgeoning experience had advanced beyond his. The older boy decided to reserve judgment.

"You jealous?" Mokey said it suddenly.

"What you talkin'?" Ordinarily Tony's English was good and contained little trace of his formative education in Italian, but he hadn't learned yet to extend his self-control to emotive situations. Evidently Mokey had touched a sensitive spot.

"You can have her if you like. I don't want her," Mokey offered. He added, by way of inducement, "She's real hot stuff."

"What makes you think I'm interested in Inchka?" Tony's guilty discomfort showed through his posture.

"I seen the way you look at her in school."

"I look at all the girls—so what?"

"Nothin'. Makes no difference to me. Just don't forget I offered."

"I don't want her either." Then he added, "I better straighten you out on one or two things." Tony's attempt to play the heavy had little conviction.

Their attention had wandered at a bad moment. The two fair-haired Polaks, square, sturdy brothers, rushed on them, one from each side of the dirt road. The Vitales' school books went flying, and an instant melee of thumping, yelling, pulling, and tearing raised a sudden cloud of dry dust. In the windless day it took only a few moments before the struggling boys could hardly be seen scuffling

12

within the dense brown curtain that their fighting generated. There was nowhere to flee; not that it would have occurred to them to do so. Tony and Mokey stood their ground and traded blow for blow.

Maria Vitale let out a shriek and recoiled at the vision confronting her across the porch of their wood-framed house. Her two dusty, torn, and bleeding sons staggered together through the doorway.

"Don't worry, Mama, it looks worse than it is." Tony tried to give her a reassuring smile, but it hurt to stretch his swollen lips. He prodded the bruised Mokey into a chair. The Polaks had made Mokey their target. A clump of his hair was missing and blood ran freely from what was now not merely a prominent, but a suspiciously misshapen, nose.

Maria, giving forth with a stream of alternately villifying and sympathetic Italian and English, ran to get towels and a bowl of water. Tony stood over her while she bathed her younger son's bruises. When the dirt was washed away, Mokey's face was a sorry sight. "How you let this happen? You the older one, you are responsible," Maria wailed at Tony.

"There was nothing I could do, Mama. It was the Polaks—they jumped us from behind a hedge."

"Why the Polaks suddenly decide to jump on you from a hedge? What you do they should be so angry?"

"Nothing, Mama. Honest."

"For nothing they jump on you from behind a hedge? Maybe you like to pull the other leg, huh? You better have a real excuse ready when you papa come home. He gonna be good and mad you let your young brother get beat up. Now go and clean yourself—you look disgusting."

Tony turned, pleased they got off so lightly, and went out to the kitchen.

Later, the two boys sat out on the porch, waiting for the sting to leave their wounds. Soon their father would return home from work. The sounds of Mama's activity in the kitchen and the piquant odors of the dinner she was preparing were somehow more reassuring than usual. Mokey took a deep breath through the pungent smell of balsam; the air whistled through his nose. "What you gonna tell Papa?" he ventured quietly.

"Same as I told Mama."

"He won't believe you—you better make up some story."

"No stories. Everyone knows the Polaks are kinda crazy. They're always trying to show how tough they are."

They lapsed into silence.

Tony spoke again. "Maybe you better tell me what really happened in that book closet."

Mokey's sideways glance told of his duplicity. It also served to gauge his brother's mood. "Like I told you, Inchka wanted to tell me she's in love with me." A moment later he decided Tony was in a receptive frame of mind. "I ask her to prove it."

"How?"

"I said, to prove she loves me, she gotta take off her bloomers."

"And did she?"

"Sure." Mokey's hand slid into his pocket and reappeared holding a pair of white cotton bloomers with elasticized waist and legs. His smile widened. "When her brothers pull her out of the closet, I hide them in my pocket."

"If they'd known about it, they'd have pulverized you. You better steer clear of that girl from now on."

"Yeah. She's all trouble."

But there was a glint of excitement in Mokey's eyes that told Tony he hadn't heard the last of the Polak girl.

CHAPTER TWO

Bruno regarded his elder son dourly across the breakfast table. "Am I making a mistake, or has school canceled summer vacation?" he asked.

Tony looked up in surprise. "No, Papa. Why you say that? This is the first day of the holiday."

"Then why you looking so down in the mouth?"

"Me? I'm O.K." He toyed with his boiled egg. "I'm just thinking."

"If thinking makes people so unhappy, maybe just as well I'm not so good at it, this thinking."

Tony reacted immediately, always defensive of and respectful toward his father. "Oh, you can think real good, Papa, when you want to." He glanced quickly across at Bruno to determine his mood, then took the plunge. "I'd like to get a job."

"What kinda job?" His father's eyes narrowed.

"A full-time job. Just for the summer vacation," he added quickly. "So I can earn some real dough, like the other guys my age."

"You have a job—your studies. That's your job."

"I won't stop my studies, Papa. I promise. I can do it in the evenings."

"And get yourself a second-rate education? No, a first-rate education, that's what you gonna have. You the ace of the school. I know—I get it straight from the horse's mouth. You forget, your teacher's a regular customer at the barber shop. I'm planning with Mr. Russell that you should go to college. He's preparing you. You got plenty of homework for the vacation, right?"

"I got a little extra," Tony agreed.

"Who knows—maybe one of these days you'll go to university? You could become a lawyer, or a doctor. You can do whatever you want with an education like that. The world at your feet. Times are hard and this no Italy—here a man gotta have an education, he wanna get on."

"I don't want to be no doctor or lawyer, Papa."

"Never mind. Get the education, that's the thing."

"I learned enough already."

"Nothin'—you don't know nothin', Tony. Take it from me, you got a lot to learn. Something I always wanted—to see my son, a Vitale, a college student."

14

"But we can't afford it, Papa."

"Let me worry about that," Bruno said sharply.

"I don't want you and Mama should have a hard time while I sit around in college."

"In your whole life, you remember a time when there was no bread on the table in this house? Answer me that question."

"No, Papa."

"So long as I am head of this family and these hands can hold scissors, there will always be bread on the table."

"I'll be seventeen when I go back to school. All the other guys are taking jobs. I'm gonna end up a class of one."

"Takes time to arrange a college education."

Tony tried a different tack. "My pal Skeeter gets a dollar a day helping out down at the Wharf. He says he can get me on his gang if I kick back ten cents to the foreman."

"I don't wanna hear about that," Bruno roared. "At your age there more important things to do than earn dollar a day."

Tony persisted. "If I go away to college, there'll be books to buy and my keep to pay for. How we gonna do it, Papa?" It was clear to him that the prospect of higher education fell into the category of unattainable objectives.

"I got savings."

"How much you saved up, Papa?" He said it casually. He knew well enough. The battered tin buried among the pots and pans on the top shelf in the kitchen held two hundred and fifteen dollars. Against a rainy day. Or sickness in the family. Or some unexpected calamity. Blood money—earned dime by dime, quarter by quarter, dollar by dollar. It was the barrier between the Vitales and destitution.

"None of your business," Bruno said gruffly.

"If you spend your savings sending me to college, you'll never get your own barber shop."

It was rarely discussed in the Vitale household, this ambition of Bruno's to become his own boss. But they all knew it was there, the vision lingering in the heart of a man who'd always known a master. There was no prospect whatsoever that he'd acquire the wealth necessary for the transition from employee to employer. Not in this life—not the way things were. Not if he saved for a hundred years. But dreams cost nothing, and they helped balance the limitless servitude that was his only true horizon. "I can wait. It maybe take a little longer, that's all," Bruno said firmly.

All this time the younger Mokey sat across the table eating quietly, watching with bright-eyed interest this exchange between his father and his brother. Maria came bustling in from the kitchen to check the progress of breakfast and her glance swept across the table to light on Mokey. Without warning she grabbed the unsuspecting youth by the scruff of the neck. "I told you change your collar. I'm not sayin' twice." She turned back one of his ears for inspection. "You don' wash your neck again."

Mokey yelped in protest. "It was clean yesterday, Mama. I put a clean collar on yesterday, honest."

"Yesterday ain' today. You wear clean collar every day, like your brother. Nobody in this town goin' say Maria Vitale sen' out dirty kids. This high-class Italian family, don' you never forget it. Get out to the kich'—wash your neck." Holding on to his ear, Maria propelled her son toward the kitchen door.

"We ain't got no school today, Mama." Mokey went, protesting. "It's bad enough we the only kids in the whole school gotta wear a clean collar every single day."

Out in the kitchen, Mokey continued grumbling. Bruno rose from the breakfast table and prepared for work.

Tony placed his forearms on the top rail of the fence, rested his chin on them, and watched the boat edging in to Market Street Wharf. When it was secure the passengers disembarked, then a gang of men began unloading bales of cotton that stood piled on deck. It was a light load this trip, and the men worked quickly. Soon the bales were neatly stacked on the wharfside. It was the last operation of the day for the workers. Their task complete, they came toward the fence in a group, then dispersed in all directions. The last and youngest of them, a tall, husky youth with a mop of unruly blonde hair, made his way across to Tony. Skeeter Froelich was second-generation American of German descent, and he and Tony had been friends since the fifth grade. Tony detached himself from the fence. They fell into step and began making their way up Market Street.

"You tell your old man about the job?" Skeeter asked. Tony nodded. "What'd he have to say?"

"He's giving me a hard time. He says I gotta stay on at school and prepare myself for college."

"You ain't going to no goddamn stupid college, are you? You wanna spend your life working in some office?"

"You kidding?" Tony gave him a caustic look. "Thing is, I have to let the old man down easy. He got his heart set on me getting a college education."

"He's crazy. You can be picking up a dollar a day right now working with me on the Wharf."

"I told him."

"There's a dozen guys I could name who'd jump at the chance."

"I gotta pass it up, Skeets. I don't wanna hurt the old man's feelings."

"What's the difference, now or later? He gonna be upset when he finds out anyway, right?"

"I gotta find a way to break it to him gently."

"Time you get around to it, there won't be no job."

"I can't do anything about that."

"He ain't right in the head, you ask me. How's he gonna fix it for you to spend all your time getting educated? He ain't got that kinda dough."

Tony frowned at Skeeter's disrespect. "It's not impossible, you know. The old man's got money he was saving so he could have his own barber shop one day. Anyhow, you never hear of people working their way through college? Lotsa guys done it. I could swing it if I wanted. But I don't wanna."

"So why don't you give it to him straight?"

16

"He ain't ready to hear it."

Skeeter shrugged and for a while they walked on in silence. Then he said, "You coming out tonight? Friday's a good night downtown."

"Sure. Where we going?"

"Bob Samos and me, we're gonna shoot crap in one of them joints around here—the one behind Lacey's butcher shop." Since Skeeter had gone to work at the Wharf, Bob, of Syrian parents, had drifted in to make the partnership a trio. "There's guys in there don't do no work—don't do nothin' but shoot crap all the time."

"They professional gamblers?"

"I dunno." He scratched his head. "It's all they seem to do."

"I ain't never gambled," Tony volunteered.

"You don't have to play. Just watch Bob and me clean out the joint."

"How about Mokey?"

"Sure, he can come, too. A couple of weeks ago, Bob won twenty bucks. We had a great night—ended up in a cathouse down on Water Street. Jeez, that was some night . . ." Skeeter swaggered a little as he said it, and Tony glanced sideways at his friend.

He was feeling his schoolboy status more keenly these days. Even some of the guys at school boasted of their experiences in the town's garish bordellos. Most of it was nothing but hot air, and they didn't have the price of a stick of gum in their pants pockets, but that didn't matter somehow. Skeeter was no longer a schoolboy and was fast throwing off the inhibitions of adolescence. Bob had the advantage of several months' headstart on both of them. There could be something in Skeeter's story, Tony decided. "Maybe you can teach me to play craps?" he suggested.

Skeeter looked across speculatively, then had second thoughts. "No, you better not play. You'll lose your money. Just come in and watch."

They'd reached the point on the street where they parted. "I'll come by after dinner," Tony said as he moved off toward home.

It was three hours later when Tony, Skeeter, and Bob stopped on the sidewalk outside Lacey's butcher shop. Skeeter turned to Tony. "I thought you said Mokey was meeting us?"

"He oughta be here by now." He squinted up the street. In the distance two figures were hurrying toward them. He recognized them both. "Oh, no," he groaned.

Mokey arrived, grinning. At his side the panting Inchka tottered on high heels, her fourteen-year-old figure enclosed in a dress so tight that the form of her young bosom stood out clear and proud. Her lips were scarlet with color, and, breathless from the fast walk, she took a theatrical puff on the cigarette burning between her fingers and blew the smoke out quickly. "Not late, am I, fellas?" Mokey said smugly.

Skeeter stared at him coldly. "You planning on keeping company with us, kid?" he asked quietly.

"Sure, that's why I'm here, ain't it? We're gonna shoot a little crap, right?" he said importantly.

"That was the general idea—nobody said nothin' about bringin' broads along."

17

"Inchka's O.K. She's just along to see the action, she won't get in the way."

"It ain't the practice for broads to go visiting gambling joints," Bob told him. "It ain't nice." The older boy took up an impatient stance.

"How was I to know?" Mokey's face lost its smile.

"Aw, I been around, fellas," Inchka piped up. "You guys don't need to worry about me."

"Who's worried? You just ain't coming in no gambling house with us. Come on, we're wasting time." Bob turned to the others.

Inchka made her final protest. "There's lots of working girls my age downtown," she said tartly. "Just because I'm still at school don't mean I'm not a woman." The flash of rebellion in her eyes was indeed womanly, and beyond her years.

"Jeez, I was hoping to watch you guys clean out the place," Mokey grumbled.

Tony stepped in. "Here." He took a handful of coins from his pocket. "Take Inchka to a movie." The cheapest seat at the Pavilion movie theater, located just outside town, was a quarter. He counted out fifty cents. "Hang around the fire exit before you spend the money. Maybe you can duck in when nobody's watching."

Mokey's spirits revived. He reached out and grabbed the money. "Sure, we'll get in. See you guys later." He turned abruptly and marched off. Inchka trotted faithfully beside him.

The remaining three strolled manfully down the alley by the side of the butcher shop. Bob stopped before a door, its blue paint faded and scarred but still bearing the words: THE KOKOMO CLUB. He pushed through the door and the others followed him into a large room pungent with cigarette smoke. The solitary source of light was a large, bare bulb swinging on its wire above a dilapidated pool table. The attention of a dozen or so men in the room was riveted on this table, pressed into service to contain the flying dice of a heavy crap game. Tony shuffled self-consciously through the sawdust on the floor and followed Skeeter and Bob to look over the shoulders of the men clustered around the table. Vaguely he recognized some of the faces in the room. In a town this size the workless and the workshy took on an appearance that was uniformly unmistakable. Around the rim of the table the players were mostly mill workers, some with the dust of the steel mills still on their clothes. He realized with surprise that he knew the young dealer controlling the game. The youth dressed in an apron and wielding the stick so expertly was Bluey Esposito, perhaps a year older than the trio, but still considered a buddy. In between yelling cryptically such expressions as "Big Six" and "Snake Eyes," Bluey's gaze momentarily swept over them, and Tony found himself wondering at the fleeting frown that creased Bluey's forehead. There was no further sign of recognition as the dealer's attention returned to the flying dice.

"I'm getting into the game," Bob said. He pulled out his diminutive roll.

"Me, too," Skeeter followed suit.

Tony pressed close up behind them as they prodded the backs of onlookers, who gave way with instant respect at the sight of men holding real folding money. The game was a total mystery to him, but he became aware that his friends' willingness to risk their money assured them immediate welcome at the table. There was an excitement in the air, new to him and more thrilling than anything he could remember. More money crossed the green felt than he'd ever seen. The excitement

18

escalated when Skeeter and Bob began to win. The dice had traveled around the table from player to player, and now the shooter was a thin character at the other end, his stained fedora pushed back on his head, throwing the bones with practiced, casual abandon and, it seemed, enormous luck. The shooter chased his ten-point and, as throw after throw miraculously side-stepped the fatal seven, the man confidently increased his bet. Tony became aware of the heightening of tension around the table. "What's happening?" he leaned forward.

"The guy's crazy. We're betting he sevens-out." Skeeter spoke out of the corner of his mouth and pushed another dollar bill across the felt. The shooter threw again, and the spots on the dice added up to six.

"What's sevens-out?" Tony whispered.

Skeeter shoveled out a little more of his and Bob's joint reserve. "He gotta make a ten to win—that's his point. If he makes a seven, the house wins and so do we."

"Oh, I see." Tony watched the dice as they came to rest; this time the spots on the bones added up to twelve.

"He's gonna blow it for sure." Skeeter's conviction got the better of him, and he pushed the remainder of their pot out onto the felt.

"How come you so positive?" Tony asked.

"It's the law of averages. The odds are stacking up against the guy. You can't beat the numbers."

The shooter was now looking worried and had stopped increasing his stake. He stood pensively shaking the dice in his hand, gazing around at the bets on the table. If they were so certain, it was worth the risk, Tony decided. He dug into his pocket and came up with the five dollars. He pushed the notes into Skeeter's hand. "Make a bet for me."

Skeeter half-turned. "Where you get this kinda money?"

"Put it on," Tony urged quietly, "before it's too late." He pushed Skeeter's arm forward.

Now the trio had their entire joint stake riding. The shooter's expressionless eyes glanced up as he pitched, as if he'd suddenly lost interest in the outcome. The dice flew from his fingers and firmly laid up a ten, making his point. Bluey's stick flew across the felt and swept up the boys' money in a movement swift and final. They'd been wiped out in a flash, and they stood there empty and awkward. Within a few moments, now that they were mere spectators, others were jostling them for a better view of the action.

"Let's get out of here," Skeeter said sourly.

Tony wondered if he was the only one to notice it. As they turned away from the rim, Bluey gave them an almost-imperceptible glance of remorse.

Disconsolately, they walked down the street three abreast. After a while, Skeeter spoke dully. "Know what I'm thinking?" he volunteered. They looked at him. "My ma takes in washing for a whole month for what we lost back there."

"Aw, shit, it cost me my week's wages," Bob put in. "So what? We were just unlucky."

They continued walking, their eyes on the ground. "Yeah," Skeeter agreed eventually. "Maybe we'd have won another twenty bucks, like last time. That was some night, eh? Boy, I could use another night like that." Unceremoniously, as he walked, the hand in his pocket scratched his testicles. He turned suddenly. "Hey, Tony, where'd you get the five bucks?"

It had all happened so quickly, he still couldn't believe it—a moment's impulse had cost him his entire savings; the result of months of scrimping and saving precious dimes and quarters. It was a costly business, this being one of the boys.

"Tony, where'd you get the dough?" Skeeter was repeating.

"Oh, it was just a little spare cash I had lying around," he said. "I could use a soda—anybody got the price?" he added bravely.

"I'm cleaned out." Bob showed his empty pockets.

"Me, too," Skeeter said.

"Let's go dig Mokey out of the movie. Maybe he still got the fifty cents I gave him," Tony suggested, "if he wasn't stupid enough to pay for the tickets.".

"Say." Skeeter brightened. "Let's go see the movie ourselves. It's a Jimmy Cagney. We can get in through the fire exit, too—I done it dozens of times."

The trio brightened considerably. They walked toward the edge of town. In the distance the colored electric bulbs outlining the canopy fronting the Pavilion formed an oasis of illumination in the otherwise unlit street. To get to the fire exit at the rear they'd have to pass the building and approach it from the opposite side. They made themselves inconspicuous by crossing the street and padding along in the dirt beyond the asphalt surface. Tony stopped suddenly and stared at the theater opposite, his face cold in the dimly reflected light.

"What's up, Tony?" Bob stopped walking and turned inquisitively.

"They the Polak brothers?" He pointed to two figures standing furtively at the edge of the pool of light.

Skeeter squinted into the distance. "Yeah, it's them all right. What's the trouble?"

"I think they're waiting to beat up Mokey."

"What for?"

"Messing around with Inchka, I guess. They hit us once already."

"That little broad's out to screw every guy in the school," Skeeter snorted. "Them brothers gonna end up fighting the whole world."

"What you say we teach 'em a lesson?" Bob suggested.

"Yeah, let's do that." Beneath his sanguine exterior Tony hadn't stopped smarting at the beating Mokey and he had received at the hands of the Polaks. He knew of no way to persuade Mokey to give up his pert little companion. Or, more likely, Inchka had no intention of losing her hold on Mokey. And force was the one thing clearly understood and respected in the eternal war between ethnic groups of adolescents in the town.

"Let's creep up on 'em." Skeeter's hand had slipped into his inner pocket and reappeared with the tight little blackjack he carried on him, now that he worked down at the Wharf. A malicious grin was spreading over his features.

"Hold it," Tony commanded. Together they had the edge on muscle and he had no intention of wasting the opportunity on a wild rush. In an untidy brawl outside the movie theater they'd lose the element of surprise; and if the cops were called, they'd be marked as troublemakers. "Let's make a plan," he suggested. "If we're gonna get 'em, let's do it good." The others listened to his scheme, then he slipped away into the darkness.

The insecure fire exit door yielded to a firm push, as always. The door to the men's room was immediately to one side. He nipped in and stood at a stall, fiddling with his fly and whistling. After a while it was apparent that his clattering entry had gone unheard. In the dark he found Mokey and Inchka seated in the front row, their heads thrown back, gazing up like feeding baby swallows at the flickering screen above them. They were entwined together across the adjoining seats, and, in the dim reflection of the projector's rays, he saw that Mokey's hand disappeared somewhere inside Inchka's clothes. On each side the seats were unoccupied. He sat down next to them and kicked Mokey's ankle. "The brothers are waiting for you outside," he hissed in Mokey's ear.

"What brothers?"

"Inchka."

"Oh." Mokey half-started out of his seat and stared around with the look of a hunted animal. "I better get out of here."

"Sit down." Tony grabbed his coat and pulled him back into the seat.

"What am I gonna do?"

Voices behind made shushing noises.

"We got everything under control," Tony said quietly in his brother's ear. "I got Bob and Skeets outside. We're gonna make 'em eat dirt."

The fear in Mokey's eyes gave way to a look of mischief. "Yeah, let's beat the crap outa them—we owe 'em one."

"We're gonna do it right. You and Inchka leave by the front entrance in about five minutes. Stand around outside so they see you, then start down the street toward home. It's my guess they'll follow and make a grab for you in the dark. But we'll get in first. When you hear me whistle, start running. We'll be waiting and the three of us'll get 'em when they come past." Inchka was leaning across Mokey inquisitively. Tony dropped his voice even lower. "Don't tell her."

Tony could see his brother's eyes glistening in the dark. "I'll come back and help when you grab 'em. We'll smash 'em to pieces," Mokey said.

"No, you go on home. We'll handle it." He was determined to stop the Polaks from making his brother a target. It was better done without Mokey's presence. He went to get up. "Give me the fifty cents," he added.

Mokey's self-possession didn't fail him. "I paid for the tickets," he said hopefully.

"Come on, give . . ." Tony repeated threateningly. Mokey resignedly reached into his pocket and handed over the money. "I oughta let 'em beat you up, you know that?" Tony said sourly. Then he was gone.

Mokey and Inchka appeared in the light at the front of the theater and the Polak brothers slid off into the concealment of the night. Watching from a distance, Tony grinned to himself. The brothers were due for a big shock—and to discover they had no monopoly on ambush. A couple of minutes later, the young couple made their way leisurely to where the trio lay in wait in the dark. Inchka's complaints that she'd missed the finish of the James Cagney movie came across to them clearly in the still of the night. In the distance Tony could make out the two shadowy forms that flitted across the edge of the pool of light and were now hardly discernible, tracking the couple at a distance. He waited until his brother and the girl drew even with them, then whistled. Mokey grabbed Inchka and, to her yells of alarm, made off down the street. The footsteps of the brothers thudded toward them in pursuit. They waited until the last moment, then the trio stepped out, timing their interception to perfection.

It was more a massacre than a fight. The Polaks were not allowed to take to their heels when it was apparent the odds were against them. They were dragged down in flight and left moaning and bloodied in the dirt.

It was a lesson in keeping with the accepted standards of youthful life in Steubenville, and one the brothers wouldn't forget, Tony decided. There'd be no more trouble with the Polaks, he was sure. He was deeply impressed with the power of muscle.

The fifty cents bought them two beers apiece, and left change.

CHAPTER THREE

Every barber shop in Steubenville did business on the side—taking bets for customers, a little bootlegging of cheap illicit booze, a heritage of the old days; it was the accepted practice. It was Saturday and Tony breathed a sigh of relief. Today he'd be able to make a few dimes and, if he got lucky, a quarter or two running betting slips across to The Club for customers at Signor Boccardi's barber shop. He waited impatiently for midday when he could set off downtown; nothing much happened before the afternoon. He was still sore that he hadn't a red cent to his name. He couldn't remember when he'd been so completely broke before, and he felt unprotected and insecure. For a few lousy coins. He disliked the feeling intensely and was determined it would never happen to him again. It wasn't a college education he needed, it was money. Nobody asked a guy with money if he had a college education.

"Am I wanted yet, Papa?"

Bruno looked up from his snipping, proud that customers could see that this straight, tall young sapling was his son Antonio. "It's a little early, boy. Just hang around, there'll be plenty of racing this afternoon. Lotsa customers—they'll want to make bets."

"O.K., Papa." He looked around for the broom and made himself busy sweeping out the shop. Vincenzo Boccardi looked away, smiling faintly to himself that the dull conscientiousness of the father was reflected in the son.

When he took the first betting slip across to The Club he found himself examining the place through new eyes. Strangely, because he'd been in and out many times.

Now, his critical faculties awakened by the incident in the Kokomo Club, he observed that this must be a slightly superior establishment in the scale of values that governed gambling joints. "I got one for you, Gimpy," he called out eagerly.

"Hi, there, Doc. How's tricks?"

Tony grinned self-consciously as he always did when the crippled, friendly ex-prizefighter called him Doc. Gimpy Moran ran the bar occupying one corner of the large room. The bar doubled as a grill for hungry patrons, and it was said that Gimpy made the best hamburgers and french fries in town. It was also said that Gimpy was an easy touch for a bum without the price of a meal. "Doing fine, Gimpy. School's out—I'm on vacation."

"Wait here, kid. I'll check with the boss." Gimpy took the slip and the dollar bill and disappeared through a door behind the bar. Somewhere in the back was the crossroader, and Tony had only seen him once or twice. The Duke was legendary for mysterious, distant exploits Tony didn't comprehend.

While he waited for Gimpy's return, he took a stroll around the room. Apart from a guy reading a newspaper, and another asleep in a chair, the place was empty. He hadn't noticed previously that the bulbs always burned, even though it was broad daylight outside. The light that entered through the high, meager windows was augmented by the hanging bulbs under green shades. Drab green walls were decorated with photographs, some yellowing now, of old-time fighters, stage actors and actresses and, he presumed from the settings, political figures. On some of the photographs there was writing. He squinted up at one of a buxom lady in a frilly dress and a big hat, to read that it was signed: WITH LOVE TO THE DUKE. Now Tony's searching gaze sought out previously missed details of his surroundings. At his feet the floorboards were lightly sawdusted, as they were in many establishments in town, to soak up slush from the streets. The main feature of the room was the central pool table, flanked by six card tables, three on each side, complete with Bentwood chairs that had seen better days. A roulette layout stood at the far end of the room. Other than the bar, which had no stools, the appointments were completed by three bench seats with torn and scuffed upholstery.

Gimpy reappeared. "You can tell the barber, the boss'll take everything he can throw at him today."

"O.K. Gimpy—I'll go tell Signor Boccardi right away."

"Someone wants a bet, you bring it over real quick, you understand, Doc? There's racing at lots of big tracks this afternoon. Move quick and you'll earn yourself some dough."

"Leave it to me."

"What you looking at, kid?" Gimpy's beat-up demeanor belied his alertness. Tony was surprised the other had noticed.

"Just lookin' around."

"At what? The place ain't no pretty sight—and you seen it lots of times."

"You play craps here?"

"Sure we play craps. Most nights we got the hottest game in town."

He was again surprised. In the afternoons there was sometimes a game of pool on the center table. On occasions he'd seen a dollar bill or two change hands. Other than that the pace was slow, and the bums hanging around looked as though they hadn't two cents to rub together. As long as they conducted themselves respectfully, Gimpy seemed to welcome them. "This craps—is it the same as they play over at the Kokomo Club?"

"That lousy clip joint?" Gimpy snorted in disgust. "Over there they play for pennies. Here we get real players." He suddenly became curious. "You been playing craps at the Kokomo?"

"I, ah, just heard about it from a friend," he said innocently.

"Keep outa that joint," Gimpy said seriously. "It ain't nothin' but trouble." He paused. "This friend of yours—he lost his dough, right?" His tone was sardonic.

"Yes. But last week they won," Tony put in brightly. "Twenty bucks."

"Yeah. And this week they lose their bankroll, right?" Tony stared at him. "How much you lose yourself?"

He hesitated. "Five dollars," he said eventually.

"Do me a favor, Doc, keep away. You wanna see craps played, you can come in here in the evenings. Just to watch, you understand. I ain't allowing you to play."

"Gee, thanks, Gimpy."

"Yeah—now get back to the barber shop. We're expecting action on the horses real soon."

He ran all the way.

It was six o'clock before the horse-racing activity had fizzled out and the flow of betting slips requiring transfer to The Club ceased. He'd run plenty that afternoon, and now the jingling of coins in his pocket restored the sense of security he'd lost along with the flash disappearance of his five bucks at the Kokomo.

"Go home now, Tony," his father said. "No sense hanging around for me. Tell Mama I'll be working till eight tonight." The barber shop was filling with tired, dusty men coming off the Saturday shift at the Mill. Bruno's snipping stopped just long enough for him to shake out his apron in readiness for the next customer.

"I don't mind waiting, Papa," Tony volunteered.

"Nothing for you here, now—go home."

"O.K., Papa. See you at supper."

As he walked along the street, he counted the coins three times. One dollar and eighty cents made his best payday yet. His step became firmer as he strode toward a corner out of sight of the barber shop. He turned quickly down the side street to make the detour he didn't want his father to see. Five minutes later he was climbing the iron stairway to the dingy New Philly poolroom, where Skeeter and Bob habitually hung out after work on Saturdays. He didn't dare mention the place at home because, when Bruno warned him of the perils of associating with the local drop-outs, he invariably mentioned the New Philly in the same breath. At the New Philly they usually planned their Saturday nights out. This week it would be different—Tony had plans of his own. Skeeter and Bob were engrossed in their game of pool, berating one another with the usual ferocity. He sat down on one of the hard wood benches, waiting for them to play out their needle match.

After the game, they came to sit by him. Bob suggested, "What you say we go over to Weirton tonight? They say there's a new jazz band at Rosie's bar. I hear they play terrific ragtime."

"Yeah, sounds great," Skeeter greeted this novel suggestion. Often they couldn't think of a single original thing to do in the whole town; and just as often they stayed where they were, at the New Philly.

"I won't be coming this evening, fellas." Tony dropped it in casually. "I been invited to The Club to watch some big-money craps."

They studied him together. "*The* Club?" Skeeter repeated.

"Yeah."

"And who did the invitin'?" Skeeter added disbelievingly.

"Gimpy Moran. Him and me, we're kinda buddies."

"Gimpy ain't nothing but a bartender," Bob put in. "He's just a rundown old-time fighter."

"Gimpy's a member of the staff. So am I, in a way," Tony said impressively.

"Running slips don't make you no member of the staff."

He thought better of arguing. "Anyhow, I'm going."

"O.K., if that's the way you feel. You're gonna miss a great band," Bob said, with a touch of envy.

"Say, why don't you guys come along, too?" Tony suggested.

"Me, I'm keeping outa them gambling joints," Bob said sorely. "I ain't gonna get cleaned out no more. I decided."

"We got no spare cash," Skeeter added lamely.

Someone was standing over them. "Who's gonna give me a game of pool?" They looked up to see the grinning face of Bluey Esposito. The three frowned at him in unison. ". . . All right, you guys, don't get sore. If I'd known you was coming in to the Kokomo to play, I'd have stopped you. Who knew, for Chrissakes?"

"How long you been working there, Bluey?" Skeeter quizzed him. "You never said nothing about it."

"I started the day you guys walked in. Before that I had a couple of weeks' training." He sat down alongside them on the bench.

"That's horseshit. Any fool can do that job," Skeeter said caustically. "You don't need training to be a dealer."

"Oh, yeah? That's what you think."

"Shoving dice around a table. There ain't no skill in that."

Bluey started to reply angrily, then a cautious look came into his eyes. "Listen, you guys don't know *nothing*. I'm telling you—stay outa joints like the Kokomo if you don't wanna get took."

Bob cut in, "You trying to tell us something? Who you kidding?" Bluey went silent, but the blood began to rise in his face. Bob sensed Bluey was about to tell them something and changed his tone. "What sort of pal are you? If there's something we oughta know, you should tell us."

Bluey glanced around the room. Nobody was within hearing distance. "Listen, you guys gotta promise me you'll keep your traps shut—the Kokomo's a bust-out joint. So just keep outa there, will ya? They took your dough once and, you go back, they'll take it again. Just listen to me."

"I'm going down there to smash up the place." Skeeter was on his feet, the blackjack from his pocket gripped in his hand.

Bob reached out and grabbed Skeeter's arm. "Hold it, hothead," he barked. He turned to Bluey and spoke coolly. "I don't believe you. You're just trying to make yourself look big. I didn't see nothin' going on. Nothin' at all."

"You didn't, huh?" Bluey said scornfully. The ache to justify himself before his buddies was overcoming his desire to retain professional secrets. "Well, now I'm gonna tell you somethin' that'll blow your heads off: There wasn't a genuine customer in the game except you guys. Everyone else at the table was a shill."

After a moment's silence, Skeeter said incredulously, "You including the shooter—the guy who got his ten-point?"

"I'm including everyone at the table. 'Specially the shooter. The guy you were betting against is a bust-out artist. He works for the house."

"You telling me he manipulated them dice when we had the big bet riding?" Bob's voice dripped with disbelief.

"Nope, he didn' manipulate no dice. He switched 'em for a pair of loads." They stared at him stonily. "Nothin' I could do about it; they got eyes like hawks. I tried to tip you off—you didn't see me."

Tony volunteered quickly, "I saw the look you gave us. I didn't understand."

"Best thing you guys can do is steer clear of the place," Bluey repeated.

"That does it." Skeeter's fury rose again. "They ain't getting away with it."

"Forget it," Bluey cut in sharply. "There's some guys around the place'll beat the hell out of you. I seen it happen."

"Just a minute," Bob said calmly. "Now I think you're giving us a load of horseshit. No way a guy could switch them dice and I wouldn't see it."

"Zat so?" Bluey got to his feet and walked across to the pool table, and the boys followed him. His hand went to his pocket. "I ain't no good at this, but I'm gonna show you how you got took by the hustler." He opened his hand. "What color the dice?"

"White," they said together.

"O.K. Now watch." He shook his closed hand theatrically, and they heard the dice rattling. He half-turned from them, still shaking. Tony moved quickly to see Bluey's hand dip clumsily into his jacket. Bluey threw the dice and they rolled up a seven. Green dice.

Skeeter goggled. "Holy fuckin' cow."

Bob wasn't so easily impressed. "You turned away so we couldn't see the switch," he snorted. "You wouldn't get away with that in a live game."

Bluey shrugged. "I told you, I'm no hustler. I ain't good enough." Two men carrying cues were approaching the pool table. The four of them moved away, and Bluey spoke from the corner of his mouth. "Listen, I better clam up, or I'm gonna get myself a busted head."

As if by mutual consent, the incident was relegated to the costly past. Except for Tony—he couldn't stop thinking about the magical way Bluey had switched the dice. Seven-thirty came around and he knew he'd have to make a move if he didn't want to be late for supper. He'd been watching Skeeter beat the pants off Bluey at the pool table, and now it was Bob's turn to take up the challenge. Bluey sat down beside him on the hard bench. "Listen, Bluey, I gotta go in a few minutes. Would you be a pal and show me that dice move again?"

Bluey shook his head. "I ain't giving away no more trade secrets."

"It ain't no secret anymore. I saw how you did it." Tony slipped his fingers inside the breast of his jacket to demonstrate how the other had plucked out the exchange dice. "It's terrific—I ain't ever seen anything so clever."

He'd judged Bluey right; the other swelled with pride. "Well, if you seen it, you seen it." Again he shook the white dice and this time made no attempt to turn away. Tony watched wide-eyed as Bluey made his clumsy dip. Tony urged him on and he dipped twice more.

Tony felt sure he could perform the same action more dexterously. "Gee, thanks, Bluey. I gotta go now. S'long fellas," he called out.

"Don't go blabbing all over town," Bluey threw at him ominously.

Tony frowned. Bluey should know him better than that. "I know how to keep my trap shut," he said seriously.

The trick fascinated him. Several times on the walk home he tried dipping his fingers into a ghostly inner pocket to extract a pair of imaginary green dice.

By the time he reached home his long, thin fingers were moving incredibly quickly.

CHAPTER FOUR

After supper, as soon as he decently could, he rushed out of the house and made his way over to The Club. With a sense of excitement, he entered the large room. A number of men were in the place, and more drifted up the stairs by the minute. There was an expectancy in the air that had been absent in the cold, harsh atmosphere of the Kokomo. Over the pool table, extra-large bulbs had been screwed into the green shades, and now several men took up a stance at the edge, an anticipation in their movements as they counted their money, or shuffled from foot to foot.

At the bar Gimpy was in close conversation with a figure Tony knew well. Angelo Boccardi, at eighteen, was the oldest of the barber shop owner's eight children. Their conversation ended abruptly as Tony approached, and there was a scowl in Angelo's nod of recognition. "What you want here?" he said shortly.

"It's O.K., Angelo," Gimpy told him. "I said Tony could come in and watch the crap game."

"We don't want kids in here disturbing things," Angelo commented irritably. His two years' seniority was a gulf as wide as the Ohio River.

"Doc knows how to behave himself," Gimpy said. "He runs bets over on Saturdays."

"Yeah, I know that." There was a belligerence in Angelo's glare. "You thinking of training him?"

Gimpy laughed. "He's still at school." He looked around to see the room filling, then glanced up at the clock on the wall. "It's time to open the game, Angelo."

"Yeah, right." Still eyeing Tony suspiciously, Angelo reached across the bar to pick up a thick cup and downed the contents in a single gulp. A whiff of the whiskey drifted across Tony's nostrils. Angelo walked over to the pool table, now covered over with a craps layout, picked up a dealer's stick, and called out: "Game's starting, gentlemen. Get your bets down."

At the other end of the bar, a customer was calling for service. "Wait here," Gimpy instructed him.

Tony had been unaware that Angelo was a dealer. He couldn't imagine why the older boy had found it necessary to be close-mouthed about it. Strange that Bluey's behavior had been similar. Perhaps they had something good going and didn't want to share. He watched Angelo's back as the older boy began to deal smoothly, voicing the same intriguing cries Bluey had used over at the Kokomo. Angelo's seniority put him outside Tony's crowd, which held him in distant awe as a renowned womanizer, boozer, and amateur vocalist, whose declared ambition it was to become a vaudeville performer. Angelo was always in demand at the vociferous local Italian weddings. Knowing now that Angelo was a dealer, too, Tony couldn't imagine a life of greater fulfillment. "What did Angelo mean, you thinking of training me?" Tony asked, when Gimpy returned to his end of the bar.

"Oh, he's got a suspicious mind. He's afraid you'll steal his job." Gimpy laughed.

"Me?" Tony said incredulously. "But I'm not old enough."

"You will be soon, Doc. Quite a few young guys in this town are dealers. They work cheap, that's why the club owners start training 'em young."

The idea stirred in him. "Gee, Gimpy, I'd sure like to train as a dealer," he said eventually.

"Forget it. It ain't no decent life." There was a sudden harshness in Gimpy's voice.

"It's better than the mill," Tony retorted instantly.

"Not for you, Doc." Gimpy studied him coolly for a moment. "Listen, you go to college and get yourself an education, like your pa wants. You're a bright kid— you'll go far."

"I ain't got no argument with a college education, and I know what it can do for a person, Gimpy. Thing is, I ain't gonna get one, and that's for sure."

"Why not?"

"Cause we can't afford it, that's why. I don't think my father's realized how much it costs." Gimpy remained silent. "Of course, if I was trained as a dealer, I'd be almost certain of a college education."

"How come?"

"I could work nights and study in the daytime. Plenty of people work their way through college."

The smile crept across Gimpy's face. "You asking me to help you, Doc?"

"You're the only guy I know could make it happen. No other way I'm gonna do it." Tony kept his gaze riveted to the other man's face.

"Yeah, I know what you mean." Gimpy studied him thoughtfully.

"You gonna be a pal and help me get educated, Gimpy?"

The smile on the beat-up face developed into a warm, open grin. "Sure, Doc, I'll help you if I can."

"How do I start?"

"Go across to the table and watch the game. I'll explain the moves later."

"I won't forget you for it, honest." Flushed with excitement, Tony turned away. Just as quickly he turned back. "Say, do you have some old dice?"

"I got a box full of bones under here." He bent below the counter. "How many you want?"

"A couple of pair." He reached out and carefully chose his first dice, selecting two distinctly different pairs. For a long moment he held them gingerly in his fingers, as if they were hot coals.

"What's wrong, kid?"

"Nothing, Gimpy. I never handled dice before."

"Don't hold them like that. You're gonna handle the bones, you gotta show 'em who's master—or they'll master you."

Tony grasped the dice firmly, examining and caressing them. His curiosity satisfied, his hand closed over them possessively. When he turned away, Gimpy couldn't help noticing that the boy's eyes were wide and bright with some secret wonder.

The summer night was still and humid as he stood quietly at the bedroom window looking out over the rooftops at the reflection in the sky of the garish downtown lights. The heat was oppressive and he wore nothing under his jacket, which was carefully closed by its three front buttons. His arms hung limp at his sides but the fingers of his right hand moved constantly, gently manipulating the dice. Occasionally he stopped the movement and, holding the dice between his thumb and the tips of his fingers, he raised his hand to feel for the precise location of a point at the lapel of his jacket. Then he allowed his arm to fall back to his side.

"You're keeping me awake." Mokey's voice came from the darkness behind him.

"I ain't making any noise."

"What you standing there for?"

"I'm thinking."

"What you thinking about?"

"Nothing—go to sleep."

"I can't sleep when you ain't in bed."

"Oh, shit. Leave me alone."

In a while, Mokey's voice said, "What's it like, in The Club?"

"It's a different world." He thought a moment, then added, "We're very poor. I didn't realize how poor we are. We ain't got much."

The bed creaked as Mokey sat up. "There's a lot poorer'n us."

"Ain't no excuse for being poor." Mokey waited for him to continue. "I saw a guy with a roll of bills bigger than his fist. I never knew there was so much dough. He lost four hundred dollars."

"Four *hundred* dollars?" Mokey echoed.

"He didn't say a word. Just walked out of the joint and didn't say a word."

"Maybe he's a millionaire?"

"Maybe." They were quiet again, then, "Gimpy says he'll train me to be a dealer. Like Angelo Boccardi."

"Wow—that's terrific."

"I'll be better than Angelo. I was watching him work the whole evening. He ain't so good."

"That Angelo—they say he sings 'Pasadena' just like Russ Columbo. I heard he only gotta lift his pinky and the broads come runnin'." Awe and envy dripped from the young voice.

"Only one problem. I don't know how to tell Papa."

"That you're gonna be a dealer?"

"That I ain't going on to college."

"Oh—yeah."

Tony's outline disappeared from the window. A switch clicked and pale light from the feeble bulb in the center of the ceiling filled the room weakly.

Mokey blinked. "What'd you do that for?"

"I'm going to practice with the dice."

"They'll hear you."

"No, they're fast asleep. They won't wake up now."

He took a clean bedsheet from a drawer of the ancient, scarred dresser, folded it, and spread it on top so that the dice would fall in silence. He sat down in front of the dresser, adjusted the three-way mirror so he could watch himself from the front and both sides, and began throwing the dice.

Mokey watched him in silence. Then: "Why you keep touching your chest after you shake the dice, Tony?" he asked inquisitively.

He stopped to look sourly at his brother's reflection in the mirror. "None of your business. Go to sleep, willya?"

"I can't sleep with the light on."

"Too bad—you better get used to it."

After a while, Mokey became bored. He lay down in the bed, drew the sheet over his head, and blocked out the light.

Soon the only sounds in the room were his sonorous breathing and the regular, quiet click of the dice in Tony's hand.

CHAPTER FIVE

At the end of the long room a couple of shabby regulars, glad of the shelter on an aimless Sunday afternoon, muttered together. Otherwise, Tony, Skeeter, and Bob had the New Philly to themselves and exclusive use of the battered pool table. As usual, Skeeter was making mincemeat of them on the felt, and the three-cornered game came to an abrupt halt while they argued the imposition of a handicap on him.

When the big guy came stomping in, they stopped arguing. He stood about six-six, with a great leathery face the size of a young bull's, and wrists so thick they blended with his massive hands like two Wisconsin hams. His flowing gut hung out over a wide belt, and the dirt of the mines was so ingrained in his clothes, they could have stood up by themselves.

"My name Olaf Johannson," he said. "I come here for play pool." The trio stared. "Anyone here play Olaf Johannson pool?" he roared out to the room in general. He was met with two blank stares and some nervous shuffling from the far end of the room. His attention returned to the trio. "Maybe one of you young guys give Swedish Olaf a game, huh?"

Tony got in first. "We only play for money here, mister," he said.

"Oh, sure, I got money. Look." He took a handful of bills out of his pocket. "I got plenty money. I work six weeks straight down mine. No day off. Make plenty money."

"Gee." The trio looked at one another. Bob gave Skeeter's ankle a kick. "Oh . . ." Skeeter said. "Ah, I'll give you a game, Swede. Yeah, glad to . . ." He stood rubbing one leg against the other. "How much you wanna play for?"

"You say."

Tony said quickly: "How about five bucks?"

"Five dollar fine with me."

Tony and Bob exploded into action, setting up the balls on the table. Behind Olaf's back they exchanged glances and winks with Skeeter. Then they stood back and waited confidently for the slaughter. Skeeter won the toss, sighted along his cue, and broke up the pack. Nothing went down. The grins went to the other sides of their faces when the huge Swede stepped in and sank six balls in a row with startling accuracy. From this bad start, Skeeter tried all he knew to catch up. He didn't make it and the final ball was an easy black for the Swede.

Skeeter stood back from the table, defeat and bad humor written all over him, and put down his cue. "You're too good for me, Swede," he said, disgruntled. "I know when I'm outclassed."

"You good player—I like." Olaf encouraged him. "You keep playing—maybe you beat me."

Skeeter shook his head, but Tony had other ideas. "Look, Swede," he said. "You a champion or something?"

"No, I not champion. Just good player."

"We got nobody around here in your class. Now, it's O.K. with us if Skeets plays you, but you gotta give him a shade of odds, an ace like you."

"What you mean?"

"For Skeeter to play, you have to give him two for one. Skeeter's five dollars against your ten."

He thought for a moment. "O.K., I agree," the Swede said blandly.

"Right, let's go," Tony said to Bob, ignoring Skeeter's frantic wave of dissent. Together they quickly set up a new frame of balls.

The reluctant Skeeter tried his best, but the Swede won again. "Good game. I enjoy," he told Skeeter. "You owe me ten dollar."

"No, you got it wrong. Five dollars," Tony said pleasantly. "You agreed—five dollars for your ten."

"I win first game for five dollar. Five and five is ten."

"Gee, I thought you meant we were starting again for the second time." Tony's face was a picture of innocence.

"No, I not mean. He owe me ten dollar, your friend."

They had a problem. Before the Swede's appearance, a count-up had revealed their joint wealth as eight dollars twenty cents. And the Swede was as big as a house. "You a sport, Olaf?" Tony was showing admirable presence of mind.

"Yes, sure, I'm sportsman."

"How about double or nothing? Skeeter's twenty against your forty?"

"Sounds good," Olaf agreed, thinking about it. He turned suddenly to Skeeter, and they winced together. "Twenty dollar a lot for kid. You got twenty dollar?"

Tony answered for him. "Sure we got it—there's three of us, ain't there? We got the twenty dollars between us."

"You show me money," Olaf said.

Skeeter and Bob looked at each other. Tony remained calm and displayed a measured annoyance. "How about you, Swede? I didn't see forty dollars there when you showed us your money."

"Sure I got forty dollar. I got more than forty—I got ninety dollar. You wanna see?"

"Yeah—I wanna see the dough. Maybe you ain't got that much."

Laboriously, the Swede counted out forty dollars from his pocket.

"O.K., that's fine," Tony said. "Now we play."

"You show me your money."

"Start the game. I got the money in a locker—I'll go get it," Tony said with a nonchalant air.

Out in the john he wrapped the single dollar bill he owned carefully around some toilet tissue. From a few feet it could be mistaken for a roll of money. He timed his return to the table for when Olaf's turn to play came up. As the big guy went to sight along his cue, Tony, from the other side of the table, waved the tight little roll at him. Olaf nodded in acknowledgment, then bent down to concentrate.

Now that he was familiar with the Swede's style, Skeeter began to get a grip on his game. It was no pushover, but he held his own—again it ended up a black-ball game, with Skeeter to play. The damn ball would have to be tight on the cushion, at an awkward angle from the pocket. It was unlikely Skeeter could sink it. Tony didn't like the odds and decided to improve them. From where he stood behind Olaf, he motioned to Bob. Then, as Skeeter sighted along his cue, Tony swooped at the Swede's feet and came up holding a half-dollar piece.

"Hey, Olaf, this your money?" Tony asked loudly. He stepped back so that Olaf had to turn his head to see the coin. "I found it by your foot."

"No, I got no half-dollar piece." The Swede frowned at the coin.

"You must have dropped it—wasn't there a minute ago."

"No, I told you, I got no half-dollar."

32

"O.K., I'm not complaining." Tony pocketed the coin with a friendly grin.

In the time it took to divert the Swede's attention, Bob had stepped up to the table and flicked out the black ball so that it stood an inch from the cushion. Now it was a different game. Olaf's head swiveled back just in time to see Skeeter's cue ball flying down the table to smash the black into the pocket.

Forty skins.

The Swede had gone and Skeeter was laying out the dollar bills in a line on the pool table. "Just look at all that loot," he whistled. "Tony, I gotta hand it to you, that was some move." There was a new respect in his eyes.

"Tell me, how much we win, Skeets?" They'd never seen him like this—his eyes were bright and he was immensely self-controlled.

Skeeter looked puzzled. "Forty dollars, right?"

"Forty dollars," Bob repeated Skeeter's words in answer to Tony's questioning look.

"You're both wrong—we won fifty. We bucked the Swede for ten dollars the first game, right?"

"Right," Skeeter agreed.

"Then we won fifty."

Skeeter studied the bills uncertainly. "How come we only got forty?"

Tony sighed patiently, then allowed himself a rare expletive, in honor of the event. "In the future, let's not hear how you're such a fucking marvelous pool player," he said.

She let them into the narrow, dilapidated house on Water Street with practiced allure. A couple of brawny miners, on their way out, shoved past impatiently in the entrance passage, and the smile on the brassy redhead's face frosted over. The miners made off wordlessly, and her features settled back into their rutted welcome. "Glad to see you again, er . . ." she began.

"Skeeter."

"Yeah, Skeeter. Nice to see you. You're getting to be quite regular, big boy."

"I brought my buddies along for a ride, Cora," he said. "This one here's Tony. That's Bob."

"Hi, fellas—you boys got dough?"

"Yeah, sure," Skeeter answered.

"Let's see the color, kiddo."

"Prices still the same, Cora?" Skeeter grinned knowingly and dug into his pocket.

"Sure—dollar straight, two bucks half-and-half. What's it gonna be?"

"We'll, ah, stick to straight." Skeeter glanced at the others.

"Three bucks." He handed over the money. "O.K., follow me, boys. This way to Paradise."

A row of small rooms led off the shabby, narrow passage. The doors to several were open, and they could see the beds in them, most with a girl sitting expectantly. In larger rooms the space was divided by a curtain hung off a rope, doubling the room's capacity.

"You got any special preference, Skeeter?" Cora turned.

"That Chinese girl, she still around?" Skeeter said eagerly. Cora nodded at a half-opened door and Skeeter disappeared through it.

Bob was staring into a room at a big, strapping blonde who gave him the eye. She came out into the passage and took his arm, and he allowed himself to be led off. This left Tony standing uncomfortably in the passage. In the next doorway, a girl came out to lean against the frame, studying him. "You ask me, he's cherry," she murmured to Cora.

"You reckon?" Cora took a new interest.

"I'll take him, if you want," the girl in the doorway said.

"Keep your hands off—he's mine," Cora said. She turned to Tony. "This way, kid," she said. "Come with me."

In the second-story room with its red shaded light, Cora wore her nakedness with total unconcern, reducing Tony to a jelly. His experience with girls was limited to surreptitious fumblings in the dark, and the odd summer glimpse of a leg, or part of a breast showing above a bathing suit. Of all the people walking around in the world, half of them had two each—an average of one for every soul in existence. He'd never seen a whole one—not since he was at his mother's breast. Now the sagging mammalian glory displayed before him confused him so much he couldn't get it up. And he couldn't stop staring at the corrugations of childbearing lines across her belly.

"You gonna get your pants off, boy, or you wanna do it through the fly? You better make up your mind, your dollar's running out fast."

"Oh, I'm sorry," He began fumbling at his belt.

"You're too slow. Here, I'll do it for you." She stood before him with deft fingers ready. He dropped his pants, then bent down to unlace his boots. "Don't bother with them," Cora said. "You ain't staying long enough to make it worthwhile. Only, remember—when you're on top, don't kick. I got marks all over my legs from guys kicking." She walked over, lay on the bed, and yawned open. He climbed on clumsily. "Nothing happening down there, boy—how about some action?" She grabbed his cock and started to work it.

The feel of her cool hand at his crotch galvanized him into movement. Doglike over her on his knees, he supported himself on his left hand and reached out with his right for the breast that had slid over the side of her chest. He kneaded this gingerly for a moment. Suddenly the realization of it hit him—a real, live woman lay beneath him, waiting to be served with his manhood. With a rush the heat came into his loins, and his sudden erection overcame the soreness Cora was creating with her rough, energetic motion. "Attaboy," she said enthusiastically, "now you got it. Bang it in and let's get to work." He let himself down on her, his cock seeking out the dark nest. But the goddamn thing didn't seem to know where to go. "Let me put it in for you." Her hand reached down to guide him.

"No, leave it. I wanna feel the way for myself." His words were suddenly harsh and urgent. He felt cheated by Cora's dominance. It was he doing the fucking, not she—she should get her priorities right. He plunged his hand roughly into her pubic hair, seeking the cleft. When he found it, her cunt was dry and loose and felt like the chamois leather Papa used to clean the windows of the house.

34

"Come on, kid, get it in. Time's wasting."

While he was groping around she'd gone back to pumping; the waves at his groin increased and he felt his climax come rushing in. Desperately he let himself down and she tried to guide him in. It was too late. He exploded in her hand, and she turned his cock so that the sperm spilled along her belly. "Oh, Jes-us," he shouted. The convulsions shook him and he collapsed on top of her.

She gave him a whole minute to recover. "That's good," she said. You did real good—now get off."

"But I didn't get it in," he complained.

"You had your time. Come on, kid, that's it."

Reluctantly he rolled off. When he was pulling on his pants, she said, "Come back any time you got dough, honey. You'll have a real good time. Always pleased to see a nice kid who knows how to behave."

They walked along the sidewalk, three abreast, as usual. "Boy, did I have a good time," Skeeter said with relish. "That little lotus blossom, boy, can she screw— fucks like a rattlesnake. It gets better every time."

"I paid the extra dollar. I ain't never been french'd before," Bob said. "Ain't that sump'n?"

They looked at Tony expectantly. He looked straight ahead as he walked and said nothing. "Who'd you have, Tony?" Skeeter said eventually.

"What?" He hadn't been listening.

"Who'd you get?"

"Oh. I had Cora."

"You crazy?" Skeeter yelled. "That old bat ain't no good for screwin'. You telling us you picked her when there's all them young broads waiting to get laid?"

"I didn't know who to choose." Tony shrugged.

"You know what you did? You wasted a buck, you prick."

"Yeah," he said quietly. "I know."

The first chance he had, he went home and thought about it.

Thing was, he couldn't decide whether or not he was still cherry.

CHAPTER SIX

"Tonight, Doc," Gimpy said from behind the bar, "you gonna see a big game of craps."

"Yeah?" Tony lifted his head from the dice he was casually rolling along the bar.

"There's a guy they call the Colonel, from the South. He'll be playing here tonight—be a big money game."

"The Colonel one of them rich guys you was telling me about, Gimpy?"

"He's rich enough to give us a headache if things go wrong at the table. So we gotta be on our toes. The Colonel's a maverick."

"What's a maverick?"

"That's some kinda professional gambler."

"He famous?"

"Ain't nobody gets famous in gambling."

"Why not?"

"Well, you just work it out: To get famous you gotta be good—if you're that good, ain't nobody gonna play with you. Nearest you're gonna get to being famous, you gotta lose big as well as win big. Only way you're gonna win big all the time is if you're crooked. Then being famous is the last thing you want."

"What you're saying is, if someone's good, he'd better keep it to himself."

"You got it, Doc. There's guys around know how to win some, I seen 'em. They just don't talk about it." Tony digested this information, and Gimpy went on, "Tonight you're gonna be helping Angelo. You'll be standing next to him learning the payouts. You don't reach out and grab any checks. You don't touch nothing he don't tell you to, and you don't touch no dough on the layout. You do exactly what you're told and nothing else. You understand?"

"Sure, I understand," Tony said eagerly.

"You don't say nothing—no back talk, no comments, and no excitement. And you stay cool at all times. You gotta remember that, it's the first rule—a good dealer always stays cool."

"I'll remember, Gimpy."

"There's something else you gotta remember: Be nice to everyone. You gotta learn to be polite, always. A lot of young guys, I wouldn't consider them for dealers because they ain't polite. No screamin' and yellin' and no loudmouthin', that's the way to behave. Guys playing at the table, they get all het-up sometimes. Maybe they gotta take a lot of shit at work, or at home, and they play craps as a kinda release, so they yell. That don't mean you gotta do the same. You're working, they're playing, and that's the difference. And when I say everyone, I mean you treat *everyone* at the table with respect. Maybe you don't like the guy—makes no difference. Maybe the lady is a whore—none of your business. Maybe it's a guy gambling like a fool with more dough'n you earn in a year. Just remember, away from the table, he's no fool—you had that guy's earning power, you don't gotta stand there awaiting his pleasure. Got me?"

"I understand. Honest."

"Now, let me take a look at you, Doc." He leaned over the table to examine Tony from head to toe. "Yeah, you look O.K. I gotta hand it to your ma, you're always well turned-out—clean collar, your pants pressed, your shoes shined. That's important. Just like your pa. I seen him over at Boccardi's barber shop. He always looks good."

"Mama says, the world's full of bums, all the more reason we gotta look sharp."

"Right, that's good thinking, for a woman." He eyed Tony. "If you're gonna be helping out permanent, maybe I'll get the Duke to spring for a new set of duds for you. Yours ain't got holes or nothin', but—well, they look kinda worn out." Tony looked down at himself in surprise. "Don't let it bother you, Doc," Gimpy added.

"I'm only speaking comparative."

"Oh. You got a minute, Gimpy? You wanna see how I'm handling the dice?"

"Sure, kid. You been practicing?"

"Yeah. I practice all the time."

"That's the way it's done. O.K., Doc, let's see you shoot the bones."

Tony held out his hand. "These are white dice, O.K.?" Gimpy nodded. Tony shook his hand energetically, close to his chest. He threw. A pair of crudely painted green dice went spinning along the bar.

There was surprise in Gimpy's voice. "Do that again, Doc, willya?"

He retrieved his green dice and, with his back to Gimpy, reset them for his trick. Again he showed Gimpy the whites in his hand. He gave an elaborate shake and shot the green dice along the bar for a second time.

Gimpy studied him. "Say, that's good. Real good."

"Honest, Gimpy?" He glowed.

"Yeah, that's as good as I seen any pro do it. I didn't see the dip, I'm gonna admit right away. And you're fast—but there's something I gotta tell you. I can see the shape of the pocket you got behind the lapel of your coat. And it's too near the edge. In a real game, that'd be spotted, and by now they'd be cuttin' off your balls."

"Oh." He was crestfallen. "I tried sewing in a thin one, but I couldn't get my fingers in the pocket quick enough, so I used a thicker cloth."

"You have to stiffen the lapel of your coat. And shape it so it stands away from your chest and gives you room to work."

"Gee, I didn't think of that."

"There's always refinements—it's refinements make it work."

"Next time I'll make sure you don't see the pocket."

"Incidentally, you ain't thinking of pullin' that move in a real game, are you, kid?"

"Me?" Tony said, astonished. "I can't even play craps. I never been in a real game in my life."

"Reason I'm asking—there's something else you better know."

"What's that?"

"Keep a straight face. If I hadn't seen the dip I'd've known you was up to something by the look on your face. It's a dead giveaway. You never hear of a poker face?"

"Yeah, sure I heard."

"O.K.—that's what you're gonna have to develop. It's the eyes. Keep the eyes down. When you look up, stare. Like a challenge."

"Something like this?" Tony looked up and grimaced.

"Keep trying, you'll get it." Gimpy studied him. I got one last piece of advice for you, Doc. If you wanna play parlor tricks, that's fine; nobody gets hurt. But if you're thinking of using them tricks in serious gambling, forget it. For that you need nerves of steel." Gimpy's attention was taken by a group of four men entering the room. His eyes flew to the clock on the wall. The strangers moved confidently, and the tallest, who wore dark clothes and a wide-brimmed Stetson, strode importantly in front of the others. "What the fuck's he doing in here this early?" Gimpy muttered.

37

"That the Colonel?" Tony swiveled around for a better look.

"Yeah. You better go get Angelo. Tell him to get his ass over here in a big hurry. We wasn't expecting to start the game till eight."

"Who're the other guys with him?" Tony began.

"Move it. Go get Angelo," Gimpy barked at him.

He ran all the way, to find the barber shop closed. Nowadays Vincenzo Boccardi lived with his family in rooms above the shop. Tony went to the side door, hammered on it, and waited. The door was opened by Francesca, second oldest after Angelo in the Boccardi tribe, and his heart, as usual, skipped a beat at the sight of her. The bursting-ripe, creamy-skinned, seventeen-year-old girl stared at him with her enormous hazel-brown eyes. He'd never before seen her like this, casually dressed for the home, her long jet-black hair flowing loosely over her shoulders. Her sturdy peasant frame, with full-rounded young breasts, resisted the constraints of the simple, printed cotton dress. He noticed that, ordinarily, she didn't enter the male environment of the barber shop proper. However, when he was around, she usually contrived to be somehow passing through, and they had exchanged smiles and glances. He'd always treated Francesca circumspectly, as the daughter of his father's employer, but it didn't prevent him from thinking about her at night. Sometimes he'd lay in bed before dropping off to sleep, picturing her as his devoted slave, subject to his every whim.

"Hello, Antonio," she said.

"Hello, Francesca." He stood looking at her.

"What you want?"

"Oh—Angelo's needed at The Club. In a big hurry."

He failed to understand the momentary anger that flashed across her face, until she said, "We're not speaking. You better tell him yourself. He's in there, in the shop." He followed her down the hallway, admiring the view as her rear swayed from side to side. She stopped at the door connecting their living quarters with the barber shop, and pointed. "You can go through."

"Thanks, Francesca."

Angelo stood at a washbowl, dabbing spirits on a small cut on his forehead and examining himself in the mirror. He looked around at Tony in surprise. "What you doing here?"

"Gimpy sent me. He says to get over there in a hurry."

"What's the rush? I ain't due in the joint till eight."

"The Colonel arrived early."

"Aw, fuck the Colonel. I ain't ready yet."

Secretly, he admired Angelo's blasé attitude and wished he had the older boy's self-confidence. He said, "You better get dressed quick. Gimpy says it'll be a big game."

"Yeah, O.K. Throw me that tie, willya?"

Tony got the tie for him. "How'd you get that cut on the head?"

Angelo's face contorted. "That goddamn bitch sister of mine—she hit me over the head with a pan."

"Francesca?"

"Yeah. The bitch."

38

"What'd you do?"

"Nothin'. Not to her, anyway. I been screwing around some with that Lucy Gancini, that friend of hers. Me and two or three other guys—I ain't the only one. Now Lucy's in trouble, and I'm getting the blame."

"You mean she's having a baby?"

"Sure she's having a baby—what you think?" Angelo looked at him sourly.

"You the father?"

"How the fuck I know? Coulda been the garbage man, all I know. Some fat chance I marry that little number. I ain't marryin' no broads. I got my career to think of. This year I won three singing contests—now I get a shot at the finals over in Philadelphia next month. No way I'm gonna screw up my singing career marryin' some broad. No way." He turned back to the mirror, stuck a small plaster on the cut on his forehead, and straightened himself up. "I look O.K.?"

"Yeah, you look fine."

"We better make a move." He walked toward the door and Tony followed. "This thing—you know what Italian families are—I don't marry her, we're gonna end up with a family feud, unless I can talk my way out of it."

"Oh, Christ."

"Yeah, and that bigmouth Frankie ain't helping any. Way she's carryin' on, you'd think she was knocked up herself. Come to think of it, that's what's wrong with the bitch. She can do with a good screwing . . ." He said it loudly as he opened the door. She stood outside, prettied-up, her eyes wide with alarm and shame. "You been listening outside the door?" Angelo blazed at her.

She recovered quickly. "I was coming to ask Antonio if he wants a cup of coffee," she said miserably.

"I bet you was listening."

"I wasn't listening, I told you." In an instant, her mood changed to match the anger of her brother. "Besides, what makes you think that what you say is so important, I have to listen outside the door?" Tony was astonished at the sudden fury that came into her voice and turned the docile girl into a spitfire.

"I know you, you little bitch," Angelo said viciously.

She glared back. "You'll be getting to know Lucy Gancini pretty well, too, when you're her husband."

"I ain't marrying your pal Lucy, or any other broad."

"But you're the father of her baby—she told me."

"How the fuck would she know? How about them other guys she been screwing around with, eh? How about them?"

"So you admit you've been making love to her."

"I ain't admitting nothing."

"I know which one of you two I'd rather believe."

"Yeah, bitch, how about believing me for once? How is it I get blamed for everything happens around here? The cat has kittens—it's gonna be Angelo screwed the cat."

"I have to tell Mama and Papa before they find out from Lucy's parents."

"Keep outa this. It ain't your business."

"Lucy's my friend."

"Yeah, and that's sump'n else worries me. Maybe you ain't quite the lady you like us all to believe, keeping company with friends like that. All them airs and graces—I seen you in your bedroom with the busy fingers when you think no one's around. You think I ain't seen that, the busy fingers?"

She let out a shriek, and her hands flew to hide the scarlet of her cheeks. She turned and tore up the stairs connecting to the rooms above the barber shop.

There was a strange excitement running through Tony, at Angelo's words. He said, "We better get going. Gimpy's waiting."

"Yeah," Angelo said sorely. "First I gotta have a drink. That bitch, she always riles me. That's her sport, riling me. I gotta have a drink to settle down."

Angelo went back into the shop and Tony watched him take the bottle of whiskey from a cabinet behind a long, narrow mirror. He took a long pull at the bottle, held the whiskey in his mouth, then gulped it down in one swallow. He returned the bottle to the cabinet, turned to Tony, and squared his shoulders. "O.K., let's go bury the Colonel," he said.

Much as he tried, for days afterward, Tony couldn't get the image of Francesca's busy fingers out of his mind.

CHAPTER SEVEN

You coming on the boat ride?" Mokey asked.

Tony opened his eyes, rolled over in the bed to look out the window and see the sun climbing into a cloudless sky. For days the temperature had hovered in the eighties; even at this hour of the morning the torpid air in the small bedroom was stifling. "Why'd you wake me, stupid?"

"It's Sunday—today they have the boat ride—you remember, the school's free vacation boat ride. Down to Kennywood Park."

"Yeah, I remember."

"You better get up. Mama's getting breakfast, I can smell it." There were sounds from the kitchen and the odor of frying bacon wafted under the bedroom door. "Boy, does that make me feel hungry."

"Open the window, for crying out loud. A guy can die for lack of air. It's murder in here."

Mokey pushed out the wood-framed window. There was some small improvement in the room, but not much, as the air outside was still. "I'll go check the time," he said. "The boat leaves at nine."

"I'm not going on the boat ride," Tony told him.

"Don't you wanna see Kennywood Park?"

"Nah, I'll see it some other time. I got more important things to do. I have to practice the dice a few hours. Then I'm meeting Skeeter and Bob, later in the afternoon. We got things to talk over."

"Business?" Mokey asked curiously.

"Yeah, big business." Telling his brother what he wanted to know was an easy way to end his constant prying, Tony had long ago discovered.

"You taking that job Skeeter says he can get for you down at the Wharf?"

"Maybe I won't need it. I think I can get a dollar a day helping out at The Club."

"When you gonna tell Papa you're not going back to school?"

"I dunno." Tony frowned.

"Better tell him soon. He's already on to you, that you ain't been studying this vacation."

"He ain't said nothing."

"I heard him talking with Mama the other night."

"What'd he say?"

"Don't remember, exactly. You better tell him, though—quiet, the way you do it. Before he gets the idea himself and blows his top." It was a sage observation, coming from Mokey.

"Maybe I'll tell him today, I get the chance."

During breakfast he tried to gauge his father's mood. They'd moved the kitchen table out onto the porch for breakfast, but even out there the heat was becoming oppressive. Everyone was complaining about the heat, except Mokey, who appeared to have no feelings. The day wasn't right for it, he felt sure. He'd better choose a day when the atmosphere was less volatile, he decided. Then Mokey dashed off to catch the boat ride and he was left at the table with his father. He surveyed the remains of the meal, wiped his forehead, and then, unexpectedly, was precipitated into it when Bruno said suddenly, "Mr. Russell, he was in the barber shop Friday for his haircut."

Tony looked up and recognized the questioning look in his father's eyes. It was now or never. "How is Mr. Russell?"

"He's fine. He ask me how you're getting on with the extra studies he give you for the vacation?" Tony remained silent. "He been expecting to see you, to check your work, but no Antonio. I tell him you study hard."

He took a deep breath. "I ain't been doing the work, Papa." He looked across the table to see only puzzlement on Bruno's face.

"Why not? Why you stop your studies? You make it harder for yourself later."

"I'm not going back to school."

Bruno visibly checked the impulse to rage, but his voice rose. "How you go on to college if you don't complete your studies at school?"

"I ain't going to college, Papa. I'm finished with school."

"What you saying?" Bruno said in disbelief.

"I'm nearly seventeen, now. I gotta start thinking like a man, not a schoolboy. We have to face the facts—the way things are, I gotta earn my keep."

"Nobody asking you for the keep. Wassamatter with you? When you last hungry? Tell me that, Antonio—tell me when I didn't see there was bread on the Vitale table, huh?"

"It ain't the point, Papa. We just can't afford for me to go to college."

"*I* decide if we got money for college, not you. Bruno Vitale the papa here, in this house, not Antonio Vitale. You understand? When Papa say you go to college, you go—finish." He ended on a bellow, and Maria put her head around the kitchen door, to withdraw it quickly at the expression on Bruno's face.

"Please sit down, Papa. We gotta talk this out."

"Nothing to talk. You do like you're told."

Something of Tony's resolution had transmitted itself to his father, and it was too big a question for histrionics. Bruno sat down again, trying to match his son's apparent calm, unaware that Tony's knees were knocking together under the table.

"How much money you got saved up, Papa? Two hundred and fifteen dollars, right? How far you think that'll go toward a college education?"

For a moment Tony thought his father would strike out across the table. "How you know what I got, hey?"

"It's in a tin box on a shelf in the kitchen. I seen it. Two hundred and fifteen dollars."

"I got more, besides."

He couldn't contradict his father. "Just how much you think a college education gonna cost?" Bruno shrugged impatiently. "I worked it out—we need three, maybe four thousand dollars to see me through college. Where you gonna get three, four thousand dollars, Papa? You gonna rob a bank?"

"Thas' a long time ahead you talking. Years. In years I find the money, somehow."

"It took ever since I can remember to get two hundred and fifteen dollars together. You gonna suddenly become a rich man and have maybe a thousand dollars a year to spare?"

"I don' gotta be a rich man to put my son through college—this America," Bruno said stubbornly.

"So where's the thousand a year coming from, Papa? Answer me that. You gonna be giving haircuts all night?"

Faced with the cold logic of Tony's argument, Bruno stared miserably across the table. He hadn't yet figured out that it suited his son's case to disregard the fact that he could earn some money by his own efforts during the period of scholarship. "This ain't Italy—this America," he repeated in a low voice. "I find a way."

"There ain't no way. Can't you see that? You're working all the hours God sends to keep body and soul together in this family. You gotta be a realist and face facts, Papa."

Bruno was already respectful of his elder son's powers of reasoning. If this was Antonio's deduction, then it had to be correct. "I had a dream—such a beautiful dream. A Vitale—a lawyer, or maybe a doctor. A Dr. Vitale . . ." His voice faded, and the aged look Tony hated came into his face.

"Dreams won't pay college fees and buy books. We just can't hack it."

"You absolute make up your mind, hey, my son? You not wanna go back to school?"

"I'm a man now. I'd be wasting time. I gotta get out there and earn some dough. Just think, Papa, I'll be bringing money into the house, instead of being a noose around your neck. You realize what that means? First time in your life, you're gonna get some help."

Bruno lifted his head. Just as he was accustomed to being the victim of circumstance, he was quick to seize on life's small joys. "Sure be a help, son, you get some money," he smiled.

"Things'll be fine for us from now on."

"You thinking of working with your friend down at the Wharf?"

Tony hesitated. "I'm not sure—maybe I got something better in view."

"You be a hard worker. I know my Antonio."

"Yeah, sure, I'll work hard, Papa. It's hard work gets the dough."

It wasn't exactly what he had in mind. And the whole thing was so nebulous he couldn't very well explain it to his father. Besides, he was too preoccupied with the pleasurable prospect of his new-found liberty.

Tonight, he decided, he'd go out with Skeeter and Bob to celebrate his step across the threshold of maturity.

They hadn't yet offered him a steady job, but it didn't stop him from hoping. Even the mysterious Duke had once nodded to him in passing, and his presence around The Club was becoming an accepted fact. Angelo, too, was coming to rely regularly on his help when the table was busy, and Tony had quickly become adept at paying out. Angelo alternated shifts with a quiet, older man called Chuck Peters, and it was the patient Chuck who familiarized Tony with the odds offered on the various bets around the table. It appeared that Chuck handled the quiet shifts, but it was always Angelo on the stick when heavy action was expected.

One evening the now-familiar smell of whiskey came wafting across as they worked the crap table together. Angelo was skillful at disguising his boozing, his constantly heavy-lidded eyes concealing his true condition, but Tony guessed that tonight he was carrying a bigger load than usual. The drink seemed to make him short-tempered. It was Tony who spotted the mistake, when Angelo paid out over the odds on a bet. The fortunate player on the other side of the table scooped up the bonus checks wordlessly and made his next bet. Tony nudged Angelo.

"What you want?" Angelo put his head to one side. Like all dealers, he rarely took his eyes off the layout.

"That guy, he won five bucks his point of eight, and eighteen dollars a double four the hard way, a two-dollar bet. That's twenty-three dollars the win. You pay out thirty-five bucks."

"You crazy?"

"I think you made a mistake," Tony said hesitantly.

"I don't make mistakes," Angelo hissed back.

"But I saw it," Tony insisted lamely.

"What the fuck you know?"

"I worked it out."

"Since when you understand all the bets, punk? Listen, just keep your trap shut. I'll do the dealing here, O.K.?" Angelo blasted whiskey-laden breath in his face.

He said nothing more, but was positive in his own mind that he'd worked out the odds correctly. He'd have to ask Chuck to explain the whole range of odds again, in case he'd missed something. He noticed, however, that Angelo was now paying winning bets with meticulous care. At the first opportunity, it seemed, Angelo told him, "O.K., the heat's off, now. Take a break. I'll call if I need you."

"Thanks, Angelo." Tony brushed his hands together professionally, the way he'd seen dealers do it at the end of a session, to show he was concealing no checks. He left the crap table to walk across to the bar.

"Hey, Doc," Gimpy called to him. "There's a guy here you gotta meet. This is Boston Bailey." Gimpy glanced around to see there were no strangers near them at the bar. "I thought you'd wanna know—Boston's a dice mechanic," he murmured, enjoying the interest that sprang into Tony's face. Tony's gaze shot to the newcomer, a gangling, thin man with a deadpan expression and humorless eyes. "Boston's only passing through," Gimpy said. "We don't allow him to play in here. No, sir, no way."

The thin man said, "Gimpy tells me you're pretty good with the bones, for a kid."

"Gee, I'm no expert. I only know how to switch the dice, that's all."

"The switcheroo's the basic move. You got that, the rest is easy."

"Is that so?" He was intrigued by this information.

"If a guy can switch, he's got options." He saw Tony's perplexed look. "There's several types of dice," Boston explained. "But if a guy can't switch 'em in and out the game, they're no use to him."

"Oh, I get it."

"Let me see your move."

Tony took the white dice from his pocket. Practicing several hours every day had made his actions economical and smooth. A quick shake and he sent his green-painted cubes spinning along the bar.

Boston's eyebrows rose. He flipped the green dice back to Tony. "Let's see that again, kid." Tony replaced the dice in his secret pocket, and, in a movement that was fast becoming automatic, he repeated the trick flawlessly. "Say, that's good— real good, for a kid. Let me see your hands." It was the first thing he'd noticed about Boston, the thin, supple fingers. Tony seemed to know instinctively that the hands were part of it, and spent an hour each morning squeezing a soft rubber ball. "Yeah," Boston announced, feeling the fingers. "He's a natural if I ever saw one."

"I told you he was good," Gimpy said, pleased.

"More than that. If he's got the nerve, he could maybe make a mechanic."

"You reckon?" There was an excitement in Gimpy's eyes. "Hey, that's some find for around these parts."

"Yeah. Only guy I ever knew could switch that smooth was Dandy Miller, out of Atlanta. And he didn't get it right until after word got around he was an operator, poor sucker." Boston paused. "I'm gonna tell you something: I didn't see the kid make the switch, second time around. That's something ain't happened to me since way back when. Not when I was looking for it, it ain't."

Tony thrilled at such praise from an expert. He hung on to every word. "I practice every day," he said. "Five, six hours—more sometimes."

Boston nodded in understanding. It was like meeting a kindred soul. "Now, watch this, kid, here's something else." He picked up Tony's green dice from the bar with his left hand, transferred them to his right hand, shook and threw. White dice rolled out along the bar. Tony goggled. "That's palming," Boston said with a small grin. "How'd I do it?" he asked. Tony scratched his head. "Simple. I had the white bones stashed in my right hand—look." He turned his right hand over. Concealed between the third and fourth fingers, and the palm of his hand, were the original green dice. "The best miffs are the simplest ones," he said.

Tony knew with immediate certainty he could perform such tricks easily. He was surprised by the voice behind him. It was a voice he knew, sonorous and free from local nasal inflections. The boss of The Club spoke over his head. "If you got the time, Boston, I'd like you to take the kid in hand and show him the ropes. I'll be training him for a dealer."

"Sure, Duke," Boston said, and Tony sensed the immediate respect in the dice mechanic's manner. "For you, it'll be a pleasure. I'll be in town three days, waiting for the big game over at Cleveland. I can teach the kid plenty in three days. The rest is practice."

"I appreciate that," the Duke said. "Shall we say a hundred dollars a day, for your time?"

"That's good money." Boston nodded a courteous acknowledgment.

"I have the feeling he'll turn out one of the best. If he's got the nerve, that is," the Duke added.

CHAPTER EIGHT

He hardly slept all night. He got out of bed for the fifth time and went to stand at the open window to watch the birth of the dawn. The wood-framed Vitale house stood high along Sixth Street; the boys' bedroom faced out over the rooftops of Steubenville, so he could look down to where the jagged panorama ceased abruptly at a line that followed the course of the Ohio River. Wide as the river was, he couldn't see the water from this flat angle, but he imagined the light reflecting off it as the sun peeped over the horizon and its rays shafted across the land. With the new day, fatigue finally overcame him and he returned to lay on the bed, listening to Mokey's snores and occasional gulps. It was five o'clock before sleep finally won. He woke again almost immediately, it seemed, but he knew it was now six; he could hear his parents moving about in their icon-and-crucifix-festooned bedroom, preparing for the morning ritual.

"What you doing up so early?" his father asked, curious. "You fall out of bed, maybe?"

"It's too hot to sleep, Papa," Tony complained. "Besides, I'm thirsty." He made a display of getting a glass of water.

"Mama's making coffee. Be ready in a few minutes."

"O.K., I'll wait." He sat down at the kitchen table.

"How things going with you, Antonio? Your friend, he didn't get you the job at the Wharf, huh?"

"Not yet."

"I got an idea. Your papa, he got a good name down at the Mill. The name Vitale, it mean something down there—it mean hard worker. You want me to talk to Karlovac, the foreman? Maybe he fit you in somewhere. Not much money, maybe, but get better later. For ten dollars he put you on the list—you don't gotta stand in line every morning. A job come up, you got it."

"Papa, I don't wanna work at the Mill."

Bruno was surprised at the vehemence in his son's voice. "Sure—what I'm saying? I'm ashamed of myself, suggesting something like that. Ain't nothing worse in this world then working in the Mill. Listen, I got a better idea—what you say I train you to be barber, like your papa? Thas' easy, we do it right here, in house. Maybe Signor Boccardi let you help out in shop, sometimes. You never go hungry. Always a guy around who needs haircut. Tonight I bring home tools, you practice on Mokey. We got deal?"

"I don't wanna be a barber either, Papa."

"Then what you gonna do?"

"I'd like to be a crap dealer."

Bruno looked at him in astonishment. "You mean in one of them sawdust joints, with the dropouts and the gamblers?"

"I won't be gambling, Papa, just working."

"I don't like that. I'm gonna tell you straight—this town, it's full of dropouts. And where they hide, when they ain't causing trouble? In them sawdust gambling joints, that's where they hang out, right? You wanna be like them dropouts?"

"I won't become a dropout, you know I won't."

Bruno shook his head sadly. "This place changed since the Vitales come to live here. Now is all gambling—everyone doing something against the law. Even Signor Boccardi, respectable businessman, he do a little bootleggin' on the side. He gotta, that's what the customers expect. Town is wide open. Break the law, you get caught, you pay the Fix, everything O.K. I hear about it all the time in barber shop. Nobody wanna go to church anymore, nobody got respect. I tell you, it frighten me what's happening around here these days."

Things hadn't changed much, that Tony was aware of. "I think the Duke is gonna offer me a job at The Club."

His father stared. "You been talking to the Duke?"

"Yeah, he spoke to me a couple of times, around the place." He was surprised at the look on his father's face.

"That Duke, they say he was an important man in his time. They say he fought with Pancho Villa, down in Mexico."

"On the wall at The Club there's pictures of him with Mexicans," Tony recalled.

"I also hear he got connections with a lot of crooks."

He shrugged. "I ain't seen no crooks."

"How come you hanging around the joint so much?" Bruno asked suddenly. "I hear you always in that place. Saturday's one thing, running the slips—I hear you in there nights, too."

"I been helping Angelo," Tony said quickly. Then he added, "Angelo's training me how to be a dealer."

46

"Oh, sure, I forget Angelo work for the Duke."

"I'm gonna be Angelo's assistant, I think."

"Maybe not so bad. Boccardi family good people—they don't do crazy things."

He guessed his father didn't know much about the true Angelo. "If I get offered the job, I'm gonna ask for a dollar a day, same as I'd get at the Wharf."

"O.K., you let me know what happens." Bruno rose. "Now I gotta make a move, or I be late opening the barber shop."

"What the heck you doing here this time of day, kid?" Boston Bailey opened the door of his hotel room only after several minutes of Tony's persistent knocking. He stood there looking dazed, the night still on his face.

"I didn't know what time you want me. I left it late, in case you wanted some extra sleep."

"What time is it?"

"Nine o'clock," Tony told him.

"In the *morning*, for Chrissakes?" Boston croaked. He glared at Tony, turned, and went back into the room. "I ain't seen this hour of day more'n once or twice since I was your age."

Tony followed him in. "Sorry, Boston, I didn't know."

"First thing you have to know is: gamblers don't get up early in the morning. It don't suit their constitution."

"I won't do it again, I promise. Want to go back to bed? I can come back later."

"Nah, I'm awake now—what the hell." He sat down on the bed, looking exhausted.

"I'm sorry. What time you want me to come along tomorrow?"

"Well," Boston said, "let me explain. Usually I get up around noon. That's when I ain't been out too late. Now, I come around slow, you understand, so it's a couple of hours before I'm cleaned up and fit to speak to. Then I gotta eat breakfast and prepare for the day. Around four o'clock should do it. Five's even better. I'm in good shape by five."

"In the evening?"

"Evening to you, son—morning to me." In answer to Tony's dubious look, he said, "Ain't as crazy as it sounds. I gotta be at my peak late at night, and the early hours of the morning. No way I'm gonna be like quicksilver if I'm yawning over the crap table, and my eyes are closing because it's my natural sleep time. You gotta think of it as shift work, get it?"

"Yes, I understand now."

"You'll be just the same, in a few years. Gamblers gotta be nocturnal, like cats. Watch a cat on a warm afternoon—if he missed his midday nap, he's likely to drop where he stands."

He decided secretly he would resist this strange conversion of night into day. Morning was the time he liked best, when everything was bright and fresh. He was young and strong, and he'd be able to survive without too much sleep. Boston was just an old man with unhealthy habits.

"Well, now I'm up, I better eat. I got this thing: when I don't get enough sleep, I get hungry. Maybe it's something to do with being thin. I dunno. You eaten, kid?"

"I had my breakfast at seven."

Boston winced. "You can eat again, can't you? I was your age, I done nothing but eat."

"Sure, I can eat any time." He grinned.

"O.K. Go down and speak to them guineas run this jerk hotel. They don't speak English so good, maybe you understand their lingo. Tell 'em Mr. Bailey wants a couple of steaks, done rare. Half a dozen eggs and a pile of toast. And plenty of coffee. Tell 'em to keep the coffee coming after breakfast. I want a fresh pot every hour—I don't wanna be falling asleep when I'm teaching you the moves."

"I'll tell them, Boston."

"Maybe, if you tell 'em in Italian, they'll get it right for once. I go down myself, I tell 'em exactly what I want, and they send me pasta. This pasta, that pasta—they drive you crazy. Don't the eyetalians eat nothing but pasta? The jerk hotel . . ." Tony was lost for a reply. "You make 'em understand down there, I want them steaks rare. And order anything you want for yourself. Anything you want, you got, O.K.?"

"Gee, thanks, Boston."

"Sure."

The grimy exterior of the hotel on Third Street, abandoned to soot like the frontage of its neighbors, belied its spic-and-span interior. He ran down the stairs, marveling again, as he had on the way up, at the luxury of rugs on every floor, the crocheted cushion covers on easy chairs at each floor level, and the embroidered damask. The dining room, which still held a few guests at breakfast, had linen tablecloths like his mother brought out for holidays, with hand-finished embroidery along the edges. The tables held classy-looking cutlery and crockery, all matching pieces. He'd never seen anything like it before. The owners were refined Italians, and they smiled respectfully and indulgently when he gave them Boston's order. In his confusion at the splendor, he couldn't decide what he wanted for himself. He ordered the same as Boston.

Back in the room, he said, "I ain't never seen a ritzy joint like this before. It sure is something, for Steub."

Boston glanced across. "It's nothing special, kid. Just another commercial hotel."

"You mean there's places like this all over?"

"Sure. Some're better than others. One like this, run by a family, it's got a little home atmosphere. Them guineas, they got a flair for running hotels, and cooking, all that stuff."

"What's your hometown like?" Tony asked interestedly.

"Ain't seen it since I was a kid. On the move since I been hustlin'—which is all of my life, I reckon."

"You mean you live in places like this all the time?"

"This ain't much, kid. In the cities they got bigger and better."

He resolved there and then he would live in nothing but classy hotels when he was a man. He wolfed down the enormous meal and sat back, satiated, to await instruction. Boston ate slowly and ceremoniously, then carefully smoked a cigar

48

right through, so that two hours passed before he finally reached down to pull out a case from under the bed.

"To begin with, you gotta know the different bones. I ain't saying I got them all here, and there's always some wise guy finds a new angle, but I got most types you're gonna find coming at you across a crap table." He took a leather pouch from the case and emptied it onto the bedcover. Tony goggled at the variety of dice that tumbled out. "But let me tell you something—if you're gonna be a top dice mechanic, you gotta learn to live without all this garbage. You gotta learn to make them straight bones talk. That means practice, plenty of practice. Like them great pianists who make it to Carnegie Hall. You heard about them pianists?"

Tony nodded. "I understand about practice, Boston. I got the hang of my trick by practicing. But Gimpy tells me there's ordinary guys around using the bogus dice. People who don't practice. How they manage that?"

Boston grinned. "Sure, there's always guys around desperate for dough who'll take a chance on getting killed. We ain't talking about them. We ain't talking about a game in the dirt with the hicks either. We're discussing a professional player—and remember, a pro ain't necessarily hustlin'. Maybe he's working in a carpet joint, so he's got to know how to protect the house. Got it?"

"I understand, Boston."

"But when he *is* hustlin', he's gotta be able to walk away from the table after the game, and nobody's gotta know they got took for their dough. Them other guys, they always end up running."

Tony smiled to himself. He'd never end up running. He'd make the bones talk, the way Boston did. He leaned forward in his chair.

Boston pointed to the dice on the bed. "I got here many different gaffed bones." He picked one up. "This here's a Load—it's a cube heavy on one side, so that's the side will face down after a roll. The simplest Loads got the spots drilled out and small weights put in. Dice loaded on the low numbers will bring four, five, and six so that both dice won't add up to seven. That way, you won't crap out after you made your point."

"They always show right side up?"

"Nothing's guaranteed. You have to understand about this business. Sometimes you get an unlucky break, but it ain't often if you know what you're doing. Take these particular dice—safest way is to use light Loads that'll give you a percentage advantage in the course of play. Heavy Loads are for a single shot, if you got any sense. Switch 'em in, score, switch 'em out."

"How do I recognize loaded dice?"

"O.K., that's a good question. The best way to check for Loads is to drop 'em in a glass of water. If they're heavy on one side, they turn as they sink to the bottom. But it ain't so easy. You're gonna imagine you're the dealer and there's a hot game running on the table—the shooter's winning bundles and you don't like the way he keeps grinning at his partner, so you wanna check he ain't switched in them gaffed cubes. You pull out the dice in play by switching in a fresh pair of straights. Now, maybe the shooter's a regular high roller, and he's gonna get awful peeved if you order up a glass of water and start dunkin' the dice. So you need something better'n that. That something's your fingers, and a delicate touch. Watch this." Boston held the die diagonally, point to point, between his thumb and forefinger. Nothing happened. He tried another diagonal. On the third try, the die slowly swiveled downward of its own volition. "We find we got here a gaffed bone," he said. "So we know we gotta bury the shooter."

"Let me try that." Tony held out an eager hand for the die.

"Take it easy. First I'm gonna show you more dice." He picked out several and held them in his hand. "Now, I'm gonna ask you a question: did you understand what I meant by percentage dice?"

"Sure I did. It means you got the edge on the other guy."

"You're a bright kid. In case it ain't crystal clear to you, however, percentage dice ain't gonna give you the result you want all the time, so you have to spread your bets—but in a whole session you're gonna be more right than wrong—savvy?" He held out his hand. "These are low-percentage dice and the great feature is, they're safer to use than Loads. This one here's a Shape. A Shape tapers a little toward one end, so it's most likely to stop on its widest side. It ain't so easy to spot Shapes, and nobody can say they ain't just poor-quality, cheap bones." He paused. "This next one is a Flat. A Flat is wider than it's high, so it gives you two faces bigger than the rest. Six-ace Flats is the most popular, and them is the numbers gonna be coming up most—the six and the one. That's good for missouts—a player's going for his point; it gives him a good chance to seven-out."

"Why does he want to seven-out, if he's going for his point? That's nuts," Tony said, mystified.

"It ain't nuts if he's betting he don't make it," Boston said testily. "People bet for and against. So does the crowd."

Tony nodded, his head bobbing up and down.

"These next ones: they're Tops and Bottoms, or Tees, as they're known. They got the same numbers both sides of the cube. You have to switch Tees in and out, and do it quick. They're real crooked dice. With these bust-out cubes you can fix it for a player to make any point, after his comeout roll. Later I'll explain the combinations of numbers you have to use."

"You say they got the same number of spots on each side?"

"Opposite sides of the cube, that's right."

"That means, with six faces, you use only three numbers."

"Yeah. The combinations you want. With two cubes rolling, you can rig the result."

"Can't people see they got the same number of spots on opposite faces?"

"Nope. Look at this . . ." Boston threw the cube he was holding onto the bedcover. "How many faces you see?" he asked Tony.

"Three. Two sides and the top."

"Right. You always see three faces, three different numbers. And that's all you're gonna see, unless you take a walk around the other side—then you'll see an exact duplicate of the first side. Now that ain't healthy for the shooter, so he don't leave bust-outs lying around. After the throw they gotta be snatched up off the table."

50

He pursed his lips. "Gee, I'm not sure I can handle all them different dice," he said uncertainly.

"Kid, you'll get the hang of it, believe me. Just remember what I told you yesterday. The key to the whole gig is the switcheroo. You get that right, the rest is like taking candy from a baby." He paused and looked at the door. "You sure you told them people downstairs to keep the coffee coming?"

"Yes. They said O.K."

"Them guineas," Boston said, more to himself than to Tony. "It ain't pasta, you don't get no service."

As if in answer, there was an immediate knock at the door. Boston threw the bedcover over the dice before he opened it. After the fresh, hot coffee, Tony found himself revived. He sat in the chair again, eager to continue.

"We're gonna take a look at the switcheroo," Boston said, "because it's the key to the whole business. Nothing works if you don't get it right. We're gonna look at the one-handed switch. Now, maybe you're the dealer—that means you're holding a stick, remember. So you have to lift the dice and make the switch entirely with the other hand. For this I gotta give you a demonstration." He pulled the bedcover forward off the dice and chose a pair of whites for Tony to examine. "They look O.K. to you?"

He examined them closely. Feeling he must have missed something, he offered them back. "I can't tell the difference, Boston. They look like straight dice to me."

"You're absolutely right. They are straight bones. Now throw them on the bed." When Tony had done so, Boston put his left hand in his pocket and picked up the dice with his right. "You notice, one hand only?" Tony nodded. "O.K., keep watching me. I'm gonna roll these straight white bones." Boston rattled the dice in his hand and threw them. They came out red.

"How in hell . . .?" Tony began.

"How'd I do that, kid? How'd I change the white bones for red ones?" Tony shook his head, which was beginning to feel like it would explode. In answer, Boston opened up his right hand. The white dice were gripped securely under the third and fourth fingers. "What does that tell you?"

"That you're using the same two fingers you used for the two-handed switch . . ." Tony said doubtfully.

"Well, that's true enough. When you think about it, you got only four usable fingers on the hand and you'll need two of 'em to pitch the gaffed bones, so you ain't got much alternative. But there's something else that's just as important: I had the two reds set up in my hand before I picked up the whites. And that's something you didn't see. I'm talking about preparation. While I was preparing the reds in my hand I was speaking to you so that you wouldn't notice what I was doing. Now, a dealer who's preparing to switch in a pair of gaffs, he can't talk in the middle of the game, so he distracts people who might be watching him. He reaches out and does something with the other hand while he's setting up the gaffs. Got it? The other hand is the one people will watch. If he's holding a stick with it, he can poke something, or move some checks about."

"I get it. That's how magicians do it—I been reading about magicians."

"We're talking about illusion, so I guess it's the same thing. Just remember, the preparation's just as important as the pitch." He paused, studying Tony's expression. "What's bothering you, kid?"

"I'm not sure," Tony said reluctantly. "It's just . . . well, all these gaffed dice. I guess there's no way to get straight dice to bring up the numbers you want, huh?"

"Waal," Boston drawled, "now, that's sump'n else again. I was gonna leave them moves till last. Yeah, sure, it's possible. Like I said, if you're aiming to be a top mechanic, you gotta make them bones talk." He thought for a moment. "I guess it makes no difference if I show you one or two moves now. Hand me over them straight whites—I'm gonna roll them on the bed." Tony handed across the first set of dice Boston had used. "If I get a seven or eleven on the comeout roll, I win. I get two, three, or twelve, I crap out. O.K.? That means I have to avoid that two, three, or twelve. Now, how'm I gonna do that little thing?" He rattled the dice in his hand and rolled them onto the bed. They laid up two fours. "That's good," Boston said. "I ain't won nothing, but I ain't crapped out either. My point is eight—I gotta get eight to win. Now, I'm telling you, make any bet you want that I'm going to win—all I gotta do is keep rolling until them spots add up to eight. Just keep watching . . ." He began rolling. On the third try, the dice laid up two and six. He grinned.

"For crying out loud, Boston, how you do that? I tried rolling for numbers—I tried for days and days. I just can't cut it."

Boston lifted the dice from the bedcover and held them up, pressed together between his thumb and forefinger for Tony to see. "Notice that I'm holding the bones with a six-point against my thumb and an ace against my forefinger," he said. "You can hold them the other way round, makes no difference. Now, I'm gonna shake 'em . . ." He closed his fist and shook, the dice rattling audibly. When he opened up again, the dice hadn't moved from their former position. "All I do is ease the pressure a little, so they knock together," he said. "This time when I roll, I'm gonna do it slow, so you can watch. You'll see the bones come off fingers one and two, just like I'm pointing the way for them to go. Them's the same fingers I use to pitch the gaffed bones. I gotta do it a special way, though, like this—they spin off my fingers like wheels and the six and the one stay on the outsides, sorta like an axle. Now keep your eyes open . . ." Boston's arm swept forward in a smooth motion, and this time Tony noticed how the dice started rotating when they left Boston's fingers. Just like little wheels.

He grinned at Tony. "Seeing as how you're gonna be a top mechanic, you no doubt already worked out that I ain't gonna crap out on two, three, or twelve, because there ain't no two numbers left to add up that way. And, out of the sixteen combinations left, I got four chances of laying up a natural seven. If that don't happen, I chase my point."

"There can be odds against repeating your point," Tony said brightly.

"Yeah, but there's something you can do about that. The same sixteen combinations give you sixteen more axles like the six-ace, right?" Tony stared. "There's a lot of odds to remember. I'll explain them to you later."

In his mind, Tony was already fingering the dice, practicing the six-ace. "Gee,

Boston, you're fantastic, throwing the dice on a bedcover and making them lay up the way you do."

"You appreciate that, huh?" Again Tony nodded. "Well, kid, I'm sorry to tell you it's just one more part of the illusion. On a soft surface, it ain't so hard to wheel the dice. On a hard surface, they bounce like crazy, and it ain't easy to get it right. Let me tell you a story: During the war the dice hustlers got to work in army camps. They was living in tents and they'd use, maybe, a blanket on the dirt floor. Them hustlers soon realized they'd found a good way to control the bones, using a throw like the six-ace. Them guys got themselves a bad name, and it got to the stage, anyone pulling a blanket off his cot to play craps was likely to get shot. That's how the Blanket Roll got its name." He walked across the room and tried the temperature of the coffeepot. He made a wry face and poured himself a cup.

"Any other moves, Boston?"

"Sure. Plenty. There's the slide shot, where the bones are thrown flat, so they don't spin." He brought his hand around in a deliberate, flat arc. "And there's variations of it, so the other players don't suspect the percentage advantage it gives you. For instance, rolling one and sliding the other, the two bones. The slide works real good on a shiny surface covered in dust or sawdust. The sawdust builds up in front of the bones as they slide and stops 'em rolling. Used to be an old icehouse miff, that one. Best to use real sharp, fresh dice, too. But don't use them sharp dice for the six-ace. For the wheel you need bevels. Them bevels, they run on forever."

"I got a lot to learn," Tony said thoughtfully.

"You sure have. We'll go back and begin with different types of bones, now you got the idea what they're for."

"O.K., Boston. Anything you say."

"Grab a handful, and tell me what each one is."

He got out of the chair and leaned across the bed, studying the dice. He hesitated. "Tell me something, Boston," he said slowly. "What did the Duke mean when he said he'd train me for a dealer if I got the nerve?"

Boston was silent, and Tony looked up at him. "That's something I just can't explain right now, kid," he said. "That's something you're gonna have to find out for yourself."

CHAPTER NINE

He strolled into The Club. In the three days that had passed he'd been elevated into a different world. There was a new confidence in his walk, and he grinned self-consciously when Gimpy caught sight of him. "Hi, Doc, you're sure looking pleased with yourself," Gimpy said.

"Hi, Gimpy." He leaned on the bar.

"Boston left town?"

"Yeah. He's gone on to Cleveland, bury them chumps over there."

Gimpy looked at him, then said, "You want a beer?"

"Thanks."

He brought the beer over. "How'd it go?"

Tony was too full of it to describe his experiences with the dice mechanic coherently. "Boston's a champ. Boy, did I learn some moves. I got it made."

Gimpy glanced at him again and, for a moment, wondered whether it wasn't all a mistake. It took a certain kind of temperament—and the kid had always given off the right signals. The rapid change in Tony's behavior bothered him. He put it down to youthful exuberance. "It ain't so easy," he said slowly. "Takes years of experience before a guy gets to handle the dice like Boston."

"Oh, I ain't saying I'm good as Boston," Tony came back. "I know I gotta practice. He showed me how it's done. He taught me a lot of moves. When I get them moves down square, I'm gonna show these people around here a thing or two."

Gimpy's expression hardened. "You ain't showing people nothing," he began. "Now, let's get something straight here right from the start . . ."

They were interrupted by a man who walked up and stood next to them at the bar. Tony hadn't seen him in the bar before. He was a down-and-out, one of many in the town these days, his suit threadbare, his attitude servile. The man took off his misshapen hat, stained where the summer heat had bled through the hatband, and stood waiting. "Yeah, Joe, what can I do for you today?" Gimpy's voice lost its harsh edge. It was clear as daylight he knew what was coming.

The man's eyes flitted uncomfortably to Tony, then back. "May I have a private word with you, Gimpy?" he said politely. He spoke well, Tony thought, like he'd had a college education. For all the good that'd done him.

"Ain't no need for privacy, Joe. You wanna ask something, ask out loud, the way you oughta."

"I don't mean to bother you." The man rubbed his unshaven chin. "Things haven't got better since I was last in here. I've been thinking about the couple of bucks I owe you."

"I'll wait, Joe. I understand."

"I was wondering if—."

"I don't reckon I can lend you any more, pal. Things ain't been too hot around here either," Gimpy put in.

"Sure, Gimpy, I know. It's the same all over. But I haven't had a decent meal in a week. I was wondering if . . ." His gaze went to the grill where Gimpy cooked up his renowned hamburgers and french fries.

Tony watched Gimpy's resolve crumble. "O.K., Joe, just this once. I'll put it on your tab."

"You're a pal, Gimpy. One of the best."

It took Gimpy a few minutes to serve up the food and return to the bar. "You crazy?" Tony shielded his mouth away from Joe. "This town's full of bums like that. The guys around, they say Gimpy's a soft touch—you know they say that about you?"

He barely concealed the cynical anger of his youth.

"Sure," Gimpy said emotionlessly. "It ain't done me any harm. People has hard times, that don't mean you gotta treat 'em like dirt. So O.K., they say I'm a soft touch. But they still got respect. That means something to me, kid. And I told you, it don't seem to have gotten into your thick skull—I said you have to be nice to people."

"I understand, Gimpy. But that guy, he's just a bum—how you gonna be nice to all them bums?"

For the first time he saw anger in Gimpy's face. "That bum," he said ominously, "is Mr. Joe Preston, the businessman, who is temporarily down on his luck, same as a lot of other respectable citizens who can't get it together this present time. What's more, you can bet your bottom dollar, the first chance Joe gets, he'll be in here to pay his tab. And, incidentally, I don't see the line-up of bums at the door, just because I extend Mr. Preston a little credit on his hamburger and french fries."

Tony winced. "Don't get sore."

"I'm gonna tell you straight, kid—I'm disappointed in you. You ain't grasped the principle. You gotta have respect. It pays to be nice to people."

"I'll remember that, Gimpy, honest."

"That's one of the house rules if you want to work here as a dealer. And there's something else I notice, while we're discussing your attitudes. Three days with a dice mechanic and suddenly you're full of shit. That's one thing gonna stop right now." He glared and pointed. Tony stared at the broom against the wall. "Your first job today, Mr. Big. Sweep this place through until there ain't a speck of dust on the floor. O.K., now hop to it."

Working industriously, it took him more than an hour to brush out The Club. When he'd finished, Gimpy inspected his work. "O.K., now go comb your hair and clean yourself up. The Duke wants to talk to you."

He hadn't been in the room behind the bar before. Occasionally, through the doorway, he'd caught a glimpse of the big roll-top desk where the Duke sat. Mostly the door was shut when the Duke was in there dealing with club business or speaking to his visitors. There was a small but regular flow of these visitors, Tony had noticed. Strangers in town, mostly, many of them prosperous looking and smart. Men who never stopped to play the tables in The Club. From all these visitors, there had been only one he had recognized—and then only because he'd seen Police Chief Linklater around town in uniform. He wasn't in uniform when he came to see the Duke.

He sat down in the chair next to the roll-top desk. "Well, Tony, how'd you get along with Boston Bailey?"

"Just fine, sir." Still shaken by Gimpy's tongue-lashing, he was cautious about his mouth.

"That all you have to say?"

"I seen all the moves—now I gotta practice."

The Duke nodded. "I want you to know, Boston thinks you got the makings. The rest is up to you—you understand?"

"Yes, sir. I'll be working on it."

"Chuck Peters will start training you. He'll be spending time with you when the table's quiet."

"Couldn't I learn under Angelo?"

"I said Chuck." The expression remained the same, and the tone of voice didn't change, but Tony knew it was an order.

"Chuck—right."

"Angelo may be a smart dealer, but I wouldn't rate him a teacher."

"Yes, sir."

"What's wrong, boy? You look uptight. Don't you want to train as a dealer? Most kids around these parts would give their eye teeth . . ."

He couldn't do a thing right today, he thought. "Oh, sure. I want that more than anything in the world," he blurted out.

For a while the Duke studied him in silence. Tony, more from fear than bravado, stared back, hoping he hadn't messed things up. It was the first opportunity he'd had to take a good long look at the Duke. The older man was no taller, when standing, than he was himself, but the middle-aged body appeared twice as sturdy as his own slim, youthful frame. The Duke's skin was brown, as if permanently tanned, and his dark eyes were set in a knowing face that never seemed to smile. His hair, almost gray, was always carefully slicked down, Tony had noticed, like those guys in the movies at the Rex. With the dark suit he always wore, it gave him a constantly groomed appearance. And the way he held his back upright, even while sitting in the chair, made him look purposeful and proud. "A few things we have to talk over before you start," the Duke said suddenly.

"Yes, sir." Tony became attentive.

"I've been watching you. I like the way you conduct yourself. You always look clean, and you're polite to your elders. These days, it seems few youngsters know how to behave. I know your father's an honest, hard-working man, and sometime I'll be over to Boccardi's barber shop and tell Mr. Vitale he should be proud of you."

Tony's mouth dropped open, that the Duke should be aware of him to the point of knowing about his father. When he closed it, he said, "It's Mama—she insists we always look good, with so many bums around."

"Good. You should listen to your mother," the Duke said. "Now, there's things about being a dealer you should know. For instance, you have to think like a bank clerk. You have to remember at all times that the money you're handling is not yours. That sound easy to you?" Tony nodded. "Well, it's not so easy as it sounds. It fools a lot of people. I'm going to tell you now: you'll be watched. In gambling there's always someone watching, often when you least expect it. Where money's concerned, people have big eyes. Just remember that."

"Yes, sir."

"You gotta learn not to be jealous of the player who's winning—or treat the one who's losing like a fool. When you're at the table, keep your personal feelings out of the game. A good dealer functions like a machine."

"I'll remember."

"Next thing: A dealer who's good becomes a valuable guy. But it takes time and

56

money to train him. I don't want you running off somewhere else soon as you're trained."

"I wouldn't do that," he started.

"How old are you, Tony?"

"Just seventeen."

"I want your father to sign that you'll stay on at The Club until you're twenty-one. Unless I discharge you."

He couldn't believe his ears. I'm sure my father will sign if I ask him," he said.

"It's like an indentured apprenticeship, you can say," the Duke added.

He nodded, although he didn't know what an indentured apprenticeship was.

"O.K., that's about it for the moment," the Duke said unexpectedly. "Go see Chuck—he knows what to do."

"Thank you, sir." He got up and stood for a moment uncertainly.

"Well, what is it, Tony?"

He wanted to say, "I won't take less than a dollar a day." It came out as, "Will I be getting wages, sir?"

"Sure. You'll be paid. You're working now."

"How much will my wages be?"

"I'll start you at ten dollars. You'll get more when you can handle the table on your own."

He couldn't believe his ears, and walked out of the Duke's office in a daze. There were men in Steubenville, grown men with families to keep, mouths to feed, who earned little more than ten dollars. Skeeter earned less, and so did Bob. What would those two wise guys have to say now? He was ahead of them in a single jump—and he hadn't started yet.

So much for a college education.

Gimpy eyed him suspiciously again. "You're looking pleased with yourself. I hope you ain't gonna be repeating them mistakes we discussed before."

"No, sir." He shook his head determinedly. "I'm here to learn. You won't have to tell me twice. Not about anything."

Gimpy appeared satisfied. "That's good, Doc," he said in the old friendly tone. "To learn, you came to the right place."

CHAPTER TEN

"You ready?" Mokey asked again.

Tony had lost count of how many times his brother had asked that question. "It's too early, yet. We don't have to be down at the barber shop before twelve," he said, tired of repeating himself.

"We don't wanna be late."

"Plenty of time, I told you."

"Maybe they got slips to send over."

"Makes no difference. Gimpy don't get into the place before twelve, Saturday. Simmer down, willya?"

Mokey paced the room, impatient at the prospect of taking over Tony's Saturday job, now that his brother had full-time work. "Maybe I should go on ahead and wait, just in case."

"Oh, for Chrissakes," Tony said crossly. He looked at the clock. "All right, we'll have a slow walk down. We'll still be too early."

"O.K., let's go." Mokey was at the door instantly.

The first couple of trips, he took Mokey across to The Club himself, just to show him the ropes. The third run, Tony sent him off on his own and watched as his brother tripped and went sprawling in the street in an excess of zeal. He winced to himself as Mokey scrabbled around, retrieving betting slips from the dust. Thankfully, nobody in the barber shop had seen—there would be hell to pay if one of the slips was lost. But that was Mokey—he couldn't do anything right. After that, the afternoon passed slowly for him, punctuated only by Mokey's periodic galloping back and forth.

Then he saw her, as she walked carefully past the shop and turned to go into the side entrance. She hesitated a moment, their eyes met, and she was gone. After a while, he said, "I'll be hanging around outside, Papa. Not much I can do in here." Bruno, clipping away busily, looked up momentarily and nodded.

He stood outside the shop, stretched, and strolled around to the side entrance. The door was kept open during the day to accommodate the ebb and flow of the Boccardi tribe. He looked down the passage and could see as far as the stairway that led to the rooms above—there was no sign of her. For a few minutes he hung around in various nonchalant poses and was about to move on when he heard one of the Boccardi kids clattering down the stairs. He knew some of the faces, but not the names. This one was a girl, about twelve. "Francesca upstairs?" he asked.

"Who wants to know?" She eyed him up and down. She knew him well enough, by sight.

"Look, kid, just answer the question."

"Maybe she is, maybe she ain't."

"I saw her go in."

"You wanna be announced?"

"Just tell her she's wanted."

"Who by?"

"Say it's Antonio."

"So that's your name, is it? I seen you around—you're the barber's kid, right?"

"You going, or not?"

"O.K. Just asking."

A few moments later she returned unhurriedly to stand in the doorway, leaning on the frame and studying him with renewed interest.

"Well?" he demanded.

"She's coming. Prettying herself up. You gonna be Frankie's boyfriend?"

"What gives you that idea?"

58

"She ain't got a steady. About time, if you ask me."

"We got things to talk about, that's all."

"Yeah, I bet. You'll have to meet Mama, you know, you wanna be Frankie's steady. She'll wanna check you out."

"Look, dummy, nobody's getting serious. Besides, I know your pa well."

"It's Mama. She's a drag. She says all the Steubenville boys are beasts. You a beast?" she added hopefully.

He was glad to see Frankie coming down the hall. The younger girl slid beneath his arm and was gone out the door.

"You want Angelo?" Frankie asked innocently. "He's out."

"No. I come to tell you—I won't be running the slips for your pa anymore."

"Oh. That means I won't be seeing you." Considering how rarely they saw each other as it was, she sounded disappointed.

"I thought maybe we oughta keep in touch."

"Yes." She stood there demurely, while he shuffled his feet. He noticed that her hair was nicely combed and she looked fresh and dewy-eyed. When his gaze reached her breasts, he looked away.

"Hey, tomorrow's Sunday. You wanna meet somewhere?"

"I don't know . . ."

"I'll call around if you want."

She thought. "Sometimes, after church, I go out walking with my sister."

"Maybe I can just tag along. I like walking, too."

"O.K."

"I'll look for you after mass. Is that the sister I was just talking to?"

"Yes—Teresa."

"We gonna have her along all the time?"

"She bothers you?"

"What, your sister?" he said stupidly.

"I'll talk to her. She's too bossy, for a twelve-year-old."

"Aw, that's all right."

"I have to go now, Antonio. I'm helping Mama bake some cookies. See you tomorrow, then."

"O.K., Francesca."

He liked the formality of using her full name. He wanted her to feel he had respect. Walking back around the corner to the barber shop, he whistled happily to himself.

"There's a package here for you, Doc." Gimpy reached under the bar. "Come in the mail today."

"For me?" Tony looked at the small, tightly sealed brown paper package in disbelief. "You sure it's for me?" He'd never received any mail before.

"Your name still Tony Vitale?"

"Yes, sure."

"Then it's for you."

He took the package gingerly and studied it. "It's from Chicago—a place called Cicero," he read.

"Uhuh."

"But I don't know anyone in Chicago."

"Well, it seems someone there knows you, Doc."

"I don't understand."

"Why don't you try opening the package?"

It had been carefully taped, and he was timorous about breaking the seals. The package looked much too important to concern him. Inside the brown paper was a cardboard box. When he removed the lid a card fell out. It said: THE GREAT LAKES GAMBLING NOVELTIES COMPANY, CHICAGO. Then he knew. He lifted out the soft leather pouch and opened it on the bar. A profusion of colored dice fell out.

"Boston Bailey," Gimpy said immediately.

"He didn't say he was gonna . . ." Tony began.

"That sly old son of a bitch—got a soft spot for you."

"Gee, just look at 'em, Gimpy. They're all here—Loads, Shapes, Mif Spots, Tops and Bottoms. Now I can get some real practice in." A look of concern crossed Gimpy's face. "What's wrong?" Tony asked.

"Make sure it's only practice, kid. You ain't ready to own them things, yet. Keep 'em home."

"Sure, Gimpy." He swept the dice back into the pouch. "I ain't stupid."

"Just remember. What you got there is dynamite. Use 'em for real the wrong time, some guy's gonna break your back."

"You crazy?" Tony laughed. "I ain't never played a serious game of craps yet. I told you."

The blanket roll was easy. He quickly mastered the art of wheeling the cubes off his fingers onto a soft surface, keeping the six-ace axis level. Taming the pitch onto a hard tabletop was a very different matter, and he spent hour after hour in utter frustration, with the dice spinning away uncontrollably in different directions. He almost gave up. Boston had said it wasn't absolutely necessary to master the hard-top action—that the felt of a crap table gave sufficient adhesion to simulate the stabilizing effect of a soft blanket. Few mechanics ever mastered it anyway. And for that very reason, Tony kept trying. If it could be done, he was going to do it. It took a couple of weeks of blind determination before the dice began to run for him, before his fingers developed the magic touch. The secret was, he found, that the cubes had to leave his fingers in a perfectly horizontal position. Any deviation, however slight, any angle imparted to the axis of the twin dice, and the throw was wasted. He taught himself to control the hard-top horizontal six-ace pitch to near-perfection.

"You been seeing Frankie, I hear," Angelo said suddenly. It was early in the evening, and there was little action on the crap table.

"Yeah," Tony admitted. "We been walking-out a few Sundays. Teresa, too."

Angelo grinned. "You won't get no hanky-panky with that one along. Boy, has that got a mouth on it, for a twelve-year-old. You make one move, you're gonna be headline news, I'm telling you."

"Aw, she ain't so bad. I kinda got used to her."

60

"That's when it gets dangerous. Them women, they get to work on you. Drop your guard for a minute—zap, they got you where they want you."

"Teresa's only a kid. What can she do?"

"Ha," Angelo said. "I can see you don't understand them women. They're born that way. The only thing they got in mind is manipulate the guy. That Teresa, she's already an expert. She's feeding ideas to Frankie all the time."

"About me?"

"Sure about you, dummy, what you think? They have the nightly conference up there—every night they talk about it, make the plans."

"What the heck's there to talk about every night?"

"They find. Believe me."

They had to give their attention to the game when three players arrived at the table together. Tony was still working as Angelo's assistant, paying out, and he performed the task mechanically. It was becoming automatic to him to calculate the odds on the various bets across the layout, and to check quietly on Angelo's payouts. He usually had time, too, for a discreet study of the faces around the rim, and the players' behavior. That was how he recognized him—the man who'd silently accepted Angelo's generous overpayment on his bet. There was no mistake. He was the same guy, making a five-dollar bet on the pass line now, with no real interest in the game. Tony got the feeling the man was just passing time, as if waiting for something. He was, and, in disbelief, Tony spotted what it was he'd been waiting for.

From his position next to Angelo at the rim, he'd noticed when Angelo's hand went to his right pants pocket and he saw Angelo make the clumsy switch. It happened when the man opposite put a hundred dollars on the pass line. The shooter threw a point of eight, and again Angelo switched the dice. Two or three throws later, the guy made his point. Angelo paid out across the table, and Tony watched covertly, fascinated to see the bogus dice switched back out of the game.

In the course of an hour the partners repeated the sham win three times. Then the other guy picked up his winnings and casually sauntered off. Angelo had used Tops and Bottoms, Tony was sure. It wasn't that he was so surprised to see the other cheating—what amazed him was the ineptitude of the switching. Angelo was working at a standard Tony had left behind weeks ago—he'd cringed inwardly at each switch, waiting for the outcry as someone spotted it. Nobody had. And it struck him forcefully how much easier it was for the dealer to cheat than the player. Most eyes at the table were on the player if the dealer timed his switch right. He thought about it. Later, in a quiet spell, he whispered in Angelo's ear: "Them Tees you got there, they ain't so clever." Angelo stood stock-still, staring forward. "I see the switcheroo," Tony added.

"You know about switching?" A nervous movement of Angelo's hand betrayed him.

"Boston showed me the moves."

"Boston Bailey?"

"Didn't you know?"

"Nobody said . . ." It was then he realized that the Duke and Gimpy hadn't taken Angelo into their confidence. In the same moment he wondered if this had been deliberate. "You know about Tops and Bottoms?" Angelo said.

"You was using Lows on the comeout roll. Then you switched to even numbers."

"What you gonna do about it?" Angelo said, without rancor. He made no attempt to deny it, and Tony made no reply. "They find out, they'll bust me. They'll bust me good . . ." His tone of voice changed to a plea.

"Maybe they already know. They could be testing me. Maybe I'm supposed to spot you're cheating."

Angelo considered this. Tony watched his hands trembling slightly. "No, I don't think so. They're too cool." He paused. "You gonna split?"

"No point . . ." He came back at once. "I wouldn't get your job, I ain't ready for it yet. They think I'm too young."

"Listen, Tony—taking from them, it ain't like stealing. They stealing themselves, from the players."

"I ain't seen no stealing."

"You will—you're around long enough, you'll see."

"I dunno," he said doubtfully. "You gotta decide. You working for the house, or for yourself—you can't mix it, way I see it."

"You're right," Angelo admitted immediately. "Keep your trap shut, and you got a hundred dollars," he suggested.

"No," Tony answered quickly. He knew instantly that he mustn't compromise himself with Angelo. That could only mean trouble.

"What, then?"

"Not when I'm at the table, you understand that? What you do when I'm not here—that's got nothing to do with me. But not when I'm around."

"O.K., you got a deal. Thanks, Tony, you're a stand-up guy. Sure you can't use a C-note?" Angelo added hopefully.

A hundred dollars was more than he dared dream about. He swallowed and made the decision. "I don't need it right now," he said.

CHAPTER ELEVEN

The dark clouds finally fulfilled their threat and rain began to fall in a fine drizzle. He looked into the distance, but there was no sign of them. For another ten minutes he walked up and down the pathway in the park, clicking the dice in his pocket impatiently, getting damper and damper, and wondering whether they'd turn up or not. Girls were very particular about their appearance, and he guessed they wouldn't like getting their hair wet, and all that, walking in the park. Then he saw her, hurrying through the entrance toward him. His heart skipped a beat. She was alone. "Where's Teresa?" he asked, when she reached him.

"Oh, she couldn't make it today," Frankie said blandly. Her big, dark, candid eyes smiled innocently at him over the cheeks flushed by her brisk walk in the rain. "She's gone to her friend's birthday party."

"That's too bad."

"Not a very nice day, is it?"

"You rather go back home?"

"No, I'm O.K.," she said quickly. "I like the rain."

They turned and began walking. The farther they got, the harder the rain fell. "It's getting worse," he said. "We're getting soaked through. Maybe we ought to get in somewhere, out of the rain."

"There's nowhere out here, in the open. I suppose we'll just have to go back." She'd stopped walking.

"There's the old summer house over there." He pointed. The broken windows of the dilapidated, unused summer house peeped over the bushes forming an island in the middle of the park. A sign, prominently displayed, said: KEEP OUT. DANGER.

"We're not supposed to go in there."

"Just for a few minutes—until this rain stops."

She followed him hestitantly as he stepped over the low, iron-link chain ringing the prohibited area. The door to the summer house was off its hinges, hanging drunkenly to one side. Inside, the floor was thick with moldering old leaves, bracken, and refuse blown in by past winds. As they walked on it, broken glass crunched beneath the foliage. "We shouldn't be in here, we'll get into trouble," she said.

"We'll only be here a few minutes—just till the rain stops," he said. "Nobody around anyway."

Over to one side, an area of the roof had remained intact and sheltered an old wooden bench. He brushed debris off the bench and they sat down. "It's awfully lonely in here," she said. There was an air of abandonment about the old summer house, which was heightened by the dismal day. "It frightens me. Let's get out." She moved closer to him.

He put a comforting arm around her shoulders. "Relax, Frankie—we're O.K. in here. A few minutes, until the rain eases off." The nearness of her excited him. They sat there just listening to the rain, until he pulled her a little closer to him. She yielded, and when she turned to look at him, he kissed her timorously on the mouth. Then she decorously pushed him off and moved away a few inches along the bench. "Don't you want me to kiss you?" he asked.

"Yes, I don't mind."

"Then, what's wrong?"

"Nothing's wrong."

"Why'd you do that?"

"Do what?"

"Push me away."

"I didn't push you—I moved away myself."

"Why'd you move away?"

"We shouldn't be here alone," she said.

After a moment, he said, "Don't you trust me?"

63

"Yes—it's not you I'm afraid of." Her sophistry came from beyond her seventeen years, and she was staring at him with a look he'd never seen before. Her eyes had become huge round pools. He felt his heart thumping away in his chest, as if he'd been running uphill. He reached out for her, but she brushed him aside. She stood up suddenly. "I'm going now," she said.

"But it's still pouring rain out there." He stood, too, and in doing so, moved a step closer.

"Doesn't matter."

When he reached for her the second time, he felt her whole body trembling. He pulled her to him and she made no protest, but remained stiff and unyielding. When he tried to kiss her she turned her face away. "What's wrong, Frankie?"

"You're not being fair." She said it quickly, breathlessly.

"I don't wanna be fair," he said roughly.

When he leaned forward to kiss her, she arched her back in an effort to evade him, but he was taller and held her so she couldn't resist. When, in desperation, she turned her face to him, their lips met. At first she gasped for air, then, when she stopped struggling, he found her mouth blending hungrily with his. Behind the kiss she began to moan, and he felt her arms go around him. When she pressed herself to him, it was with unexpected strength. In the damp, dripping summer house, the heat between them mounted rapidly.

They heard it together, the sound of footsteps crunching on broken glass behind them. They sprang apart guiltily. The twelve-year-old with the knowing eyes stood in the doorway, rain running out of her hair and down her face in rivulets. "Hi, gang," Teresa said. "Not much of a birthday party. Thought I'd come across and keep you company, like always."

"I hear you working regular over at The Club these days," Bluey Esposito said to him.

"Yeah. I got a job helping Angelo Boccardi," Tony said.

"Word is he's a top dealer, that Angelo. Best in town, they say."

"I didn't know that." He was surprised.

"Yeah, that's what they say." They were watching Skeeter and Bob berate each other in the regular, bad-tempered Sunday game of pool. The New Philly had attracted a few more customers than usual, and they'd had to wait for the table. "I wish I could get work in a better-class joint. The Kokomo, where I am—boy, is that place a dump. Even the sawdust on the floor is secondhand."

"So why don't you find something else?" Tony said, only half-interested.

Bluey looked at him. "You kidding? There ain't a job around. I'm only holding on to mine by the skin of my teeth. There's a dozen guys waiting to step into my shoes, I make a wrong move."

"That bad, huh?"

"Where you been? Don't you know how bad things are in this town?"

"Oh, I got some idea," he said.

"Everybody's stealin'. Thing is, there ain't nothing left to steal."

"Tell you something," Tony said. "There's still some guys around with dough. We get some real action over there, at The Club. High rollers. The Duke, he knows

64

lots of people from out of town. I seen as much as a grand on the layout at times."

"Gee, I'd like to see some of that action. In the Kokomo, all we got is garbage, local dropouts, bums. Ain't often we see an out-of-towner with real money, not over there."

"What you expect? Nobody in his right mind gonna go into that fly-blown joint."

"Don't I know it."

An idea was forming in Tony's mind. He glanced across at his morose companion. "Say, Bluey, what you say we play craps? I never played a real game of craps yet."

"Aw, I can't be bothered."

"I mean for money. If you beat me, you keep the winnings. I got seven, eight dollars here." He pulled out the money and waved it temptingly under Bluey's nose.

"You'll lose your dough, that's for certain," the other said. But he sat up.

"I'll take the chance. I gotta get live experience somewhere."

"O.K." Bluey brightened. "We'll use the pool table when they finish the game."

He had the dice ready in his hand. Plain whites. They matched the Loads and Tees he had ready in the other pocket. Skeeter, never one to be left out of a game, was in from the first throw, and Bob soon followed. But it was Bluey he watched, closely, for any change of expression, any sign of awareness. A dealer used to handling dice constantly would spot the moves quicker than anyone else. That was the test. And it was a safe test, here between friends. At least he wouldn't get his head kicked in if he couldn't cut it.

At first he played straight and was soon down to his last dollar. He reflected wryly to himself that, with his luck, there was little future in straight play. Bluey didn't notice when he switched in a pair of Tees as passers. To the others it seemed Tony had a miraculous change of luck. When he had his money back, he switched the gaffed dice out of the game and let the straights go to Bob. He bet cautiously until the dice came around to him again. This time he introduced a pair of six-ace Flats and slowly took their money away, to the accompaniment of Skeeter's indignant protests. He was about to clean out his friends completely, grinning to himself, when a new man appeared at the table. He wasn't a total stranger—they'd seen the white-faced guy around the New Philly from time to time. "This a private game? Whiteface asked. "I'm feeling lucky."

Skeeter, almost out of money, gave a belligerent grunt. The other two looked up from the table indifferently. "There's always room for one more," Tony said, and moved over to make space. It was a good opportunity for a live trial—any trouble, they were four to one.

Whiteface pulled out his roll. The other three gave quick, envious glances at the money. "First bet a buck." The man stripped off a bill.

"Nothing under two dollars. Two dollars the smallest bet," Tony said. The others looked at him sharply, but he maintained an even expression.

Whiteface wilted. "That's a little strong, fellas."

"That's the game. You in or out?" Tony said firmly. He waited, and his friends remained silent, wondering what he was up to.

The guy shrugged. "O.K., I'm in."

"Let's go."

Skeeter and Bob were soon cleaned out. Bluey recovered his losses, and Whiteface held his own. When the dice came to Tony, he was ready. His comeout roll gave him a point of six. They didn't notice him wheeling the straight dice on the six-ace axis. Then he switched the straights for a pair of even-numbered Passers and began to pitch. And the damn six just refused to appear. He was throwing everything else but. He felt sure they must be noticing the succession of even numbers turning up, unless they were blind. He decided it had gone too far—he'd have to pull the gaffed dice out of the game and start again. He felt the beginning of panic as Bob and Skeeter, borrowing from Bluey, placed what they could on the layout, betting against him and watching each throw of the dice with eagle eyes. He would give it just two more rolls, he decided, certain that they would discover his deception. On the very last roll, the cubes lay up the elusive six. He let out his breath in a sigh of relief as Skeeter yelled and thumped the table. Then he almost forgot to snatch the gaffed dice from the layout.

He'd taken everybody's money. All of it. "Remind me the fuck to find some unlucky players in the future, willya?" Whiteface said sourly, and stomped out of the club.

He let them cool off. Then he called them back to the table and spread his winnings across the layout. He gave the three of them their money back, and added five dollars each from Whiteface's losses. They looked at him in consternation. "What's this for?" Bluey was the first to speak. "It's your dough. You won it."

"It's to celebrate the event," Tony said.

"What event?" Bob put in.

"The first and last time you guys are ever gonna play a game of craps with me."

"What you talking about, prick?" Skeeter said. "So you had a lucky streak, so what? You ain't gonna win every time you play, believe me." He laughed.

"I can win any time I want."

"What you talking about?" Skeeter said again.

"I'll show you." Tony looked across the table. "Name my point, Skeets," he said.

"O.K., make it a nine," Skeeter said suspiciously.

He had the odd-and-even gaffs ready in his right hand. As Boston had said, preparation was everything, and he'd planned the move before he started the discussion. He pitched the odd pair and, as luck would have it, they laid up an instant nine. When he looked up, it was to see three confounded expressions.

With a yell, Bluey stepped across, grabbed Tony's right hand, and turned it over to reveal the remaining dice concealed by two fingers. "Jes-us," he said in admiration, "if only you could do that in the Kokomo, we'd clean out the motherfuckers."

"Maybe I could," Tony said.

CHAPTER TWELVE

They stood in the dark watching the Ku Klux Klan cross burning in the hills above the town. "We got Italians—we got plenty Italians," Skeeter said. "Also we got them Yugoslavs, Greeks, Germans, Syrians, Poles, and Russians. We got the Irish and we got the Jews." He counted off the races on his fingers. "Now, who the fuck them Klan pricks burning them crosses for?"

"You ain't mentioned the niggers. It's the niggers they don't want in town, most of all," Bob said.

"We ain't got many niggers. Not like some places, we ain't."

"Yeah. There's a nigger doctor moved into a house up on North Jefferson. The guy just moved in and put up his shingle. They don't want no niggers on North Jefferson, that's a high-class neighborhood. Them Wasps, they're going crazy. Last night the KKK stuck a cross in his front garden and set it on fire. They threw rocks through his windows."

"What they afraid of?" Tony said. "One nigger doctor ain't nothing to get upset about."

"It don't stop there. They figure, once the niggers move in, the whites'll start getting out of the street. Nobody wants a nigger for a neighbor. That way, them niggers get to grab the whole street. Then, the whites not only gotta sell out, they get a shafting on the prices. They can't get fancy prices when there's niggers in the street."

Tony wasn't convinced. "It don't have to happen that way, not just because of one black doctor," he said stubbornly.

"You gotta be realistic," Skeeter said. "Just look at your own street. All guineas—ain't hardly nobody but Italians live on the street where you are. That's how ghettos get started up."

"Our street's no ghetto," Tony said indignantly. Inside him a small apprehension had begun. Bruno Vitale's efforts, over the years, to assimilate himself and his family into an alien society, had not been without cost. Part of this cost had been the transmission, to his sons, of a fear of the Establishment. As with many of his contemporaries, this fear emerged in Tony as a resolve to avoid the Establishment like the plague, or at worst to defy it and its representatives. Then the fear was replaced by the anger of youth. He had the same rights as a native-born American. He was as good as any of them.

Skeeter cut into his thoughts. "Let's go up in the hills and take a look," he suggested.

It was some distance on foot, considerably more than it appeared, to where the cross burned in the night. When they finally turned off the road onto the wide dirt track that led to the high point in the hillside forest, they could see the flames from the burning cross leaping above the trees into the sky. They rounded the last bend and the clearing came into view. There were at least a hundred robed, hooded figures standing at the base of the huge, flaming wooden cross that burned so intensely white in the night. They stopped where the parked cars began. The cars stretched along the track all the way up into the clearing. "We going on up there?" Bob said doubtfully.

"Sure. Why not?" Skeeter could always be counted on for bravado—the right sort and the wrong. "Let's take a closer look." He strode forward resolutely, and Bob fell into step beside him. Tony took up the rear uncertainly.

They got no more than four paces when the hulking figure in uniform stepped out from between two cars, arms spread wide to bar their path. They stopped; all three were familiar with the beefy silhouette of Hoyle, the cop. "Where you boys think you're going?" Hoyle said.

"Up there." Skeeter pointed toward the gathering.

"That's a private meeting," Hoyle said in a neutral tone. "You're not invited."

"We don't aim to join the meeting," Skeeter said. "We just wanna take a look."

"You ain't looking at nothing. Just turn your butts around in the opposite direction and get back where you came from."

Skeeter considered this, then said, "Listen, cop, it's a free country, ain't it? There's no law says we can't take a look just because it's the KKK up there."

"Who says it's the KKK?"

"What the fuck they doing in them bedsheets, it ain't the KKK?" Skeeter said.

"I don't see no KKK. Seems to me you come up here just to make trouble."

"We ain't making no trouble. Just taking a peaceful walk, like we got a right to."

"Only rights you got are the ones I say. Now, I'm gonna tell you for the last time—get out of here before I run you in. You understand? You already committed misdemeanors, abusing a police officer and telling lies. I ain't gonna warn you again about your behavior."

Skeeter stood his ground. "I ain't causing no trouble," he insisted.

"And he's not telling lies either." Tony, from behind, added his support.

Hoyle stared past Skeeter at Tony. "Now we got two making trouble. You're the guinea kid, ain't you—one of them guineas from Sixth Street?"

Tony felt the fury running through his veins. He made an effort to control his response. "I'm an American, same as you. Same as them people up there . . ." He pointed toward the leaping flames. "I got the same rights they got—the law says so."

"Not in my book, you ain't, guinea." The hate percolated through Hoyle's words. "And I represent the law in these parts; don't you forget it." He took a threatening step forward. "I got the feeling a night in the pokey's what you kids need—teach you young jerks a thing or two."

Bob, who'd stood silent this far, reacted badly. At the cop's threat, he hopped to one side evasively. Hoyle bridled up, and Skeeter and Tony moved instinctively into defensive attitudes. It was enough for Hoyle. "O.K., boys, let's get 'em," he called out to the dark.

Tony sensed rather than saw the fleeting figures come from behind. There was a rush of feet and some flying dirt, then the sudden crack on the side of his head came as an unbelievable shock. His knees buckled, and he felt himself sinking to the ground, absorbing the blows as heavy boots sank into his body. The next thing he knew, he found himself on all fours, the night sky going around above him. His head hurt, and putting his hand to it meant he fell to the ground once again. He took his hand away from his head to stare stupidly at the blood. Then someone wrenched his arms behind him and he felt the handcuff's snap together on his wrists.

From a great distance, he heard Hoyle's voice saying, "Take 'em down and lock 'em up. A night in jail's just what they been asking for."

It was too much of an effort to stay awake. He felt his eyes rolling in his head before he lost consciousness.

Through the bars of his cell Tony watched anxiously as Hoyle, swinging a bunch of keys imperiously, led his father through the Third Street Jail to claim him. Bruno was dressed carefully in his Sunday suit and hat, and he wore a new starched collar as a mark of respect for the law—and to expedite Hoyle's promise to release his son into his custody and control. When his father sighted Tony's bandaged head, he ran forward and a cry of anguish left his lips, his dignity forgotten, to reach for Tony through the bars.

"My Antonio—you're hurt." Bruno's lips quivered and tears filled his eyes.

"I'm all right, Papa. It's just a scratch, honest."

"My son."

"Not here, Papa. Don't cry in here—not in front of them." The vehemence in Tony's voice brought Bruno up short.

"Antonio, what they do to you?" he asked in a breaking voice.

"I'm O.K. Pull yourself together. Nothing to worry about, honest, Papa. Just get me outa here, willya?"

Bruno quelled the tears, but he couldn't control his quivering lower lip. When the cell door swung open, he claimed his son with a firm, protective clasp and, under the mocking leer of Hoyle, led him from the jail. He propelled Tony through the streets, arms linked, in grim silence, not trusting himself to speak until they reached home. Safely behind his own front door, he allowed his emotions their reign. To the accompaniment of Maria's evocation of the Deity's protection, he enfolded Tony in his arms, and the tears flowed freely down his cheeks.

Eventually, Bruno gained enough control of himself to say, "Antonio, you must promise your mama and me, no more fights with the police. We got trouble enough already, this town, without a good boy like you getting arrested."

"Honest, Papa, we weren't doing a thing."

"I know what happen. That officer, Hoyle, he explain—you get into bad company. You make bad friends and they lead you astray. I understand that. You not bad boy."

"I was with Skeeter and Bob, nobody else. They been my buddies for years," Tony protested.

"He say you go up on the hill to make trouble."

"That ain't true." He contained his impulse to call Hoyle a dirty liar. "You gotta believe me, Papa. We just wanted to take a look at the KKK doing their stuff, that's all."

Bruno's eyes rounded in horror. "You keep away from them people, you hear? For the love of Jesus, promise me you never again go to make trouble with them bad people."

He looked up as Bruno's cry permeated the room. He was more concerned for his father's peace of mind than his own satisfaction. "All right, Papa, I promise. We never again go near the KKK. You got my word."

"They got all the power, all the money, them people. Us foreigners, we ain't got no power. Best thing, keep outa their way, and hope they leave us in peace."

Bruno had never before seen the cold challenge that flickered into his son's eyes. Tony spoke in a flat voice. "We ain't foreigners no more. We're Americans, same as them. We got equal rights—the law says so. They ain't better'n we are, and I ain't afraid of 'em.

"I ain't afraid of anyone, Papa."

"Let me explain the whole thing to you," Skeeter was saying slowly. "There's no risk and we just can't go wrong. The biggest danger at the crap table is the dealer, right? It's the dealer's job to spot the hustler, right?" Tony nodded cautiously. "O.K., then that angle we got tied up."

"How about the other players at the table? They got eyes, too, you know," Tony said doubtfully.

"Aw, forget 'em. They'll be too busy trying to save their own hides to worry about what you're doing. Once you start winning, they'll be more likely to follow your bets than play against you. Players are like sheep, you know that. It's only the dealer you gotta worry about."

"He's right," Bluey put in. "If the dealer don't spot your moves, you got it made. Now, this game, we know the dealer ain't gonna be seeing nothing—we know the dealer's gonna be looking the other way. How we know that? Simple—I'm the dealer."

"I don't like it. Maybe I'm just not good enough. I never played against a house, out in the open like that."

"Jeez, I wish I could handle the dice like you," Skeeter said in exasperation. "I wouldn't hesitate. I'd go in there and give that Kokomo the screwing it deserves."

"There's something else bothers me. No sense going in there for revenge, the way you wanna do it, just because they took us once. They take everyone who goes into the joint. We deserved it and they don't owe us a thing. If I go in it'll be to hit them for money—no other reason, understand that."

"Yeah, he's right," Bluey agreed. "If we aim to wipe 'em out, we're asking for trouble."

"O.K., I agree." Some of the excitement went out of Skeeter's eyes. "If that's the way you want it, it's all right with me. Just so long as we take 'em. How much we going for?"

Tony turned to Bluey. "How much can we go for without them getting suspicious?"

"More'n a hundred bucks and they're gonna get real interested in what you're doing. I'm telling you. Ain't often a guy comes outa the Kokomo with a hundred fish their money."

"O.K., then, we make it a hundred bucks. That's the target," Tony said.

"How about me? I got any part in this?" Bob put in.

"No. Two people is a normal gambling party," Bluey said. "Three's a gang. More reason they'll keep an eye on you."

"Yeah, you stay out, Bob. Tony and me, we'll do it. We're gonna screw them bastards real good," Skeeter said.

"Maybe I better come along, just in case there's trouble," Bob offered.

"Let's get one thing straight," Tony said. "We ain't going in the joint looking for trouble. Just to collect some money, quiet and peaceful."

"I hope you're right," Bob said.

The interior of the Kokomo was even seedier than he remembered it. The insignificant stakes on the layout told him all he needed to know about the group standing desultorily around the table. Bluey was dealing the game in a measured, detached manner and gave no sign of recognition when they stepped up to the table. But their presence hadn't gone unnoticed. Two men at the back of the room put their heads together, and the bigger of them approached Tony from behind to tap him on the shoulder. Tony turned around. "Ain't you the kid works over at The Club?" the man said quietly.

"That's right," Tony agreed.

"What you doing in here?"

"Night out with my buddy." The man looked around and Skeeter nodded to him.

"Do I got it wrong, or you a dealer over there, at The Club?"

"I'm learning," Tony said, with an excess of adolescent pride. "I'm helping out at the table."

The man chuckled. "This wouldn't be my idea of a night out, kid, if I worked in a club. Myself, I was your age, I'd be out chasing myself some tail."

"Yeah, that's what I say." Tony smiled. "My buddy, he's kinda a compulsive gambler—you know how they are. He lost his dough in here a while back. He's hoping I'm gonna give him some tips and show him how to win his money back."

"Uhuh, I get it." The man stepped back.

"So it's O.K. with you if we play?" Tony took some bills from his pocket.

"Oh, sure, kid. Be my guest. And good luck."

"Gee, thanks."

He thought carefully about how best to do it. His first preference was for the secret pocket, but he decided against using it. The risk of discovery in the Kokomo was an unknown quantity and the secret pocket would be undeniable proof of his guilt. Exposure would leave him of little use to the Duke, so he could say goodbye to his job. Then the idea hit him—he would use Skeeter as a feeder. Boston had explained how this was done. In Skeeter's pockets would be a selection of gaffed dice to be fed to him on prearranged signals.

At the table the action was straight, Tony decided, when he started betting. Skeeter stood pressing into his back, gazing over his shoulder in readiness. Bluey wielded the stick in his right hand, which they had agreed meant there was no dice hustler operating at the table. When Tony became the shooter, he used the six-ace pitch to draw two sevens, one after the other. Interest quickened among the jaded players at the table. He let his bet ride and drew a point of four. At the third attempt, the dice obligingly laid up the twin deuces. Now he was fifty dollars in front, and this evoked sufficient comment to cause the appearance of some new faces at the rim. He made a small bet, allowing it to lose, and let the dice pass to the next shooter. So far he hadn't used the gaffs, and he continued making minor bets on the others' play so that there would be no significant change in his winnings. He'd always wondered how he would react under live conditions and was delighted to find he remained completely calm, although secretly elated. He knew only too well that the dexterity of his fingers would prove useless if he couldn't keep his cool. Minute by minute, the baptism by fire was confirming him in his career. But the game wasn't over. When he saw Bluey suddenly transfer the stick to his left hand, he looked up sharply. He found himself gazing into the curious eyes of the dice hustler who'd stripped Skeeter of their money on their first visit.

He felt Skeeter stir behind him. "That's the guy—the one Bluey says works for the house," Skeeter hissed in his ear.

"Yeah, I know . . ." Tony said, matter-of-factly, hoping the hustler hadn't noticed Skeeter's quick stirring. That was when he realized something else. It would be dangerous to use Skeeter as a feeder under this man's eyes. Skeeter wore his emotions on his face, and it was open to doubt how well he could conceal his movements. "Just keep still," Tony continued in the same routine voice, without turning his head. "I won't be using what you got."

"Whaddayamean?"

"I'm not gonna use the gaffs."

"Why not?" Skeeter nudged him again.

"Keep still, willya?" He stared at the house dice coming across the layout toward him on the end of Bluey's stick. Without the benefit of the gaffs in Skeeter's pockets, his repertoire was strictly limited. He decided to keep the action to the minimum by going for the hundred dollars in a single bet. He pushed the money up to the pass line and reached out for the dice. It meant using the six-ace pitch again, and it worried him that the hustler watching from the other side of the table was probably familiar with the move. His brain raced as he shook the dice in his hand. Out of the corner of his mouth he muttered to Skeeter, "Quick, put one hand on the rim of the table."

"Eh?"

"Do it now." Tony watched the hustler from under his eyebrows. When Skeeter's hand appeared mysteriously from behind Tony, his gaze shot to the rim of the table. In the same instant, Tony released the dice from his fingers and, when the hustler's gaze found them again, it was too late. The two cubes had stopped on a natural seven. A murmur went around the table as Bluey paid out on the bet. Tony's next bet was a small one, and he allowed it to lose so that the dice went to the next shooter. He gathered up his winnings and turned to Skeeter. "O.K., let's get out of here."

Just before they got to the door, the big guy who'd spoken to him before stepped in front of Tony. "We want a word with you, mister," he said. "Private."

"What the fuck you want with us? We're going . . ." Skeeter turned on him.

The big guy put out his hand and placed it on Skeeter's chest. "Not you, buddy," he said coldly, and gave a small push. "Just the kid. In there." He nodded toward a door at the side.

Skeeter stepped back, bristling. "I go where he goes. And who you think you're pushing anyway?"

Tony spoke quickly, in a quiet voice. "It's O.K., Skeets. Go outside and wait for me. I won't be long."

"I ain't leaving you on your own with these sharks."

"Do what I say." The big guy was watching Skeeter closely, waiting for him to make a move. He didn't see the wink and the tap on the pocket from Tony.

Skeeter cooled. "All right," he said reluctantly. "I'll be waiting just outside the door. If you ain't out in three minutes, I'm coming back in."

"Just wait outside," Tony repeated.

When he stepped into the bare, dusty room, it was to face a wizened old man who sat on a chair in the middle of the floorboards. He had only an instant to absorb his surroundings before two toughs grabbed him from behind, lifted him off his feet, and ran him backward, slamming him up against a wall. "Frisk him—frisk him good," the man on the chair said.

By the time they'd been through his pockets and examined his clothes, he'd got his breath back. Then, when they were down to his shoes, the dice hustler entered the room. He stood for a moment, studying Tony. "Find anything?" he said to the two men.

"Not a thing," one of them said. "Only the dough." He held up Tony's money.

"Give it here," the man on the chair said.

"How'd you do it, kid?" the hustler said to Tony.

"What you talking about?" He mustered as much anger as he could. He tried to shake off the two guys manhandling him, but they held him firmly against the wall.

"O.K., that's enough—let him go," the man on the chair said.

Tony straightened his clothes and stepped back into his shoes. "You treat all your customers this way?" he said sorely.

"What you think, Johnny?" The wizened old man said to the hustler. "It possible the kid got lucky?"

"I dunno, the punk. Either that, or he's got the smoothest action I ever see in my whole life."

"Couldn't be, I guess. He's just a kid."

"Yeah, I suppose you're right."

Skeeter chose this moment to burst into the room. The door smashed open and he strode in defiantly, fists at face level. "O.K., I'm ready for you bastards," he barked. "Who's gonna be first?"

Staring at Skeeter, the hustler's eyes lit up. "I got it now," he yelled. "He's the one—he's the feeder. Grab him; he's got the gaffed dice in his pocket."

Skeeter's attention had gone to the hustler and he'd turned his back on the two toughs. It took them and the big guy no more than a moment to overpower him. It was his turn to be slammed against the wall. The big guy pinned him back while the others went through his pockets. Tony prayed to himself that Skeeter had the sense to get rid of the dice. "Nothing here," one of the men announced.

"I don't get it." The hustler scratched his head.

"Listen, kid," the man on the chair said to Tony. "I don't know how you did it, but I'm warning you, don't ever come in this place again."

"You kidding?" Tony retorted. "This is one joint gets crossed off my social list as of now."

"Go on, get out. Both of you."

"How about my dough?" Tony said.

"We're keeping it."

"You can't do that, it's our money." Skeeter stepped forward. So did the two toughs.

The man on the chair became thoughtful. "Hold it." He held up his hand. "I'm gonna ask you a question, kid, and I want a straight answer. I ain't gonna bother you if you tell me the truth. Was it the Duke sent you in here?" His look was penetrating.

"No." Tony answered instantly. "Nothing to do with the Duke. And that's the truth." The implication was too serious to be taken lightly. "Look, you can keep the dough—just forget the whole thing." He stared at the wizened man, his facetiousness gone, and there was a sudden communication between them. For a silent moment the man returned Tony's stare, then he said, "O.K., I understand." He inclined his head toward the door. "You better go now."

They moved toward the door and the hustler followed them. "Listen, you punks, if I see you around this place again, you're gonna get more than you bargain for . . ."

"Hey, you—shut your big mouth," the man on the chair said disgustedly. "For a dice ace you're nothing but a pain in the ass."

They put distance between themselves and the Kokomo. "Them jerks in there," Skeeter said, "They got their gall, keeping our dough. I got a mind to go back there with a few guys from the Wharf. That's what I got a mind to do."

"Forget it," Tony said.

"We just gonna let them keep our dough?"

"Yes. I made a mistake." He looked into the distance thoughtfully. "I ain't doing things right."

"We won, didn't we? That's doing things right. They take our dough away, that's another thing."

"That hustler, he knew. He guessed right away. How the heck he knew like that—I don't get it."

"He couldn't prove a thing. Same as the old guy, the boss. He didn't know for sure either."

"Yes, he did."

"He was only guessing."

"No, I told him. Not in so many words, but I told him—so he would know it wasn't the Duke put us up to it."

"You crazy? We're lucky we didn't get beat up."

"I don't think so." He brought his full attention back to the present. "Anyhow, it's a good thing you got rid of them gaffed dice. We'd have been in big trouble back there if they found 'em on you."

"I didn't get rid of 'em. I got 'em right here."

"What you mean?" He stopped walking.

"I came back ready for a fight, so I held the dice in my hand to make a hard ball. I punch better that way. Look, I still got the dice here in my hand. When they searched me they didn't think to look if I was holding anything."

Tony swallowed. When he could speak, he said slowly, "Skeets, I got news for you—you just failed to qualify as my permanent gambling assistant."

CHAPTER THIRTEEN

When he walked into The Club he knew immediately, from Gimpy's expression, that he had problems. "You're wanted in the back." Gimpy hooked his thumb toward the Duke's office.

"O.K., I'll see the Duke in a few minutes," he said warily. He wanted time to prepare his excuses.

"Now."

Inside, the Duke sat at his roll-top desk busy over his papers. For a while he ignored Tony, who stood shuffling from foot to foot. When he spoke, he didn't lift his head. "What you did last night—that could have made me a whole pack of trouble," he said. "There's something you better get straight once and for all: You want to go on working here, you're gonna have to behave. If you can't handle it, I got no place for you in this club."

"I didn't know I was out of line," Tony said. "Nobody told me. I wouldn't have done it if I knew."

His words sounded unconvincing and incensed the Duke. The swivel chair turned sharply. "Don't fool around with me, boy."

"I thought it made no difference what I do on my own time. Honest." There was an urgency in his tone now.

The Duke studied his face, and his anger dissolved as quickly as it had come. "Maybe I shouldn't believe you, but I do." He paused. "You're no mechanic yet, you know. You're just a kid who's learning—get that through your head and don't forget it. You got a long way to go. What you did last night, a guy can get beat up bad in that type joint. One thing they don't take kindly to is losing their dough."

"How come you know what happened? I mean, it ain't so important, I win a few bucks."

"It might have been if they decided I sent you over there to bury 'em," the Duke said briefly.

"I told him straight, the old man, it had nothing to do with you," Tony said. "Yeah, he said."

"Before that, he wasn't sure I took 'em or not."

"That's what you think—nobody gets lucky in that Kokomo."

"They didn't see the moves. He admitted it. They didn't find the gaffed dice on us neither."

"Just as well for you. You'd have been nursing a busted head this morning."

"So how they knew?"

"You never hear of miracles? It takes one to win a hundred bucks straight in that joint. They don't believe in miracles over there. That's how they knew." Tony nodded slowly. "You understand what I'm saying? While you work here you don't play in no local joints. That's out. You get known around here, you're no good to me. What you do out of town's your affair, but in Steubenville the last thing we need is for you to become a dice celebrity."

"I understand—it won't happen again."

"You're damn right it won't." Tony stood in miserable silence. "What in hell you doing in that dive anyway?"

"A friend of mine, this Skeeter Froelich, they took him for his dough."

"And you went in to get it back for him?" It was the first time he'd seen even the ghost of a smile on the Duke's face. "Forget it, that's one-way money."

"O.K., boss. Thanks for giving me another chance." He turned to go.

"There's something else." Tony stopped. "We got a high roller coming in tonight. A guy called Rafe Connolly. We're gonna take him for all he's got. I'm telling you now so you won't look surprised at what happens on the table."

"Do I get a crack at him?" The excitement crept into his voice.

"No. What you do, you help Angelo, same as always. Watch and learn. And don't jump through the roof if you spot Angelo switching the dice. Now that you know the moves, I want you to try and follow what happens. Don't talk, just look." Tony bit his tongue. It would be presumptuous to tell the Duke that some of Angelo's action was transparent and clumsy. "It's important you stay cool. Can you handle it?"

"Sure, Duke. I won't let you down."

"In a gambling house you learn to act, but never to react. Fix that in your head. Tonight you'll see what this business is all about." Again he paused. "I know you're good with the dice, kid, and you're getting better. But it's not enough. You have to absorb the atmosphere and get to know people's behavior. Then, we don't know yet if you got the nerve for it."

Tony was surprised at the harshness in his own voice. "Just let me deal, and you'll find out," he shot back.

"That's a risk I can't take, boy. Not yet—you're not ready for it."

"I practice four, five, six hours every day. Ain't nobody gonna be a better mechanic than me." The words tumbled out of him.

"That's a tall order, son."

"That's the way it's gonna be."

"To be a mechanic, you not only need to be good with the dice, you need a great deal of personal discipline," the Duke said patiently. "That's something few men have. To be a *top* mechanic you need nerve of a special sort, and that's something you gotta be born with. No other way you can get iron nerve, kid. Let me tell you something, in case you think it's easy: I spent my life in gambling joints, clear across the country. I seen plenty of dice hustlers, good and bad. From all them guys I can count on the fingers of one hand the men who had what it takes to become a top mechanic. And even out of them, there's only one I know of had the true iron nerve. He was the only one—this guy called Duane Fisk."

"He still around?"

"No, he dropped out of sight a few years back, when Capone organized the gambling houses over in Chicago. A lot of the mobsters this side of the country got the message. Ain't healthy for a mechanic to go up against them people. It's my guess Duane got himself lost somewhere in the West. Nobody took his place, I know of."

"If he was so good, he didn't have to be afraid of nobody." It might have sounded like adolescent bravado, except that Tony's voice was perfectly serious.

For an instant, the Duke lifted his eyes to the youthful face, then dropped them. "There's a lot of pressure on a guy who's good. Maybe someone caught up with him—who knows?" He shrugged. "Hell, I got work to do—get out of here."

When Angelo walked up to them at the bar, Tony could smell the drink on his breath. "Give me a blast, Gimpy," he said.

Gimpy produced a bottle of Two Naturals and poured Angelo a stiff shot. Angelo downed it in a gulp. "Take it easy with that stuff," Gimpy said. "You gotta be in top form for tonight."

"Aw, it don't bother me none. Sharpens up my reflexes."

"Way I hear it, the effect is just the opposite," Gimpy said disapprovingly. He watched Angelo reach out for the bottle and pour himself another.

"You heard wrong," Angelo threw off, sucking at the second glass of whiskey.

Tony saw the glass tremble slightly in Angelo's hand. Gimpy had noticed it, too. His eyes flickered to Tony, then returned. Angelo swallowed the rest of the drink and studied the empty glass for a moment. He reached out for the bottle and again splashed whiskey into the glass. Taking it along, he walked away to prepare for the evening game. "He don't look like he's in good condition," Tony said, watching Angelo cross the room.

"Angelo's always that way before a big game. Some dealers get the shakes, and some don't. Angelo's one of them gotta have a drink to give 'em confidence."

"I wouldn't need a drink if I was dealing," he said.

"Let's say you don't know."

"Oh, yeah, I know—honest, Gimpy. Say, how about them dice hustlers around—they get the shakes, too?"

"It ain't the same thing. A hustler can pull out of the game if he don't feel right. But a dealer who's a mechanic, he gotta stand there and do it. That's his job."

Tony's gaze fell to his hands and he unfolded his long, delicate fingers and studied them. He looked up. "Gimpy," he said, "gimme a glass of whiskey. I need a drink, too."

"Now hold on, don't you start picking up Angelo's habits," Gimpy said. "Just a small one."

Reluctantly Gimpy produced a glass and poured a mean drink. Tony lifted the glass and drank carefully until the whiskey was gone. When he removed the glass from his lips, he allowed it to brush his chest before handing it back to Gimpy, who reached for it involuntarily. "Don't much like the stuff," Tony said. Gimpy grunted and accepted the glass. Then he did a double-take and found himself staring into it. Nestling in the bottom of the glass was a pair of yellow dice, their top faces showing an ace and a six. "You ain't keeping them glasses clean, Gimpy." Tony grinned at him. "All kinds of junk in 'em. Ain't no wonder the drink don't taste good."

The guy didn't even carry his own money. A man stood behind Rafe Connolly and handed him a wad of bills when he ran short. Rafe would throw the wad nonchalantly on the layout, and Tony passed a thousand dollars in checks across to Angelo, who verified the count before sliding them on the end of his stick across to Rafe. This had happened for the fifth time in a couple of hours, and Tony's wonderment at the size of the bets abated as, between rolls of the dice, he studied Rafe's demeanor and style of dress. Everything about the man spoke of money, from the most beautiful hand-tailored suit Tony had ever seen to the heavy gold of his cigar-holder and the thick ring on his pinky sporting a ruby as big as a walnut. Everything about the man told you he was *somebody*. If he learned anything from watching Rafe Connolly that night, it was that appearance was significant in a gambling house. He resolved that, when he was a mechanic, he would always look important. The artistry of the suit intrigued him. He was sure that Rafe, a middle-aged man with deep rivers of dissipation on his face, hadn't the athletic build the shape of the shoulders suggested. Tony was equally impressed with the fact that Rafe appeared blandly undisturbed by the fact that he was five thousand bucks poorer than when he'd entered The Club. Then the guy began to win, and Tony observed the power of his bankroll as Rafe changed his style and loaded his bets fiercely against the house. The tide of money began running in the reverse direction, and soon double his original stake was piled carelessly on his side of the layout.

It was then Tony saw the signal pass between the Duke, who was standing quietly back behind Rafe in the crowd, and Angelo. He saw the immediate change in Angelo—a change so obvious that he glanced at Rafe to see if the player had noticed the sudden tension in the dealer. But Rafe was engrossed in his sudden change of fortune and had seen nothing, not even the tiny beads of sweat that started on Angelo's upper lip. Tony saw the first switch coming up like a train entering the Steubenville railroad station. He watched Angelo's fingers fumbling beneath the rim of the table, then the Tees went into play on another shooter, wiping out Rafe's biggest bet yet. When the time came to pull out the gaffed dice, Angelo gripped them so firmly in his left hand that Tony saw the knuckles whiten on the two fingers concealing the gaffs. In his anxiety Angelo made his left hand into a ball so tight that Tony squirmed and glanced around the table to see if anyone else had noticed. Angelo hit Rafe with the Tees twice more, and his technique was the same each time. When the house recovered its money and was a couple of thousand in front, Angelo switched the Tees out on a signal from the Duke. It was downhill for Rafe from then on. Tony watched from the corner of his eye as Angelo replaced the gaffs under the rim of the table. Soon the Duke strolled around to stand behind them, openly watching the game, a look of friendly sympathy for Rafe on his face. Tony happened to glance around just in time to sense an almost imperceptible change in that look, and his gaze instantly followed the Duke's to the floor, by Angelo's feet. One of the gaffs had fallen from beneath the rim of the table and now it lay openly, undeniable proof of deception.

It happened that Rafe chose that moment to buy in some checks. Tony thought rapidly as he prepared a stack for Angelo's approval. Instead of sliding the stack across the layout in the normal manner, he lifted the stack and, in an apparently clumsy movement, allowed the checks to spray out of his hand. Some went over the rim and fell to the floor. Before anyone could follow his movements, he was on the floor, reaching for the guilty die. Angelo stepped out of his way. "You punk," he snarled angrily. "You gonna get your ass kicked outa this place, you do that again."

"Sorry, Angelo," Tony said innocently, as Angelo grabbed the checks from him. When the game was under way again, he glanced behind him. His gaze again brushed the Duke's face and he received a small nod of approval.

They won six thousand, six hundred and fifty dollars from Rafe before he decided to call it a night. Tony had kept track of every change in the balance of money. It was quite a feat, the Duke told him, and handed him a ten-dollar bonus at the end of his night's work. "I got the feeling you'll make it. I like the way you handled yourself back there," the Duke told him.

"A mechanic?" he said eagerly.

"Maybe, yeah—I think maybe you'll make a mechanic. One of these days. I got that feeling."

When he went to the door, he was walking on air. He passed Angelo. "Good night, Angelo," he said cheerfully.

Angelo glowered at him. The effects of the drink had worn off; he looked tired and his eyes were red-rimmed. "That ham-fisted little punk," he said.

CHAPTER FOURTEEN

He had the feeling he was going to end up the oldest male virgin in town. Somehow he'd just been too busy to do anything about it. He'd been thinking, and now he was quite sure that what had occurred in Cora's cathouse on Water Street didn't amount to intercourse. He hadn't actually achieved penetration, he decided; in fact, in a way, it amounted to enforced masturbation which, on reflection, was of no value for his dollar. After all, he hadn't wanted the old bag to whip him off, even if he couldn't get it up quickly enough to please her. Ever since, he'd been busy with matters that weighed heavily on his mind. Things such as the law of probabilities as it applied to dice percentages, and the improving dexterity of his fingers, which called for constant practice and absorbed most of his spare time. Although sex was a constant theme for discussion, he wasn't inclined to talk much about it himself. That made it all the harder to live with Mokey who, as he grew, took every opportunity to indulge his phallic preoccupation. And who reveled in discussing the intimate details.

In his logical way he enumerated his options, which were few. He hadn't the opportunity to get to know girls by hanging around with them, the way the other guys did. There was still Frankie, who was the finest sex object anyone could wish for. But he was never going to reach first base with that ruthlessly perceptive little bitch Teresa making their meetings a perennial threesome. In any case, when it came to screwing, he had about as much chance of an accommodating arrangement with Frankie as he had of flying to the moon. She came with a tag saying the price was marriage, the terms of payment were time, and the goods were not to be sampled before the contract was formalized. With her parochial Italian background and puritanical upbringing, even a surreptitious grope took on the significance of a criminal act. Yet, in their dozens of meetings, there had been moments when his dispirited advances had been met with sudden and unexpected flashes of passion, so he knew her need was as great as his own. But there was no future in it; not for him. Although he secretly enjoyed how she found every opportunity to touch him and hang on to his arm and gaze into his eyes with adoration.

The cathouse was left as the only alternative, he supposed. It hadn't worked out too well the first time, but that was a year ago; now he was at a different level of awareness. Again he felt the stirring in his loins that lately was becoming too strong to ignore. He put on his coat and went out to find Skeeter and Bob. He picked up Bob in the New Philly and they cruised the usual haunts looking for Skeeter. "We're not going to find him," Bob told him morosely. "I ain't seen him in a couple of weeks."

"What you talking about?"

"He got a girl."

"So what—don't change things, does it?"

"He never had a steady before. He always screwed around, same as everyone. But you know what he's like—he gets an interest, he goes overboard. That Ellen Hinkley, she got her hooks into him. I never seen such a change in a guy. He follows her around like a little puppy."

Tony laughed. "Ain't like Skeeter to let someone boss him around."

"You're in for one big surprise. She got him on a piece of string."

"I don't believe it."

"When you last see him?"

"Same as you, I suppose. Maybe a couple of weeks ago. I been busy—I don't have much time to get out and about these days."

"Skeeter say anything to you about a broad last time you see him?"

"No. Not a thing."

"See what I mean?"

"What in hell you talking about?"

"How long you think he's been seeing this Ellen?"

"How should I know?"

"Four, five months at least. I find out from my sister—she's a friend. Seems everyone knows about it except us."

"You're kidding," Tony was astounded.

80

"No. He don't say a word, like it's a big secret. Like someone's gonna steal her away if he tells about it."

"Aw, come on, Bob," Tony said impulsively. "Cut the crap."

"Tell you something else. This Ellen, she ain't got no nice reputation. They say she been knocked off by every other guy in town."

"We better find Skeets and have a talk," Tony said seriously.

"Yeah. I'm telling you, the guy's out of his head."

At Skeeter's house they were told he came home late to sleep each night, and that was about as much as his family saw of him. So they waited outside in the dark until after one in the morning. Long before he appeared, they heard him whistling stridently as he came along the street. He stopped whistling when he saw them. "What you guys doing here this time of night?"

"Waiting for you—what you think, prick?" Bob said.

"So what's up?"

"Nothing's up, Skeets," Tony said. "We don't see you around much anymore. We was wondering why, that's all."

In the reflection from a distant streetlight they saw the furtive look cross his face. "I got other business" he said. "Things to do besides wasting my time hanging around them pool parlors."

"Yeah, so we hear," Bob said sourly.

"What you mean by that?"

"We hear you seeing that Ellen Hinkley kinda regular," Bob came back. "So what's the big secret?"

"Ain't none of your affair," Skeeter said, suddenly belligerent.

"All right, can it." Tony stepped in front of Bob. "He don't wanna talk about it, that's O.K. Ain't no sense being bad friends over some broad. We been buddies a long time and that's important. A broad's just a broad."

"Who says?" Skeeter glared at them.

"Say, what's got under your skin, Skeets?" Tony said sharply to him.

He dropped it on them from out of the blue. "Ellen and me, we're planning on getting married soon. If that don't suit you two, ain't nothing I care to do about it."

When it got through to them, Tony croaked, "Ain't you a little young to be putting your neck in a noose?"

"I'm nearly twenty. It's old enough to be married. Ain't no objection from my family."

"You crazy . . ." Bob began, then stopped when Tony stepped on his foot.

"O.K., fine," Tony said. "That's up to you, you wanna get married. What I don't understand—why you making such a big mystery of the whole thing?"

"I got my reasons. I don't want you guys making no cracks about my girl. We're in love, see. Ellen told me she loves me, and I love her. I don't want no jerk spoiling things for us. You better understand that and show the proper respect for my fiancée."

"Sure. Wouldn't have it any other way," Tony said soberly. "Only thing is, we don't know Ellen—not to speak to, that is."

Skeeter disregarded him and continued, "Don't matter what them bigmouths around town been saying. It's all lies."

"I ain't heard a thing. You hear anything, Bob?" Tony said with a shrug.

"Not a thing," Bob said.

Skeeter regarded them suspiciously. "You ain't, huh? Well, I'm telling you now, case you do hear something. I'll kill any guy repeats them rumors."

"We ain't heard no remarks, Skeets. What the hell, we're your pals, ain't we? We're on your side. Bob or me hear them rumors, we're gonna ram them down the throat of any guy opens his big mouth, same as you."

"Yeah, you can count on us, Skeets," Bob said.

"Thanks, guys." There was an uncomfortable moment of silence. "Well, I have to get to bed now. I gotta be up at five. Wharf starts early."

"Yeah, sure. We'll see you another time."

"Maybe you wanna meet Ellen sometime," Skeeter added hopefully. "See what a fine girl she is."

"Glad to, Skeets."

"O.K." He brightened. "I'll fix it up. Maybe, that case, I'll see you guys at the New Philly, Sunday, same as always. Just to chew the fat for a while, before I go meet Ellen," he added.

"Sure. We'll be there, Skeets, same as always."

"O.K., then, I'll see ya."

When they were out of earshot, Bob exploded. "He's crazy. That broad, she got into his head. You ever see anything like that? He's gonna break up, he goes on that way." Tony made no reply. "Well, what you say?"

"I say we gotta do something about it."

"Now you're talking. What we gonna do?"

"I dunno. Ain't never come across this situation before. We'll have to work something out. Not much we can do right now. Tomorrow, you start asking around. Let's find out the truth about this Ellen Hinkley."

"That's an idea."

"If she's no good, like you say, we gotta get Skeets off the hook somehow." For a while they walked on in silence, then he said, "Reason I come out tonight, I was thinking of going on up to Seventh and Washington. You know, Molly Whiter's place."

"The high-class cathouse—you horny?"

"Yeah. And how."

"Me, too. I'm always that way. Boy, I'd like to go up there myself. I heard about them broads in the fancy French underwear. I get a hard-on just thinking about it. That's some joint, they say. I ain't got laid lately. Seems everyone's getting it except me."

"Yeah, I feel the same way. What you say we go on up there now?"

"Ain't got no dough."

"I got dough," he said. "You can owe me."

Bob's eyes lit up. "Why we wasting time talking?" he said.

They walked Indian file down the hall behind Molly Whiter's swaying hips. He'd never seen anything like it before. Red velvet drapes reached to the floor. The rugs under his feet were soft and deep like the forest in the fall, when the ground was thick with leaves. He hadn't seen anything like the clothes the girls wore either. Six of them lounged around the parlor in satin and lace underwear, sheer black stockings and suspenders, breasts and thighs bulging provocatively from the frilly decorations. The girls looked them over, and Bob quickly made his goggling choice.

Tony chose a petite, dark-haired, black-eyed girl called Prima, Molly's latest, according to her. Her hair shone, her skin was satin-smooth and he suspected a touch of Mexican in her blood. It seemed Molly's assertion that the girl was new was true. She was no more than eighteen or nineteen, and she eyed Tony warily from the moment they entered the bedroom. The robe she wore, which had been open in the downstairs parlor, displaying her scantily covered wares, was now defensively wrapped about her body. She stood, unsure of herself, waiting for him to make the first move. "Well, what happens now?" Tony said impatiently. He was somehow reluctant to reach out and grab. But he intended to make sure he wasn't taken for a ride again.

"You're supposed to get undressed," Prima said self-consciously.

"You don't seem too sure of yourself." He took off his shoes, then his pants.

"It's my first week. I haven't gotten used to it yet."

"Oh. How come you get a job like this anyway?"

"I don't want to talk about it."

"Suits me." He reached for her and sensed a slight withdrawal. "What's wrong?"

"Nothing—let's get on the bed." He realized that every movement was designed to delay the moment of truth. He found her reluctance a strange stimulation as he followed her onto the bed. There was nowhere else for her to go when he pulled the robe away. By now he'd acquired a massive hard-on, and he surveyed her charms with lascivious anticipation. "How you wanna do it?" she asked.

"With my *prick,* how you think?" he said, grasping crudely for her. There was no time for further discussion. He entered her with all the frustration of his youthful, waiting years, and began a primitive, rapid movement. He was surprised when she began gasping along with him, and then she threw her arms and legs around him so that she, too, began to approach orgasm. In short order he climaxed and drained himself into her, knowing then what it was he'd been waiting for. A moment later she followed as she, too, reached her peak. They lay gasping together.

When he could speak, he said, "Jes-us Christ, this screwing, it's really something."

"Molly says we shouldn't come. Not with clients," Prima said. "She says it wears us out, we keep coming."

"That a fact?"

"It's no good for us. You finished now? I have to wash up."

"Stay where you are." He kept the weight of his body on her, greedy for the sensation of her firm flesh.

"You had your time."

"Maybe I wanna do it again, a coupla minutes."

"You only paid for once."

"So I'll pay again. What the fuck? Now shut up." He felt the powerful sensuality as strength flowed back into his body.

She moved slightly beneath him, and he sensed her pleasurable anticipation. "If you're gonna do it again, do it slow. Take it easy—it's nicer that way."

After a time, his sex grew again and he began a slow grind. She responded rhythmically. "Sometimes, when it's with a nice young guy, this job ain't so bad," Prima told him.

CHAPTER FIFTEEN

"I got here a solid-gold watch," Bluey said to him.

"Where you get it?"

"Where you think? This chump in the joint the other night—he loses his dough, so he wants to sell his watch, right? Swears he paid twenty-five bucks, over to Pittsburgh, in one them classy jewelry stores."

"How much you pay?"

"The chump asks me five bucks. I give him four. You want it for five?"

"Can't spare five bucks this week, Bluey."

"I could get the five bucks easy from the broads down on Water Street." Bluey held it out. "Don't you even wanna see the watch?"

"What's the use? I can't buy it."

"How come," Bluey said slowly, "a hot dice mechanic like you ain't got a measly five bucks?"

Tony looked up to take in with his gaze the dilapidated interior of the New Philly. He'd just demonstrated to Bluey a variation of the six-ace roll in which he wheeled one die and made the other slide, chosen face up. It had taken him a full month of practice to teach his two index fingers to operate independently. Now his fingers dispatched the dice as if they had minds of their own. "I ain't no mechanic yet," he said. "The Duke says I got a lot to learn."

"If I could pitch them dice good as you, I wouldn't be short no five bucks."

"Ain't talking about how good I am with the dice," he said impatiently. "I gotta learn more about people—faces, things like that. According to the Duke," he added.

"That's shit," Bluey responded. "In the Kokomo we don't worry about that stuff. All we wanna know is how much dough a guy's got in his kick—then we take it away from him."

"Yeah. That's why the place is such a dump," Tony said caustically. "It ain't got no class, not like our place. You don't gotta hit a guy over the head to get his dough. Treat him right and he gives it to you."

"Look, you wanna buy the goddamn watch or not?"

"I told you, I ain't got no five bucks for a watch."

Bluey returned the watch to his pocket. "You ain't never gonna be no big shot, the way you carrying on. Why don't you wise up?"

"What you mean?"

"You're always playing around with them dice. Why don't you get out there and make 'em pay off?"

"I'm not allowed to play in local joints," Tony said. "You remember what happened the time I took out the Kokomo. The Duke says I get the boot, he finds out I play any local joints."

"There's other places, besides them local traps, where they play craps."

"I ain't ready for that yet." Tony picked up the dice and absently began rolling them between his fingers. "First I gotta be a hundred percent sure I won't make any mistakes."

"No such thing as a hundred percent."

"Yeah—when the time comes, I'll be a hundred percent sure," Tony said calmly.

Bluey's expression was cynical, but he didn't argue. "Meantime, while you're only ninety-nine percent, you gotta eat, right?"

"I ain't exactly starving, this time."

"You're just a small-town bum, you know that? You got no ambition."

"Sure I got ambition," he said angrily. "I'm gonna be the best there is. That means I gotta train right."

"So, O.K." Bluey raised his hands. "O.K., you wanna know all there is to know—you gotta get in some rough games, too. It ain't no classroom out there."

Again Tony looked up. If there was some angle of dice-play he was unfamiliar with, he wanted to know about it. "What you mean by that?"

"I mean the real craps is played on the floor, in the dirt. Or wherever a game gets started up. It ain't all happening on them nice green felt tables, you know. I seen some pretty big games played, and they wasn't in no clubs. Them dice hustlers, sometimes they get a game together in a hotel room or in a bar. That sort of thing."

"I ain't no use to the Duke if I get known around this town as a hustler. The town's too small."

"Right—so what's to stop you stepping outside Steubenville?"

"I got no time to go traveling," Tony said impatiently.

"I ain't talking about a trip to the Rockies. You don't gotta go far." Bluey was silent a moment. "Listen, I got an idea. You seen them mill workers around here on payday—the mill workers and the miners? Well, some of 'em, they earn real dough. And some of 'em, they only gotta clap eyes on a pair of dice to get hot."

"You kidding?" Tony said. "The miners, they're so poor they can't afford to eat. What do they get—three, four bucks a day? They live in company houses and they gotta buy from the company store. Listen, Gimpy changed a pay check for one of them guys this week. You know how much? Eighty cents, after deductions."

"That's just the scum," Bluey came back. "I know a steel roller at the Weirton Mill, he's picking up fifty, sixty bucks a week."

"He must be top dog. Ain't many earn that kinda dough."

"What I'm saying is, them mill workers coming outa there payday got dough in their pockets. A lot of times I seen a game of craps start up right there, on the sidewalk. Just anywhere. Them guys, they been working their butts off all week, they need some excitement."

85

"So what you suggesting?"

"I'm saying we could go around the mills paydays. We start up a game in the street, and we take their dough while it's still hot."

"Just you and me?"

"No, we need a crew, or it don't look natural. We get the gang together, you and me, Skeeter, Bob . . ." He stopped. "We need a lookout, too, someone to spot for us. Them cops, if they don't get their share, they're gonna wipe us off the sidewalk, they get the chance."

"How about my brother, Mokey?" Tony suggested.

"Sure, he'll do. We gotta teach him a few things. Them mill workers, they're dumb, but they're tough, too. If they get the idea we're cheating, they're likely to break our backs. When we've won what the traffic will bear, we give Mokey the signal—you know, maybe you take out a handkerchief and wipe the back of your neck. Mokey shouts "Cops," we grab the money and take off."

Tony's imagination was going to work. "Yeah, I get it. Sounds good. Maybe I'll give it a swing."

"Great. You'll make some real dough. Boy, it'll be like taking candy off a baby."

They started at Wheeling Steel on Friday afternoon. Workers pouring out through the plant gates, to the siren call of the shift whistle, found themselves walking around, or tripping over, Tony and his crew, on their knees on the dusty sidewalk. The dice hurtled back and forth among the boys to their excited yells of: "High man shoots" or "No dice, you bum" or Nine your point, dummy." Shortly a crowd gathered and side bets were offered and taken in the crowd. Tony switched his gaffed dice in and out for some cautious wins, and it wasn't long before the boys were outnumbered by a growing circle of brawny mill workers who dropped to their knees to join in, outyelling and outbetting them. Soon the hard nosed gamblers among them had made their presence felt; they began dipping deeper into their pockets so that the nickels, dimes, and quarters hitting the sidewalk were exchanged for green bills, and the serious play began.

Tony waited until there was over fifty dollars in the pot. The dice came around to him again, and it was his turn to pitch. With a few smooth, deft moves he became the sudden owner of the money, to the agonized shouts of the players. He thought he sensed a sudden change of mood in the circle of players, and it was a sensation he didn't like. He drew his handkerchief and wiped the back of his neck, the prearranged signal for Mokey, at the back of the crowd, to yell "Cops."

Nothing happened. Mokey, watching the mill workers increase their stakes, was looking anywhere but at his brother. Tony put his handkerchief away and picked up the dice once more. He threw a four for his point, then threw twice more without making it. This was a good time to leave, he knew. To give some money back and initiate the procedure again later meant prolonging the risk. He'd proved to himself it was a practicable operation. Now he wanted to go away and develop a technique appropriate to the play. For the second time he pulled out his handkerchief.

"Keep your hands out front when you're handling them dice, boy," one of the men growled at him. "Specially when you're holding my dough."

"Oh, sure . . ." Tony said. He let the handkerchief fall in his lap. "Just getting a little hot under the collar, hoping my luck holds out," he said pleasantly.

"Get on with the goddamn game, willya?" someone else called out.

Tony obliged and pitched for the four. He got the four at the third attempt, using his percentage dice, and picked up another ten dollars. When he thought none of the workers would notice, he threw an appealing glance at Bluey, touching the handkerchief in his lap. Bluey sized up the situation immediately. He waited until the players were giving their attention to Tony's next shot, then turned to catch Mokey's eye. His urgent grimace told Tony's brother the story.

The cry that leaped from Mokey's lips startled those at the back of the crowd, causing a shock to ripple through the spectators. "Cops—cops," he yelled at the top of his voice. "Run, it's the cops." He jumped up and down in a frenzy.

Tony looked up with an appearance of concern. "Sorry, fellas," he said quickly, "gotta bust up the game. Don't wanna get arrested for gambling." He reached out apologetically and grabbed his take, scattering the other players' money purposely; then he was on his feet and running.

They took off in different directions, just in case the mill workers had their doubts about the propriety of the game and came after them when no cops appeared. But there was no trouble, and they weren't pursued. The players were too busy ensuring they got their correct shares of the money strewn about the sidewalk.

They met again at the Meanspot, the corner of Sixth and Market. "We coulda taken them chumps for a whole C-note. They was just begging us to take their money," Bluey complained. "Why the heck'd you call it quits?"

"Because it was time to stop." Tony frowned.

"What's the difference, a few bucks here or there? It's free money, ain't it?"

"No," Tony said thoughtfully. "It didn't feel right. I was watching the faces, like the Duke taught me. Some of them guys, they was suspicious. You heard him, the biggie, when I took out my handkerchief."

"Them jerks, they always suspicious." Bluey shrugged it off. "So what—they couldn't prove a thing."

"Them people don't prove nothing, they just let fly. We didn't plan it right."

"What you mean?"

"Look, I'm hustling, right? And we're using a signal that means I gotta put my hand in my pocket. We're crazy, using a signal like that—them guys are watching my hands, and they're gonna keep on watching them, once they got ideas."

"Yeah, you got a point. And that Mokey, the prick, he didn't help any."

"He ain't used to it yet," Tony said. "We have to make sure he knows exactly what to do and when to do it."

"We better use someone else."

"No—I'll see to it he don't make no more mistakes."

"I know he's your brother, Tony," Bluey said, "but he just ain't got the grift sense. Know what I mean?"

"Listen, it's my neck, too. He stays in or I don't operate."

Bluey shrugged. O.K., if that's the way you want it."

"That's the way it's gonna be."

"O.K.—that's O.K. with me. Let's have the shareout."

Tony took the sixty dollars from his pocket. "I'm giving you guys ten bucks apiece. Mokey gets five."

"But we agreed equal shares," Bluey objected.

"I changed my mind," Tony said. "Now that I got the picture, I know you guys are only there to make up the number. I don't gotta share with you. I take the risk and I do the work. If I ain't got the nerve, we don't get the dough, right? So this is the way we'll do it: I get half, you guys get the rest." It was entirely up to Tony, and they knew it. Nobody argued. "Where's next?" Tony asked.

"There's High Shaft Mine, up on Ninth and Washington," Bob suggested. "We could knock that over for a start."

"No," Tony said immediately. "It's a mine. Them miners don't earn any real money."

"Sometimes they got dough," Bluey put in. "We get 'em coming in the Kokomo. Always some of them miners killing themselves to get a few extra bucks. When they come up outa that hole in the ground, they just ready for anything. We'll take 'em easy."

Tony waited for Bluey to finish, then went on, "And the other reason, they're mostly Poles work in that High Shaft Mine. Them Poles, maybe they're dumb— they also the most suspicious bunch of people we got in this town. We get in trouble with them, we won't be able to handle it. We'll leave High Shaft Mine out until we get the routine good and straight."

"That leaves Weirton Mill the nearest," Bob suggested.

"Right. That's next, then. We take Weirton, next time around."

"Next week," Bluey said. "Payday."

"It depends," Tony said. "First we get the routine straight. I gotta train you guys so you don't make no mistakes."

"Hey, Tony, how about my five bucks," Mokey complained. "I ain't had it yet."

"You owe me. I'm taking it off the tab," Tony said.

"But I don't owe you five bucks—it's only four," Mokey said.

"So you're a dollar in credit. Enjoy the new experience," Tony told him.

CHAPTER SIXTEEN

It took him longer than a week to teach them to react the way he wanted so that the game had an appearance of spontaneity. After each visit to a plant, he subjected them to a debriefing in which he analyzed the action move by move, seeking out any combination of factors that could throw suspicion on his apparent good luck. The others were unaccustomed to the high standard of personal discipline that had become habitual in Tony, but he persevered, and the result was a very smooth dice crew, alert to the tactics he used at each stage of the bogus games. He devised a secret code with which they could communicate, signaling by finger positions, touching various parts of his body, and using numbers. They trained by squatting down and playing a game of craps in utter silence. Tony manipulated the game so that the heat was directed toward the others, and he only became the focus of attention when it suited his purpose. When the time was ripe to win.

Now that they were proficient as a team, they had another problem. They were rapidly running out of local plants to set up a game. The further out of town they tramped or bussed, the more remote and wide open the location, the more difficult it became to make a sudden run for it without staying in view of the players for longer than was healthy. Tony came up with the solution. "I got it," he said. "We need transportation. We kill two birds with one stone. With a car we can get to dozens of plants all over the valley. What's more, when it's time to scat, we're sure of making a clean break. So far we've been lucky. One of these days them chumps are gonna wake up and come after us. I doan know about you guys, but I ain't so good at running."

"We gonna steal a car?" Mokey's eyes lit up.

"No, we ain't stealing no car, *stupido,*" Tony said impatiently. "We buy one. As a business investment. We don't gotta steal nothing."

"A car can cost a grand. We ain't got that sort of dough," Skeeter said.

"I ain't talking about no limousine," Tony said. "We get something cheap."

"I know a car salesman," Bluey said. "He's got an old ragtop Chevy he's been trying to sell for a hundred bucks. I seen him driving it around town—seems to go O.K."

"That sounds good," Tony said.

". . . How I know him, he comes in the Kokomo. He don't play—he's wise to the kind of action we got in there. He just likes to see the chumps lose their dough."

"Pity he don't play," Tony said regretfully.

"I said he don't play in the Kokomo," Bluey asserted. "That don't mean he's not partial to a game of craps now and then, in the right company."

Tony looked at him. "Can you set something up?"

"Yeah, sure. Couple of times I put him into a good private game, and he won. He's just ripe for us. He ain't sold the ragtop that I know of," Bluey added. "Maybe he'll be happy to do a deal to cover his losses."

Skeeter, always impatient, cut in, "O.K., that's fine, so we get a car. Meanwhile, what we gonna do today? We said we'll take in the Mingo Junction Mill today, right? That's why we're here, right?"

"Yeah," Bluey agreed. "It's the only plant left around we ain't been to."

"So how we get down there—you tell me that? The plant's four, five miles outa town, and there ain't no bus."

"Well, it all depends," Tony said.

"On what, for Chrissakes?"

"On how bad you want the money."

"Sure I want the money. I want it real bad. Don't everyone?" Skeeter gave a laugh.

"You gotta want it bad enough to walk down to Mingo. And walk back," Tony said.

"Screw that," Skeeter groaned. "It must be ninety degrees today. It's gonna be like a goddamn furnace out on that road."

"Who said getting dough was easy?" Tony smiled at him.

The car salesman was named Caplan. He was the luckiest craps player Tony had ever come up against. The guy simply didn't make a bad bet, and he countered Tony's moves with a degree of good fortune most players only dream about. Fast as Tony took his money, he took it back. He refused to be snowballed into making larger bets, and Tony had to win his money dollar by dollar, until he began to despair of ever owning the Chevy. Because the balance of money between them didn't change significantly in any one bet, Caplan didn't realize, as Tony did, that had he been pitching such dice in a straight game, he'd have won a fortune. Lady Luck drifted through Caplan's life that day, an unseen phantom. But in the end, science overcame Caplan's good fortune, and Tony laboriously took the automobile dealer up to an eighty-dollar loss. "That's it," Caplan said suddenly. "I'm finished. I got in way over my head."

"Aw, come on," Tony urged. "Let's shoot for the straight C. No sense stopping twenty bucks short of a regular number. Maybe you'll get your money back. You're a lucky player—just haven't had the breaks."

"No, I know my limit," Caplan said, unmoved. "I'm over the top."

"Well, I tell you, buddy," Tony drawled. "There's an idea been sorta creeping up on me. Bluey here tells me you have a car that's good for a hundred bucks. You wanna settle for the eighty dollars you lost? Here's your dough back—I'll take the car and we'll call it square. What you say?" Tony held out the bunch of bills temptingly.

Caplan stared at him thoughtfully for a moment. "No," he said. "The Chevy's got to make a straight hundred. That's the price. I already been offered the eighty."

"Oh," Tony said.

"If you want the car, I'll be glad to sell it to you. You'll have to make up the difference."

"Tell you what I'm prepared to do. I'm prepared to be generous," Tony went on. "I want that car of yours. I'll play you for forty dollars, straight. If you win, I'll pay forty. If I win, I settle for the car—that is, the odd twenty bucks, and I give you back the eighty. I'm giving you odds of two to one on an even bet. What you say, sportsman?"

Caplan thought again, "The odds are good," he said, "but I'm finished gambling. You want the car, it's gonna cost you twenty bucks over the eighty you already won." The initiative had passed to Caplan, and he was back at being a salesman.

Tony knew he was wasting his time. "O.K., Caplan, you got a deal." He threw across the man's eighty dollars and added twenty of his own.

Now they had wheels.

The Chevy made a healthy difference in their operations. They could reach targets all over the valley, and outside, within an hour or two. They felt good, too, roaring over the bridge downtown into West Virginia, or out through Weirton into Pennsylvania. Suddenly they were able to benefit from living at the corner of three states. In the open car they explored the summer countryside, with the sun beating down on them, leaving the main highways to run fast in the dirt and raise enormous, swirling wakes of dust. These days there weren't many young guys around town who owned a car. Out in the country they could drive for miles without seeing another one.

It was all beyond the understanding of Bruno Vitale, who doubtfully accepted Tony's explanation that the Chevy was a joint venture among him and his buddies.

Then, early one morning, Tony found himself being roughly shaken by the shoulder. "Get outa bed," Bruno ordered him.

"It's too early, Papa," he complained drowsily. "I was working late last night. I gotta get some sleep."

"I said get outa bed," Bruno repeated. "I only got a few minutes, I gotta go to work soon." The anger in his father's voice brought him to wakefulness, and he rose, rubbing the sleep from his eyes, to follow Bruno into the kitchen. His mother stood quietly to one side, her arms folded, a look of serious concern on her face. "Your mama, this morning she take your pants to wash."

"So?" He was still dazed, and it came out surly.

His mother rounded on him instantly. "Antonio, you have respect for your father," she snapped. He knew immediately that she was overreacting. Something was worrying her. He went silent.

"In your pants pocket, your mama, she find this." Bruno threw the roll of dollar bills onto the kitchen table, and it sprang apart so that tens and twenties projected from among the many singles, making the bundle of money appear huge. Tony glanced at it and waited. "There's five, six hundred dollars there—I never see so much money in all my life. Where you get all that money, Antonio?" He made no reply. "Where you get that fine automobile you running around in? I wanna know the truth—you stealing this money? You stealing from your employer, maybe? No boy your age get this much money legitimate. I wanna know whose money it is . . ." Bruno's voice rose and behind it Tony sensed the fear, the outright terror. It poured across from his father in a wave. A lifetime of deprivation caused him to fear money, as if he had no right to own it. The fact that his son carried a fortune in his pants pocket pointed clearly to crime.

"It's my money, Papa. There ain't nothing to be afraid of. I didn't steal it."

"This town nothing but jail bait for kids." Bruno's voice trembled. "You explain. I wanna know where the money comes from."

He spoke carefully. "We're in business for ourselves. Me and the guys. We go around to plants in the district and we set up a game of craps. It ain't just for fun. Instead of waiting for these people to come into the joints in town, we go out and find them. Bluey and me, we're both dealers, so we know how to handle things, that's all—there's nothing else to it." It was unwise to enlighten his father as to his own particular skills.

Bruno stopped shaking and his brows knitted. "This gambling—it's so profitable?"

"Sure, Papa, it's my business, ain't it? We're not doing nothing don't happen in the joints every day. And we ain't stealing. You don't got a thing to worry about."

"How come I know lots of gamblers—they don't make no profit?"

"The gambler don't make the profit, Papa. He just got a license to give his money away. The house usually wins. How you think all them traps in town get a living?

91

What we're doing, we sorta take the house out to them. In a small way," he added.

Bruno, uncertain, but wanting desperately to be convinced that his son was not the subject of a police file, looked across at his wife. Maria appeared satisfied with Tony's explanation. He knew from experience that her instincts were usually right. "What you think, Mama?" he asked.

"Antonio wouldn't tell you lies," she said firmly. "He say that's how he got the money, then I believe my son. He's a clever boy, not cheap thief. O.K., I believe him—he make lotsa money, like he say."

Bruno was relieved. "I'm glad everything O.K. Now I gotta go open up the barber shop." At the door he turned. "Tony, maybe you shouldn't walk aroun' with all that dough in your pocket. There's lotsa thieves aroun'. Or maybe you just lose it. What you say, son, you put it somewhere safe—in the bank, maybe, huh?"

"Don't worry about the dough, Papa. There's plenty more where that came from." He grinned.

Bruno went out, shaking his head.

He found another use for the Chevy. When he could spare the time, he took Francesca for rides in the countryside. Teresa came too, of course, sitting in the back. He'd gotten used to the presence of Frankie's younger sister now, and it hardly bothered him. Until the day Teresa, a little too eager to ensure they had no opportunity to be alone, made a mistake. It happened when he ran out of gas a couple of miles out of town. "You two wait here," he told the girls. "I'll walk into town and get a can of gas from the garage. Won't be long."

He set off briskly along the road. Around the bend, he came across a farmer in trouble. The farmer's old Model-T truck, loaded with hay, had been negotiating the bend when its load had shifted. The truck stood at a crazy angle, two wheels off the ground, half its load spilled, looking as if one push would send it over. "I'd be obliged if you'd give me a hand with the rig, son," the old farmer pleaded. The only useful articles Tony found on the truck were a hammer and a long rope. He banged a stake into the ground and, tying the rope to one side of the truck, wound it around the stake. He took the strain while the farmer eased the truck out of the ditch and back onto its four wheels. Then they gathered in the bales of hay. The farmer drove Tony to the garage.

Walking briskly back along the road carrying the can of gas, he saw Frankie coming toward him. "What happened?" she asked. "You were so long, we didn't know what to think."

"I gave a farmer a hand getting his truck out of the ditch. You should have stayed back there. Where's Teresa?"

"I left her in the car."

They stepped out together along the road. Then they took a short cut across a field where the road rounded a bend and almost doubled back on itself. And that was where they must have missed Teresa, for, when they reached the Chevy, the note said: "Don't feel like sitting here anymore. Walking down the road to meet you. Love, Teresa." A seemingly purposeless note, suddenly useful.

Frankie said, "We must have missed her back there at the bend."

When he'd emptied the can of gas into the tank, he came back to sit in the car. He didn't press the starter. In the warmth of the summer afternoon, in the quiet of the countryside, they looked at each other. Such total privacy was rare and it showed in their eyes. "You know, the note could have been blown out of the car, or something. We could have drove away and missed her," he said.

"How could that happen? It's only a couple of miles into town, down the same road."

"Well, we missed her walking, didn't we? Stranger things happen."

He didn't wait for her reply. The look on her face was enough. His eye was on a dirt track to their right, going off into the distance across someone's land. The Chevy's motor came to life and he swung out, then turned onto the track. For a while he drove fast, the car pitching and wallowing on the uneven surface until he'd put an impossible walking distance between themselves and the road. In the middle of a vast meadow the track reached away, empty, into the distance. He pulled off to one side and stopped the motor. They sat in silence.

"Tony, we shouldn't be out here alone," Frankie whispered. Her hand, holding on to his arm since they began the rough ride, squeezed until her nails dug into his flesh. Her eyes were wide and dark.

For a reply he turned and planted his mouth fully on hers. They'd kissed often enough—embraced briefly in the odd moments when Teresa wasn't around, but this was different. After a moment's hesitation, Frankie relaxed enough to allow him to crush her to him in the full, pliant softness of her form. In the appetite of their youth, he tasted the ripeness of her lips, the sweet scent of her mouth. He felt the excitement growing in her, and after a moment's perfunctory defense, she allowed him to fondle her breasts gently. Under his fingers he felt the nipples harden, and the soft moaning that came from the back of her throat encouraged him to drop his hand down to her knees, which were tightly locked together. She blocked him at first, and it took him a few moments to get his fingers past the tight protection of the leg of her bloomers. He parted the thin pubic hair to enter the soft, moist cleft. Now her moans had turned to little gasps as she relaxed her knees, and he began to explore her mystery. He felt her bearing down on his hand as her passion mounted. Instinctively he found her clitoris and began massaging slowly and delicately. He started to remove his hand, but she grasped his arm tight. "No." Her voice was low and urgent. "Keep doing it. Don't stop now—please, don't stop now."

She relaxed her legs, urging him to more and frenzied activity. She reached her orgasm and climaxed with a succession of gasps and shudders to his great interest and delight.

"Let's really make love." His hand went to the painful bulge in his pants in full expectancy of all the joys of the long-anticipated moment.

She snapped her knees shut and straightened her clothes. "No, Tony, we mustn't. I can't do that—you know I can't. I have to save myself for when I'm married."

Stunned, he said, "How about me?"

She thought a moment. "I'll do the same for you."

He got his member out, and she stared at it. Then she took hold of him gingerly. When she began pumping him, her movements were so fierce, he had to tell her to take it easy. He came very quickly, and she let go before he was properly into the orgasm so that it was unsatisfactory.

They sat for a while, recovering. "We'd better get back," Frankie suggested. "If we stay away too long, Teresa will get ideas."

"Yeah, I'll make it quick." He pushed the Chevy so hard, Frankie had to hold on to the door to keep herself from being thrown about. When he turned onto the road, he floored the accelerator. As he slowed down at the outskirts of town, they caught sight of Teresa. He stopped alongside her. "Jump in, kid," he said. "We been looking all over for you."

"Where have you two been?" Her eyes were accusing, looking from one to the other.

"We been looking for you, Teresa. Must have missed you, back there on the road, when I got back with the gas."

"How could you possibly have missed me? Didn't you come back along the road with the car?"

"Sure thing. No sign of you anywhere. Couldn't imagine where in hell you'd got to."

"I went back to where the car was, but you were gone. I waited there for a while, in case you came back for me. When you didn't come along, I started walking home." There was a break in her voice, and the start of tears in her eyes. She'd failed in her duty to her sister, and the responsibility weighed heavily on her shoulders.

"Aw, don't be upset, Teresa," Tony said. "I just don't understand how we passed each other like that. Sure is something funny going on back there, on that road. You understand it, Frankie?" He turned to the older girl.

"No, I just don't understand it, Tony."

"Well, you better hop in, kid. No use worrying about mysteries. I gotta get you two home."

Teresa climbed in. "It sure is funny," she said.

She couldn't make out how they'd evaded her. But her look of reproval told them she didn't trust them one bit.

CHAPTER SEVENTEEN

He felt restless when he parked the Chevy in the alley at the side of The Club. It was around five o'clock, an hour before he was due to take over the crap table from Chuck for the evening shift, and the place was dead, with not a solitary player seeking its refuge from the hot afternoon. The only movement was at the bar, where a couple of guys idled over coffee. Gimpy stood behind it, resting on his elbows, leafing through a boxing magazine. Tony strolled up to him.

"You know, Doc," Gimpy said suddenly, "if things had been different, you might have seen my picture here in this magazine, just like them other guys."

"What went wrong, Gimpy?" Tony asked curiously. He'd often wondered about the old-time fighter, who rarely talked about himself. When he described the old days he usually left out his own experiences.

"They said I coulda been the heavyweight champ. Lotsa people said it. There wasn't nobody in my class, back in twenty-six. I coulda beat the world—the whole damn world."

"That so? Gee, that's really something. I hear there was a lot of tough fighters around, them days," he prompted.

"Right. The Manassa Mauler, outa Colorado. Jack Dempsey, a real tough cookie. But I coulda beat him when I was ready. He didn't bother me, not one bit. The guy bothered me was the contender, Gene Tunney. Boy, was he good—when he came to fight you couldn't buy a ticket, the show he put on. A real crowd-puller that Gene Tunney."

"How about you, Gimpy? What happened with you?"

"Me?" It was like opening a window to his subconscious. There was a hurt in Gimpy's eyes Tony hadn't seen before. "Oh, you know, things happen . . ."

"Was it something to do with your leg?" Tony guessed out loud.

"Yeah. Bootlegging. Everybody was bootlegging, them days, earning a lot of dough. I needed dough—I was living real high. I was gonna be champ, wasn't I? I spent money like it was water coming from a faucet. Me and the guys, we used to have spending contests. We'd spend five hundred, a thousand bucks, in a nightclub. There was always more. We'd run a couple of truckloads of booze down from Canada and earn five thousand bucks apiece from the racket bosses—for a couple of days' work. What'd they care—they got fifty grand. It was wild. Crazy."

"You should be a rich man today, Gimpy."

"Some got rich. The guys running the rackets, they got rich. People like me, we lived like there was no tomorrow."

"And your leg?"

"There was a lot of stick-ups on the road. One mob used to hijack another mob's booze. Got held up one night—we made a fight of it, and they turned a couple of Tommy guns loose on us. There was six of us, and only one got away. Four got dead and I took the bullets in the leg—shot the bone to pieces. They found me next day in a ditch by the side of the road. I should have died, they reckoned. I was pretty fit in those days—it's what saved me, I guess." Tony stayed silent, waiting for Gimpy to continue. "The Duke, he took me in. He didn't have to— didn't owe me a thing, being one of the bosses . . ." Gimpy stopped suddenly, and the glassy look went out of his eyes. "Yeah, the Duke took care of me. We been together ever since."

"So the Duke's a good guy, huh?" Tony said.

"Yeah, the best—he's one of the best." It came out almost a whisper. "Don't you ever let him down, Doc, you hear me? He'll look after you, you don't let him down."

"I'll remember."

Of the two men at the bar, one left and the other looked over at Gimpy, pointing to his coffee cup. Gimpy picked up the hot coffeepot and refilled the man's cup. When he returned, he said, "Sure is hot. Say, what you doing in the joint this early anyway? Ain't much doing this time of day."

"Need an hour's practice with the dice, Gimpy. Don't get much privacy at home. You know how it is, a small house and all. My ma's got it into her head to take the place apart today, know what I mean? She got everything upside down, the furniture all moved around. In this heat, too. Can't practice around there today. I was wondering if I could use the Duke's office for a while."

"Sure you could, 'cept he's in there right now. Matter of fact, it wouldn't be a bad idea for you to have a little talk with him."

"What about?"

"Well, you been doing fine here. You're earning the house real dough. I know the Duke's tickled to death, seeing you come along the way you have—I heard him talking on the telephone to some friends, telling them how you're coming along. He says you're already as good as Angelo, and Angelo's got a couple of years head start on you. The thing is—well, we all see you ain't short of dough. Angelo, we know when he's got dough, he drinks it up, changes to a better brand of booze. But you, you're different. You're dressing better, and you're running an automobile. Can't be done on the forty bucks a week you're getting here."

"I ain't made no secret of the fact that me and my buddies been taking a crap game out to the hicks," Tony retorted.

"Sure, I know, you told me. What you ain't done, you ain't said it straight to the Duke. You left it to his imagination. It ain't his business to ask what you do in your own time. He's like that—he'll wait for you to tell him."

"He got ideas I'm stealing?"

"Why don't you ask him?" Gimpy said enigmatically.

"I will. Right now." He moved toward the door behind the bar as Gimpy leaned back to give it a light tap.

The shades were closed and there was little light in the room. The Duke sat in a big wicker chair, a dead cheroot between his lips, his eyelids half-closed. The solitary window was shut, and the atmosphere in the room was stifling. "Come in, Tony," the Duke said in a quiet voice.

He realized that the Duke had been resting. "I didn't mean to disturb you, Duke. Maybe we can talk later." He half-turned.

"No, it's all right. I've had my rest. Gimpy has orders to call me at five. I suppose it's that now." The Duke's voice became stronger as Tony heard Gimpy close the door behind him. "Open the shade if you want."

He walked across to the window. "It sure is hot in here, Duke. How d' you stand it?"

"Open the window, too." Tony did so, and, warm as the day was outside, the air made a welcome change. "Years ago, many years ago, I fought with Pancho Villa down in Mexico. If you think this is hot . . ." He paused. "That was when I got into the habit of taking a siesta in the afternoon. It helps, running a gambling house. Lots of gamblers lose money because they're dopey with fatigue late at night. You realize that?"

"Boston mentioned it."

"Sit down, Tony. Gimpy will bring us some coffee soon."

"Thanks, boss."

Now the Duke's eyes were wide open and studying him. "What is it, Tony? You have a problem you need some help with?"

"Not a problem, exactly. I was just talking to Gimpy. He seems to think maybe you got the idea I . . ." He stopped, and began again. "I ain't stealing from the house, Duke. That's what I wanted to say."

"I never thought you were," the Duke said immediately.

"Oh—Gimpy got the idea you might be thinking that because I got some dough these days, and the car . . ."

"Gimpy's judgment is sometimes at fault," the Duke said.

"He thought I better explain what I been doing. Me and the boys, we been taking a little game of craps out of town. You know, around the mills and places, payday."

"Yes, I know you have."

"You do?" He was surprised.

"It's an old miff, that one. You stand a chance of getting yourself beat up."

"We ain't had no trouble yet. Nothing we couldn't handle."

"You must be conducting the game well."

"Oh, sure. I trained the crew real good. We use a secret code."

The Duke nodded his approval. "You're not still short of money?"

"Not now, I ain't." Tony grinned.

"I should have realized you're growing older. You're twenty now, right?" Tony nodded. "It's time you had a raise. Tell Gimpy you'll be getting fifty dollars in the future."

"Gee, thanks, boss." It was over a year since the last raise. Even on forty dollars he often took home far more money than his father, and that was before he went out with the crew to get the real dough.

"I appreciate you haven't let the extra money you're earning go to your head— and that you haven't let it influence you to give up your training here."

"Nothing's gonna make me give up my job. Not unless you throw me out on my ear. Like I said, I'm gonna be a mechanic. But the best. Whatever I know, I learned it here, just like you said I would."

"It's also time I was a little more frank with you, Tony. You done the right thing all the way down the line. It's no mean feat for a youngster to be a stand-up guy—and it seems you got the nerve, too. It's a little early to tell yet. Your real test won't come here, it'll come later—sometime when you're out there on your own." Tony looked at him, but the Duke's eyes were fathomless. "I don't want to discuss that now. What I want to say is: you got the capability, but there's a third quality a mechanic needs, and only time can tell if you have it."

They were interrupted by Gimpy, who limped in with two cups of coffee, put them down, and departed in silence. He moved forward on his chair. "Duke, I looked at the dice all ways—I mean all ways. There ain't nothing I missed out. The nerve—that ain't no problem for me. I got nothing to be afraid of, long as I do things right. That's what I found out. I don't make a move until I practice so much, it comes natural to me. So what's missing?"

"I'm talking about integrity—the integrity of a professional mechanic." Tony frowned at this strange phrase. "Most people will tell you honor among thieves is a heap of horseshit, and they'd be right. Where a mechanic is concerned, it's one of the cardinal rules. It's the difference between a top man and a cheap hustler. One of the reasons there's no more than a handful of top mechanics in the country is they don't have the integrity."

"That's honesty, ain't it?" Tony said.

"Not in the accepted sense of the word. For a mechanic it means this: the man you're working for has to trust you completely. He can't do your job; you can cheat him, and maybe he'll never know. But these things have a habit of getting out, and a mechanic only makes the wrong move once, usually."

"That ain't my style," Tony began, and the Duke held up his hand to silence him.

"Forget about Steubenville—this is only a start. I'm talking about later, when you'll be operating in carpet joints around the country—New York, Chicago, Florida. Places where clients are the cream of society, politicians, industrialists, top people. Where ladies come dressed in evening gowns and furs, their fingers sparkling with diamonds. Where more money crosses a table in a single night than this town sees in a year. Carpet joints, expensive rugs on the floor, glittering chandeliers half as big as this room swinging from the ceiling, lit by a hundred bulbs. You never seen. You'll live like a prince—the finest food, the finest women, the finest clothes. It can all be yours, and you'll be the kingpin of the whole operation." He stopped, a faraway look in his eyes. When he spoke again, he said, "But it only works for you if you're a hundred-percent stand-up guy."

"Just being a mechanic—all that?"

"Yes, and more. Of course, it's not quite that easy. It takes introductions to get into those ritzy joints, even if you're an ace. You gotta get known—to the right people."

"How do I get over that problem?"

"I'll arrange it all for you when the time comes."

"Can I ask a question?"

"Go ahead."

"It crossed my mind—if I don't make it as a mechanic, what's to stop me operating for myself? I mean solo—that thought's gonna cross my mind, right?"

"There's nothing to stop you. Except this: you can always hustle, win small. You can only win big once or twice. You'll get known. Nobody gets known quicker than a hot dice player. Once you're known you're dead—they'll bury you. There's more profit in being a good dice mechanic. You understand what I'm saying?"

"I think so," Tony said. "These people you know, like the Fix, and them other important guys come here to see you, they the ones you're talking about?"

"Linklater?" the Duke said. "No, he's just a local police chief, small fry. The others are state contacts mostly, people bringing deals, looking to make connections. When I came home here to be among my people, I didn't think . . ." Scorn had crept into his voice, and it was the nearest Tony had seen to emotion on his face. Just as suddenly, he switched off. "No, not them. Other people outside this town, outside the state. I spent my life in gambling, up and down the country. I know a lot of people who matter in the business."

"I guess you're solving all my problems for me," Tony said.

"Yes, I can help. But there's something you must do, too. Always touch base. By that I mean keep in contact with me from time to time. No matter what happens to

you, good or bad, so long as I'm here. There'll come a time when I'll be useful."
Tony gave a small, uncertain laugh. For the first time the Duke had said something illogical. Why should the old guy maintain an interest once he'd outgrown the joint, as he was bound to do? There was no sentimentality in business. The Duke went on, "I know what you're thinking, and I can't explain now. Just take me on trust that it's necessary. You'll understand, in time. Will you give me your word that you'll always touch base?"

It was crazy, but his word was his word. "Sure, boss, I'll remember." But he maintained a puzzled expression.

"What's bothering you?"

"Something else. Them carpet joints you mention. They there right now, this very minute?"

"Yes."

"I thought things were tough around the country, the Depression and all. How come there's places like that, with rich clients?"

"Take my word for it, they're there. Gambling's a funny business. The tougher things are on the outside, the better it gets. More people look for escape when times get hard. That includes the rich and the poor. For instance, I hear they're taking down fortunes with the numbers racket in New York and Chicago. That's big business now, a Niagara of nickels and dimes."

"Gee." He thought again. "I got one more question."

"Yes?"

"Why me? Why not Angelo? He's been with you longer than I have."

"You can answer that yourself. Is he a good dealer?"

"He ain't bad—he works the table O.K."

"Is he as good as you?"

Tony looked across. "No," he said. "Not when the chips are down."

"That's your answer. You can add to that, he's got a problem with booze—and more important, he's not a hundred-percent stand-up guy."

"You mean he ain't got that integrity?" He couldn't believe that the Duke was aware of Angelo's occasional divergencies.

"He brought in his own shill a few times and made bogus payoffs on the dice. He's not very ambitious—I estimate his stealing don't cost me more'n a couple of dollars a day, on average." He added quietly, "I reckon maybe you know about it."

"Me?" Tony said casually.

"Sure, you spotted him. He can't hide it from you."

Act, not react. He didn't change his expression. "Why d' you keep him?"

"I have to trust someone," the Duke said. "A couple of dollars extra a day is reasonable for a reliable dealer. If I change him, I got the same problem over again. You understand?"

"I think so," Tony said.

"With you, it has to be different, or you don't make it up there. One wrong move from you, you're out on your ear."

He nodded and got up from the chair. Somehow the room had become stifling hot again. "I gotta get ready to take over from Chuck," he said.

99

CHAPTER EIGHTEEN

Usually the last customer had left The Club by two in the morning, and Tony went home to bed as promptly as he could. For several nights now the joint had been invaded by a group of engineers from Cincinnati, in town for a special retooling job at the Wheeling Mill. These guys seemed to revel in staying up late, and they'd put his bedtime back an hour or two. It was after four in the morning when he turned into a darkened, silent Sixth Street. Except for his house. When he saw the lights burning in the kitchen and his parents' bedroom, he knew there was trouble. When he stopped outside the house, his father rushed to the door. Before he got out of the car, his father was at his side. "Mokey, he's not home," Bruno said. "We ain't seen him since seven o'clock last night. You mama, she very worried. Is not like Mokey."

He got out of the car and walked indoors with his father. "Maybe he's just staying out late with his friends, Papa. He's nineteen, now. He ain't a baby no more. You gotta accept that. He'll turn up."

His mother sat at the kitchen table in her nightgown, looking anxious. When he came in, she got up. "Not like my Mokey to stay out late," she said. "He always come home early—he like sleep."

It was true. Mokey loved his bed. Whatever scrape he got into, he was almost always in bed before midnight, and his buddies could never persuade him to stay out late. Given the opportunity, he'd happily sleep through the night and the following day.

"Aw, don't worry, Mama, he's O.K. I just know it. You go on to bed. I'll stay up and wait for him. There ain't much we can do right now. He don't turn up by the time it gets light, I'll go out and look for him. You, too, Papa. Go on to bed—you need your sleep."

"No, I stay up," they said, almost in unison.

He took a cup and reached for the coffeepot on the ever-warm potbellied stove. He was glad to turn his face away from them. A feeling was stirring in him he didn't like. Mokey had never stayed out this late before. Usually he was voluble, so they knew what his intentions were. Tony was certain something was wrong, but he didn't want to alarm his parents. He turned back to them, his features passive. "Papa, you gotta face up to it, Mokey likes the broads. Maybe he just got shacked up somewhere and fell asleep. You know how he is—once he's asleep, nothing wakes him. Just relax." It sounded plausible. He hoped he was right, but he doubted it.

When it got light, he took the Chevy and cruised Mokey's usual haunts, but there was no sign of his brother. He woke two or three of Mokey's friends—none of them had seen him the previous day, and none had a clue as to his whereabouts. When he returned home, it was after seven. He said to Bruno, "Papa, I think we gotta go to the police, now. Maybe they know something. Anything gets reported, they know. We got nothing to lose, so let's go."

At the city jail on Third Street a tired, sallow-faced deputy was completing night duty. "What was that name?" he repeated.

"Vitale."

"How you spell that name?"

The deputy went into an inner office and took a cursory glance at a register. When he'd let Tony see him do that, he kicked the door shut from the inside. Then he sat down at a desk, put up his feet, and lit a cigarette, unaware that a light behind the desk threw his shadow onto the frosted glass in the door so that they could see his movements. When the deputy emerged, after finishing his cigarette, Tony said immediately, "Look, you have any information?"

"Can't tell you a thing," the deputy said, but he avoided Tony's gaze. "Maybe Officer Hoyle knows something. You wanna wait for him, that's O.K. He'll be here at eight."

The deputy was being evasive, he was certain. He knew then, they had trouble. He started to argue, but the expression on the deputy's face told him he was wasting his time. He glanced at the clock on the wall; it said seven-thirty. He guided his father to the bench across the room.

When Hoyle came in, Tony and Bruno jumped to their feet, but Hoyle strode past them, ignoring Tony's call. He conferred with the deputy in the inner office, then reappeared. "Your name Vitale, from Sixth Street?"

"Yes, it is." Tony answered. Hoyle knew damn well what his name was.

"I got your brother here in jail."

"You got him?" Tony echoed.

"Yeah, that's what I said."

"Why weren't we told?" He exploded. "We been waiting here, been out looking all night—."

Hoyle cut him short. "I'm telling you now, buster. He's in on a charge of burglary—breaking into a food store."

"What?" He couldn't believe his ears.

"You heard me. He was found on the store premises last night. Lately we got a spate of burglaries downtown. Gang of kids your brother's age. We been looking for them. He was caught in the yard behind a store been burglarized twice. The owner reported a prowler, and we found him hiding. He ain't got no explanation. That's enough for me—I'm charging him."

He was stunned. "Mokey's no thief. There's something wrong here" was all he could find to say.

"Oh, yeah? That's what they all say."

"Can we see him?"

"Sure. You got five minutes, that's all."

Mokey sat miserably on a wooden bench in the cell. When he saw them coming toward him, led by the deputy, he jumped to his feet. "What you doing in there, Mokey—you been stealing?" Tony said.

"No, I ain't no thief. You know that," Mokey muttered.

He studied his brother. Usually he knew when the other was lying. This wasn't one of those times. He said, "What you doing in the yard of that food store, like Hoyle says?"

Mokey looked across at his father, then down at his feet. He turned his face to direct his voice to Tony. "I been seeing that Myra Wilmot—you know, the wife of the guy got the shoe store next to Hyme's delicatessen. I ain't the only one, she likes the young guys. Well, her old man, he's been away, out of town. Last night he came back sort of unexpected. When he came in the front, I went out the back, fast. Thing is, the only way to the street's over the wall and through Hyme's yard. I knock over a bin and Hyme starts yelling for the cops. Well, that wall—you know, it runs along the sidewalk—that prick's spread broken glass all along the top. The time I find something to put over the glass so I can climb over, the cops arrive and grab me."

"I don't hear what he say," Bruno said. "What he say about a wife?"

"Leave it to me, Papa, Tony said. He turned back to Mokey. "You tell this to the cop who arrested you?"

"You crazy or sump'n? I tell them that, Myra's in trouble. And that Wilmot, her old man, he'll fucking kill me."

"Jes-us Christ, you just gotta tell the truth, that's all."

"No way."

"But you got a witness—Myra."

"I ain't talking. Forget it."

"That Hoyle, he's gonna throw the book at you, you know that? He's got burglaries he ain't solved. You'll get blamed for all of them, you don't speak up."

"I ain't saying nothing, I told you."

"This town's full of broads looking for action. Why in hell you gotta go screwing some guy's wife?"

Mokey shrugged. Then the deputy was behind them, ushering them out. "Time's up. You gotta go now."

In the front office, Tony approached Hoyle. "Listen, Mokey's no burglar. He was in the shoe store, next to Hyme's place. He's been messing with that Myra Wilmot, so he don't wanna talk about it. Wilmot came in and Mokey, he went out the back way. That's how he comes to be in Hyme's yard, trying to get back to the street." He had no compunctions about revealing Mokey's tryst with Wilmot's wife. It was clearly the lesser of the two evils.

Hoyle laughed at him. "That's cute—real cute. You sure made that one up quick."

"It's the truth. Honest."

"Mrs. Wilmot a friend of yours, maybe?"

"No, sir, I never met her."

"She gonna give evidence when you talk to her, maybe?" Hoyle's voice had soured.

"Listen, that ain't possible. You can see the trouble it would cause—."

"Get out of here," Hoyle said suddenly, "before I lock you up for trying to drag a decent citizen's wife through the dirt. The guinea kid's stuck with burglary. I don't wanna hear no more of this shit, you understand?" He walked away.

102

Hoyle wasn't interested in getting at the truth, he was making it plain. He's captured his "burglar" and an easy conviction would follow. Then Tony's brain began to work—this was Steubenville, and there were ways of dealing with this sort of thing. He said to his father, "Sit down, Papa, and wait here. I won't be long." He ran out to the car and raced for home.

When he returned, he walked past Bruno and caught Hoyle again, just entering the inner office. "There's something else," he said. "Private."

"Yeah—what's that?"

"Let's go inside." Tony shut the door behind him, so that they were in the inner office alone. Hoyle's eyes were wary and, at the same time, mocking as they faced each other. "Listen, he didn't do nothing, but I can't prove it, right? O.K., I accept that, but I got another way out of the problem." He took a deep breath. "Eight hundred bucks."

Hoyle was silent a moment. "You got eight hundred bucks?"

"Yes," Tony said.

Hoyle stared at him thoughtfully, then went to sit down behind the desk. "Let's see the dough," he said.

"Mokey walks out free and clear, right?"

"He ain't done nothing. I know that. It was all a mistake."

"I appreciate your cooperation." This was the way business was done. It was costly, but worth it. He took the roll of bills from his pocket and threw it onto the desk.

Hoyle picked it up and looked at it. "Eight hundred here?"

"Exactly."

He leisurely opened a drawer in the desk and dropped in the roll of bills. "Where you get this sort of dough, kid?"

"Gambling," he said instantly.

"You never hear, gambling is illegal?" Hoyle gave a sour smile and Tony knew immediately he was in trouble.

"Aw, come on—how about all them traps in this town?"

"You accusing me of allowing people to break the law?"

"I ain't saying nothing," Tony said desperately.

"Maybe you got that dough robbing them stores with your brother."

"That ain't right and you know it. How about our deal?"

"I don't do deals with guinea kids who got big dough and can't explain proper where it comes from."

He felt the anger pouring through him. "Give me my money, you don't wanna let my brother out. I gotta get a lawyer for Mokey."

"You better get out of here, kid, before I arrest you for attempting to bribe an officer of the law."

Something snapped, and he found himself lunging across the desk, trying to get at the drawer. But Hoyle was faster, and stronger. In a moment he had Tony's face pressed to the desk and an arm twisted up behind his back. Hoyle hollered for his deputy.

He fought all the way down, but it didn't help. He was thrown, bruised, into the cell with Mokey.

On the second day, Bruno was allowed to visit them. In that time, Tony reflected on how badly he'd handled the whole affair. He should have guessed that Hoyle was a dog and not to be trusted. Worse, he'd reacted to the situation, and not acted. When he saw his father coming down the corridor toward them, his blood boiled at the apprehension on Bruno's face. His father was again dressed in his Sunday best, as a sign of deference to Authority. "You don't gotta get dressed up to come to this stinking jail, Papa," he said.

"A man gotta have respect," Bruno said, lost.

"Give me your pencil, Papa." Bruno took out the pencil that always sat in his breast pocket, along with his comb. Tony began writing on the piece of paper he had ready. When he finished, he handed it through the bars to his father. "Take this to the Duke. Do it right away, Papa."

"First we gotta talk. They make me wait a long time to see you—," Bruno began.

"Fuck 'em." It was the first time he'd sworn in front of his father. "Go, now, Papa—go see the Duke. We gotta get out of here," he said, pushing his father off the bars of the cell.

He sat down to wait. The time passed slowly; it was late at night and he'd almost given up hope when he heard the footsteps echoing down the corridor. He kept his fingers crossed. The footsteps stopped and he leaped off the bunk. He found himself staring at Hoyle, dressed in civilian clothes and holding a bunch of keys. Hoyle stood there for a moment and they stared at each other. Then he stepped forward and unlocked the door of the cell. "You been sprung," he said stiffly. "You two crumbs get your hides outa this jail real quick, before I change my mind."

Tony stayed where he was and put out a hand to restrain the eager Mokey. "You ain't got no mind to change, Hoyle," he said coolly. "You just follow orders like you're told. Now—where's my dough?"

"You ain't getting that dough back, guinea. You seen the last of that."

"Too bad," Tony said. "We ain't moving out of here till you come up with my eight-hundred fish."

"I'm giving you just one more chance. You wanna be sprung or not?"

Now Hoyle was in his ball park, and he knew what to do. "No, that's O.K., Hoyle—we'll just stay here." He turned. "Get your head down, Mokey. We're staying. Might as well get some sleep."

"Listen, you creep," Hoyle began, confusion in his voice. "You're getting out of here, you like it or not."

"Tomorrow I'll have someone get word to the Fix," Tony said. "Maybe he can get my dough back from his crooked cop."

"What you know about Linklater?" Hoyle's voice had changed.

"Your boss? Only that he's gonna cut off your balls, he finds out what you done to me."

After a moment, Hoyle grated, "I got your dough up in the office."

"O.K., then we'll be happy to leave," he said.

Mokey didn't stop talking as they climbed into the Chevy and drove out of the police compound. Tony didn't hear a word. He only knew that the Duke had come through. The Duke had juice, just like he said.

And he was a step closer to a bright new world.

CHAPTER NINETEEN

He looked sideways at Angelo. "You're gonna introduce me personally to Dick Powell, the movie actor?"

"I promise—the man himself."

"How come you acquainted with Dick Powell?"

"Well, you remember when he was in town, the Capitol Movie Theater, Sundays?"

"Yeah, I think so," Tony said.

"Sure you remember. No Sunday shows in Pittsburgh, so Warner Brothers brought his show over here."

"So?"

"Don't you know anything going on around you, outside of gambling?" Angelo said impatiently.

"What else I gotta know? I'm doing O.K."

"You remember the amateur talent contests at the Capitol? On stage—to publicize *The Broadway Melody of 1937*. You remember that, don't you?"

"Sure, that was the contest you won. Oh, I get it. Dick Powell was the master of ceremonies. I remember now."

"Right. When I was winning the heats, we got to be real buddies. He's a real nice guy, that movie actor."

"Buddies, huh?"

"I got a letter, from Warner Brothers themselves. All the finalists, from all over the state, they're gonna appear at a grand gala final contest over to Pittsburgh, next month. The winning party gets a screen test with Warner Brothers Studios and goes on to a nationwide all-winners festival in Hollywood. Maybe even gets to appear in a movie with Dick Powell himself."

"That so?"

"Yeah. What you think of your friend Angelo now, hey?"

"Sounds good. You wanna be a movie actor, Angelo?"

"First I gotta win the contest. I got a good voice—Dick Powell said so himself. And I got personality, up there on the stage. Some of them chumps, they got voices, but they got no stage personality."

"Gee, I hope you make it, Angelo."

"There's something you gotta do for me."

"What's that?"

"The day of the contest, it's the fifth of the month. You gotta be a pal and take me across to Pittsburgh in your car. Who wants to go on the bus, the biggest day of his life, wearing a tux and all? Besides, you're leading the cheer team."

"Team?"

"Yeah—Frankie's coming, too. She turned eighteen now, and she ain't hardly been outa Steubenville. Now her brother's gonna appear in a big-city theater with

105

Dick Powell, no way you gonna keep her away."

"Frankie, too, huh? How we gonna manage that? You and me, we can't both be out of the club together, the same night."

"Yeah. Chuck takes over. For twenty bucks he goes straight through the two shifts. I O.K.'d it with the Duke."

"Frankie excited?"

"You bet. She never stayed overnight in a big city before."

"What we staying overnight for? Ain't more than an hour's drive or so to Pittsburgh."

"They're providing hotel accommodations for all contestants. Might as well use 'em. People coming from all over Ohio, remember. I put in for two rooms. One for me and my manager, that's you. One for my dresser."

"Your dresser?"

"Frankie."

"Oh, I get it."

"Boy, it's gonna be some night."

And it was. They felt like celebrities, shepherded together with other contestants and their supporters under the protection of the Warner publicity machine. Two thousand seats in the theater were filled, as near as Tony could judge, with friends and relatives of the performers. They'd come from all over Ohio, and it was like a big party. There appeared to be countless finalists, and it was obviously going to be a long program. As Dick Powell introduced each performer, and announced his or her hometown, a cheering and whistling arose instantly from a small island in the sea of faces. The applause was taken up by the whole audience, clapping and yelling enthusiastically, even though most of them privately wished failure on that particular individual and success for their own. It was in the air that this was a big night, the culmination of months of effort, of sweat and hope, and prayer. Fame beckoned this night—the gate to stardom was about to open. Almost as one, the performers were determined to pass through those gilded portals. Hollywood, the silver screen, lay before them, and tonight anything was possible. So the dancers danced energetically; the magicians performed their entirely original feats of wonder; the comedians clowned through their finest routines; the ventriloquists' dummies might have had blood in their wooden veins; and the singers sang their hearts out.

"That guy, the number twelve, he was damn good," Tony said to her. "He sings just like Crosby. If I hear that voice on a record, I don't know that's not Crosby. He got real style. Boy, Angelo's got some competition here tonight. I hope he's in top form."

Frankie, seated next to him in her new red velvet gown, her face flushed with the excitement of it all, looked anxiously across. "You think so? I didn't think number twelve was *that* good—not original good. I'd rather hear Angelo sing anytime."

She was bound to say it, he thought. "What's he gonna be singing?"

" 'Donkey Serenade' and 'Where or When.' "

"He shoulda chose something jazzy—something that swings."

"They're his best numbers. He always sings them at the weddings. Everyone asks for them."

106

"Oh, in that case, maybe you're right." He smiled at her reassuringly. Inwardly, he didn't imagine Angelo had a chance. Of the three singers he'd heard so far, he thought all of them good enough to match the voices that came daily over the air from Radio City. Worse, Angelo was more nervous than Tony had ever seen him—even during a tough game at The Club. The half-bottle of Two Naturals he'd downed at the hotel wouldn't help his performance either, Tony mused. He waited to see Dick Powell's expression when Angelo breathed whiskey fumes into his puss.

Then, "He's next—number nineteen, that's Angelo," came from Frankie in a strangulated voice, and they were instantly on their feet, yelling and clapping in a frenzy. It was their turn to lead the applause that dutifully followed from the tireless audience.

Angelo walked out onto the stage, and Dick Powell announced the Steubenville entry as "Johnny Angel." Tony grinned to himself. But then, he was prepared to concede that "Angelo Boccardi" was hardly romantic enough for a singer about to set the world on fire.

When the first words of the song came rolling over him, massively amplified so that every tremor in Angelo's voice vibrated in his ears, it was the voice of a stranger. He realized with sudden surprise that he'd never actually heard Angelo sing. There were odd moments, around The Club, when Angelo gave forth with a note or two, as if to clear his throat, but he was too serious about his ambitions to go around yodeling at the drop of a hat.

He had a good voice, Tony thought, with surprise. It had depth and a wholesome, carefree quality that was pleasing. A compelling voice that made the listener pause and wait to catch the next phrase. But what Tony found incredible was the élan with which Angelo handled himself on the stage. Style and confidence poured out over the footlights. Up there the vocalist with the charismatic manner was an entirely different person from the unknown kid—the one with the slightly Roman nose. The guinea from Steel Town. Up there Angelo was in his element and it showed. Tony closed his eyes and listened to the pleasing sounds filling the auditorium. Then he opened them to glance at the faces of people sitting nearby. All eyes were on the stage—nobody glanced away, bored or disinterested. The women's eyes gleamed, and their lips were parted, their mouths smiling with pleasure. The men stared thoughtfully, as if the romance portrayed in Angelo's song had somehow passed them by, and they secretly wondered how and what might have been. The applause was genuine and stronger than that evoked by any other performer. Frankie, hanging on Tony's arm, was ecstatic with joy.

Afterward came the judges' decisions and the cliff-hanging moments before the announcement of the six finalists. "Johnny Angel" was one of the names. Then the final votes for one, two, three—given in reverse order. "Johnny Angel" hadn't been called by the time the two runners-up had been named. They waited, their hearts pounding, hardly daring to breathe. The roll of drums ended and Dick Powell stepped up. The movie star was grinning from ear to ear when he finally reached out to Angelo. The words had hardly been spoken when a tumultuous thunder swept through the audience. Then they were on their feet, and Frankie's screams were lost in the deafening acclaim around them.

He'd done it. The whiskey-swilling, hook-nosed, unprincipled, clumsy, friend-of-his-sister's screwing, fumble-fingered son of a Steubenville barber had hit the jackpot. And the road to stardom was open.

Angelo was still dazed when they got him back to his hotel room. They drank to his success in what was left of the Two Naturals, then grandly ordered a bottle of champagne from room service. Angelo proceeded to give them a full-bodied recital of his entire repertoire—until the guy in the next room, who'd been banging on the wall for ten minutes, came to the door and threatened to bust some heads if the guy with the tonsils didn't quit and let him get some sleep. Tony had taken only a couple of drinks, and Frankie seemed to make her glass of whiskey last the whole evening, but the amount of champagne had been steadily reduced. Then it all caught up with Angelo, and he subsided slowly onto the carpeted floor, closed his eyes, and promptly went to sleep.

They didn't bother with him for a while, the aura of the evening glowing around them. Then Frankie, a little light-headed, said, "We can't just leave him there." She giggled.

"Why not? He's happy enough." Tony stepped over the inert body and sat down in an armchair.

"You don't mean it?"

"Sure I mean it."

"Come on, get up and help me put him to bed."

"Do I gotta?" he complained.

"Yes."

"O.K.—if you say so."

He took Angelo's head, Frankie took his feet, and together they hauled him onto the bed. They undressed him and threw the bedcover over him. He looked like he was dead.

"He's out cold." Tony grinned.

"Will he be O.K.?" she asked anxiously.

"He'll be a new man in the morning."

Now it was their night, their time to celebrate. When they kissed, it was a blend of the evening's excitement, their own heat, and the smell of cheap whiskey on their breath. Their mouths melted together. Then they were touching each other. Eventually, Frankie said, "No. Not in front of Angelo."

"Don't worry, he wouldn't hear if the roof fell in."

"He might."

"He won't."

"But he might."

"Let's go to your room."

She'd never allowed him to undress her before. Now she lay naked on the bed and he explored the subtle curves of her body freely. Then his weight was on her and smothering her, and she was moaning. "No, we mustn't—I can't do that."

"Jes-us Christ, I gotta," he gasped. "I can't stand it."

"Let me do it for you. Same as we do sometimes." Her fingers probed between their joined flesh, seeking him. "You'll feel better then."

"No. I don't want that. Not now. I gotta go all the way." He was using his strength to force her to part her legs. "Come on, Frankie, I'm gonna explode."

"I can't. Don't you understand that I mustn't? Suddenly tears were spilling down her face from eyes that were darker and more huge than he'd ever seen them. "My family will kill me," she whispered.

"They don't have to know about it. We ain't gonna send 'em no cablegram," he persisted. They were both sweating, and her scent came over him in waves, tormenting him. He managed to get his body between her legs, but she blocked him with her hands.

"An Italian girl . . . you know it . . . she has to be a virgin, or she don't get a husband . . ." Frankie got the words out urgently, in between fighting him off.

"Who's gonna know, for Chrissakes? Only us. What difference now or later?"

"What are you saying?" Her breath caught in her throat.

"We get married, I'll tell 'em there was blood if that's what they want to hear. Leave it to me."

"They come to see the bedsheet."

"That's the old days—oh, all right, so I'll cut my finger. Don't worry, they'll see blood, I promise you. Come on, Frankie, let's do it."

"Tony, you gonna marry me? Is that what you're saying?" There was a new excitement in her voice.

"Sure, we'll get married. Come on, now, let's screw."

"Oh, Tony, darling—I love you so much." Suddenly he felt the tension go out of her, and she threw her arms around him, engulfing him.

"I love you, too, Frankie."

"It's all right for us now, isn't it?"

He didn't answer. When he sank himself into the warm, moist flesh he uttered a groan of delight. She exhaled with a great sigh as he penetrated the tight ring of her virginity. She bit into his shoulder. The pain from her teeth was excruciating, but he couldn't stop now. He forced himself deeper, past the resistance of unstretched vaginal tissue, opening her up, until she had consumed his full length.

They lost their inhibition in the joy of union. They made love several times, through the night, resting in between in each other's arms. They were still awake when the first gray light of a Pittsburgh dawn touched the window of their room.

CHAPTER TWENTY

It was unlike Tony to arrive at work late. Usually he was in The Club well before time so that he could begin work cool and unflustered. That evening it was ten minutes after time when he walked through the door to take over the shift from Chuck. The Duke was at the far end of the room and Tony walked up to him. "What the hell's going on around here?" the Duke said gruffly. "First Angelo goes missing, and now I got you rolling in when you damn well feel like it."

109

"That's why I'm late. I been out looking for him. I covered everywhere in town he's likely to be."

"So, where is the bum?"

"He just dropped out of sight. Ain't nobody seen him." Tony shrugged.

"That don't sound good. It's not like Angelo not to turn up for work three days in a row." He paused. "Chuck's about beat, doing double duty. You'll have to work the table tonight without relief. Can you handle it?"

"Oh, sure, I'm in great shape." He watched the thoughtful expression on his boss's face for a moment. "I went to Angelo's house, like you said. His family hasn't seen him for three days neither. Not since he left to come to work that afternoon. I tried the police and the hospitals—no dice."

"He worked his shift here O.K.," the Duke said, puzzled. "So that means he's missing since he left here two nights ago."

"Yeah. I asked around—the guys who know him. Ain't anybody seen him." He paused, then went on. "What you're thinking—I don't reckon his going missing has any connection with The Club. Things been pretty tame around here lately. I'm sure Angelo ain't been getting no new ideas about stealing. He's too busy thinking about his singing career."

"I hope you're right," the Duke said. His face was impassive when he turned away.

Angelo's sudden disappearance bothered him. It was unlike his work partner to take off without warning. Angelo was usually clear in his intentions, and his limited capability as a dealer forced him to adopt a responsible attitude toward his work. He was no movie star yet, and there were guys in Steubenville who'd quickly fill his shoes at The Club if he got out of line. Worse, around this town there could be some very unpleasant explanations for a person's disappearance. There were guys Tony knew of, down at The Hole and places like that, who would arrange a convenient removal for fifty bucks, or a cracked skull for twenty. Over at the Boccardi household that afternoon, Frankie had been in tears, and Vincenzo and his wife were panicking. He'd promised them he would keep searching, but there was little he could do without going outside Steubenville. And he had no idea where to begin. Perhaps, when he'd thought enough about it, he'd come up with a clue. He knew as much as anyone about Angelo's lifestyle—or did he? He cleared his mind of the problem when he took over the table from a thankful Chuck. It was going to be a long night, and a guy with a wandering mind had no business being in control of a dice table. Saturday night, the busiest night of the week—he wished it were any night but Saturday.

The betting was light but steady. In a couple of hours he'd hardly lifted his eyes from the layout and the flying bones. When he called the bets, he directed his patter at the table and the game. The people at the rim were not personalities to him, merely ciphers who initiated functions he completed at the command of the dice. The dice were the masters of the court, and each courtier unquestioningly bowed his head to their fickle pronouncements. Then he noticed a change in the pattern of play. The bets had progressively increased, and he looked up.

When he glanced toward the source of the new money, he already knew the guy had been betting steadily and quietly for an hour or more, losing some, winning

110

some. The action hadn't been spectacular, and Tony had taken no special interest. Now he found himself curious about the diffident stranger on the other side of the table. The man was from out of town, he was sure. He was dressed carelessly, but his clothes were of good quality and fairly new. It was his smooth movements that intrigued Tony, and especially his hands. They were soft and slim, the fingers supple, the skin white and unblemished by the callouses so common around these parts. And although they were as graceful as a woman's hands, they were purposeful and direct, almost masterly. Tony's curiosity increased as he observed the quietly confident demeanor of the stranger. He completed his covert survey of the man with a sweeping glance, an unobtrusive, slow movement of the head from side to side that allowed him to study the stranger's face for a couple of seconds. What had begun as a tickling sensation at the back of his neck became an electrical charge, surging down his spine. Everything about the man was a carbon copy of what he had modeled himself on—the action, the smooth, certain movements, the diffident air belying the quiet, capable skill of the dexterous fingers. And he knew the man was a dice hustler.

An expert, no ordinary cheat. Not like the dozens of amateur cheats he regularly unmasked. Tony was developing an instinct about cheats—and learning to trust his instincts.

He could have had the man thrown out on his ear. The appropriate signal and the house "guards" would come running to escort him out through the front door, no questions asked. But that would be too easy—and he reminded himself that he was here to learn. He continued to deal, calling the bets in a lower key than before, hoping he'd given no outward sign of his suspicions. While he worked, he tried to retrace, step by step, the action of the last hour, since the hustler's arrival. He found it difficult to decide if the man was a winner or a loser. It wasn't possible to tell from a check tally; others had been winning and losing, and the hustler seemed to keep some of his checks in his pocket, bringing them out to replenish his stock at the rail as he used them. Or replacing them in his pocket when he won. And, incidentally, giving his fingers a frequent opportunity to disappear from view, Tony thought to himself. He was aware that the table float was two or three hundred dollars down since he'd last taken account. Nothing remarkable about that in the course of the game. But most of what was missing was in the hustler's pocket, he felt sure. He tried to estimate, from the bulge in the pocket, how much the guy had picked up. It was a hopeless task. If the hustler knew his business, the inside of the pocket was lined with a stiff material to defeat a telltale bulge.

Then the Duke, who'd been wandering around behind the crowd, was at his side. "What's up, Tony?" he murmured.

From the corner of his eye, he saw the hustler's gaze shift to them. He let a moment pass, maintaining an unconcerned expression, before he said quietly, "Hang around—I got a live one."

The Duke stepped back and waited until they no longer had the hustler's attention. He heard the voice in his ear again. "The guy with the hands?"

Tony nodded once, without looking around. "How the heck'd you know—did I make it so obvious?" he said quietly.

"No. Nobody else would have guessed something was wrong."

"Well, *you* guessed. I didn't show out or nothing. I didn't move a goddamn muscle."

"I know your style. Just forget it." But it bothered him that the Duke could read him so easily. "How much of our dough's he got?" the Duke added.

"Difficult to tell—I just started counting. The float's down three, four hundred. A couple of others had wins."

"O.K. We'll see."

"You wanna throw the guy out?"

"You seen his action yet?" the Duke asked.

"No."

"Maybe he's straight."

"Wanna bet?" Tony was that certain.

The Duke made no reply. When Tony glanced around, his boss had gone, and he was on his own. He didn't have long to wait. Ten minutes later the hustler was shooter. The man dipped lightly into his pocket, using his left hand. When the hand emerged, Tony knew it was the wrong shape. Then the left hand brushed the right, and he knew that the gaffed dice had been passed across, ready to come into play. The guy was good, he thought to himself—if he hadn't been looking for the move, he'd never have spotted it. The hustler increased his bets in careful stages, and Tony decided he was using percentage dice. As sometimes happens when a player gets hot, other players at the table followed the hustler in increasing their bets. When the hustler put five hundred dollars on the pass line, it had become a big game and Tony decided to go into action. With a flourish, he delivered the dice to the hustler for the big one—but they weren't the dice the hustler was expecting. A moment later Tony was raking in the hustler's five hundred and the bets of the others who'd taken the ride. In the same movement, he switched out his own gaffs and replaced them with straight house dice. He didn't have to look at the hustler to see an expression of confusion cross the man's face. As if nothing had happened, he continued his smooth movements and flipped the dice across to the next shooter. As play continued, he watched for the hustler's reactions, without making it apparent. Surely the guy had guessed what had happened? Apparently not—Tony raked in another three hundred dollars before the hustler stopped pressing his bets, having finally realized that the dice in action were no longer the percentage dice he'd introduced into the game.

Now it was Tony's turn to be puzzled as the hustler calmly produced more checks from his pocket and placed them at the rail in readiness. Then the realization of what had happened struck him like a bolt from the blue. The hustler had presumed Tony had made a legitimate dice change, and that somehow he'd missed the changeover. Dealers sometimes changed the dice if a game escalated—especially if the house was losing. It was the chance a dice cheat took, and several pairs of house dice stood in open view on the layout for this purpose. Tony had to force himself not to grin. To encourage the man in his misconception, when the next shooter came on the line, Tony deliberately changed the house dice, making sure the hustler saw the changeover. He caught the pursing of the man's lips.

When the dice reached the hustler again, there was an excitement growing in Tony. To avoid showing his feelings, he slowed the action down a little and dealt the game in a more deliberate manner. If anything, his slower movements would lull the hustler into an even greater sense of safety. When he came to bury the guy, it would be that much sweeter.

Two sides of five spots each faced upward. The hustler had made a point of ten. Tony took his time over paying a couple of small bets on the layout, waiting to see the hustler's move. When Tony was ready to pull in the dice, the hustler had lined up seven small stacks of bills—a seven-hundred dollar bet. In cash, which probably meant that he was out of checks and the house money had been recovered. Tony was intensely curious to know which gaffs the hustler had introduced to insure such a bet. As he hooked the dice toward him on the end of his stick, a twist of his wrist flipped one cube over. The five spots on the side going under reappeared immediately on the side coming up and he recognized the dice instantly as Tops and Bottoms. He delayed the sequence of actions for a fraction of a moment, aware that the hustler was watching him, hawkeyed. Tony switched in his own set of gaffs, bust-outs showing one, three, five on opposite sides of one die, and two, four, six on opposite sides of the other. There was now no way the hustler could repeat his point of ten to win. On the second roll, the hustler sevened-out. No sooner had the dice stopped rolling than Tony's stick was across the table, culling the hustler's money.

Now the man knew. But nobody else at the table had been aware of the silent contest going on under his nose. Tony could almost feel the wave of savage, muted anger coming at him across the table. He couldn't resist looking up, and he couldn't prevent the hint of a triumphant grin that crept onto his face. The light was dim beyond the green shade that projected a glare onto the layout, and the hustler had stepped back, but Tony caught the eyes glaring venomously at him. For an instant he met the challenge in those eyes. Then he dismissed it with a curt, "Next shooter, please. Get your bets down, gentlemen."

The hustler's place was taken by another player, and the game went on. Through his self-satisfaction, he tried to concentrate on his work. But the image of the eyes remained, and occasionally the spite in that look drifted across his thoughts. He hoped he was wrong—he had the feeling he hadn't seen the last of his opponent.

CHAPTER TWENTY-ONE

When he opened his eyes, he knew instinctively, from the different sounds, that it was Sunday. Outside, none of the weekday commercial hubbub reached the house, and, through the thin partition separating his bedroom from the kitchen, he could hear his father and mother talking softly in Italian. They spoke in subdued tones so as not to wake him. Even the smells were different, Sunday. The aroma of a roast in the oven crept under the door and pervaded his nostrils. He looked at his watch. It said twelve-thirty, and the events of the previous day came crowding back into his mind. He relaxed on the pillow and smiled to himself at how he'd buried the hustler with sheer professionalism. It meant a lot to him that he'd beaten a man skilled enough to be a mechanic. He turned the phrase over in his mind—it still evoked a thrill in him, even after all this time. It was no challenge to cheat some high-rolling chump out of his dough at the crap table, but to defeat someone like the hustler in a straight contest was different. He pulled himself up short. He had to beware of thinking of players as fools, he told himself. The Duke had warned him that it was a sign of a bad dealer. The vicious look in the hustler's eyes drifted across his mind, and he found himself frowning. He dismissed the vision impatiently. What did he expect from a hustler he'd put down—a vote of thanks and a smile?

And, what in hell's name had happened to Angelo?

He threw off the covers and rolled out of bed, determined to make a real effort to find his work partner. When he emerged from the bedroom, he said to his father, "Hey, Papa, they found Angelo yet?"

"No, they not find him," Bruno said. "He disappear, like that invisible man in the movies. Francesca, she's over this morning. I tell her, we got no fresh news."

"You should have woke me."

"No reason to wake you. You need your sleep. I send out Mokey to ask around. He got lots of friends in town."

"Frankie been down to the cops again?"

"Yes. They know nothing."

"Gee, it's real weird, him going off like that, without a word—it ain't like Angelo, you ask me." Remembering Mokey's experience, he'd wondered if the police had a hand in Angelo's disappearance. The Duke had put out feelers, and the reply came back negative. He made for the bathroom. "I'll get going," he said. "Maybe I can pick up a lead somewhere."

His mother jumped to her feet. "Your lunch be ready soon, Antonio. You eat before you go out . . ."

"Ain't staying to eat, Mama. I gotta get going. Sure appreciate a cup of coffee, though," he threw back over his shoulder.

At the New Philly he sought out Bob and Bluey. They piled into the Chevy and, on the quiet Sunday streets, headed for the Boccardi barber shop. "Listen, you guys," Tony said, "a person don't just disappear into thin air, not even in Steubenville. He gotta be around somewhere, and we're gonna find him."

Bluey said, "Angelo's always hankerin' after being a singer. Maybe he was offered a rush singing spot and grabbed it while it was hot. That'd be out of town, right? Ain't no singing jobs in this town."

"No, he'd have said," Tony answered. "Or he'd have called home on the telephone by now. Besides, I'd have known—he don't stop chewing my ear about the singing. He got this audition coming up in a couple of weeks, over to Chicago. Besides the visit to Hollywood, later in the year, there's nothing else."

"Everyone's looking for him. Ain't nowhere else in town he can hide," Bob said, "except maybe over to Weirton."

"O.K., we'll go over there and look around, after I see Frankie," Tony said. He added, "Anyone ask Skeeter if he seen him?"

"Come on, Tony," Bob grunted. "Nobody sees Skeets these days—but nobody. Since that broad hooked him he's dropped out of sight."

"He still holding down his job at the Wharf?" Tony asked.

"Oh, sure," Bob said. "After work he runs straight home to his little tootsie. The prick," he added sourly.

It was a sore point with them that Skeeter had vacated the social scene abruptly, dropping his lifelong friends like hot coals. Skeeter's secretive romance and sudden marriage to Ellen Hinkley had ruffled their chauvinistic solidarity. "He didn't even ask us to the wedding, the crumb," Bluey said.

"So who the fuck wants to go to a whore's wedding anyhow?" Bob put in sorely. "That Ellen, I told you, she ain't got no good reputation. The way I hear it, she been seen up at Molly Whiter's place."

"You seen her there yourself?" Tony asked.

"No."

"Then keep your trap shut."

"O.K., so she's a lady—so what's Skeeter afraid of? Maybe he thinks we're gonna steal her away from him? Why's he hiding her away? We ain't never even met the broad. Not formal."

"Listen," Tony said sharply. "That's Skeets' business. His private life ain't our affair. Personally, I'm leaving him strictly alone. He wants me, he knows where to find me." He peered over the wheel, and they rode on in uncomfortable silence.

Her eyes were red from crying. In the background Vincenzo and his wife hovered, their faces creased with anxiety. "Something terrible's happened to Angelo—I know it," Frankie said.

"Angelo can take care of himself, Frankie. He's O.K., take it from me. We'll find him soon, and it'll be a big laugh." Tony spoke with a confidence he didn't feel. It didn't seem long since he was saying the same thing about Mokey.

"This town, I hate it," she said suddenly and ferociously. "The best we've got here is prejudice and ignorance. It's a town full of savages. Decent people don't stand a chance. Places like Water Street and The Hole—anything you want to name, anything rotten, it's all here." She burst into tears.

"Aw, it ain't that bad," Tony said uncomfortably.

"What if he got into a fight with one of those gangs? What if he got rolled, and he's lying hurt somewhere?"

"We'd have heard by now."

"From who, the police? What do they care if there's nothing in it for them?"

"O.K., Frankie, that's enough," Tony said. "You just stop upsetting yourself now. Me and the guys, we're going out again to look around. Just relax—it ain't no help, you getting hysterical." He signaled Bob and Bluey that it was time to leave.

It seemed a hopeless task. They scoured the bars, the clubs, and the pool halls. They spoke to anyone they could find who had even a nodding acquaintance with Angelo. They crossed the river to Weirton and started all over again. They drew a blank. Late in the evening they admitted defeat, and when they finally returned, it

115

had been dark for a long time. The lights burned in every window of the Boccardi household, and Frankie waited anxiously in the doorway. Her face fell when she caught sight of their downcast expressions. She turned away and they followed her up the stairs to the parlor above the barber shop.

Gratefully they sipped the hot minestrone Signora Boccardi served them. "Let's go over this again," Tony suggested to Frankie. "Did Angelo do or say anything unusual before he left for work that last day?"

"Nothing." She shook her head. "He spent a long time getting ready before he went off to work, that's all."

"Longer than usual?"

She stood up. "Yes. In fact, he had Papa give him a haircut and shave that day. He usually shaves himself."

"Meeting a dame?" Bob suggested.

"He left for work the normal time, and we know he was in The Club all evening," Tony said.

"How about after work?"

"It's possible." He turned to Frankie. "Was Angelo dating any girl you know of?"

"No," she said. Then she lifted her head thoughtfully. ". . . I just remembered, he was talking on the telephone a couple of days before he went missing."

"That mean anything?"

"I don't know. Why I mention it, I think it was a girl on the telephone—the way he said goodbye. I was walking upstairs when he was hanging up."

"Could have been arranging the meet," Bluey speculated.

"O.K. Let's work on the supposition that he had a date after work that night," Tony said. "Question is, with who?"

Frankie shrugged again. "Lately he doesn't discuss his girl friends with me."

"Well, how about Lucy—that friend of yours, remember?"

"Lucy's married and living in Toledo," Frankie said.

"Anyone else you can think of?"

"He says he only has time for his singing career these days," she said.

Tony knew different. He'd come to recognize the self-satisfied smirk on Angelo's face when he'd made a new conquest. But Angelo, expansive on any other subject, didn't talk names where his women were concerned. It was always: "The broad with the legs" or "The blonde dame with the body." Angelo had learned the hard way how to keep out of trouble. "Who was his last steady girl friend?"

"The last one I knew of was Ellen Hinkley. It was an on-and-off affair for a couple of years. The reason I know, she was the only girl Angelo ever went back to."

The three of them sat up and exchanged glances. "How long since Angelo last seen her?" Tony said.

She looked at them. "About six months, I think. Does it mean anything?"

"I don't know—we'll check it out," Tony said. He got to his feet. "Come on, you guys, it's time we paid Skeets a visit."

The isolated house was located a couple of miles outside town along a dirt road. It was the first time any of them had seen the place Skeeter had taken his bride. He cut the motor of the Chevy and they sat there staring at it. "This can't be the place," Bob said eventually. "Skeeter's a town guy. He ain't gonna be living out here with the pigs and the chickens."

"Yeah, it checks out." Tony peered through the windshield at the house number on the mailbox. "It says Froelich."

"He's gotta be crazy, living out here," Bluey said.

"Don't look like anybody's home," Bob said. "There ain't a light nowhere."

"Let's take a look," Tony said.

They got out of the car and walked up to the darkened house. Tony banged on the door; they waited, but there was no reply.

"Let's go," Bluey said. "We're wasting our time—there's nobody home."

"Wonder why all the drapes are drawn?" Tony said, curious.

The others looked up. "Yeah, that's strange," Bob said, "all the windows."

"Let's take a look at the back of the house. Bob, you bring the car around so we got some light," Tony said.

At the back of the house, the drapes were again drawn across every window. Bob said, "Jeez, this place gives me the creeps."

"Say, there's a light on in there." Tony pointed to a tiny crack where the drapes fitted imperfectly.

"Think there's someone inside?" Bluey asked.

"I dunno—there's something funny going on here," Tony said, puzzled. On impulse, he stepped up to the window and rapped on it sharply, the sound echoing in the quiet night.

Almost immediately the drapes parted an inch, and they found themselves staring into a single, wild eye. The drapes snapped shut. "Who the fuck was that?" Bob burst out.

"Let's go find out," Tony said grimly.

Nobody answered their hammering at the front door. They put their shoulders to it and the door burst inward. Tony switched on the light, and the parlor was revealed in riotous disarray, the remains of several days' living strewn about the room. The door facing them on the other side of the room was locked. "He's in there," Bob said. "That's the room where the window is . . ."

They hammered on the second door and a voice they could hardly recognize suddenly screamed, "Go away—get out of my house."

They looked at each other in disbelief. "Was that Skeets?" Bluey asked.

"Yeah, I think it was," Tony said soberly. He called out: "Hey, Skeets, it's your buddies. It's me—and Bob and Bluey."

"Go away. You got no right coming in here. I'm not talking to nobody."

"Skeets, come on out of there. If you don't come out, we're coming in."

"No, you can't come in here. Go away—go away, damn you." Skeeter's voice rose in rage.

Tony waved the others away. He stepped back a couple of paces, then took a flying leap at the door, feet first. The door crashed inward.

The stench came out to meet them before anything else. For a moment they couldn't comprehend what met their gaze in the dim light. Then it all crowded in on them. Skeeter stood frenziedly in the middle of the room, his arms hanging before him like an ape's, staring at them with wild, bloodshot eyes. On a bed a girl lay trussed hand and foot with rope, a filthy rag gagging her, from behind which she moaned desperately as she stared at them in mute apprehension. Over in a corner of the room a familiar form cowered, half-crouching, one forearm swinging loose at an unnatural angle from a broken elbow. The face was almost unrecognizable, the prominent nose smashed to one side, the swollen mouth and lower part of the face covered in dried, caked blood. "For God's sakes, get me out of here," the pitiful figure in the corner croaked.

"Is it Angelo?" Bob said incredulously.

"Yeah, it's Angelo all right." Tony blew breath out between his teeth, hardly able to accept what he saw.

"What in hell's been going on?" Bluey said.

Then Skeeter rushed them, but the tough guy was in a weak condition, and they soon pinned him down. When they sat on him on the floor, he capitulated and burst into frame-racking sobs. "O.K., he won't be any trouble now," Tony said.

Bluey and Bob released the girl, who collapsed on the floor when she tried to stand up. Angelo, too, was barely able to stand. They stood supporting him. "That guy, he should be put away in a sanitarium," Angelo got out through a mouthful of rust. "He's out of his mind. He was gonna kill us. He meant it, I swear."

"You ain't dead yet," Tony said. He turned to the others. "Get these two to a hospital right away."

"How about Skeeter?"

"I'll stay here with him."

"You want us to send for the police?"

"No, keep the cops out of this—I'll handle it. Wait at Angelo's house. There's a telephone over there, I'll call you when I want you."

The others had gone, and he sat on the floor nursing Skeeter in his arms. As the hours passed and his friend became calm, Tony found out what had happened: The night Angelo went missing, Skeeter had arranged to help out with an urgent repair on a boat down at the Wharf. The plan was for work to continue on board when the boat made a trip to Wheeling early the next day. The repair was finished ahead of schedule, before the sailing; Skeeter tramped home at dawn to find Angelo in bed with his wife, Ellen, Angelo's old flame. Apparently he went berserk.

Skeeter rocked gently back and forth in Tony's arms. "Why'd you keep them prisoners, Skeets? That don't help nothing," Tony said eventually.

"I was gonna kill them," Skeeter whispered. "I couldn't bring myself to do it. I wanted them to die, what they done to me."

"Maybe it's wrong, what they done. Maybe they're dogs, them two—it don't justify no murder, old buddy," Tony said softly.

"Yes. I'm dead inside. Why should they go on living when I'm dead?"

"You ain't dead—you'll get over it."

"No. You don't understand. I loved her—I loved her more than life, my Ellen. Now I'm dead."

"Maybe I should have listened to the other guys when they tried to tell me about her," Tony said ruefully. "I didn't wanna know—I was too busy. Maybe I'd have

118

been a better friend if I'd listened. I could have done something about it."

"No, there was nothing you could do," Skeeter said in a moment of logic. "I was under her spell. She held me under a spell, like a witch. Now the spell's broken, isn't it?"

"Sure. You'll be O.K. now."

"Yes." Then, a moment later, "But I'm frightened, Tony. She took part of me away. I ain't whole anymore. What am I gonna do?"

"I'll look after you. We're buddies, ain't we? We always been buddies, since we was kids. Nothing's changed. I won't let you down, Skeets. I promise. I'll always be there—any time you want me."

Skeeter was calm again. Soon, he began humming softly to himself.

CHAPTER TWENTY-TWO

He beat the deadline by a minute. For months it had been his ambition to get out of The Club by one in the morning. It had been one of the quietest nights he could remember, and they'd shut the doors at ten minutes of one. Now that he'd finally made it, the damn Chevy wouldn't start, and it looked as if he'd be out in the cold night trying to fix the thing, he reflected ironically. For some time it had been his intention to change the worn-out car for something better. It wasn't that he couldn't afford a newer car—he just hadn't got around to changing. The starter ground on, draining the life out of the battery. Unexpectedly, the motor coughed, caught, and a welcome roar rose from under the hood as he prodded at the pedal with his foot.

He had his hand on the gear shift when the passenger door opened and a guy slid in beside him. He surveyed the grizzled-looking stranger. "What you want, mac?" he said.

"Just relax," the man said levelly. "Let's move off."

"We ain't going nowhere," Tony began, his voice hardening. Then he saw the gun. "This a stick-up?"

"It's no stick-up. Just do like I tell you—now, drive . . ."

He knew better than to argue with a gun. He put the Chevy into gear. "If it's dough you want, I don't carry more than ten bucks," Tony said.

The man ignored him. "Turn left onto Market Street." Two blocks down, he said, "O.K. Stop here."

Then he began to understand. The dice hustler he'd defeated in The Club came out of the shadows. For a moment the man stood staring into the car. The eyes were the same as he remembered them, piercing and cold. The hustler motioned to the other man, who moved over so that the hustler could slide into the rear seat. "O.K., punk," the gunsel said, "move off."

He was coming to the end of Market Street and they hadn't said a word. Tony spoke out. "Where to now?"

In the rearview mirror he saw the hustler glance out at a road leading off to the right. "Where does that road go?"

"Runs along the river," Tony said.

"Take it." He swung the wheel, drove unhurriedly, and the town dropped away behind them. If it was the hustler's intention to harm him, he certainly seemed in no hurry. Then the voice from the back said, "O.K., it's quiet enough here. Pull off the road." For an instant he disregarded the hustler, but when he saw the gun rise menacingly, he took his foot off the pedal and pulled to one side. *This is it,* he thought to himself as the wheels stopped rolling. He felt the tension building up in him, and he looked again at the gun, now pointed unwaveringly at his stomach, knowing it would be suicidal to make a dive for it. He had little choice, it seemed. "Cut the motor," the hustler said. "We're gonna talk."

Tony breathed a little easier. "I had trouble starting. We oughta let it run."

"O.K., leave it." There was little animosity in the hustler's voice, and Tony's hopes rose.

"What you want with me? I was only doing my job." He poured out a torrent of words. "Nothing personal in it—you'd have done the same thing yourself. A guy walks into a sawdust joint to hustle the bones, he's taking his chances. Win some, lose some—that's the way, ain't it? In another trap, you'd have got beat up and thrown out on your ear."

The hustler was silent and Tony's words echoed in the interior of the car. The man said, "What's your name, kid?"

"Tony Vitale."

"How old are you?"

"Twenty."

"You ever been outside this town?"

"Sure. I been in a few big cities, up and down the state."

"I mean you worked somewhere else?"

"No . . ." Tony said. "This is the only job I had."

"Something I have to tell you, kid. I never see a mechanic good as you. I seen 'em around—high-class joints in Chicago and Kentucky. Nobody ever pulled a switcheroo on me like you did and got away with it."

"Why, you something special?" Despite his predicament, he felt the old thrill at the hustler's recognition of his skill. He decided not to aggravate the situation and spoke in a quieter tone. "You ain't so bad yourself. Usually I spot a hustler right away. Most of 'em are just amateurs—they wanna steal some dough and run. I knew you was different as soon as I picked up your moves."

"Yeah . . ." the hustler said. Tony waited in the heavy silence. "Don't make no difference to what you gotta do," he went on eventually. "You're gonna get me my dough back, with a profit."

"I don't get it," Tony said.

"You're gonna lay it on to pay out a five-grand win."

It took him a moment to assimilate the hustler's meaning. He shook his head.

120

"Wouldn't work," he said. "The boss, he's got your number. I told him you was hustling. You wouldn't get past the door."

"Sure, I know that," the hustler said. "It ain't me you'll be paying. It's my partner here."

"We don't play for that kinda dough in The Club." He was beginning to feel very uncomfortable.

"My partner's a high roller from out of town. He's gonna be playing with a stake of a couple of grand. That'll look good, right? A man walks into your joint with a couple of grand, you don't tell him he ain't welcome, right?"

"It won't work," Tony repeated.

"Why not?"

"I let a stranger walk out with that size win, the boss is gonna ask why I don't get to work on him."

"That's after the game—after you pay the win."

"Yeah, sure," he said. "There'll be an inquest."

"You don't understand. That's *your* problem, kid. We'll be long gone."

"Oh." Tony went silent.

"I didn't say. You got a choice."

"What's that?"

Suddenly the hustler's voice was behind his ear, and he could feel the man's breath on his neck. He could picture the vicious eyes boring into the back of his head. "You can agree, or you can get shot right here and now. I wanna tell you, that's my partner's specialty, shooting people. The way you took me at the table, I ain't particular which way you wanna play."

Tony shot a glance at the gunsel at his side. The man's eyes were gleaming, and the angle of the gun's barrel hadn't altered. It was still pointed at his stomach. "What's to stop me saying I agree now, then bilking you in The Club?"

"That's a good question, and the answer's nothing—there's nothing to stop you doing that thing." The hustler sat back again and spoke calmly. "What we do, we shoot you later. We ain't in no hurry. Maybe we leave it for now, and we come through town in a month or so to do the job. One day you walk out of that joint, and your feet don't hit the sidewalk. You land on your face, full of holes. Same thing happens if my partner here don't walk out of that club in one piece, with the dough in his pocket."

"Seems you covered all the angles."

"Right," the hustler said.

"Well, I suppose we better get back," he said, positioning himself behind the wheel.

"Hey—this punk, he ain't agreed to the plan yet." The gunsel came alive and glared into the back of the car.

"Sure he agreed. He got no alternative. That right, Tony Vitale?" There was mockery in the hustler's voice.

He turned the car and headed back to town, anger boiling in him. He had no intention of cooperating in the plan to rob The Club of five grand. But the danger of getting shot was very real. These days a guy could get shot for a lot less than five thousand dollars. A guy could get shot because he'd dented a hustler's ego. He found no way out of his predicament by the time they reached the Steubenville streetlights.

The junction with Market Street came into sight ahead, and the hustler said, "Stop here." Tony rolled the car into the curb and the hustler spoke to his partner. "You better walk in from here. We don't wanna be seen in town together."

The gunsel opened the door and stepped out onto the running board. "Here, you take the piece," he said to the hustler. He turned and leaned back into the car.

Tony acted. He'd quietly slipped into first gear, and now he let out the clutch with a slam, throwing the gunsel off balance. The man went sprawling across the sidewalk, and at the same time the gun spun up into the air, fell into the car, and went rattling down somewhere by Tony's feet. He steered with one hand, his chin on the wheel, as he fished around for it. He found it and his fingers closed over the butt.

The Chevy was accelerating fast. The light at Market Street was red, but he ignored it, roaring across the junction, his toe to the floor. From the corner of his eye he saw Hoyle's cruising police Ford come out of Market Street, then swerve as Hoyle tried to miss the Chevy. There was a crash as the Chevy's fender carved into the side of the Ford. It was a glancing blow, and Tony managed to keep control. His instinctive reaction was to keep going, and he blasted away from the downtown area through the sleeping streets.

The next thing he knew, the hustler's arms were around his throat, pulling his head back so that he couldn't see the road ahead. The hustler was throttling him; he couldn't breathe and the car ran on blindly. In desperation he pointed the gun behind his head and pulled the trigger. There was a massive explosion in his ear, and the pressure on his throat eased. When his head stopped ringing, he could just see the outline of the road ahead through watery eyes. Fortunately, the car had been running along a wide, straight stretch. He jammed his foot on the brake and the car came to a screeching halt. He spun around in his seat. The hustler lay half on and half off the seat. A shaft of light from the last of the town's streetlights cut across the hustler's face. The eyes were wide open, cold and vicious, staring at Tony for the last time. They were lifeless and the man was dead.

The wail of Hoyle's police siren reached him—Hoyle must have recovered from the crash and taken up the chase. He put the car into gear and roared off. But the Chevy was low on power, and, within a mile or two, he knew the police car was gaining on him. He could kick himself that he hadn't stopped to think. Now, with the police in pursuit and the body of a man, complete with evidence of the shooting, in the car, he was in deep trouble. Worse, Hoyle would like nothing better than to pin a murder rap on him, which wouldn't be difficult if the hustler's partner came forward to give evidence. Nobody would believe he was being threatened, and a plea of self-defense would sound ludicrous. The hustler's presence in the car suggested a conspiracy against The Club—and his death a falling-out among thieves. There was no avoiding the facts: Hoyle had had a clear view of Tony at the wheel and a guy in the back when the cars struck.

The full extent of his peril sank into his bones and he shouted at the night in despair.

On a long straight, the headlights of the police car appeared in his mirror, and the banshee wail of its siren reached out for him. He fought down the panic in his throat and tried to think. Hoyle would catch up with him in a few minutes and that would be the end if he didn't act. In the bouncing splash of light on the road ahead, a dirt road running off to the right appeared. He slammed on the brakes and barely managed to make the turn. The car raced, pitching and crashing along the broken track, while Tony tried desperately to figure out a plan of action. The decision was made for him. As the car breasted a rise and started down the slope beyond, the track suddenly disappeared into blackness ahead and the headlights shone out into vacant space. He remembered instantly where he was. The track led to nothing but a stony cliff top, part of a deserted mining area, now nothing but a place for lovers' assignations, a hundred feet above the Ohio River.

He hit the brakes in desperation, but the downhill momentum of the car carried it on, the wheels locking and sliding on the loose surface toward the edge of the cliff. The car had lost most of its speed before he knew he no longer had control. In the last few feet before the drop, he opened the door and threw himself out. He rolled a couple of times on the rough, hard surface and picked himself up. The car, unfettered, had run on freely and was gone. For a crazy moment, as it fell, the headlights inscribed a leisurely arc in the black sky. Then, from way down below, he heard the splash as it went into the river, carrying with it its gruesome cargo of death.

Now the howl of the police siren, echoing shrilly in the empty darkness, pierced the air around him, and almost immediately the headlights of Hoyle's car came over the rise and started cautiously down toward him. Panic in his heart and mind, he turned and made off, bruised and stumbling, across the rough terrain.

A murderer and a fugitive, Tony fled into the night.

BOOK TWO Outside

CHAPTER ONE

The gaudy mobile home leading the long caravan of huge, lumbering carnival vehicles turned south off Ogden Avenue and bumped its way over the open ground leading to nearby Sportsmen's Park. At one side the racetrack stretched off into the distance. One by one, and slowly, like a line of lethargic lemmings trailing each other blindly, the heavy, colorful trucks turned right and followed the lead vehicle. The crunching of great cogs told of cumbersome gears being changed, and smoke belched from muscular, steam-driven prime movers, as old as the hills, riding on ancient solid tires and hauling gargantuan trailers. On the highway, traffic from both directions came to a standstill as the lumbering caterpillar of carnival equipment left the road. On the sides of the vehicles, colorful paintings depicted the various carnival attractions: the Jungle House and the Swamp Ride, Shooting Galleries and sideshows, Dracula's Castle and the Western Tavern, the Roller Coaster, bumper cars and the Airplane Ride, the Haunted House and the House of Mirrors. The Big Top, miraculously compressed into the largest, longest truck of all, bumped and swayed across the rough land. For the first time in many days the drivers relaxed their strict caravan discipline and churned off in different directions, seeking favored parking spots. The air of somber purposefulness changed to one of relaxed abandon as they rejoiced at the sight of the new resting place, the end of their long haul—the Chicago suburb of Cicero.

Paddy O'Herly, looking even smaller than his diminutive five foot three as he wrestled with the huge steering wheel of his leviathan, gave Tony, seated on the other side of the driving cab, a sweat and grease-stained grin. Conversation had been impossible for hours in the din from the massive diesel engine thundering between them; Tony grinned back from the pile of ropes that formed his seat. They both had seen enough of the open road to last them some time. When the engine stopped, they sat in silence while the awesome echo died away and their hearing returned to normal. "Well, that's that," Paddy said gratefully, "and I can tell you—I'll be glad to crawl into the cot and lay me head down tonight."

Tony nodded in agreement. He got to his feet and winced. It was as if the ropes had cut a permanent impression into his pants. "I can think of better ways to make a

125

living," he said. "I was glad of the job, but I gotta tell you—it's beginning to lose some of its charm."

Paddy laughed. "You're too soft. The Carny's not a job, it's a way of life. You'll get used to it."

They jumped down together, stretched, and stood watching the last of the vehicles leave the road. "If this is Chicago, I don't think much of it," Tony said, looking around. "Don't look any different from some of them midstate towns we been in."

"We're not in Chicago proper," Paddy said. "They don't like the Carny too close to the city." He pointed east. "Downtown Chicago's that way, a few miles, on the shore of Lake Michigan."

"So what's this place?"

"Cicero—you never heard of it?"

"Yeah, I heard the name," Tony said.

"The place is wide open. Around here's where Al Capone was king. Over there, over on South Wabash Avenue, they got everything—bars, broads, nightclubs, gambling—anything you want."

"I'd like to see that."

"Keep away. You'll blow your dough."

"So, what else I need dough for?"

"Yeah, you got a point." Paddy grinned.

"Let's get cleaned up and shoot over there. I'm buying the drinks," Tony said.

The fatigue dropped away from Paddy and his grin broadened. "No good Irishman refuses a drink," he said. "First we gotta get this equipment bedded down. Come on, let's get to work."

Tony found his gloves. Before he put them on he looked ruefully at his hands, rough and stained from months of work as a roustabout. It wasn't that he minded the work; he'd been glad of the job. There were plenty of workless men on the roads and jobs were few and far between. It had been a stroke of luck, finding the traveling carnival. He'd come across it in a storm when, bogged down in mud, the Carny people needed every hand they could muster. The Irishman took a liking to him and had let him sleep in the truck cabin a few nights, and even shared his food. Then the carnival had stopped in a hick town, and Tony was put on the payroll for fifteen dollars a week, handling the electric bumper cars. He didn't find it easy, adapting to the primitive living conditions and lack of sophistication of the Carny people. But he felt a distant affinity with them, realizing that beneath the show most of the sidegames were crude gambling gyps. Living in a state of limbo, unquestioned and unquestioning, he slowly found himself again. His calm had returned and now he was hankering after the suppressed excitement and muted competition of a gambling house. And he knew the time had come for him to move on.

They strolled leisurely along South Wabash Avenue, ignoring the soliciting pimps. "Hey, that's the tenth cigar store we passed in five minutes," Tony said. "What the heck—everyone around here hooked on cigars?"

"No," Paddy laughed. "The cigar stores are fronts. In the back they got gambling games. Each store runs an individual game—poker, faro, baccarat, craps. You go in one of them joints to buy a cigar, you're likely to get shot. They'll think you're looking to rob the place." They stopped at a bar, the biggest on the street. "This is where we wanna be," Paddy said, "the Three Aces."

Tony looked into the garish saloon. "What's in here?" he asked.

"Everything," Paddy told him. "Booze downstairs, gambling and women upstairs. You name it . . ."

When they sat down in the Three Aces, the first thing he noticed was the number of unattached females. They were at the bar, or occupying tables in groups and singly, always with an eye on the door. Several of the women were looking at them and preening themselves. "This is one place you won't suffer from night starvation," Paddy grinned. "As for me, let me get the taste of some honest whiskey down my throat first." For Paddy drinking was a ceremony. He was on his third glass before Tony had finished his first. "What's holding you up, son?" he said. "You're wasting valuable drinking time."

"I been watching them people going upstairs."

"The couples?"

"No, the guys. They must have some real action up there. Never seen so many people coming and going in a joint."

"The gambling saloon's one of the biggest around these parts."

"I'd sure like to see it," he said nonchalantly.

"Well, gambling don't hold no interest for me," Paddy said. "A couple more drinks and I'll be ready for some female company. But don't let me hold you up. Go ahead, if you want, and I'll see you afterward."

"O.K." Tony got up.

"You want to borrow a few dollars?"

"I got enough," he said. "I don't need much."

"See you when your money's gone," Paddy said.

"Don't bank on it."

He walked through the door and saw the crowd at the crap table, tasted the excitement in the air, and it was like coming home. The familiar cries across the room stirred his blood and, for a moment, made him homesick for Steubenville. It was a much bigger joint than The Club. There was something new here—an atmosphere of primeval ruthlessness, an air of sardonic contempt for the players. It came across in the cries of the dealers, the faces of the toughs lounging against the walls. They surveyed the action with a bored, cynical air, their occasional stirrings revealing ominous bulges under their coats. Three dice tables were in operation and for a few moments he watched the action, moving from one to the other. He'd been flexing his fingers unobtrusively and he hoped the lack of practice hadn't diminished his capability too much. Then he took out the four five-dollar bills representing his entire capital. He had no gaffs and he'd be limited to manipulating the straight house dice. It would be slow, and his options would be limited. But there was no rush, and time was another weapon in his armory of moves. When he was shooter, he placed a five-dollar bet and set out to give himself a simple percentage advantage. His fingers hadn't lost their skill, and he restricted himself to his two best and least obvious pitches. His basic six-ace specialty gave him good table odds— occasionally he used a slideshot, spinning one die with an exaggerated action to distract the attention of the other players so they didn't notice how the other die revolved in the horizontal plane. He worked unostentatiously, and a couple of hours passed before he'd won the three hundred dollars he considered the least he needed for his purpose.

When he returned to the saloon, Paddy was sitting alone, contemplating a collection of empty whiskey glasses. His eyes were beginning to swim when he looked up at Tony. "How'd it go, bhoyo?" he said cheerfully.

"Not bad," Tony said. "I won a few bucks. It's more than most of them suckers up there can say."

"That's because I asked the little people to look after you. What you say we blow some of that fine money on a good time? There are some very accommodating ladies in this establishment. They're all eager to see your needs are attended to." He leered drunkenly around the room.

"I need the dough, Paddy. I got plans."

"There's been a Protestant influence on your good Catholic upbringing," Paddy said resignedly.

"Something else I gotta tell you—I ain't coming back. I'm finished with the Carny."

Paddy sat up. "You know what you're saying, boy? Things're hard out there on the streets. You'll not be getting another job easily."

"I'll be O.K. I'm going back to my own work."

"And what is that? You're a secretive son of a gun—you never did tell me what it is you do."

"I'm a mechanic," Tony said, on impulse.

"Ah, now we've plenty of work for a good mechanical man on the Carny equipment. You should have said so. I'll tell the boss that's what you want to do."

"I sort of specialize. I can't explain. It's goodbye, Paddy. I want to thank you for your help." He held out his hand.

"Well, if you've made up your mind . . ." Paddy took the hand and shook it heartily. Remember, there's always a place for you with the Carny."

"You've been a real friend—I won't forget." Tony looked at him thoughtfully. "You gonna be O.K., with all that booze inside you? Maybe I ought to get you back."

"Me? Need a nursemaid? I haven't started drinking yet, me bucko. The night's young." Through the haze, he viewed Tony's concern with enjoyment. "And don't you worry about me, sonny. The Irish have a guardian angel who guides us home when we're in our cups. He's the most overworked angel in Christendom. Away with you—and do what you have to."

It wasn't much of a hotel, sandwiched between a cabaret and a dance hall on Twenty-second Street, and they weren't particular about accepting his business. He realized why when he lay down to sleep in the sleazy room. The regular slamming of doors and the tramping of feet kept him awake at first. After a while he closed his ears to the traffic and slept like a log in his first real bed in months.

128

CHAPTER TWO

Chicago. Cicero. And then he remembered it was the home of The Great Lakes Gambling Novelties Company. He found the place eventually, on the second floor of a blank-walled building near the Hawthorne Inn. He walked down a long passage and knocked on a frosted-glass panel in a door. The panel opened and a bespectacled man looked out. "I've come to buy some gaffs," he said.

The man gave him a reproving look and glanced past him down the passage. "You made a mistake, sonny," he said. "You've come to the wrong place."

"We done business before," Tony said. "I'm a friend of Boston Bailey. You sent me a box of gaffs about three years ago, on his order. My name's Tony Vitale. From Steubenville," he added.

The man half-closed the panel, and Tony saw him glancing through a ledger. He closed the panel and opened the door. "Come in, Mr. Vitale," he said. "You understand, we don't deal with guys who come in off the street looking for joke dice. Now, what can I do for you?"

"I want the works. Everything—same as I had before. The best you got."

"We have most of them in stock, but if you want a full variety of percentage shapes, they'll have to be specially cut. Aren't many people have a use for the full range. It'll take a day or so."

"How much?" Tony said.

"Five hundred dollars for the complete outfit."

"Jes-us."

"You said you want the best."

"I do—look, here's two hundred bucks. Give me a set of Tops and Bottoms, high and low numbers. I'll come back tomorrow with the rest of the dough."

"Certainly, Mr. Vitale." Then, when Tony was leaving, "Give our respects to Mr. Bailey."

"Sure will, if I ever see him." He grinned.

That night, in the Three Aces, his confidence came pouring in. He'd spent an hour that day in the hotel room, scrubbing and kneading his hands; then he'd rubbed oil into them so that some of the old flexibility had returned, and he felt good. He was careful to ensure that his play was inconspicuous. He won some, gave a little back, won some more. He was luxuriating in six hundred dollars' worth of house checks when he sensed he was being watched. He glanced up to realize he was looking at a familiar face at the other end of the table. It was the Colonel, the high roller who occasionally visited The Club. The Colonel's usually benign, indulgent expression was missing. He'd recognized Tony immediately, and it was in his face: What was an insignificant young dealer from Steubenville doing in a high-stakes game in Cicero? The Colonel was transmitting his suspicions to the man at his side, who scowled across the table in no uncertain manner.

He didn't get long to think about it. The man at the Colonel's side disappeared, and a moment later Tony was grabbed from behind and led away from the game. Two bulky hoods locked his arms tightly behind his back and frog-marched him out. He lost his balance on the second flight of stairs and they gave him no chance to recover, dragging him down from step to step, giving his knees a violent hammering. Briefly they searched his pockets, then threw him into a downstairs room. The hoods walked out, locking the door behind them.

When he recovered, he examined the room. The only furniture was a chair and a wooden table, above which a fly-spotted bulb burned weakly. The door he'd come through was fitted with a strong lock. Another door, on the other side of the room, was equally well locked and covered with a steel plate. Above it a small, high window was fitted with iron bars. From the sounds, he guessed that the steel door led into an alley. He had no more time to look around. The inner door opened again. The bigger of the two hoods came in and, locking the door behind him, stood there leering. Tony found the gun pointing at him very disturbing. "You treat all your customers this way?" he said sorely.

The hood's grin widened. "Nah," he said. "Only the special ones. In a couple of minutes you'll be walking out of that door, a free man." He pointed at the steel door.

"Oh, yeah?" Tony said suspiciously.

"First I got a job to do. Take the chair and sit down at the table." Tony hesitated, but the look on the hood's face changed like quicksilver, and he did as he was told. "Put your hands on the table."

"What for?"

"I'm gonna give you our standard treatment for hustlers, pal."

"What's that?"

"I'm gonna have to break your fingers. Seems a pity—they told me up there you're good with the bones." Now the hood was behind him. Tony went cold. Fear and desperation raced through him. He started to get out of the chair and a sudden blow on the back of his head sent him reeling. He was forced back down and his hands were slammed onto the table. Dazed, through the pain, he felt the cold snout of the gun pressing into the back of his neck. "I don't wanna have to shoot you, kid, so just do what you're told. Now, wake up. I like to see a guy's face when I do this to him." A hard slap across his face brought him to full consciousness. "Spread your fingers out on the table."

He kept his hands balled. From the corner of his eye he watched the hood reverse the gun in his hand, ready to use the butt as a hammer. He shook his head, forcing himself to think. If he panicked now, he was lost forever. He forced down the terror that choked him. "Listen," he got out. "Listen to me."

He couldn't see the man clearly through his blurred vision, but he sensed that the hood had paused. "What you want?"

"I got a way out of the problem," Tony said quickly.

"I ain't got no problem, kid." Tony shook his head again, and things were coming back into focus. "It's you got the problem—how you're gonna hold your knife and fork." The hood gave a gruff laugh.

"You're throwing away a lot of money."

"What you mean?"

"I'm willing to pay to get out of this spot."

"Yeah?" A note of curiosity entered the hood's voice.

"Sure. What's the difference to you? You can break my fingers and throw me out—what you gonna get, a medal? My way, you collect five grand. Either way, you don't see me again. I'm passing through. I ain't from this town. Nobody'll ever know what happened. You got my word."

"You got five grand?"

"Yeah." Tony talked quickly. He could see the indecision on the hood's face. "You gotta be rich to throw away good money, right? That's what you're throwing away, you don't listen to me." He met the hood's stare. "You got my absolute word. A guy like me, he's gotta mean what he says."

The hood looked toward the door and passed his tongue over his lips. "Where's the dough?"

"Skidmore's," Tony said without hesitation. It was the only name in Chicago he could think of."

"That's a high-class joint, one of the best in town. You connected?"

"I got a friend. All you have to do is get me over there. You'll get your dough immediately. Nothing'll be said—you got my word," he repeated. The hood made no reply, and Tony pressed on. "Look, you heard 'em say up there that I'm good. Five grand ain't much to me, I can get it any night of the week. It ain't worth losing my fingers for. You stay right with me all the time and you got a gun, so I can't argue." He waited.

"Make it ten grand." The hood was testing him.

"Can't do that." He shook his head. "Five grand's what I can get right now." There was another silence. "Maybe you're yellow?"

"I ain't afraid of nothin'."

"Then, let's go get the dough."

It was a strange way to see a new town, Tony thought, as the streets of Chicago flashed by the windows of the cab. He stole a glance at the hood seated by his side, one hand in his pocket fingering his gun. From the look on the hood's face, he knew he could expect a bullet if things went wrong. Perhaps it would be preferable to spending the rest of his life regretting his mutilated fingers. This was a game in which the stakes were higher than five thousand dollars. Again he forced himself to be cool. It was the only way he could carry it off. When they got out of the cab he walked straight into Skidmore's. At first he couldn't believe his eyes. It was like a Busby Berkely movie set, complete with characters in evening dress, some apparently straight from dinner engagements. Fortunately, some were dressed informally, otherwise they'd have been conspicuous. There was an air of prosperity about everything that overwhelmed him almost as much as his fear of the hood with the gun. He was taking in the marble and the high mirrors when the hood nudged him. "The dough—let's get the dough."

"Sure," Tony said. Ahead was a wide salon, busy with people at the gambling tables. He walked through, awed by the opulence and the sheer size of the place. He pulled himself together and made a beeline for the nearest crap table. A healthy game was in progress.

The hood was right behind him. "Where's the dough?" he hissed.

"Right here," Tony said.

"What you talking about?"

"Gimme a hundred bucks. I'll get it for you."

"You crazy?"

"You want your five grand, or don't you?"

It dawned on the hood what was Tony's intention. "I ought to plug you right here," he grated.

"I wouldn't bring out that gun in here if I was you. Here they got real guards. Use that gun and you won't get to the door in one piece. Anyhow, that way, you don't get your dough."

After a moment, the hood said, "You mean you're still gonna pay me?"

"Look, prick, I gave my word, didn't I?" His indignation was real, and the hood stared. "Gimme the hundred bucks. I'll get your dough for you."

The hood's hand went to his pocket.

They hadn't searched him thoroughly when they threw him into the downstairs room at the Three Aces, and the Tops and Bottoms were still tucked into the waistband of his pants. When it was his turn to pitch, the bogus dice were ready in his fingers, and he went to work. If it hadn't been for the large amounts of money in play on the table, he'd never have got away with it. As it was, he didn't hesitate, and his sheer desperation was his strength. He simply hit the table as hard and as quickly as he could.

Probably the speed saved him, because he was getting some funny looks by the time he'd collected the five thousand dollars. He unhesitatingly picked up the checks, turned, and stuffed them into the hood's hands. "I gotta say it," the hood said admiringly. "You got balls."

"Hell, that's standard equipment for a mechanic," Tony said. "Now we're clear, right?"

"Right."

"Then do me a favor, will ya, pal?"

"Sure, kid."

"Go fuck yourself." He walked away from the hood.

When he got to the street, he kept walking, without looking back.

CHAPTER THREE

He couldn't get the place out of his mind. As he walked, he pictured again the opulence, the gentility that was so far from the world he knew outside. His world, his jungle. Perilous arenas like the Kokomo, the Three Aces, or even The Club, he supposed, where a thin veneer of sociability disguised a latent savagery so easily evoked. The jungle where only the fit, the strong, and the astute survived. It'd be nice to work in the easy atmosphere of a place like Skidmore's, he mused. It

132

must be the type of carpet joint the Duke used to talk about. That was so long ago now he'd forgotten such places existed. They weren't any part of his life and probably never would be. It just wasn't the life for him—he wasn't equipped for the subtleties, the niceties of social behavior. He couldn't remember ever feeling like a hick before—but he sure felt out of place in there, rubbing shoulders with them swells. Even if he did manage to steal their five grand before they knew what hit them. Funny, but in a sawdust joint he could stand up to the raucous bellowing of an irate miner, not turn a hair, and still steal the man blind. Yet he wasn't sure how he'd feel about switching dice on a classy society broad with diamonds sparkling on her fingers. Somehow it wasn't the same thing—or was it? Fingers . . . He put his hands out before him and studied them as he walked. He'd been lucky back there with that dumb hood. He'd been within an ace of being out of business for good. He put his hands down and felt in his pockets. He hadn't a bean—not a red cent to his name. And where the hell was he walking to anyway? He slowed his pace and for the first time took a good look around, to realize he was totally lost.

The street up ahead looked bright for a short distance, with neon signs and store lights shining out into the darkness. But it was an illusion, a desert mirage. The stores were silent and locked, and, except for an occasional passing vehicle, the street was deserted. When he came to the end of the block, again the road stretched dark before him. It was at this moment that the loneliness of it closed in on him—the utter solitude, no soul in the world to turn to, no place to go. An inner fear touched him, and he shivered.

Then he saw it, in the distance, a beacon in the night. He could make out forms moving near the light and he turned, a moth to a candle, to investigate the unexpected phenomenon.

Beneath a wide railway arch, on a piece of uneven ground that served as a garbage dump, a dozen or so down-and-outs had gathered, warming themselves by a blazing fire. As he drew near he could feel the welcome heat. He hesitated when a couple of the bums glanced around at him curiously, but they seemed peaceful enough, and when he edged closer to the flames, one on them moved over to make room for him. "Thanks, buddy," Tony said. "Sure is cold tonight." He put out his hands, grateful for the warmth.

"Sure is."

He didn't have to stare to see that most of them were hardened wanderers. The collection of castoffs they wore told its own story. He glanced down at his own clothes—next to them he must have seemed a prince. Preoccupied with their own misery, they didn't take much notice. "Say, pal, where is this place?" he said to the bum who'd moved over for him.

The man looked at him. "Chicago."

"Chicago's a big place," he said. "I mean what section?"

". . . Yeah, Chicago," the man repeated after a while, looking into the fire. Tony glanced across and saw the sullen lifelessness in the man's eyes. He didn't push the question. A moment later the man said, "Got a butt?"

"Don't smoke much."

"I need a butt—need it bad," the man said, as much to himself as to Tony. His gaze traveled over the group and returned to the fire. "Been on the road long?"

"Me?" Tony said.

"Who else?"

"Not long. Coupla days, maybe."

"Things got tough, huh?"

"Sure did," he said.

"Things're bad all over. They say Roosevelt's the guy can pull the country through. You believe that?" Before Tony could think of a reply, he went on, "You got any dough?"

"Nope. Not a nickel."

"Me neither. Could do with something to eat." He touched his stomach.

"Ain't got a thing," Tony said apologetically.

"You don't look hungry. You ain't got that hungry look."

"Reckon I got it to come."

A little later the bum said, "You sure you ain't got a butt?"

"Yeah, I'm sure," Tony said patiently. They didn't speak again until he noticed that, one by one, they were drifting across to lay down by a nearby wall. The lucky ones tucked old newspapers inside their clothes, or laid them on the cold ground to insulate themselves. When the bum moved, Tony followed him. "O.K. if I sleep here tonight?" he asked.

"Guess that's what you're here for," the man said. He went to a cardboard box and turned it over to reveal a couple of thick, rolled newspapers. "You can have one of these, if you want."

"Gee, thanks," he said gratefully. In a crazy way, he felt privileged to have the use of the bum's newspaper. When he lay down, the exhaustion came over him in waves. Putting his head back meant resting on the bump the hood had raised with his gun. He turned on his side and wrapped himself in paper as best he could. Even at this distance, the fire took the chill out of the night air, and watching the dancing flames was curiously comforting. He fell asleep.

Through the mist of semiconsciousness, he couldn't make out why his feet were moving. They seemed to be imparting a jerking motion to his body. That's strange, he thought—doesn't feel right, he thought. Then, through lidded eyes, he made out the form of a man at his feet. He came awake fast. The bum already had one of his shoes off and was working on the other. Tony sat up sharply, grabbed the bum by his head, and pulled him down so that the man lost his balance. Tony dived for his shoe and turned, ready to defend himself. But the bum had rolled away and lay where he had stopped, staring at him through listless eyes. Tony put on his shoe and stood up. In the distance a dull, steel gray on the horizon heralded the dawn. Now that he knew which way was east, he knew which direction he should take. With a last glance at the bundles of human rags, he turned and started walking.

The milk truck rattled south on Lake Shore Drive. Tony looked across the driver at the sun rising out of the leaden waters of Lake Michigan. The sky was crystal clear, and the sun, a brilliant searchlight, was so bright that when it hit his eyes it blinded him. He turned away and rubbed his eyes with his knuckles. "Best time of day, sunup," the driver said. Tony nodded assent. "Ain't often I got someone to talk to, this hour of the morning."

134

"I'd have thought, with the number of guys on the road, there's plenty hitching rides."

"Too early. 'Sides, I don't stop for just anyone. Some of them people, they look real mean. Women, too—kinda desperate. Can be dangerous, picking up people like that, you know what I mean?"

"Sure." Tony focused on his shoes.

"Where you headed for?"

"Know a place called Calumet City?" The driver looked across at him from under his eyebrows. "What's wrong?" Tony said.

"Nothing." The driver's eyes were back on the road.

"I heard someone mention the place last night. It's down this way, isn't it?"

"Oh, sure," the driver said. "I'll drop you off the other side of Calumet Harbor. It's a few miles south of there. Maybe you can hitch another ride."

"Thanks."

"What you gonna be doing in Calumet City?"

"Looking for work."

"What work you do?"

"I'm a dealer."

"What you deal in?"

"A dealer in a gambling house."

"Oh, I get you." Then, after a moment, "What you hear about the place?"

"Nothing," Tony said. "I was in a club last night. I hear a guy say he's been to the gambling house in Calumet City, just south of Chicago, near Lake Shore."

"Plenty of them gambling places in Chicago, I hear."

"I want to get out of the city."

"Ain't got a nice reputation, that Calumet place."

"That so?" Tony said.

"Small town, right on the state line, Illinois. Five blocks by ten, maybe three thousand people—and a hundred and fifty bars. Other side of the street is Hammond, Indiana. Over at Hammond, everything shuts down at twelve, and Sundays. In Calumet City nothing closes, ever. People come from all over. Them bars, every one's got two or three B girls."

"B girls?"

"Yeah, hustling the guys. The women get a commission on the booze. Plenty of brothels, too."

"And gambling?"

"There's a place called the Border Club. I hear it's mob-owned. Them Italians, they rule Chi." He looked across at Tony. "You Italian?"

"Yeah," he said.

"I don't mean nothing."

"That's O.K. If they own it, they own it."

"Toughest town around, they say, Calumet."

"Ain't they all?" Tony said laconically.

"I guess you're right." Now the road became arrow-straight along the shore, and he could take his attention away from the road ahead to study the beauty of the early-morning sun on the bay.

135

When the milk truck dropped him off and continued along the shore, he made no attempt to hitch a second ride. He turned south and strolled, glorying in the morning sunshine. He could see his direction for some way ahead. He walked through Eggers Woods, skirting Wolf Lake by going a mile inside Indiana, then came back into Illinois at the other end. By the time he reached Calumet City, the sun was high in the sky and getting too hot for comfort. First he located the Border Club—a big joint, by the look of it, only yards from the state line and near the railroad track that ran through the town. After a while he found himself standing on State Street looking to the right into Calumet itself. The long line of garish bars, just coming alive at midday, stretched away along the block. He looked left into Indiana and could see the residential and business areas of Hammond, just across the line. It wasn't a good hour to visit a gambling house. He turned left and made for Hammond to familiarize himself with the district.

When he entered the Border Club he could smell the action in the air. The chumps must be lucky to get out of the place with their own skins, he thought to himself. It was a large room with a small bar over in the corner. The whole back section was occupied with a horse book, and eight betting writers were busy handling slips and posting information on a board that covered the entire wall behind them. Further into the room, three double-ended roulette wheels served a few interested players. Over to one side, a couple of poker tables were already occupied. And one crap table. He moved closer. The dealer was no youngster. Unlike the kids in the Steubenville joints, he was a thin, active man with something of the appearance of Boston Bailey, Tony thought. And, by his movements in the busy game, very experienced. But experience wasn't enough—and Tony wanted his job. There were a few Sicilian faces about the place, mostly concerned with the function of the club, apparently. He brushed himself off and made for the door marked MANAGER'S OFFICE.

"Who you wanna see?" The Sicilian bruiser stopped him when he reached the door.

"The boss," Tony said.

"What's your business?"

"I got some dough for him."

"Wait here."

After a moment, he was ushered into the inner office. The man who looked up at him from the leather Chesterfield was dressed in an expensive blue suit, the bulk packed onto his frame from an excess of macaroni, but the flesh was firm over the fat. His black-button eyes penetrated Tony. "I'm Willie Freschia," he said. "You got something for me?"

"Yeah—dough. How much you want, a thousand or two thousand?"

"What the fuck you talking about, punk?"

"Give me two minutes of your time."

"You dago?"

"Yeah."

"Make it quick, wise guy."

"O.K." Tony paused. "I could go out there right now, take a couple of grand off

136

your crap table, and you'd never know how. But I ain't gonna do it, so I reckon, that way, I'm giving you two grand."

Freschia sat up. "You must be nuts."

"I'm a mechanic," Tony said. "One of the best. The guy you got working out there's experienced, but he's a fumbler."

"Why you telling me this?" The black eyes gleamed.

"I need a job," he said.

"How come, if you're so good, you need work? A good mechanic can take his pick."

"I had to leave my hometown. Something personal," he added quickly. "I play it straight with the house. I only play one side of the table."

"There ain't many mechanics in that class," Freschia said cynically.

"I'm one of them. I earn my dough for you, and plenty besides."

"Where you from?"

"Ohio," Tony said, after a moment. Freschia looked at him, but didn't pursue it. "If you want to see me work, come outside. Name a sensible figure and I'll get it for you."

An amused grin crossed the Sicilian's face. "O.K., I'll settle for the two grand. You beat my guy on the crap table and we're gonna have a serious talk."

"Let's go." As they walked out of the office, Tony said, "You want me to make it look natural, or you want the dough real quick?"

"Make it quick."

"I'm gonna need some house checks for a stake."

"O.K."

Freschia stood back and watched detachedly. The crowd at the table was thin, and Tony soon became shooter. By the time the dice had been in his hands five minutes, he'd won the two thousand dollars. Then he noticed the dealer was looking toward Freschia and he saw Freschia give the dealer the eye. Tony watched the dealer's gaffs come into the game. He instantly switched them out and replaced them with his own. When he doubled up the two thousand dollars he saw the dealer's mouth swing open.

In the manager's office, Freschia turned to him, his eyes again bright. "I ain't never seen a mechanic that good, *paisan*. I'm gonna admit to you I don't see you make a fucking move."

"I got the job?" Tony said calmly.

"You bet. If you're straight, like you say, you're a walking gold mine. If you ain't, we'll break your back."

"I'm straight," he repeated, unconcerned. Then, for good measure, he added, "If I'm working for the house, you better know: that clumsy prick you got out there— it's a wonder you ain't had a bomb thrown in the joint."

CHAPTER FOUR

He never hated a place, before or after, as much as he hated the Border Club. In the three months he spent there, he developed an aversion that became painful. He avoided contact with other employees and, when he wasn't working, spent most of his time practicing the dice and studying the laws of probability that determined the outcome of straight games. There were no decent hotels in Calumet City, other than the whore cribs and brothels, and he took a room over in Hammond, where he paid five dollars a week, including laundry, in a featureless flop. A few times he made the trip to The Great Lakes Gambling Novelties Company, over in Cicero, where he discussed with the makers the finer points of dice balance and explored every area of gaff performance so that no freak result would surprise him.

He wanted a woman badly, but he couldn't bring himself to go with one of the town's iron whores, working three shifts a day on their backs in bare-board hostelries. Their patrons were mostly laborers from the mills around Hammond and Indiana Harbor, or U.S. Steel over in Gary, or Inland Steel. Drunken, rampaging workhorses whose relaxation appeared to be beating one another to pulp. To dissuade them from smashing each other's skulls, it was the practice for tables and chairs to be nailed to the floor in the town's amenities. But the urge finally overcame his scruples, and he found himself in a trap called The Barn. He was ushered, along with a couple of other johns, into a large room furnished with a long wooden bench and two slot machines. From a parade of six hip-swinging broads wearing see-through shifts, high heels, and big, childlike ribbon bows at their throats, the hairiest detached herself and claimed him. "I'm French Monica," she said in a hoarse, syrupy southside Chicago accent. "I'll give you a good time, honey, any way you want." The pancake of rouge did little to enhance her charm, and it was doubtful he had bigger muscles than she. He shoved a couple of dollars into her hand and made for the door.

He gave some thought to his Italian ancestry these days. He was distinctly aware of a warm affinity with Catholicism and its colorful, intimate ceremonies. In rare moments of reflection he would imagine himself back in Steubenville, at Fifth and Slack, going humbly into the Holy Name Church hand-in-hand with his parents and his brother. Giving himself up to his devotions so that he basked in the benign, peaceful bliss of an innocent childhood once again. He would put the thought quickly out of his mind and try not to think about his parents—about the anguish they must be suffering at his disappearance. Better that than they should have a son convicted of murder, and be pointed at in the streets. In time, when things had cooled, he would quietly let them know he was alive and well. Perhaps, one day, he would even arrange to see them again. But it was too soon now, and he must wait.

He wondered why it was he'd become conscious of his background. Perhaps because the Border Club was run by Italians, and the expressions and mannerisms reminded him of home. But then, they weren't mainland Italians, they were Sicil-

138

ians. He was Neopolitan, and that was very different. Neopolitans were one thing—he understood them, the cafoni's philosophical expectation of life's misfortunes, engendered in his lineage by centuries of feudal oppression. Calabrians were another, and he knew they looked down on Southern Italians as prone to poverty and ignorance, and besotted with superstition. The Sicilians were something else again—a mystery to all, and mostly to themselves, it seemed, as their ancient culture of internecine genocide suggested. Whether it was the Black Hand or historic, savage, and mortal family feuds, nobody harmed the Sicilians more than they themselves. In the Border Club he quickly learned how to handle them, once he understood that "face" was an important ingredient of their philosophy. The Duke had taught him well—he quietly gave them the respect they craved and they, in turn, respected his ability as a technician.

Freschia's orders were straightforward: "Whack 'em out, get the loot." The Border Club was a bust-out joint, plain and simple. It operated as a short-season house, with steerers out on State Street looking for chumps when the action sagged. A less formidable management wouldn't have survived, but the Sicilians displayed little interest in repeat business. In his short tenure, Tony gained more experience switching dice than he'd have got in years elsewhere. In some sessions, he dealt almost repeatedly in gaffs so that he raped game after game for the house, leaving customers soured and confused, and often suspicious. But the Sicilians were always there, steely faced, to regulate the unfortunate players' conduct if they carped. In all this time not one soul spotted him at work with his gaffs, and, unwittingly, he achieved his longed-for hundred-percent success rate. But he drew no pleasure from this achievement, and now rarely looked up, working robotlike without fear of, or interest in, the consequences.

Which was why he'd come to loathe the whole scene. The art, the joy, the fine balance of plausibility was gone from the game. He grieved inwardly, and the Sicilian sweetheart deal couldn't last.

Freschia had been screaming at someone in his office for ten minutes. When he came to the door, his eyes were blazing. "What the fuck you all looking at?" he yelled out at the room. Everyone turned back and got on with his work. Unfortunately, Tony, at the crap table, was nearest the door. Freschia walked up and stood behind him, spoiling for a fight. "You," he snapped. "Fingers—how I know you're not stealing?" Tony stopped dealing and turned to stare at him. For an instant he boiled, then just as quickly brought himself under control. The rules for a Sicilian caper were different. Self-control was one of his tools. "Well, *contadino,* I ask you a question." Freschia bawled.

"You don't," Tony said.

"Yeah? Maybe I'm having you watched, smart ass."

"Then you know I'm not stealing."

"The take on this table's down."

"Not to my knowledge—and not in my shift."

Tony's sterile attitude was getting to Freschia. "I ain't sure whose shift. I'm going back right now and check that out." He stared Tony in the eye. "If you're stealing, you're gonna be sorry the day you first saw this fucking joint."

"Mr. Freschia," Tony said carefully. I been here thirteen weeks now. In my shifts, the tables show you a gross of eighty-two thousand dollars up to today. I cost you a hundred bucks a week, and I'll triple that to include your overhead, so I make it I cost you three thousand, nine hundred dollars. That leaves you a profit of seventy-eight thousand. I estimate, if the table is straight, you don't make a tenth of that figure, so I guess I'm earning my bread." He said it loud enough for the players at the table to hear. They exchanged angry glances.

"Keep your voice down, jerk," Freschia hissed. His gaze shot to the scowling players.

He spoke more softly. "I'm only justifying the figures to you, Mr. Freschia," he said. "It's unlikely I'm stealing on them numbers."

Freschia turned to the players disarmingly. "Yeah, gents," he said, "this kid's new here and he ain't got the grift yet. He don't know what he's talking about." A couple of the players were making unhappy noises, and the resident guards were moving up to take care of any situation. The table was suddenly empty. "Now see what you done," he spat at Tony.

"I didn't think they heard me."

"Goddamn jerk." Freschia walked off, muttering, to his office.

He was fast sickening of the whole rotten operation, longing for word of home. He desperately wanted to contact his parents to let them know he was alive and well. The more he thought about it, the more he knew he had to make the call. The Duke's words came from the back of his brain. "Keep in touch," the Duke had said, "no matter what." If there was one person in the world he could trust, it was his mentor.

"Hullo." The Duke's voice came over the long wire.

He savored the word and the sound. He took a deep breath. "Duke, this is Tony."

"Who's that?"

"Tony—Tony Vitale." There was a silence at the other end of the line. His heart was thumping in his chest.

"Tony!" The voice rose, and he sensed the great relief in it. "So you're O.K.? Dammit, you're O.K. . . ."

"Yeah, I'm O.K., Duke. Gee, it's great to hear your voice."

"Where the hell—everybody here . . . we all thought maybe you got hurt in that car and . . ."

"No, I'm O.K."

"The car—they found it where it went off Green's Bluff into the river. It looked real bad."

"I wasn't in it, Duke. I got out. How's my folks?" he said quickly.

"They had a bad time of it, but they'll be all right now."

"I got out before the car went over the cliff. Then I took it on the lam before the cop could grab me."

"I don't understand. Why did you run?" He sensed the puzzlement at the other end of the line.

"Because of the guy in the car."

"What guy, for Chrissakes?"

"The hustler—I killed him. He was in the car when it went over the cliff. Didn't they find the body?" he asked incredulously.

140

"There was *no* body in the car, Tony." Suddenly the voice was coming from a million miles away. "Nobody knows anything about a body. Hoyle says he was chasing you because you rammed his car." He paused. "Tell me exactly what happened."

"The hustler and this other guy, the one with the gun. That night when I left The Club they were waiting for me. You remember the hustler, don't you—the guy with the eyes. I took him for his dough, a couple of nights previous."

"I remember him," the Duke said.

"He wanted me to shake down the joint for five grand. Otherwise it was a bullet. The other guy looked like he meant it, too. I let them think I was going along with their plan . . ." He paused. "I wouldn't have done it, you know that."

"Sure I know."

"The gunsel was getting out and I jerked the car forward. The gun was somewhere around my feet, but I still had the hustler in the back when I come racing into town. Of all the luck, Hoyle comes cruising down Market Street in the squad car. I run smack into him."

"What happened then?"

"I dunno, exactly. It all got mixed up. I couldn't stop or the hustler would have got me. By the time I found the gun on the floor, he was trying to choke me. I fired the gun over my shoulder so he'd let go. Then he was dead—I couldn't believe it. Hoyle was closing in on me and I guess I panicked. I didn't wanna be found with a body in the car. With that Hoyle, it'd be curtains for me for sure."

"Now I understand," the Duke said slowly.

"What you think happened to the body?"

"It was a ragtop car. The body must've been washed away downstream. They're always finding bodies in the river. It wasn't you they found, and Hoyle knows it was you driving, so nobody's connected the body with the accident."

Hope roared through him and welled up in his throat. "So you think maybe I ain't wanted for murder?"

"I *know* you're not wanted for murder. You never were." Tony was so choked, he couldn't answer. "And don't worry about Hoyle, you can leave him to me. You're a free man—you hear me?"

"Yeah, I hear you." He got it out eventually. "Duke, tell my folks. Just let them know I'm O.K., will you? They ain't on the telephone."

"I'll do it right away. Now, listen carefully to me. You're not to mention what happened. Ever. To anyone. There was no hustler and there was no shooting. If anything comes up afterward I'll handle it. You understand?"

"Yes, I understand, Duke."

"Where are you?"

"Calumet City—I'm working here."

"The Border Club?"

"Right."

The Duke was silent, then he spoke softly. "Tony, you a mechanic yet?"

"Oh, yes, I'm a mechanic," Tony said. "I made it—the one hundred percent."

"Come home now," the Duke said.

He'd been away only a few months, but everything looked different. Smaller and less significant than he remembered it. Compared to the viciousness of Chicago, Steubenville appeared a haven of peace. The warmth of his homecoming, his parents' joy, his belonging again, and the banishment of that fearful ghost, Antonio Vitale—fugitive, combined to mellow him. Suddenly he'd matured. But he couldn't turn back the clock, and the outside world was beckoning. "It's time for you to move on," the Duke said.

"Yes."

"It's a big world out there. Trust me. I'll guide you."

He didn't pretend to understand. He only knew that his mentor was responsible for his extraordinary proficiency with the dice. That the Duke's patronage lay over him, a warm, secure blanket, protecting and comforting him. "Where do I go now?" he asked.

"New York." Tony sat up. "It's time for you to move up."

"A carpet joint?"

"Yes."

"Like Skidmore's?"

"Better."

"That must really be something."

"I had a call from a friend, Louis Miranda. He has a joint on Park Avenue. He's looking for a top mechanic. I told him you're available."

"Gee, Park Avenue. What better? New York, here I come."

"One thing. Wherever you go from there, don't lose contact with me."

"Sure, I remember," he said. "Keep in touch."

CHAPTER FIVE

New York, New York. A whole new ball game.

A carpet joint—what more could he ask? And New York. What was so exhilarating about it? He could sense magic in the air and knew instinctively he was going to fall in love with the city. He would possess it and it would possess him. He strolled leisurely along Madison Avenue, humming a few bars from "The Lullaby of Broadway," ogling the pretty girls out to snatch a quick sandwich on their lunchbreak. They walked and talked quickly together, the words pouring from their mouths as if they had to get their talking, as well as their eating, over in a hurry. At each corner he paused to watch the rush of traffic. Why the hell was everyone in such a hurry, he wondered? It puzzled him that people were looking at him. He caught their sidelong, curious glances. One or two bolder ones stared directly, looking him up and down as if he were a sideshow freak or something. A cab made an urgent squealing turn in traffic and the sudden eruption of honking and irate howls took his attention. He stood there until the wall of people moving along the sidewalk jostled him, carrying him along with it. On the next block the crowd thinned and he was able to resume his unhurried, relaxed pace. It was a good feeling. Here he was, his first day in the big city—as yet he hadn't spoken a word to a soul and he knew he had it made. He clicked his fingers softly together in rhythm.

He knew that he must be near Miranda's, and he began looking for numbers. His attention was drawn to a store packed with shirts of every variety and color. He had a thing about nice shirts. Probably because his mother had a fetish about her men's appearance—the basis of which was the customary clean collar—he saw the shirt as the primary article of clothing. He stood for a while admiring the creamy fabrics and comparing prices. The wide storefront formed a perfect mirror, framing his snappy reflection. Since Chicago he'd become more conscious of his appearance. At the Border Club, Freschia wore a different suit every day, bringing home to Tony the paucity of his own wardrobe. He'd tried to do something about that and the result stood before him, looking back at him from the store-window's reflection. He ran his eye down the figure, from the wide, silver-gray fedora, the dark, broad-striped business suit, the dazzling floral tie, to the pointed black-and-white patents on his feet. He felt good. Which was when he noticed the bulky form standing behind him. If the bull of a man was studying the contents of the store window, it meant he was looking straight through him, Tony decided. He moved over and saw the man's gaze follow him. He turned around and stared the stranger in the eye. The man stared back, unblinking. "We acquainted?" Tony said.

"No," the man said.

"You looking at them shirts in the window, or you looking at me?"

"I'm looking at you, big shot."

In the clubs, it had got so he could spot a crazy a mile off. This guy wasn't one. There was a hard, cynical look on his face, and he had an air of brutal authority. "What's bothering you, mister?" Tony said levelly.

"You're bothering me, wise guy. I don't like the way you look. I wanna know why you ain't back on Mulberry Street, with them other dagos, where you belong."

"Mulberry Street?" Tony repeated.

"Yeah. I don't want you guinea punks up here on Madison Avenue. Maybe you're looking to steal something."

It had a familiar ring to it, he decided. "So I'm a shirt thief. What business is it of yours?"

"Everything happens around here is my business." The hand snapped open and Tony was staring at a detective's badge.

"O.K., cop, I surrender," he said. "What you gonna bust me for, looking at shirts in a store window?"

The cop continued to stare, ignoring his words. "Where you from?" he said suddenly.

He thought about it. "Chicago," he said. It sounded better than Steubenville—people didn't mess with guys from Chicago.

This one did. "Got some identification?"

"No," Tony said.

"What you doing up here on Madison Avenue?"

"This a free country, or ain't it?"

"The first wop comic," the cop sneered. "What's your name?"

"Frank Smith."

"Of course. The Smiths of Milan, I presume."

"You got it," he said.

"Listen, punk, cut the lip or I'm gonna get real sore. I asked you once—I ain't asking again. What are you doing here on Madison Avenue?"

"I got a new job here."

"Oh, yeah. Where?"

He paused. Gambling houses were still illegal, even if they were carpet joints. And he was unfamiliar with New York cops. "I ain't saying."

"What's your work?"

"I'm a helper."

The cop got red in the face. "You ain't saying nothing to help yourself, turkey. You carrying a piece?"

"No."

"I'm gonna search you. Turn around and put your hands on the window."

"You ain't frisking me," Tony said belligerently. The leather pouch in his pocket was loaded with gaffed dice. The cop would make a meal out of that, he supposed.

He had no choice. The hand that had held a badge held a gun. "Put your hands up," the cop said. "I'm taking you in."

"What's the charge?" he protested.

"Suspicion," the cop said. "You the most suspicious character I see lately around Madison Avenue."

Shit, he thought. So much for the romance of New York.

The man who came to get him out was dressed like a banker. The shoulders of his quiet suit were narrow and subtly rounded to give a natural shape, unlike the massive padded extrusions Tony had come to admire. His iron-gray hair was carefully smoothed down, and he moved with a decorum Tony didn't associate with the world of gambling joints. A casino owner—and the guy didn't even wear a diamond ring on his pinkie. "You Louis Miranda?" he said suspiciously.

"Yes."

"What sort of town is this, for Chrissakes? A guy can't walk down the street peaceful without getting pinched . . ." He noticed the amused smile on the man's face. "What's so funny?"

"Nothing." The man was serious again. "It's your appearance. To Broderick it must have been like a red rag to a bull."

"Broderick the cop?" Miranda nodded. "What's wrong with my appearance?"

"Everything. You look like a Sicilian hood. They part their hair in the middle like that and wear those long sideburns. And that suit—if you got out of it, maybe it'd march away on its own."

"I got the suit in Chicago. Over there all the sharp dressers look like this."

"Chicago's its own world. This is New York—here we don't advertise."

Tony thought about it. "So, what do I do?"

144

"When we get out of here, I'm taking you straight to Brooks Brothers. We'll get you some decent clothes and see if we can't make you look human."

"I ain't a hick, you know," he said crossly. "I been around."

"Yes, you are," Miranda said bluntly. "Let's start from there and we'll get it right." There was a silence between them, then he added, "The Duke tells me you're a good mechanic."

"Uhuh," Tony said, glad the other had found some redeeming feature in him. "I'm the best. One hundred percent. I never made a mistake yet, at the table. They don't come better'n one hundred percent."

"You're sure of yourself."

"You want a mechanic in your house ain't got nerve?" Tony said simply.

"I guess you're right. We'll find out soon enough. I tell you this—the way you look, and the way you talk, if anyone except the Duke had sent you, I think you'd be on your way back by now."

"You wanna get the chumps' dough, or you want I should be Cary Grant?"

"We'll see how you behave at the table."

"I got the feeling I ain't gonna get along in this town," Tony said miserably. "Listen, that cop, he's got my gaffs. They were in my pocket when he frisked me."

"We'll get your dice back," Miranda said.

"That cop, he didn't look too cooperative."

"Broderick's on the payroll."

"That mother?"

"He's useful for keeping out the hoods."

"He wouldn't last a day, back in Chicago."

"I told you, this isn't Chicago."

On the street, Miranda hailed a cab. Two yellow buckets were cruising by and both acknowledged his signal. They arrived together, missing each other by a hair's breadth. "You want I should travel separate?" Tony suggested. "That way, you don't gotta be seen in public with a freak."

The humor came back into Miranda's eyes. "Maybe there's hope for you yet," he said.

CHAPTER SIX

It made Skidmore's look like a Salvation Army refuge. There were rose-tinted mirrors everywhere and, as he moved around, he studied himself constantly. He couldn't get over the change in his appearance. Yesterday's slick, provincial hotshot was gone, and in his place was a suave, youthful gentleman, who looked at home in the elegant surroundings. The haircut was a great improvement, he decided. And he knew with certainty that he was going to be a sucker for expensive clothes from now on.

"Let's see what you can do," Miranda said, as they stood at a craps table. It was early afternoon and a small army of workers beavered about, preparing the club for the evening.

"I don't give demonstrations," Tony said.

"You want to work here or not?" Miranda demanded.

"Sure I wanna work here. That's why I come to New York. But let me tell you something, Mr. Miranda, I ain't no performer. You want to see a performance, there's plenty of them theaters down there around Times Square."

"What in hell you think I'm paying you for?" It was the nearest he'd seen Miranda to losing his temper, and he guessed it was a rarity. But this was his new life, and he was determined to start out right.

"Let's get one thing straight, boss," he said soberly. "When you hired me, you hired a mechanic, not some two-bit hustler. I don't gotta prove a thing—not to you or nobody."

"So I have to take it for granted you're as good as you say, is that it?" Miranda had quickly regained his self-control.

"I come highly recommended, and I got my own standards. That's the difference between me and some guy off the street. What's it mean if I show you a few moves now? Tonight I could be stealing you blind and you'd never know it. If I'm in your shoes, that's the question I'm asking myself now—can the guy be trusted?" He stared coolly at Miranda.

For the first time Tony sensed an uncertainty in the other man. "If there's any question of your integrity toward the house, maybe we better forget the whole thing," Miranda said stiffly.

"Right. So now we skip the matinee and we come to the part that matters: Are you asking me whether you can trust me? You got a right to ask that straight out."

"O.K., I'm asking."

"Then, I'm telling you—I'm straight up. With me, that's part of what you get for your dough."

"How do I know that?" Tony had given him a lead and now his new employer was pursuing it.

He thought about it. "You'll never know for certain, but there's one thing you can do. You can take insurance, in case you find me stealing. Is the Duke's word good around here?"

"Yes." He saw the light of caution come into Miranda's eyes.

"The Duke will guarantee me. If I steal your dough, the Duke will pay. Call him. Tell him that's what I said."

"That won't be necessary," Miranda said, without hesitation. There was new respect in his voice.

"Fine," Tony said. "Now that we got that straight, we come to the part that matters—how you want the game conducted. When to hit and when not to hit. If you wanna leave it up to me, that's O.K., but first I have to get the hang of your operation. Or I'll clean 'em all out, if you say. You only gotta tell me."

"We don't work that way here," Miranda said quickly. "This is no bust-out joint.

146

We have regular patrons—society people, politicians, big names in this city. They all come to Miranda's."

"Just tell me the ones you wanna send home broke," Tony repeated, unimpressed.

"Look, most of the time it'll be a regular game. A lot of people will lose, like normal craps. Some will win, naturally, and some will win big. That's O.K."

"When ain't it O.K.?"

"Let me explain something," Miranda said patiently. "The biggest money in gambling is the legit money. If the day comes when gambling's legalized—our sort of gambling—you'll see fortunes made beyond your wildest dreams. And the play will be absolutely straight. I'm talking about profits as a percentage of the gross take, you understand. So it follows that the take has to be high. Now, that's the sort of operation we have here. We turn over a lot of money."

"I understand," Tony said. "But you didn't answer my question."

"I'm coming to that. We need you for two reasons: the first is protection. A setup like this is a magnet for hustlers and we get our share."

"O.K., I can handle that. What's the other reason?"

"We get a lot of high rollers. Sometimes, guys like that, they don't know when to stop. They can get lucky and really hurt the house."

"I got a good line in brakes," Tony said. "Anything else?"

"Nothing that won't wait." Miranda went to walk away.

"Just a minute," he said. "We gotta work out a code."

"Is that necessary?"

"How else am I gonna know when you want me to hit, and for how much? You gonna yell across the table? Or come whispering in my ear, maybe?"

"We always managed, so far."

"Yeah—and what's it cost you, so far? That's something else you'll never know. One thing the hustler's always on the lookout for is signals. You come within ten feet of me when I'm working, that hustler's gonna be watching you like a hawk. If he thinks he's spotted, he pulls out fast. And when is he spotted? When he's winning your dough, that's when. I don't work that way, boss, it ain't professional."

"I suppose you got a point."

"O.K. Now, I'm gonna teach you the signals—oh, and I gotta tell you before we start: You have to be careful where you put your hands. When you come near me, and there's nothing doing, just remember to keep your hands in your pockets."

"I'll remember."

"And stand back from the table, somewhere behind the players."

"Yes."

"O.K. Number one, you pick your nose, the right nostril. That's a hit on the shooter. The player takes a bath."

"You kidding?"

"Fingers curled, that's hundreds—fingers straight, that's thousands."

"How many of these signals are there?"

"Twenty oughta do it, for starters."

"I better get a pencil and paper."

"Yeah—and don't forget . . ."

"Don't forget what?"

"Make a mistake, put your finger in the wrong hole, and it's tough shit on you."

Miranda's was superbly luxurious, all gold-and-crystal chandeliers, warm carpets, and tall, gilt-framed mirrors. The house staff and casino dealers had been chosen for their maturity and their impeccable conduct, as well as their experience; they were decorous, efficient, and courteous. A large area to one side operated as a high-class restaurant. Snowy with white linen, it vied with the best eating places in town. It offered one attraction other restaurants couldn't: important patrons were habitually "comped," eating and drinking at the expense of the management. The warm feelings these patrons took with them to the gambling tables frequently turned the meal into a ruinously expensive repast.

At first the place unsettled him. The sheer civility of it all overwhelmed him. He found himself waiting for the old, familiar yells and screams to begin, the fights to start up. On the rare occasion when a contentious voice rose, or changed its tone to anger, he lifted his head, anticipating the customary "I wuz robbed" or "You cock-suckin' son of a whore bitch" to go ringing through the elegant halls—to be followed by the usual sequel of crashing furniture and the thudding of blows as security guards moved in to quell the disturbance. It never came. And he couldn't rid himself of the feeling the place was likely to erupt at any moment. It just didn't seem natural for everyone to behave so well in the volatile atmosphere of a gambling house.

The carriage trade was very different from what he'd become accustomed to: Confident, prosperous, rounded men with soft white skins, smelling of barber shops, and their beautifully turned-out, gowned, bejeweled and coiffed women, who gloried in parading their finery around the restaurant and casino tables. The place filled up nightly when the Broadway shows turned out and usually ran to capacity until the early hours of the morning. He was surprised to find drunks a rarity. Now and then someone had a few too many and was discreetly removed by solicitous hands. The number of well-dressed, beautiful, unattached women who frequented the place intrigued him, until he discovered they were sent in on a rotating basis by Polly Adler, New York's best-known madam, on the orders of Miranda. The cream of the crop.

It was all a far cry from Calumet City.

For three nights he did nothing. He hung around watching the crap games, familiarizing himself with the routine, and waiting for orders. He suspected that Miranda was having trouble memorizing the signals. The thought amused him, but he said nothing and enjoyed the temporary idleness. The volume of money going across the tables astonished him. They came into the club with rolls that made him blink. And something new—credit. Some of the players simply signed a marker and went on to play with thousands of dollars of house checks. He'd have to learn about that.

Then he found a guy who was winning nervously. It took him only a few moments to discover the man was an amateur hustler, proficient in a simple way, and giving off signals like NBC. Tony was surprised the dealer running the crap game hadn't discovered him. "He's making the fatal mistake of most amateurs,"

Tony told Miranda. "The guy's rolling up his winnings for the big one. The table's very busy—if the dealer don't spot him soon, he can pull it off."

"How much?"

"I estimate, next time he's shooter, he'll go for maybe ten grand. If he goes further than that, he's crazy. But you never know with them amateurs. The dealer know what to do?" he asked.

"No, he's straight. Only thing he can do is stop the guy from playing."

"Aw, that creates bad feeling at the table. Why not let me take over the game for a few minutes?"

"O.K." Miranda said, "in you go."

When it was the amateur's turn to pitch the dice, he pushed his entire winnings out on the pass line, as Tony had expected. Tony deftly switched in a pair of Tees and served them to the man with an engaging smile. The player sevened-out immediately. He went white, turned, and stole guiltily away from the table. Tony serviced the game for another half-hour, enjoying the pleasant atmosphere, before calling back the original dealer.

"Hey, what you think of that?" Miranda said when he joined him. "The guy sevens-out at the crucial moment. Some dummies never know when to stop. Luck for the house, eh?"

"Luck?"

"Sure—what else you call it? The guy made a wrong move before you got started. I saw the whole thing."

"Oh, yeah? And these little babes had nothing to do with it, I suppose?" A pair of dice appeared at his fingertips.

"What are they?"

"The guy's gaffs. I switched 'em for Tops and Bottoms."

Miranda stared at him disbelievingly. "You're kidding. I didn't see you make a move. I didn't take my eyes off you once, and I didn't see a goddamn thing."

"Right—the day you *do* see me work is the day I'm finished." Miranda was silent. "That roll won the house thirty-two thousand, if you noticed," Tony went on. "A few of the players were following him, chasing his luck. Sometimes it happens. I pick up another twenty-two grand, along with his money. I hope I didn't make you no bad friends."

"No, that's O.K. I mean, that's fine." Again Miranda showed a quick recovery. Soon he was smiling. "I'm glad you're on our side of the table," he said.

"You think I'm something special, huh?"

"Yes, I'll agree with that."

"Do I rate special treatment?"

"What you getting at—there something you want?"

"You got an Italian chef here in the restaurant," Tony said. "I hear he's making stuffed peppers tonight. I got this thing about stuffed peppers—my mouth ain't stopped watering. I guess I miss my ma's home cooking. Look, I know you don't allow staff to eat in the restaurant, so, if it's O.K. with you, I'll grab a little of them peppers out in the kitchen." He looked at Miranda hopefully.

The boss's grin widened. "You'll eat out here in the restaurant. Special deluxe service—you earned it."

"The kitchen's fine with me, honest."

"Eat at my table in the restaurant," Miranda reaffirmed.

CHAPTER SEVEN

Because the man came into the club consistently night after night and lost money, the other dealers secretly took him for a chump. Tony knew better. He knew the man was a hustler. Not the sort he was always coming up against—Jack Shelley was a stocks-and-bonds hustler. Miranda told Tony one night, when he was puzzling over how a guy could afford to throw away so much money on gambling. Apparently, when a stock promotion turned out to be so much ballyhoo, it often had Jack Shelley's name behind it. Tony reasoned to himself that a man with a seemingly endless supply of money had to be good at whatever it was he did. As a gambler, he wasn't so hot. Jack Shelley was an insatiable craps addict. To Tony he was just another customer to be treated with respect.

Business had been steady, and Tony was working straight as a dealer. No dice cowboys had appeared and he hadn't been ordered in against a player for days. "How much am I down tonight?" Jack said to him.

"Twenty-four thou."

"O.K., keep 'em coming." His red-rimmed eyes followed the dice across the green felt. "I'm fucking starved," he said.

"What you say I order up some breakfast for you? How about some nice ham and eggs?" He hoped Jack Shelley would be tempted—he'd been on his feet a long time and his limbs were stiffening. If Jack left the table, he could break off.

"What's the time?"

"Four forty-five."

"I'll play till five. Then I'll eat."

"O.K." Tony flicked a finger and a waiter was at Jack's side to take his order. He liked Jack; the man's style amused him. But Jack's propensity for grinding on when the game was cold, or until everyone else was long gone, was wearying. Jack always took up a position at the layout as close to the dealer as possible. Tony humored him over his ridiculous losses, and Jack seemed appreciative of Tony's companionship as he whiled away the night over the dice. Sometimes, when it was very late, they were left alone at the table, playing almost as two friends. Tony sensed the isolation in the man who gambled like there was no tomorrow. In between leisurely throws of the dice they chatted. "Say, Jack, you here all night—what time you go in to the office in the morning?"

"Nine o'clock, on the nose, every day. With my operation, you have to be on the ball."

"Man, I'd be dead. Ain't seen a morning since I got to New York. How you get by on so little sleep?"

"Who's got time for sleep, for Chrissakes? I got my work cut out, making dough so you guys can get rich."

"I'm not rich." Tony laughed, then added, "But I guess the boss is."

"Yeah, that Miranda, he's rich all right. He's rich on my losses, the crook." Suddenly he wailed at the uncooperative dice. "Oh, I'm never gonna make my point."

They played on. After a moment, Tony said, "Why you say that?"

"What?"

"Miranda—the man's got a lot of principle from what I see."

"What you see," Jack said sardonically.

"Listen, after the traps I been in, this place is a joy ride."

"Where you been?"

"Chicago—around there."

"Gambling joints?" Tony nodded. "I know what you mean. That's another bunch of crooks. That Torrio, he left 'em a great heritage up there."

"Who's Torrio?"

"You don't know?" Jack looked at him. "He's the man taught Capone to organize the mobs."

After a moment, Tony said, "I know where I'd rather be."

"You think it's any better down here?"

"Come on—it's a different world."

"Sure, this section of New York. Try going over to Brooklyn on business some day. If Murder Incorporated don't shake you down, let me know. Maybe I'll go myself."

"I don't know nothing about that." He shrugged.

"You read the papers, don't you?"

"It don't sink in—I guess I live in a little world of my own. Nothing like that here on Park Avenue. I suppose the mobs don't get over this far."

Jack burst out laughing. The laughter finally stopped his game and he turned away from the table. "I've had enough for one night," he said. He took out a handkerchief and wiped his eyes.

"I don't see what's so funny."

"You—you're funny. You said . . . you don't know a thing."

"So what's there to know?" Tony showed a rare trace of annoyance.

"You're like a blind man walking across a busy street—the only reason he don't get hit is he's lucky. Look, who you think owns this joint?"

"Miranda."

"There's no way he can operate without muscle behind him. I'm talking about the mobs. Haven't you noticed those fine, manicured gentlemen who call in here regularly? The ones who talk the loudest, usually from the corners of their mouths?"

"We get real high-society people in here," Tony protested. "Politicians, industrialists, police chiefs—they all come to Miranda's."

"Sure they do. Where else the mobsters gonna meet 'em?"

"Whoever they are, they don't cause no trouble."

"Why should they? They own the joint. Most other joints in town, too."

151

"It's not my business," Tony said blandly. "I only work here." A waiter was beckoning. "Your food is ready," he said.

"I'm going to educate you, one of these days," Jack said. "Somebody ought to wise you up to what's going on around here." He turned and walked across to the restaurant.

A month had passed and Jack Shelley hadn't mentioned the New York mobsters again. He continued to play regularly, always insisting Tony deal for him. Tony noticed his bets were becoming larger than ever, and a touch of desperation began creeping into his play. Because Tony was so familiar with Jack's game, he noticed the subtle differences, the hint of urgency. One evening Miranda spoke to him before he went on duty. "Word's out that Jack Shelley's in trouble," he told Tony. "I just had a look at his markers. He's in to us for sixty thousand. If he comes in tonight, I want to see him in my office before he plays. And no more credit."

"He never bilked us, has he?" Tony asked.

"There's always a first time."

"Maybe he's just going through a bad time. You could frighten away a good customer, you don't treat him right."

Miranda glared at him. "Let me worry about that. Your business is handling the dice. Just stick to that, will you?"

"Sure, boss," Tony said easily. But somehow he felt sad that the colorful Jack Shelley was about to be downed. A rapport of sorts had grown up between them that went beyond the relationship of dealer and player. He'd even grown to respect the man's reckless disregard for the value of money. Now it looked as if the wily stock raider was about to get his. Tony would miss his freewheeling friend. Sometimes he regretted that his position in the club made it undesirable to become friendly with other members of the staff. It meant there was hardly a soul in New York who cared about his existence. Perhaps it was because of that, the gloss of the city was beginning to pale.

Jack came into the club about one in the morning. His table was busy, but Tony was keeping an eye open for him. At times Jack came straight to the table, where Tony would arrange his credit. Other times he went straight to the cage to sign markers, or settle his account before playing. Tonight Jack chose the cage, and Tony was glad. Within a few moments, Jack began waving his arms about in an argument, and then he disappeared into Miranda's office. When he emerged, he came across and shouldered his way in next to Tony. He pushed a bundle of money across the felt. "I'm playing for cash tonight," he said. "Give me checks for this five grand."

"Certainly," Tony said pleasantly. He changed up the money. When he passed the checks across he stole a glance at Jack's drawn face and murmured, "Be lucky, Jack."

"Thanks, pal." Jack didn't look at him.

The way Jack played, he deserved to lose every cent. The old rule was "Desperate money never wins." Probably because Jack habitually defied convention, and fortune sometimes favors the bold, his pile increased steadily. A couple of hours had passed and the club was becoming empty. Besides Jack, only a couple of minor

152

players remained at the table. Miranda kept his distance on the other side of the room. When Jack came to count his money, he was holding sixty thousand dollars in checks. The amount he owed the club. "Listen, Jack, you had a good night for a change. Why don't you quit while you're ahead?" Tony suggested.

"Oh, hell, you know me," Jack said stubbornly. "I have to see the night out."

He thought carefully before he said softly to Jack, "You know, they're saying you're on the skids—any truth in that?" The other stiffened, but made no reply. "How much you in a hole for, Jack?" His words were hardly audible. A crazy idea was running through his mind. It was something he'd told himself he'd never do. He felt an obstinacy driving him, filling him with a weird sense of justice. Inside him the battle raged, but he maintained a bland expression.

He felt, rather than saw the other's glance. After a moment, Jack said, "Fifty— and the sixty I owe the house. Hundred and ten and I'm off the hook."

"Take what you got there and go. You're gonna blow what you won if you keep playing." Tony spoke quietly as he worked.

"The name's Jack Shelley, my young provincial friend. I appreciate your concern, but I don't settle for half measures."

"You're staying?" He said it almost with a sigh.

"Absolutely. I don't walk out on my luck."

"O.K.," Tony said. "This is your last bet, you understand? Shove it all on the line—everything you got." Tony waited in the silence that followed. "You heard me—do it now, prick."

Jack came alive. Miranda saw the bet go on from across the room. For a moment he stared, then, frowning, strode across the room toward them. As he approached Tony saw, from the corner of his eye, the urgent signal for a hit on Jack. He deliberately kept his head down. Under Miranda's direct gaze he switched the dice and fed Jack a winning pair. Miranda dug fiercely into his nostril, but there was no double tap from Tony's stick to signify the instruction had been accepted. When the dice flew from Jack's hand Tony called out, "Last bet for Mr. Shelley." He lifted his head. His gaze immediately connected with Miranda's and he allowed himself a look of surprise.

With a whoop of delight, Jack scooped up the hundred and twenty thousand dollars' worth of checks. "There y'are, jerk, I said my luck was in tonight," he yelled at Tony.

"Yes, you had a very good night tonight, Mr. Shelley," Tony said formally. While Miranda glared around in anger, he switched the house dice back in.

"Clear my markers up for me, will you?" Jack said. He threw sixty thousand dollars in checks on the felt and turned to give Miranda a sardonic scowl. "Oh, and there's something for you." He dug into his pocket and came up with a ten-dollar bill, which he threw on the table for Tony.

"Thank you, sir," Tony said politely.

Later, he faced Miranda in his office. "I gave you the signal for the hit," Miranda stormed at him. "You lost the house a hundred and twenty grand."

"You were too late, Mr. Miranda," Tony said calmly. "It's no good coming across the room when the bet's down and I've served the dice. I can't work miracles."

"I got there in time."

"Face it, that's just wishful thinking. I didn't know you were at the table until it was too late. Look at it this way: I spend night after night dealing for a high roller and you never mention we're gonna hit him. I ain't got any reason to be looking for signals. I don't want to be disrespectful, Mr. Miranda, but you gotta do better than that. You gotta put me in the picture."

"You blaming me now?"

"Let's say the system didn't work."

"Look—just get out of here, will you?" Miranda looked as if he might explode.

"I don't wanna be blamed if it ain't my fault," Tony persisted. "I teach you the signals, you gotta learn to use 'em properly." He paused. "If you ain't satisfied with my services, I guess I can find another job."

"All right. That's enough. We'll leave it at that."

"Leave it at what?"

"The system."

"So you agree it ain't my fault," Tony said dogmatically. It was the best entertainment he'd had for some time.

"Please. Just get out of here." A boiling Miranda contained himself.

CHAPTER EIGHT

Yesterday was dying and tomorrow wasn't yet born. The hours before dawn were magical. Around him the city slept, its usually teeming pavements quiet in the receding night. There was little traffic to disturb the echo of his footsteps against the tall office buildings and darkened, bolted stores along Lexington Avenue. It was a dozen blocks to the rooming house where he lived, and he enjoyed the walk.

The shiny, black LaSalle coupe slid up to the curb alongside him. "Hey, diceman," the voice called. "Need a ride?"

He stopped and looked up and down the street before he spoke to Jack Shelley. "We shouldn't be seen together. Someone might get ideas."

"Screw someone. Jump in."

There was more prospect of being recognized on the sidewalk than in the car, so he got in. The LaSalle whirred off. "Nice." Tony looked around the interior of the car appreciatively.

"You want it? It's yours."

"No . . ." He laughed.

"I mean it. I have a couple of other cars. I won't miss it."

"I can't afford to run no fancy car. Besides, I got no use for it. I ain't going nowhere."

Jack looked across at him. "We have to talk," he said seriously. "I'm in your debt."

"Best thing you can do is forget it," Tony said. "It won't happen again."

"That wasn't what I had in mind—." Jack started.

"Look, I ain't never done that before. I guess I felt they owed you, that's all."

"There's something I have to ask."

"I told you. That was it—first time and the last."

"Will you listen to me, for Chrissakes?" Jack roared suddenly. Tony went silent. "What I wanna know is: All these months—you could have taken me any time you wanted, right?"

"Any time."

"And I wouldn't know?"

"You'd never know it, that's right."

"But you didn't . . ." Jack said with certainty.

"No." He looked out the window and watched the street roll by. "Your losses were all straight."

"Why not? You could have taken big money from me."

"I wasn't ordered to." He shrugged. He didn't mention the episode with Miranda. "Besides, it wasn't necessary."

"What do you mean?"

"I mean you're a lousy dice player. Even when you win, you keep playing until you blow your money."

"Listen, I been playing craps since I was a kid in knee pants," Jack objected.

"You burned off an awful lot of dough."

Jack drove in silence for a moment. Then he said, "What's wrong with my game?"

"One of the few things a player can control is time—when he starts and when he stops. You don't stop. You go on until the game swallows you up," he said pointedly.

"Is that all?"

"And I guess you never heard of the laws of probability."

"I'd rather trust my luck."

"Luck's a fickle lady," Tony said.

"It might surprise you to know that for years I was a scientific player."

"Oh—what happened to science?"

"What the fuck you think? I lost. Worse, it took all the fun out of the game."

"Yeah, I can believe it." He looked out the window again, a smile on his lips.

"I have to say: I've been a player all my life. I never saw anything like the way you switched those dice in the game."

"You saw me make the switch?" Tony swung around.

"Hey, take it easy. No, I didn't see a damn thing. That's what I'm saying." He paused. "You're a mechanic, right?" Tony looked at him, but said nothing. "You have to be, switching the dice under Miranda's nose the way you did. They say it takes balls—and a lot of skill." Again he paused. "You're not saying much."

"Nothing to say."

"I know what I'm talking about. I've been around dice a long time. What I don't

155

understand is: Why'd you get me out of the hole?"

"I already told you."

"Why should it concern you, that they owe me?" Tony shrugged, and Jack went on, "I'd have given anything to be a mechanic myself. Matter of fact, I always wanted to meet one."

"So now you met one—shut up about it, willya?"

"I won't talk. You can rely on me, I understand how important your cover is. Are you what they call a master?"

"I hadn't thought about it."

"They say there's only two or three in the whole country."

His mind went back to Boston Bailey. The realization dawned on him that he'd become a better mechanic than Boston. He recalled the skill and dexterity of those fingers. Even back through the years he could remember vividly every move Boston had made. He knew with absolute certainty that if he were to come up against Boston now, he would beat him. He'd be able to spot Boston's action while, at the same time, concealing his own. He'd become too fast to be spotted, he was sure. And the man at Great Lakes had told him—Boston was a master mechanic. He gave a small, dry laugh.

"What's funny?" Jack said.

"I just realized. I made it."

"Made what?"

"Nothing—forget it."

"I don't want to sound corny, but there's something I don't understand—if you're so good, why ain't you rich?"

"A mechanic don't operate for himself. Only for the house."

"That's crazy."

"It don't work no other way," Tony said. Then, "Say, where the hell you taking me?" They'd long passed the street where he lived.

"Just driving . . ." Jack said.

"Well, turn around and drive back, willya? I live the other way."

"Aw, it's too early to go to bed. Let's go get some coffee."

"Where?"

"Broadway—everybody goes." Jack took the next turn. "There's Lindy's, Reuben's, Dade's Blue Room . . ."

"I don't know them joints. Besides, I told you, we shouldn't be seen together. It don't look good for me to be out with a high roller who's a regular at the Club."

"I'm finished with Miranda's."

"Well, that makes a difference," Tony admitted.

"What kind of social life do you have?"

"What?"

"Friends—broads. What do you do for kicks?"

He took his time answering. "Don't know anybody here in New York, outside of where I work."

"My friend, that's an achievement. Here you are, living in the greatest little city in the western world, holding the key to a fortune, and you haven't found out yet you're alive. Something wrong with you?"

156

"I guess it's the job."

"We're going to change all that, my young friend. I'm going to bring you out socially. I'm going to teach you how to live. And, in return, there's something you can teach me."

"What's that?" He guessed what was coming.

"How to play dice."

"Look, you ain't never gonna make no mechanic—," Tony began.

"I know it. That wasn't what I said—just teach me to play dice."

"O.K.," he said. "Here's lesson number one: Keep your lip buttoned."

"That you're teaching me? I won't tell a soul."

"Not that. You know what I mean—what I am."

"Sure. You can depend on me."

"I dunno. I got the feeling you're likely to run off at the mouth," Tony said doubtfully.

"Don't be confused," Jack said. "The flamboyant front suits my work. There's no better way to make contacts. Who would you rather buy stock from—a guy who's broke, or one who's got so much dough he can't give it away quick enough?"

"I never took you for a fool," Tony said.

"You may be an expert with the dice, but you have a lot to learn." The lights of Broadway came into view. "O.K.," Jack said, grinning. "Play time. Start talking big. We're having coffee at Lindy's."

Jack leaped to his feet and yelled dramatically across the room above the hubbub: "Hold it. I want you for my next picture."

For a moment the place went quiet, and all eyes turned to the stunning, tall brunette who'd walked in alone. At this hour Lindy's was crowded with late-night revelers and big-city insomniacs. Suddenly the slim, shapely girl realized she was the center of attention, and a flush started from her neck and worked upward. A few guffaws from those who knew Jack broke the ice, and the chatter began again. "I think we hit pay dirt," Jack muttered.

"Oh, yeah?" Tony said. "What's a girl with them looks doing loose on Broadway this time of night?"

"Let's find out, shall we?" Jack strode quickly across to the girl's side. Tony watched her unfreeze and answer Jack hesitantly. It was difficult for anybody to resist Jack's gregarious approach for long. A few moments later he was leading her across to their table. When she sat down, Tony realized she was just as beautiful close up as she appeared from across the room. The cornflower blue of her eyes was accentuated by dark rings beneath, showing her tiredness. She looked around nervously, and only partially relaxed when she was no longer the focus of people's attention. "This is Miss Rita Sheridan," Jack said. "Rita, I want you to meet my casting director, Anthony . . ." He stopped.

"There's no need for pretense, Mr. Shelley," the girl said. "I doubt very much if you're in the picture business. And if you are, I want you to know I'm not interested. Not even when you find out your friend's last name."

"Call me Jack," he said innocuously.

"Jack," she said. "If you don't mind, I'll just sit here with you for a while. It's tiresome walking the streets around here."

"Want some coffee?"

"I'd love some. And a Danish . . . I'll pay." She reached for her purse.

"That's not necessary." He signaled a waiter and gave the order.

Tony studied her for a moment. "What you doing, hanging around Broadway this hour of the night, Rita?" he said. He had already presumed the answer.

He was wrong. "Not what you think," she said defiantly. "If you must know, I'm waiting for a bus."

"That's good—very good." Jack chuckled.

"I really am," she said, annoyed. "I was waiting at the bus station, and men were bothering me. So I started to walk. It's difficult for a girl on her own . . ." She stopped.

"Where's your baggage?" Tony said.

"In a locker at the bus station," she said promptly. She went on, "I'm from Charleston, West Virginia. I missed the last bus. First one in the morning goes at seven. I'd given up my hotel room, so like a fool I decided to wait at the bus station until the morning. Silly thing to do, I realize that now."

"What are you doing here in New York, Rita?" Tony asked.

"I was promised a job. A very good job, by standards back home. I thought it would be exciting, living in New York and all that."

"So what went wrong?"

"The job was there O.K. What he didn't mention were the strings attached. Stenography was only part of it." Jack was grinning. "It's not funny," she said.

"A girl with your looks, what you expect?" Tony said coolly.

"I expect to be treated like a lady," she said indignantly.

"Whoops." Jack was still amused.

"So much for glamorous New York," she said.

"I think the lady's telling you to shove it," Tony said to Jack.

They were interrupted by the arrival of the coffee. A few minutes later, Jack called for the check. He got to his feet. "You coming?" he said to Rita.

"Where?"

"Up to my place."

"Thanks—I don't think so."

"O.K. Have it your way. I'm getting tired, and I have to be up in the morning."

"You're not going to leave me here alone, are you?" Her blue eyes widened.

"You'll be O.K. in here."

". . . Please."

"Babe, I just offered you—."

"Can't you stay with me a while longer?"

"You kidding?"

"It's only a couple of hours now. I'm afraid to be on my own again."

"Got better things to do. Sorry, honey."

Tony recognized the fear in her eyes. In his memory he was back in Calumet City. His mouth could taste the yawning emptiness, the solitude, and the fear. The awful loneliness when there wasn't a soul in the world to whom he could turn. "Rita," he said, "it's crazy, sitting around here till the morning. Come along with

158

us. You'll be O.K. You got my personal word on it."

She looked at him and an instant bond sprang up between them. "Honest?"

"Yeah . . ." To make it stronger, he said, "If you don't believe me, I'll stay here with you myself. It's O.K."

"All right, I trust you." She made up her mind suddenly, and got to her feet.

Jack's apartment on Central Park West was vast, with rooms high and airy, and more elegant than anything he could have imagined. The brilliant white and cream decor was matched by custom-built furniture in ivory, decorated with gold filigree. Thick, ostentatiously valuable Chinese rugs covered every inch of floor. An open staircase ran from the entrance hall in a rising ellipse to a gallery above, where several doors led off to upper rooms.

Jack certainly had style, Tony decided.

"Well, guys, I'm off to bed," Jack announced, almost as soon as they'd looked around. "Tony, if you want to sleep here, the rooms at the top of the stairs are guest bedrooms. Take your pick."

"I think maybe I will," Tony said. "This sure beats my chicken coop."

"O.K., you're welcome—you too, Rita. If you want a drink, press the button on the wall." Then he was gone.

Intrigued, Tony walked across and examined the button. Just how it would deliver a drink was beyond him, unless it summoned a servant. Out of curiosity, he pressed it. He jumped aside when the wall parted and a large, mirrored bar, complete with stools, rolled out.

"Now, ain't that sump'n?" he said admiringly.

"Your friend Jack must be very rich," Rita said cautiously.

"Let's have a drink to celebrate. What'll you have?"

"What are you having?"

"Scotch."

"Fine. No ice." Then she added, "To celebrate what?"

"You, me, today, this place. Just anything."

"A general celebration."

"Right." He poured the drinks and lifted his glass. "To you, Rita. And to me. All the way to the gates of hell." He drained the glass in a swallow, then coughed. "You can see I'm no drinker," he grinned through watering eyes. "Hey, you didn't touch your drink."

"The toast isn't one I'd care to drink to." She put her glass down. "Do you think it's O.K. if I take a shower? Some of those people out on the street, they smell like goats." She shuddered. "Just being near them made me feel dirty."

"Go right ahead," he said. "Try upstairs."

He watched her walk up the stairs. She moved well, he thought. She disappeared through one of the doors leading off the gallery as he poured himself another drink, a stiff one. This time he drank carefully. He got off the stool and walked across to the black button. The bar jerked convulsively a couple of times, but failed to return into the wall. He made a wry face, turned, and walked up the stairs.

The bedroom was decorated in pink and gold. He kicked off his shoes and wriggled his toes in the thick carpet. He walked across to the bed and studied her

159

clothes, laid out tidily on the bed. He touched them gently with his fingers. Through the closed bathroom door he could hear water smacking against her body. He walked around the king-size bed, lay down on it, stretched out, and waited.

When she appeared in the bathroom doorway, wrapped in a thick terry robe, she stood stock still at the sight of him. He studied her shiny, gleaming face. "I ain't gonna hurt you," he said. "You got nothing to be afraid of—I gave you my word."

"Yes, you did," she said tightly. "And I believed you."

"So just make like I'm not here."

"But you *are* here. Look, I'm so tired I can hardly keep my eyes open. I was hoping to lie down for a few minutes."

"Go ahead," he said. He moved further to the edge of the bed.

"Not with you on the bed."

"Take a chance—maybe it'll restore your faith in humanity."

The fatigue was beginning to glaze her eyes. It was a look he'd seen often in the eyes of losers, gamblers who'd stayed too long to chase their losses. It was a good time to strike, when they had that look in their eyes. She eyed the bed yearningly. "Will you promise me to stay over on your side?"

"Yes. I promise," he said.

She lay down cautiously near the edge of the bed on her side and wrapped the bathrobe tightly around her. When she put her head down and closed her eyes, she said, "God, I'm exhausted. This city life doesn't suit a country girl. Will you wake me? I want to catch the seven o'clock bus."

"What for?"

"It's the first one."

"So what happens if you take the next one—the world gonna end?"

"I suppose not." Her breathing was becoming steady and her body was relaxed.

"Go to sleep," he said quietly. He reached out and pressed the switch that turned off the bedside lights.

Outside, the daylight was strengthening and beginning to filter into the room. He didn't bother to get up and close the drapes. After a while, he turned on his side and studied the sleeping shape.

His eyes followed the tempting curves of her long limbs, and he wanted to reach out and touch her. Into his mind came the memory of Chicago and the down-and-out who tried to steal his shoes while he slept.

He pondered the thought for a while. Then he was asleep.

160

CHAPTER NINE

She was a thousand miles away, calling his name. He wished she wouldn't do that. He'd only just fallen asleep and he was so very tired. He struggled slowly to consciousness. "What time is it?" he croaked.

"Nine o'clock."

"You're kidding."

"No, it's nine. I brought you some breakfast."

"It's sleep I need, not food. You wake me up so early, how am I gonna be able to work tonight? How am I gonna concentrate?"

"Oh, I didn't know you work at night. I'm sorry—I'll let you sleep."

A lot of good now. Painfully he cracked open his eyelids. He regarded her through the slits. "What you got there?"

"Scrambled eggs, toast, and coffee."

"Yeah. O.K., I'll take it." he sat up in bed, rubbing his eyes. She brought the tray across and placed it on his knees. She looked bright and freshly scrubbed, he noticed. It was one of the things he liked about her. He sniffed at her fragrance as she leaned over him. "You smell good," he said. "How long you been up?"

"Oh, an hour. Jack's gone off to the office. He said to wake you at nine."

"The son of a . . ." She sat on the end of the bed and watched while he downed a cup of coffee. "You didn't take the bus," he said.

"No."

"Changed your mind about going home?"

"As you said, there's no rush. I can take a later bus."

He began to eat, studying her. Now that she was rested, the dark rings had gone from under her eyes. Her beauty stood up well to daylight, he thought. Finding her on Broadway at night was like finding a fresh apple in a barrel of rotting fruit. He chewed thoughtfully, studying her breasts, her shapely thighs.

"Please don't look at me that way," she said, suddenly angry.

"Why not? I ain't hurting you, am I? That's what a girl's beautiful for, to look at."

"Last night you said I could trust you."

"I kept my word, didn't I?"

"Yes, I have to admit it," she said.

"Ain't never slept with no broad before, and not touched her."

"You behaved like a gentleman."

He chewed again. "Don't give me that garbage—I ain't no gentleman."

"But it's true."

"That was last night—today it's different."

"Perhaps I'd better go now." But she remained sitting on the end of the bed.

He poured himself another cup of coffee. "You still mean that, about taking the bus home? You still chicken?"

"That's not fair. I tried."

"You ain't tried hard enough. What if Jack or me can find you a spot? A straight job, no monkey business . . ." She was silent. "Yeah, that's what I thought—you're chicken."

"But there's nothing for me here." Her eyes glistened with sudden tears.

"Same as there is for everyone else, honey. And I'm gonna make a guess—there ain't much back home neither, right?" She avoided his gaze. "I know what it is in them small towns that ain't doing so good. You go back home and you're finished. You gonna be singing the blues forever, down there."

"I can always try again, some other time." It was almost a protest.

"Nope—this is it. Now, here. If you can't hack it, chances are you ain't gonna make it some other time. You gonna spend the rest of your life, down there, dreaming about what might have been." Then she was sobbing, helpless as a baby. He put the tray to one side and crossed the bed to take her in his arms. The damp of her tears was warm on his shoulder. "Let it all out, honey," he said gently. "Let it all go. It ain't gonna do no good, all choked up inside." After a while, her tears ceased, and he said, "Now, you wanna tell me what's really bothering you? I guess I didn't have it right—there has to be a guy mixed up in this somewhere."

The words were almost inaudible and she pressed her face into his shoulder so that the moist heat of her mouth was live on his flesh. "I love him—and he's married to my best friend."

"That gives you two choices," Tony said. "Steal him, or forget him. Ain't nothing else. Make up your mind."

"My mind's made up. That's why I came to New York. I can't go back now—I just can't. It would start up all over again."

After a while, he said, "You been screwing this guy?" He felt her stiffen, but he held her tight, her face in his shoulder so she couldn't move. "Well?" he demanded.

He felt the slight nod. "He's the only one. There's been nobody else." Her words were muted, spoken into his flesh.

"You ain't got nothing to be ashamed of, 'cause that's your problem—you need some, same as everyone else. Me, too. I ain't no different. I need you, and I'm admitting it. If we screw, you won't be thinking about this other guy. I guarantee."

She said nothing, and in a moment his hands were busy at the buttons of her dress. "That's the reason you brought me here last night, isn't it?"

"Nah," he lied.

"Do I excite you?" There was a new curiosity in her voice.

"Honey, with them looks, you'd excite a Benedictine monk. You driving me crazy." The blood was pulsing through his veins.

"You must know plenty of beautiful girls, living here in New York."

"Sure. Where I work there's dozens of them classy broads from Polly Adler's. I ain't never touched one. Somehow it turns me off, knowing there's a million guys been there first."

"Polly Adler's?"

"Never mind. Let's get in the bed."

The dress came off. When she slipped out of her brassiere, he expanded into hard

162

tumescence. He whipped away her garter belt and when she bent over to roll off her stockings, he stopped her. "Leave them," he gasped, "there's no time for that." He rolled her roughly over on her back and touched his probing, bursting self into her glistening pubic nest.

"Oh, God, I'm on fire." She pulled him into her. "Now, Tony, please . . ."

She was so tight, he thought he'd never enter. He forced himself against the barrier of her vaginal muscles and, succeeding, fed the engorged length of himself into her hot moisture. It was only a few seconds before he was groaning at his rapidly mounting climax.

"Don't finish inside, whatever you do . . ." She tore her lips away to plead in his ear.

"I gotta finish now." The words rushed from him desperately.

"Please, Tony, not inside . . ."

For the last fraction of a second, he held on. When he collapsed on top of her, the semen streamed along her stomach. "Jes-us, what a letdown."

"I don't want to have a baby."

"Sure, I know."

"You should have worn something if you wanted to come inside."

"Next time I'll come prepared." Together they laughed at the silly joke, squirming in the sticky mess between them.

"Was that good?" she whispered.

"Best I ever had."

"I'm glad—I wanted it to be good for you."

"Hell, I'm tired. Now I'm feeling it," he said.

"Go to sleep, honey, if you want."

"Yeah." He rolled over onto his side, keeping her locked to him. Within a few minutes his breathing had taken on the rhythm of deep sleep.

For a while, lying entwined with him, her cornflower-blue eyes studied his face. Then her eyelids drooped and she, too, fell asleep.

The phone rang. They were still joined together. He reached out and picked it up. "Hi, pal," Jack said. "Screwed the broad yet?"

"What's the time?" Tony said.

"Quarter after twelve."

"That's better." Now he felt rested.

"Rita still around?"

"Yeah. She's gonna be staying in New York. Can you get her fixed up with a job? She's a stenographer."

"There's an employment agent in this building—buddy of mine. He'll find something for her."

"Sure of that?"

"Guaranteed. He owes me. She gets the first job comes along."

"Thanks, Jack."

"So you have screwed her."

"The kid needs a break."

"Where is she?"

He looked down at her, beneath him. She'd heard the conversation. Now she was smiling expectantly. "Around," he said.

"Give her one for me, will you? What you say, you two come along and have lunch with me?"

"First I gotta take a shower—your call woke me."

"You have time. Make it one-fifteen—the Waldorf."

"O.K. See you then." Tony replaced the receiver. As he did so, she pulled him down. "I'll take the one for Jack now," she said.

Rita was wide-eyed in the elegant dining room of the Waldorf-Astoria. "You speak to your guy yet about a job for her?" Tony asked Jack.

"It's all fixed up. A merchant bank in our building needs a stenographer. She has an appointment for ten o'clock tomorrow."

"Thanks, Jack."

"I just can't believe it's true," Rita said. "Yesterday I was all washed up. Today it's a new world."

Tony and Jack exchanged amused glances. "What time you go to work at Miranda's tonight?" Jack asked.

"Six," he said.

"Pity. I thought maybe we'd pay a visit to some other joint. You could come along and advise me, sort of."

"Jack, don't start trying to use me," Tony said immediately. "That way we'll fall out."

"It wasn't what I had in mind, honest."

"I told you, I'll show you where your play's wrong. I'll help you with instruction any time you want. But it stops there."

"That's fine with me. Say, how much they pay you over at Miranda's?"

"Three hundred bucks a week."

"That's peanuts," Jack snorted.

"I'm the highest-paid dealer in the house," Tony said.

Jack looked around and dropped his voice. "How about when you bury a guy— you on a commission?"

"Don't happen often in that joint. You gotta understand, mostly I'm there to protect the house."

"How about the money?" Jack insisted.

"Coupla times Miranda gives me five hundred bucks, when there was action," he said unwillingly.

"They know, over there, that you could wipe 'em out if you want?"

"Sure, they know."

"I'm sorry, Tony, but I don't understand . . ." Jack shook his head. "You could earn yourself a fortune, the skill you have in your hands."

"I told you, Jack, it don't go like that."

"The hell with all that garbage. Come in with me—I'll put up a big stake and we'll go to town. Clean up. What you say?"

"No," Tony said positively. "But thanks for the offer."

"You're a damn fool."

"Jack, it's not what it appears. The fact is, I wouldn't last five minutes if I got mixed up in something like that. Sure, I know it's possible to sting short-season joints, out in the boondocks. Hit 'em and keep moving. But that ain't the life I want. I'm a professional—I got my standards. I don't wanna get no bad name in the big cities. I'm gonna be top guy in the business, one of these days."

"Now I know why there's only a handful of mechanics," Jack grumbled into his soup. "You must be crazy."

Outside the hotel, Jack took a cab back to his office and they began walking. They turned the corner of 50th Street and strolled along Madison Avenue, looking in store windows. "That true, you earn three hundred dollars a week?" It must have been going around in her mind.

"Yes."

"I never knew anyone who earned that much."

"It ain't no fortune. Sometimes I get more."

"What do you do with all that money?"

"Let it roll up—I don't spend much, maybe some clothes."

"I didn't understand what you were saying. What work do you do?"

"I'm a dealer in a gambling house."

"Aren't those places illegal?"

"I guess. It don't seem to bother us none. In our place we get society people, politicians, businessmen. They all come to Miranda's."

"And those women you spoke about?"

"The Polly Adler broads?"

"Yes, the ones you said."

"They kinda hang around, make themselves available."

"Don't you ever get the feeling you want to . . .?"

"Strictly business. Never enters my head," he lied. "I gotta be careful who I'm friendly with. Mostly I keep to myself."

She looked thoughtful as they walked along. Then she said, "For a guy who earns three hundred dollars, you sure do speak badly."

"What you getting at?"

"You should try to speak more correctly."

"What for? What I do, I ain't got no need for culture," he said, annoyed.

"You say *ain't* too much."

"All right, then, I haven't got no need for culture."

"Now you're mocking me." They walked on a little way. "Where you from, Tony? You asked me a lot of questions, but you don't say much about yourself."

"I'm from Steubenville, Ohio. It ain't so far from West Virginia."

"What grade did you finish in school?"

"Say, what is this, an inquisition?" He stopped walking. "Oh, I get it. Listen, you gotta understand something, Rita, right from the start. I don't wanna lead you down no blind alley, like the other guy you knew."

"Understand what?"

"No attachments. We can be friends and that's fine with me. But I got no intention of going any further—you got that?"

165

For a moment she frowned. Then she straightened her back. "Yes, I understand. You make it perfectly clear."

"Getting married I *ain't,*" he said positively.

CHAPTER TEN

The backslapping, the pretentious, emotional Mustache-Pete embraces, the wild generosity of some of the iron-jawed men who visited the club barely concealed their brittle, Lower East Side origins, or the savagery that lived shallow beneath their acquired, costly veneer of sophistication. When they came over from the City of Churches, they left behind them the more horrendous aspects of Brooklyn's fame.

He'd long come to realize that the joint was mob-owned. He also understood now how it was that Miranda's remained serene at the center of the seething cauldron of New York's mob interests. It was neutral ground, a place for hosting judicial administrators, politicians, dealers in the marketplace of influence and power. That explained the discretion shown to wayward gamblers—the downbeat, velvet-glove approach. It also explained why Miranda rarely brought Tony's talents into use. The rich pickings were clearly being forgone in the interests of wider, more important objectives.

He found that it suited him. It gave him a peaceful, luxurious environment in which to work. He maintained his incurious detachment from mob affairs, preferring to concentrate on refining his efficiency, constantly honing the fine edge of his skill—treading softly, with single-minded stubbornness, the long, arduous path to his goal.

Apparently his businesslike conduct hadn't gone unnoticed. There was a name that evoked immediate respect in Miranda, Tony had noticed. The name was Lombardo. It was rumored in the club that Lombardo was the real owner, and Miranda little more than a front. One evening Tony was working as pit boss when Miranda touched him on the shoulder. Tony looked up. "Come with me," Miranda said.

Tony signaled for a replacement and followed Miranda to his office. "What is it?"

"Mr. Lombardo wants to meet you."

"Something wrong?"

"No. He rarely comes around. He heard about you and he wants to meet you himself."

The two stern, athletic-looking bodyguards eyed him expressionlessly and moved away from the door as he followed Miranda through. The dapper, white-faced man with the coal-black eyes seated at Miranda's desk extended a soft hand. "Pleased to meet you, Mr. Lombardo," Tony said.

"You're the kid from Steubenville." It was more a statement than a question.

"Yes."

"I was talking to the Duke on the telephone. He says to say hello."

"You know the Duke?" Tony said, surprised.

There was a questioning look in Lombardo's eyes, then it was gone. "Many years." He went to say something else, then changed his mind. "How d' you like it here, at the club?"

"Just fine. Best joint I been in." He allowed himself a small smile.

"Good. You've probably realized by now that this house is something special—a showplace of sorts. There are more exciting clubs, but I want you to get the hang of this operation before we decide what we're gonna do with you."

"You got plans for me?" It was the first he'd heard of it.

"You have a very special talent, Tony. What's more, you don't let it go to your head. I like that. Also, you have respect. All good points. We're in a business with a big future. I'm sure there'll always be a place in the outfit for a guy with ability. One who can keep a cool head."

"Outfit?" Tony queried.

Lombardo nodded, but didn't explain. "Now, I'd like to see a few of your dice moves." He sat back expectantly in his chair. Tony looked uncomfortable. "What's wrong?" Lombardo said.

"I know you're an important guy, Mr. Lombardo . . ." he began slowly.

Miranda came to his rescue. "He doesn't like giving demonstrations," he said. "Oh—why's that?"

"Well, maybe you won't understand this, Mr. Lombardo," Tony said. "I gotta make certain rules for myself—one of them rules is that I must never make a mistake, outside of when I'm practicing privately."

"Is that possible?"

"It's possible. I already done it. I got a hundred-percent record."

". . . Incredible." Lombardo was impressed.

"Thing is, I sorta get tuned in to the action at the table, and that's part of what it's about. I ain't gonna make no mistake there, when the game's swinging. If I make a mistake, it'll come when I'm frigging around showing some guy how it's done— know what I mean?"

"Aren't you making things a little hard for yourself? What you want—that takes some living up to."

"It ain't easy to become top guy."

"And that's your ambition?"

"I talk it over with the Duke. We decide I can make it, with a little luck. In fact, I already done it, I guess. Unless some other guy got a hundred-percent record. Ain't likely," he added.

Lombardo nodded carefully. "I agree. Well, Tony, as you're a specialist, I will, of course, extend you the same courtesy you give me. Perhaps, one of these days, I'll be lucky enough to see you work."

"Thanks, Mr. Lombardo." He turned to go.

"How much he being paid?" Lombardo said to Miranda.

"Three hundred."

"He's worth more. Make it four."

167

"That's a lot of money," Miranda growled.

"Make it five," Lombardo said.

They were seated three abreast across the front seat of Jack's new Imperial as he headed south for New York on the hot cement of Interstate 78. The sun was sinking into the August evening, a fireball on the horizon, setting the sky ablaze with a red glow. Rita put her head out of the window to cool herself off. When she came back in, her hair an unruly mop, she lay down across Tony's lap and closed her eyes, humming contentedly to herself.

Jack glanced across at them and grinned. "Had a good time?" he said.

"I gotta say it—this is what living is all about," Tony said.

"Mmm," Rita agreed, from his lap.

"Those *schmucks* up there. Every August they immigrate to Saratoga Springs—countless, like tropical birds. One of them regulars, if he missed Saratoga in August, he probably wouldn't survive the winter without a heart attack."

"I could get used to it myself," Tony said laconically.

"Only reason I go personally is to make new contacts," Jack said.

"Yeah, I know." Tony smiled. Most of the contacts conveniently arranged to be out at the racetrack, or at Piping Rock Casino, where they'd found themselves each evening. Four days at the Arrowhead Hotel and Jack was returning home thirty grand light. Tony was becoming hardened to it.

"If you'd stuck with me in the casino, maybe I wouldn't have lost so much," Jack said regretfully.

"You know I can't do that, Jack. A lot of people there recognize me as a dealer from Miranda's. Besides, I hear a rumor Lombardo has an interest in the place. If I so much as put a five-dollar bet down on the crap table, he hears it as me trying to knock over the joint."

"You're on vacation—you play up a few bucks—so what?"

Tony sighed. "If you'd listen to me, instead of playing up the way you do, you'd maybe cut your losses."

"How about winning?"

"You gotta face it, Jack, you're a loser—you're determined."

Jack muttered to himself. Out loud, he said, "I go into a casino with a guy who could clean out the place if he chose, and I come out losing thirty grand. There's gotta be a moral in there somewhere."

"Yeah—quit gambling, Jack," Tony advised.

He'd only agreed to accompany Jack to the casino on the condition that, once inside, they had no contact. There were too many people around to put two and two together and come up with five. So, each evening, while Jack went off to play craps at the crowded tables, he sat down with Rita to a leisurely dinner. Sometimes, strolling around later, he'd watched the players from a respectful distance, while he exuded a vacation air. He couldn't help Jack—he recognized that now. A lifetime of conditioning had returned the gambler to his wasteful, spontaneous gambling habits. He'd already thrown out the window all that Tony had taught him. Jack lacked the necessary disciplines and had to continue paying dearly for his indulgence.

168

"We'll hit town in time for dinner," Jack said. "Where would you like to eat? How about Gallagher's? Or maybe you two'd prefer the Copa? There's a good show and you can dance if you want."

Rita opened her eyes. "How about you, Jack? I haven't seen you dance yet."

"I'm particular where I dance."

"Oh?"

"Yeah. Roseland—ten cents a hit. That's the only time I dance."

"You're kidding."

"No, I'm perfectly serious."

"That's crazy—a guy like you." She sat up and stared at him.

"Is it? I think it's quite logical. For a ten-cent ticket I have a choice of beautiful girls. I take the one I like best in my arms, and I dance. Usually she gives me a nice smile, or maybe more than one, despite the fact I probably step on her feet. I gotta tell you, I'm no Fred Astaire. Now—this beautiful broad I'm dancing with—she don't complain about my gambling habits, and she don't expect diamonds and furs. She don't expect a thing except a ten-cent dance ticket, and maybe some bruises where I handle her rough. When the dance is over, maybe she even says thanks, and maybe I get another smile." He concentrated on the view through the windshield. "And if she jumps in the sack with the next guy who buys a ten-cent ticket—who cares?"

Now he understood. Tony had wondered why such a warm, generous guy led such a solitary existence. From experience he knew that gambling addicts were sometimes on an endless trip away from reality. He hadn't realized before that Jack was bearing a cross.

"She must have hurt you real bad," Rita said softly.

He shrugged. "What's six years out of your life?" He negotiated a curve in silence. When the car was running straight, he said, "Funny thing, I met her at this dance . . ." He said nothing more.

Rita started to speak again. "All right, Rita, that's enough. Drop it now," Tony said.

"Oh, that's O.K." Jack grinned ruefully. "I got over her a long time ago. Thing is, I just can't bring myself to try again."

She ignored Tony. "All women aren't the same, Jack. You owe it to yourself to give it another chance.

"Maybe, one of these days . . ." He glanced across at them, faintly apologetic. "Hey, now, how about you two lovers? Heading for something more permanent, perhaps?" When he saw the looks on their faces, he added resignedly, ". . . Oh, guess I boobed again, eh?"

"We have an understanding," Tony said quietly.

"Yeah, ain't that the truth," Rita said, the joy of the day now completely gone from her features.

"Well, for what it's worth, I just have to say it—she loves you, kid. A blind man could see it . . ." Jack spoke softly. "You better think carefully about that. I hear it's the most precious thing in the world." Tony didn't move or change his expression. "It's something all the dough in the world can't buy. If you throw it away, maybe you're an even bigger fool than me."

"Marriage don't figure in my plans. I got things to do. I explained it to Rita right at the start." He spoke woodenly.

She sat up dead straight in the seat. "Jack," she said suddenly, "would you say I'm good looking?"

"Sure, honey, you're beautiful."

"As beautiful as the girls over at Roseland, maybe?"

"Oh, you got them taxi-dancers beat hands down."

"O.K., then—tonight I want you to pay me ten cents and dance with me." Jack began to protest, but she stopped him. "I promise you the greatest ten cents' worth you ever had in your whole life."

Jack frowned, and busied himself with his driving. Absently he reached out and flicked on the headlights.

The sun slipped below the horizon. Night engulfed the car as they rode on toward the city, three souls, each encapsulated in a thoroughly private world of contemplation.

CHAPTER ELEVEN

The pay phone in the hall outside his room rang just as he closed the door on his way out to work. He stopped, undecided whether or not to answer. Chances were the call wasn't for him anyway. He had few calls at the rooming house where he lived. He looked at his watch. It was five-fifteen and he wasn't due at the club until six. He was deliberately early. Rita, who had a room on the same floor, would be coming in from work soon, and he wanted to avoid a meeting. The phone rang insistently, and nobody seemed to be coming to answer it. He reached out and picked up the receiver. "Who'd you want?"

"Mr. Vitale."

"Speaking."

"Tony—that you, Tony?"

"Yeah. Who's this?"

"Skeeter."

"Who?" The voice wasn't right.

"Skeeter Froelich, from Steubenville."

"Hey, Skeets, that you, old buddy?" he yelled into the phone. He hadn't recognized the husky, deflated tones. "Son of a gun, it's great to hear from you. Where you calling from?"

"I'm here—right here in New York, same as you."

"You just arrived?"

"No, I been here some time. I'm working over to Brooklyn." There was a tremor in the voice Tony didn't like.

"Why didn't you call me before?"

Skeeter hesitated. "I didn't have your number. I just called your old man to get it."

"Oh. How's things back home?"

"O.K. Your pa said to tell you love. You should write."

"Yeah . . . Say, Skeets, you don't sound so good."

Long ago he'd learned to beware of the crawling sensation on the back of his neck. It was there now, and he became alert. They'd grown together, gone through adolescence together. In those days he'd been familiar with every facet of the tough guy's moods—until the marriage that blasted Skeeter into cataclysm. But there was enough of his old pal left for Tony to know instinctively something was seriously wrong.

"I don't wanna bother you, Tony, but . . ." He caught the break in Skeeter's voice. It dropped suddenly to a shaky whisper. "Help me, for God's sakes, help me—I'm coming apart. I think I'm losing my mind. Please help me, Tony . . ."

A thousand questions raced through his mind. He pushed them aside to speak reassuringly. "Sure. Take it easy, old buddy. Whatever it is that's botherin' you, I'll come over there right now and fix it. Just you relax and leave it to Tony— everything's gonna be O.K."

"Help me."

"Just give me the address, Skeets, that's all you gotta do."

He strained to hear the words. "I'm working . . . Brooklyn, a building at State and Court Streets." In the background he heard a sudden noise, the clash of dishes, and a man's voice yelling an order. The shock of it seemed to bring Skeeter back to himself. In a firmer voice, he said, "Just ask for the Court Street crap game. Everyone around here knows where it is."

"What you doing working in a crap game?"

"What else a guy from Steubenville gonna do, for Chrissakes? Anyhow, I'm only helping out in the kitchen, now." Tony heard the voice somewhere in the background yelling again. "I gotta go," Skeeter said.

"You O.K. now?" Tony said.

"Yeah, I feel better. I had a bad moment there."

"Walk outa there. I'll meet you outside the joint, in the street."

"I can't do that."

"Why not?"

"I told you, I can't do that." The shake returned to his voice. He was in a bad way, his emotions rising and falling like waves on a beach.

"Hold on, then. I'm coming right over."

"Tony . . ."

"Yeah?"

"I'm sorry I give you this trouble—I ain't got no one else."

"Hey, now, I owe you too, remember. I ain't forgot them kickings you took for me when we used to get into trouble, back in the old days—back in The Hole."

171

The memory of his youthful prowess seemed to grab at Skeeter's throat. Tony heard the choking sound at the other end of the line. "I'm grabbing a cab right now," Tony said. "Just hold on."

In numbers of players it was the biggest crap game he'd seen outside of a regular gambling house. There was a brutish air of purposefulness about the hoodlums and hangers-on who seemed to outnumber the local businessmen by two to one. And Tony knew at a glance that the group held the worst types of dissipated gamblers. There was no sign of Skeeter. He looked around for a door that might lead him to a kitchen. "What you want here, fella?" A plug-ugly stood before him.

"I've come for my friend Skeeter."

"Who?"

"Skeeter Froelich."

"Never heard of him." The surly hood eyed him suspiciously.

"I think he works in the kitchen. He's my age, same height, comes from Steubenville."

"He means Bananas." One of the others had been listening.

"Oh, you mean the loony. Yeah, he's out in the kitchen." The man pointed to a door. "He ain't going nowhere," he added.

"Why's that?" Tony asked quietly.

"He owes the house a hunnert bucks, that's why. He stays in the kitchen till it's paid."

"Gambling money?"

"Yeah, he's working off the debt." He grinned at his pal.

"Maybe I can help him out. Is it O.K. if I see him?"

The man shrugged and turned away.

Tony walked through the door to get the shock of his life. The thin guy with a peppering of white hair, the dissolute stoop, and the red-rimmed, dull eyes was wearing dirty coveralls and down-at-heel shoes. When he caught sight of Tony, his face began to work. He clearly could not control his emotions. "Hi, old buddy." Tony tried to smile, but couldn't. "Come on, I'm taking you out of here now."

"I can't." Skeeter began to shiver. "They won't let me leave. Besides, where would I go? I got nowhere to go."

"You'll come with me."

"No—I'm sorry I called, Tony. I'm sorry if I gave you all this trouble. I didn't mean to bother you. Just forget it happened."

"I ain't forgetting nothing. You're coming with me."

"I can't—I owe them. I gotta stay here." He meant it. Tortured though he was, he was even more afraid to leave the haven of the dirty kitchen. Tony knew then that Skeeter was hanging on to his equilibrium by a meager thread.

"I know about the hundred bucks. I'll square that. How long you been here?"

". . . I don't know." The eyes were clouded.

"Think about it, Skeets—a year, a day? You gotta have some idea."

Skeeter's brow creased. "A couple of months, maybe. It was the only job I could get, here in the kitchen."

"So how come you lose the dough—the hundred bucks?" He didn't have to ask.

"First week I'm here, I get into a crap game. When I lose, they tell me I can work it off."

"So how about the weeks you worked?"

"They say it only pays the vigorish on the hundred bucks. I still owe the principal."

Tony stared at him. The hoods had made a slave out of Skeeter, and, if he knew anything, had got him into a rigged game for the hundred dollars. His friend's self-confidence had been savaged to the point where he was totally unsure of himself. Tony's thoughts went back to the night Skeeter had kept his wife, Ellen, and Angelo prisoner in that remote house. Now, it seemed, he was a prisoner of his own terror. Tony had no idea whether or not Skeeter could be saved from himself. He knew one thing—he had to try to save his friend. "O.K., let's go, Skeets," he said.

Passing the crowd around the crap table, the hood stepped out in front of them. "Hey, Bananas, where you think you're going?" he said to Skeeter, ignoring Tony. Another tough closed in from behind.

Skeeter hung his head. "My buddy's taking me home," he said, as if in shame.

"You ain't going nowhere. You gotta work off your debt. Ain't you honest? You make a move out of this joint and we'll put out a hit team to get you—the guys from Chicago. Ain't no place you can hide. When they find you—bang, bang, bang, you dead." The hood and his partner roared with laughter.

Tony saw Skeeter's lower lip trembling. Although he boiled with rage inwardly, he remained expressionless. "I'll pay the hundred dollars he owes," he said evenly.

"Oh, yeah?" The hood's evil grin expanded. "That don't include the vigorish on the loan. With interest it comes to a hunnert and fifty."

Tony avoided the challenge in the hood's eyes. He pulled out his roll, letting the hoods get a good look at the money, and peeled off a hundred and fifty dollars. "Say, while I'm here, is it O.K if I shoot a few rolls of the dice? I'm feeling lucky."

"Yeah. Sure, pal."

"Gee, thanks." Tony hadn't missed the look that passed between the hoods.

He hit with four naturals in a row, while they were still thinking up ways to screw him. He yelled with manufactured excitement so that they knew for sure, each time, on the next roll, he was going to bury himself. That he was going to do the job for them.

Then he stopped suddenly, the look on his face changing to greed and amazement at his unexpected good fortune. He drew from the gallery of expressions he knew—seen on the thousands of players he'd watched over the years. He grabbed the handful of bills possessively and, hauling Skeeter along by the arm, was out of the building and into the waiting cab before they had time to think it over.

It had been dangerous, and a stupid thing for him to do, he knew. Now that his repressed fury was subsiding, he allowed himself to relax. For a couple of minutes he kept watch through the rear window of the cab. He was reasonably certain they weren't being followed. He turned and stuffed the money into Skeeter's pocket.

The Court Street crap game had paid dearly for the feeble services of its loony kitchen hand.

He knocked on Rita's door. When she opened it, she said, "They've been calling you from Miranda's."

"Yeah, I'm late. Listen, there's something you gotta do for me. Look after this guy."

She stared out into the hallway at the shrinking figure of Skeeter in his grimy coveralls and grimaced. "Who is that bum?"

"He's my buddy. I want you to get him fixed up with a room here. I'll be paying."

"Is he all right?" She was staring at his glazed eyes.

"Yeah, he's had a hard time the last few weeks. He'll be O.K. when he snaps out of it. Go get a bottle of whiskey—pour it down his throat if you have to, but make sure he drinks enough to knock him out. Then put him to bed. I'll explain later."

"I don't know," she said doubtfully. "He looks so dirty."

"Then make him take a shower, for Chrissakes," Tony said impatiently. He turned. "Skeets, you do whatever Rita tells you, you understand? She's gonna be like your sister." Skeeter nodded dully. "I have to go to work now. I'll see you when I get home."

"Tony . . ." She grabbed his sleeve, suddenly anxious. "Is he safe? I don't know if I can handle something like this."

"You gotta handle it. He needs our help, don't you understand? He ain't got no one else. Listen, Skeeter and me, we go back a long way—he's my best pal." She still looked doubtful, and he was in a hurry. He spoke roughly. "Look, you had a taste yourself of what it's like to be alone, helpless, in the city. Skeeter ain't just been waiting for some bus. They got hold of him, over there in Brooklyn, and they twisted his mind. Now, what you say—you gonna help, or not?"

"Yes, all right, Tony, I'll try."

"I gotta go now." He strode off down the hall, leaving them there staring at each other.

CHAPTER TWELVE

Miranda called him into the office and closed the door. "Lombardo has a job for you," he said.

"I don't work for Lombardo," Tony said.

Miranda looked at him curiously. "Put it this way—I'm hiring you out," he said.

"That's up to you."

"There's a guy called Valentine, has a joint over in New Jersey, the Acapulco. He needs a little help. Your kind of help." Tony waited. "He's one of ours," Miranda went on. "The joint's protected."

174

"As I said, Mr. Miranda, it's up to you."

"Lombardo thinks highly of you. He says he knows you'll do him a favor and get his friend out of a spot."

Tony found Miranda's sudden deference interesting. "What's the problem?"

"There's a high roller been hurting the house. Big money."

"Straight?"

"That's it—they're not sure. Nobody's been able to spot any moves so far. Either the guy's incredibly lucky, or he's the most skillful craps player ever rolled a pair of bones."

He was even more interested. Both propositions were highly unlikely. "How many times this player beat the house?"

"I don't know. But it must be getting serious if Lombardo's taking a personal interest."

"The guy never loses?"

"I didn't say that. He's had his losses, apparently. But when he wins, the house takes a bath."

"Why not just bar him?"

"It's a very tricky situation. The guy's connected. It needs careful handling. Lombardo says you're the man for the job."

"Tell Mr. Lombardo I'll be happy to be of service to him." He thought for a moment. "If the guy's hustling, it won't be no trouble for me to bust him out, but it could give you problems."

"Why's that?"

"When he starts losing, he'll guess I'm there to bury him. The hustler usually knows."

"Yeah, I get your point," Miranda said thoughtfully. "I'll talk to Lombardo about that. You'll be told what to do."

"And if the guy is straight?"

"Then we teach him a lesson," Miranda said. "Nobody's entitled to be that lucky."

"O.K. When I'm finished with him, I guarantee you, the sight of a pair of dice will give him the heaves."

"Be discreet. Anything goes wrong, it could mean trouble."

"Nothing'll go wrong. When do I leave?"

"Soon as possible."

"I'll go today." At the door, Tony turned. "No way the guy can be straight," he decided. "I never seen anyone do that—come back and hit the house again and again."

Miranda nodded. "That's what I think, too."

"Leave him to me," Tony said.

The Acapulco Club was big, resplendent, and the restaurant section was large enough to include a cabaret. The casino was vibrant with the expectations of players at its busy games. The waves hit Tony as soon as he entered, and he savored them the way a connoisseur sniffs a vintage wine. Immediately he was struck by how he'd become used to the subtlety and sophistication of Miranda's, which was unlike this high-class but commercial operation, where the air was vital, charged with the electricity of gambling fever.

He was surprised at his reception. Valentine treated him with deference. When they were alone, the other extended his hand as if it were a privilege. "Lombardo tells me you're a master," he said. "To be honest, I was expecting an older guy."

"I started early." Tony smiled.

"Lombardo says you're top man."

He was pleasantly surprised. "Who knows? There's no competition I know of."

Valentine smiled. "Lombardo's word is good enough for me."

Tony changed the subject. "What's been happening?"

"There's this guy, Cusik. He's very close with the Schwarz mob. You know what that means to Lombardo."

"No, I don't," Tony said dryly.

Valentine looked at him. "Everybody knows Lombardo and Schwarz hate each other's guts."

"Everybody except me, apparently."

"I thought you worked for the outfit?"

"I'm just a dealer at Miranda's."

"If you work for Miranda, you work for Lombardo."

"I keep my nose out of things don't concern me."

"Oh, sure, I understand." Unwittingly, he'd evoked even more respect from Valentine. "You're right—loose talk is for fools. Well, the situation is this," he went on. "Cusik's giving us a hard time. He's putting us on the spot. If we force a confrontation with him, Schwarz gets a lever to start something with Lombardo. Word is, he's spoiling for a fight."

"So—what's stopping him?"

"He'd lose face with the other mobs if he didn't have a reason. Maybe they'd want to join up with Lombardo and push Schwarz out. The mobs have territorial agreements and now the fucking asshole wants a bigger slice of the cake."

Tony gave no sign of interest. "Mr. Valentine," he said, "I only want to know about the player, nothing else. I got my own troubles. All you gotta do is give me your instructions and put me to work. I don't wanna know your reasons, and I'm not interested in the consequences. That's your affair—it ain't mine."

Valentine nodded. "I understand. You're strictly a professional—I like that in a guy. Well, what I'm saying, we have to handle this Cusik with kid gloves. We have to let him down easy."

"Yes, I got it."

"It's important to avoid friction."

"The game I can control, but there's nothing I can do about the man's reactions when he realizes he's being hit."

"How will he know that?" Valentine shot back.

"Because he's cheating. How else can he keep coming back at you? Players who bring back their winnings are making a present of them to the house—you ever know it any different?"

"We looked at every angle—," Valentine began.

176

Tony stopped him. "No way he can hit the house regular. We both know it. Not if he's straight."

"Not even with no limit on his bets?"

"You *crazy*?" A twinge of doubt shot though him.

"You gotta understand, this is no ordinary player. We have to extend to Cusik special privileges, just like he was Schwarz himself—we can't treat him like any john. Lombardo would be a laughing stock if we put a limit on Cusik's bets."

"Maybe he's setting you up. Maybe he's waiting for you to bring in a mechanic so he can scream you're robbing him."

"I didn't think of that." Valentine stared.

"I'll find out what he's up to, and we'll take it from there," Tony decided. "When do you expect him in the club?"

"He comes in maybe once, twice a week."

"I'll start work on the floor as a dealer, to get the feel of the house. And so the help get used to having me around."

He knew within the first five minutes that Cusik wasn't cheating. He was the most expert dice player Tony had come up against in his entire career. Tony realized quickly that the man had an exceptional mathematical mind and combined his ability with a highly expert understanding of the laws of probability. He watched, fascinated, as Cusik made impeccable, complex points bets. Except in the physical handling of the dice, Cusik's understanding of the game was almost equal to his own. He felt a genuine regret at having to destroy Cusik's polished game. But the player had a lever no house could afford to leave in the hands of a gambler—he was free to escalate his bets. And he had the money to do it. Worse, he knew just when to stop.

Tony found himself admiring the suave mobster's quicksilver mind. It didn't take him long to form a plan of action. He began to chip away gently at Cusik's stake, taking the edge off his finely balanced points bets, nudging him down with percentage losses. He worked carefully so that the player never became frustrated enough to suspect a loaded game. Now and then, when Cusik's natural losses weighted the pressure Tony was putting on his game, he reversed the process and put Cusik into a win. It maintained an apparent average and avoided the suspicion of a man who understood what ought to be happening at the table. Tony had never been extended the way he was in this game, playing to tire Cusik rather than overwhelm him. Bringing him in, letting him out some. Having to calculate rapidly the value of Cusik's points bet in order to serve the appropriate dice. It was hard, fast work. But then, Cusik was a worthy opponent and it was a gratifying experience.

Cusik had started playing at eight o'clock. It was two in the morning when he walked away from the table to sign a marker for eighty thousand dollars to cover his losses. He wasn't to know that, by this time, Tony was ready to go under—that his brain and his fingers had had about as much as they could take. The hundred-dollar bill Cusik threw across the felt for the dealer proved he didn't suspect a thing. For Tony it had been another memorable, mute page in the manual of his career as a mechanic.

Valentine waited anxiously in his office. When Tony sank down onto a chair, he realized just how tired he was. He pointed to a crystal whiskey decanter. "I can do with a drink."

"Sure." Valentine poured it out. "Something in it?"

"No, thanks." Tony downed the whiskey. The fire in his veins revived him a little. He sat with his eyes closed for a minute. He opened them and cleared his throat "Cusik's straight," he said. "He's one solid craps player."

"You're absolutely certain?"

"No question. He's the finest dice player I ever come up against, bar none. Got a tremendous feel for the game. The guy has a brain like a calculating machine. He uses a system of points betting that can blow your mind, and he don't make a bum move the whole night. I never met an evens-chance player before. Not one who knows enough to quit when he's ahead. Add to that the weight of his money and no betting limit, and you got a lethal combination. You can see why you been having problems, right?"

"And, with all his clever play, it took him all night to lose eighty grand . . ." Valentine rubbed his hands. "Looks as if things are improving." Tony stared in disbelief. He'd just explained, and the prick didn't understand a thing he'd said. Valentine sat down. "That's great—just great," he went on expansively. "Now we know where we stand. That's a big problem eliminated, thanks to you. All we have to do now is work out a plan to bury the jerk . . ."

"What the fuck you think I been doing all night long?" Tony burst out in exasperation.

Valentine stared across. "No—it couldn't be. I watched every move you made for six hours. Cusik was just unlucky tonight—." But now he was unsure.

"What's luck got to do with it, for Chrissakes?"

Valentine had gone perceptibly whiter. "You telling me you already made some moves?"

Tony stopped the retort in his throat. He took a moment to compose himself. "I been reeling Cusik in slowly since I got the hang of his action," he said levelly, "which was about five and three-quarter hours ago—give or take."

Valentine's reply was unexpected. "That wasn't the plan. You were told to wait till Lombardo gave you the word."

"It wasn't necessary. I knew what I had to do. And there's something else I gotta tell you—the guy was in great form. I saved you maybe a hundred grand out there tonight. With his losses, you're a hundred and eighty grand in front."

"You should have waited for Lombardo. What if you were wrong? What if you'd made a mistake and Cusik was cheating?"

The guy was crazy. "I don't make that kinda mistake, Mr. Valentine. I can't afford to."

"Don't you realize?" Valentine's voice rose as the implications of Tony's actions penetrated. "You could have started a mob war that would have set New York on fire."

Tony stared back coolly. He took his time replying. "Dice is my business," he said carefully. "If you ask Lombardo, he'll tell you. I just don't make mistakes."

CHAPTER THIRTEEN

He closed the door softly behind him and stood for a moment until his eyes were accustomed to the gloom. The edges of the closely drawn shades showed it was bright daylight outside, but little of it penetrated the darkened room. He looked across at the silent form on the bed, completely enveloped in a blanket. A pillow covered the telephone. "Hey, old buddy, how you feeling today?" he said quietly.

The blanket moved. "I'm O.K., Tony," Skeeter said.

"Rita tells me you went out this morning."

"I was at the zoo."

"Talk to your friends over there? The lions and the tigers?"

"Uhuh."

It had been a slow, patient haul, getting Skeeter back into shape. His physical strength had returned, but he'd remained uncommunicative. The break came one day when they took him to the zoo. Tony drew Rita back when they found him in a quiet corner, talking to the animals. After that, step by step, they'd been guiding him back to normality. Now something had gone wrong, and he was back to hiding under the bedclothes. "Something wrong, Skeets?"

"I got a bad feeling."

"What about?"

"There's a new keeper over there. The animals don't like him."

"Now, how d' you know a thing like that?"

"They told me."

Tony was silent a moment. "Maybe things'll change, once he's settled in."

"He don't like animals."

"You ain't gonna tell me a guy don't like animals becomes a keeper at the zoo?"

Skeeter thought about it. "They depend on the keeper."

"Well, them other keepers, they'll spot it soon enough, this guy steps out of line. Now, just stop worrying about them."

"It's not just that. I was thinking—I'm helpless, too, aren't I? Just like the animals over there."

"Why you say that, Skeets?"

"I depend on you, same way they depend on the keeper."

"I'm not your keeper, I'm your buddy."

"I wouldn't know what to do if you . . . maybe they'd lock me up. Send me to one of them places . . ."

"Nobody's gonna lock you up while I'm around. You got nothing to be afraid of."

"Tony, I got a bad feeling. I don't like it."

"What about?"

"You, me—I dunno."

"Nothing's wrong. Everything's fine and dandy."

"You sure?"

"Yeah." He dismissed Skeeter's fears. "Hey, I was gonna practice the dice for a couple hours. You wanna watch me?"

"Wow, I'll say." Skeeter scrambled out of the bed.

"I'll need some light. What you say, you get them shades?" Skeeter opened them, blinking at the bright day. Tony frowned at the drawn, blanched face revealed by the daylight. Even so, Skeeter was a thousand times the man he'd rescued from the Brooklyn hoods. "O.K., now," Tony said cheerfully. "When I'm finished practicing, I'm gonna play you a real game of craps, for money. Ten cents a shot, just like the old days."

"You kidding?" A wan smile crossed Skeeter's face. "I ain't that crazy."

"No cheating, you got my word. And I'm gonna make the game interesting for you. If you beat me out of one whole dollar, I'll send up one of them Polly Adler broads tonight. You know, sorta put some color in your cheeks."

Skeeter's expression became rigid. "Maybe she won't like me," he said.

"She ain't getting paid to like you. She's getting paid to screw you," Tony said.

"I don't think Rita would like that, if she got to know," Skeeter said quickly. His eyes were wide with fear, and evasive.

He thought better of it. "Yeah, maybe you're right. Another time, O.K.?"

"Sure, another time."

He was walking briskly along Park Avenue toward Miranda's when the two guys closed in on him, one on either side. "Mr. Lombardo wants to talk to you," one of them muttered.

"Lombardo knows where I am. Why don't he get me at the club? What's the idea picking me up in the street?"

"He said to grab you before you get to Miranda's. We went to your place, but we missed you."

He had serious doubts. He didn't recognize either of the toughs who were guiding him to the curb, one on each arm. He didn't get much time to think about it. A car stopped in front, the door was opened, and he found himself inside. The car was rolling before he'd sat down. Sitting between them, he said, "How do I know you're from Lombardo?"

He'd asked the question a little late. They grinned at each other. "You don't," one of them said.

But they were. The trip to Central Park West took only a few minutes. He recognized the building; it was next door to the one where Jack Shelley lived. He was led up to Lombardo's splendrous apartment. He walked across the dense rugs, so thick the pile stood up stiff and hardly gave under his footsteps. The walls were adorned with oil paintings, each lit by an individual strip light behind a gilt cover.

"You like my paintings?" Lombardo had come into the room behind him. "They're all originals. That one's a Cézanne. The one next to it's a Gauguin."

"Gee, that so?" Tony glanced at them again. The names didn't mean much to him, except that they sounded foreign and expensive. A guy had to have real dough

180

to afford extras like that. He turned. "What's the trouble?" he said.

"Why do you presume there's trouble?" Lombardo's eyes bored suddenly into his.

"You don't send them two guys out to pick me up off the street for nothing. Not when you know where to find me eight, ten hours, six nights a week."

"Yes, you're right." The heat went out of Lombardo's gaze. "Fact is, you have to leave town. Drop out of sight. Cusik found out that Valentine brought in a mechanic. We worked out that someone at the Acapulco has a grudge against Valentine and told Cusik, or maybe even Schwarz, about you. Now Schwarz's mob is out looking for Valentine, and he's out of town until the situation cools. You better go, too, for your own sake. You understand?" Tony remained silent. "This is for you." He held out a fat envelope. "There's ten grand in there. Get in touch with me in a couple of months and I'll tell you the position."

He ignored the envelope. "There's something wrong here," he said.

"What do you mean?"

"Nobody in Valentine's place knew me, except him. Not unless he told someone after I left."

"He says he didn't. I find that hard to swallow."

"I believe him. Valentine's too close-mouthed. It wasn't in his own interests to talk, and he knows I got strong views on that. There's nobody around that joint he's so close to anyhow—that's the feeling I got."

"So you think it might have been someone from Miranda's?"

"Not possible. Nobody else at Miranda's knows I'm a mechanic," Tony said.

"After all these months? There has to be someone who's spotted you."

"Nobody. Except Miranda himself, of course. In fact, there's only one guy besides yourself and a couple of personal friends in the whole of New York knows what I do. And that guy didn't know I was out in New Jersey."

"Who's that?"

"A guy named Jack Shelley—he's a neighbor of yours."

"I know Jack well. Forget it, he's a hundred-percent stand-up guy."

"That's what I was afraid of," Tony said slowly.

"What you mean?" Lombardo's piercing look had returned.

"You better take a closer look at your business partner."

"Miranda." The word hissed from Lombardo's lips. "That fucking asshole."

"I hope I'm wrong," Tony said grimly.

"It would clear up a few mysteries." The power had come into Lombardo's face, and Tony didn't care much for what he saw there.

He reached out and picked up the envelope. "So long, Mr. Lombardo," he said.

When he reached the door, Lombardo called him. "Where will you be?" he said.

"California," Tony said immediately. "Taking the sun."

The West Coast was as far from Steubenville as anywhere he could think of at a moment's notice. He wasn't about to tell Lombardo he was thinking of going home. He'd had enough of the machinations of New Yorkers, for a while. If they wanted him, they'd have to look real hard.

CHAPTER FOURTEEN

The thought nagged at him and the Duke's words echoed in his brain. "Touch base." It was time. He had one small regret—Rita. He'd been deliberately playing it cool with her for some time now. There was no place for a permanent attachment in the life of a dice mechanic. He took Skeeter and headed for home.

There was something else he'd learned: caution. They got off the train at Pittsburgh, leaving an hour's run into town by car. Mokey was waiting for them, bigger, more disproportionate and apelike than Tony remembered him. He came rushing along the platform to embrace them both in an excess of exuberance. They collected their bags and found a coffee shop, to wait for darkness.

"The old folks, they're ready to flip," Mokey grinned at his brother. "How long's it been now?"

"Nearly three years," Tony said.

"You changed, you know that? You changed a lot. Boy, you sure look swell." He fingered the lapel of Tony's vicuna overcoat. "I bet the duds set you back a few bucks."

"You spoke to the Duke?"

"Yes, he's expecting you. And I been keeping my eyes peeled, like you said. Been nobody hanging around near the house that I could see." He was eyeing Skeeter as he talked. "Hey, Skeets, you been starving yourself? You're sure looking thin."

"He's been sick," Tony said. "He's just getting over it."

"You need some of your ma's home cooking to set you up," Mokey said to Skeeter.

"He's looking forward to it. When you've dropped me off, I want you to take him straight home to his ma. She's expecting him. I wrote her a letter."

"Sure, Tony."

"Another few minutes and we'll get going." He looked out the window. "It'll be dark, the time we hit Steubenville. What car you get, Mokey?"

"I bought a Ford. That Caplan, he's got a special deal on Fords right now—he gave me a good price. Leaves three hundred bucks from the money you sent."

"Keep it. And you can use the car when I'm not around. Just remember to take Mama and Papa out for a trip sometimes."

"Gee, thanks, Tony, I'll remember." He was bursting to ask a question. "Say, in New York, it really like on the movies—all them beautiful broads and all that?"

"Oh, sure," Tony said. "The girls are wild. In New York it's the broads who proposition the guys, you know that?"

"You don't say?" Mokey's eyes popped.

"Yeah, it's murder. A guy ain't safe on the streets."

Mokey licked his lips. "I always knew we was behind the times out here."

182

Tony looked out the window again at the fading light. "Oh, shit, I can't hang around here any longer," he said. "Let's get moving."

It seemed to him as if the town had shrunk. As they rode through the emptying evening streets, he found everything about the place he thought he knew so well to be diminutive, dusty, and insignificant. It was an anticlimax after the roar of Manhattan and the elegance of Park Avenue.

When he stepped from the car he could smell Mama's cooking. They were waiting for him inside, Bruno and Maria, standing guard at a table that groaned under a mountain of food. There were a dozen varieties of pasta, and the table held every delicacy he liked, every taste for which he'd ever expressed a preference. When his parents had wept their tears of joy at his homecoming, the celebration feast got under way. For his parents it was an important occasion and, with many toasts, they made it last most of the evening. Much later, satiated with food and Chianti, he sat alone with his father. Bruno reached out for a long, fat cigar from the box of Monte Christos Tony had brought him. He lit it and, wreathed in smoke, his features proudly, if atypically, reflected his son's prosperity. "And now, Antonio, your mama and me, we been dying to ask the question. Are you home to stay?"

"No, Papa." Tony gave a small laugh. "I guess I've outgrown this town. I won't be going back to New York neither. There's a big, wide world out there, and I aim to get my fill of it."

"Where you going next?"

He hesitated. "I don't know yet. First I gotta talk to the Duke."

"That old man, you always taking his advice." There was a hint of resentment in Bruno's voice, an envy that another had usurped his authority. He bit his tongue, knowing there was nothing he could do for Tony himself.

"You can see for yourself, Papa, I ain't short of anything, listening to the Duke."

"I hear some funny things about that man. You know what it is in a barber shop, people's tongues wag."

"Take no notice. He's never been anything but a friend to me, even when I was working in The Club. You know that."

"I only wish it was something else, not gambling. Your mama, she so proud of her elder son . . ."

"I got a pretty good way of life. I can go just about any place I choose and pick up a living. Ain't many guys can say that."

"Sure, is a wonderful thing." Bruno was nodding, happy to have made the point without dispute. "It's just that—he's sorta mysterious, the Duke."

"Forget it, Papa. A guy can go crazy listening to them rumors."

"I got another question. Your mama, she was asking, is there anyone . . . I mean, you maybe gonna marry and settle down soon?" He looked apologetic. "It's no question for one man to ask another. I think Mama aches to hold a bambino in her arms again. You know what Italian women are—she worried that she got two big sons and no sign yet of grandchildren." He finished lamely, but the question was still in his eyes.

"No, Papa. There's no one. I got a long way to go yet. If I was tied to a family I wouldn't feel free to go where the action is—to learn what I gotta learn. I gotta be free to move off in case something . . ." He stopped.

"Yes, son?" Bruno had stopped puffing on the cigar and was watching him closely.

"Aw, forget it, Papa." He grinned. "I ain't ready to give up my freedom and miss out on all them beautiful broads." When Bruno had resumed puffing, he said, "So how's things over at the barber shop these days?"

"Same as ever," Bruno said.

"You, ah, see Francesca these days?"

"Not much. She married now—gone to live in Cleveland."

"Yeah, Mokey told me."

"She got fat." Bruno grinned at him. "Two bambinos, one after the other. Now I hear Vincenzo talking, I think she's expecting the third."

"Jes-us Christ, three kids." How the years had gone by. They might have been his children if things had been different. He tried to imagine himself the father of three children, and gave up. "And Angelo? You hear of him, Papa?"

"Oh, sure, all the time. In the barber shop we got pictures of him on the walls. He's a singer with a big band now—excuse me, I can never remember the name."

"That's O.K., Papa."

"Vincenzo say Angelo been offered a part in a Hollywood movie."

"With that nose?" Tony said disbelievingly.

"Ha, you never recognize him. A few months back he come in the shop and I think he's a stranger. He have the nose rebuilt by a doctor. They say they take the skin from here . . ." He patted his butt. "And they make patches."

"Yeah, I heard about that. Skin grafts. I don't think it's the same thing."

"You just can't see a thing. Not a damn thing, I'm telling you."

Tony shook his head in amusement. He said, when he'd stopped smiling, "And you, Papa—you still working them long hours?"

"Nothing's changed." Bruno looked at his son. "Barberin's easy, and I'm doing the work I like. Not the same as the Mill. Lots a guys in town, they still work at the Mill. For them life stand still."

"I'm gonna make sure it don't stand still for you, Papa." He got up and walked over to his coat. From an inner pocket he took the envelope Lombardo had given him. He handed it to his father and sat down again.

"What's this?"

"Open it."

Bruno's eyes opened wide at the sight of the money, and Tony didn't miss the tremor in his hands. "Must be a fortune here—I never see so much money in all my life," Bruno got out. "Antonio, tell me the truth—you not been doing something wrong to get all this money?"

"No, Papa." he laughed. "I ain't done nothing wrong, honest. A guy I worked for, he gave it to me. A sort of going-away present."

"How much is here?"

"Ten thousand dollars."

"In New York they give away ten thousand dollars because you a good worker? You expect me to believe that?"

Bruno was badly worried, so Tony spoke seriously. "Gambling's not like any

184

other job. I did the guy a favor. Because of me he saved a lot of money." Bruno searched his son's face. "It's O.K., Papa, believe me," he went on quietly. "Anyhow, what I was gonna say, the money—it's yours. It's for you."

"For me?" It didn't register with Bruno.

"Yes. I want you to open your own barber shop."

"I can't take your money, Antonio." He shoved it back.

"I want you to take it. I don't need it. I ain't never short of dough, Papa. I get all the money I need."

Bruno found his voice again. "Is impossible. Look, my son is rich—and I should be the one to take his money? Never . . ."

"Papa, ten grand ain't so much." He was making no impression, so he tried a different method. "Listen, what I'm saying, it's like I'm making an investment. We start a family business. We get our roots down, you understand? Maybe we get Mokey to train as a barber instead of screwing around like a punk. It's for all of us. Listen, if you don't take the dough off me, I'll only blow it. Don't you see, you'll be doing me a favor?"

Disbelief ran across Bruno's face. "Our own barber shop?"

"Sure. You gotta do it—you wanted it all your life. I'm depending on you, Papa. I'm depending on you to look after my investment."

His father was on his feet. "But, what will Vincenzo Boccardi say, I open my own shop?"

"What you care?"

"All my regular customers, they'll come to me—I know they will."

"Sure. You the best barber in town. It's you they come to for the haircut, not Boccardi."

"It'll ruin his business."

"You think he worries about you? He'll survive, don't let it bother you. Hey, listen, I got a better idea—why don't you offer to buy him out?"

"Me—buy out Vincenzo Boccardi?"

"Sure. Ain't no way that shop's worth ten grand. You'll have money to spare if you can talk him into selling."

"Antonio, am I dreaming?"

He laughed. "No, you ain't dreaming, Papa. Here, give me the dough . . ." He took the envelope from his father's hand and walked across to the table, still loaded with untouched platters of food. He took the bills from the envelope, fanned them out in his hand, then scattered them at random across the food. He called out to the kitchen: "Hey, Mama, come and see, your old man's rich. He's throwing money all over like a crazy man . . ."

When Maria came in from the kitchen, she stopped with a gasp, startled by the sight of the money. Tony walked around the table, took her by the waist, then did the same to his father, using the other arm. Slowly he started to dance around the table. Soon his parents caught on and joined in.

Maria didn't understand yet, but she knew it was a joyous family occasion, and it had to do with the fortune in money lying in the food and everywhere. Money meant security. And there was a look on Bruno's face she hadn't seen since he was a young man, the handsomest of young men, conscientious and industrious, clever with his hands, back in those days, back on the overheated, poverty-ridden streets of Salerno.

Her heart filled to overflowing, and she danced to celebrate the happiness of her beloved husband and her eldest son.

He got Mokey to drive him around the block a couple of times before stopping at the entrance. At one o'clock in the morning there were few people on the streets of this working town, and nobody strange appeared to be hanging around outside The Club. He'd already spoken to the Duke on the telephone, and he was expected, so there would be no surprises inside. The back door had been left open. He slipped through and flicked the bolt across behind him. The Duke was waiting for him in his office with a bottle of whiskey and two glasses. Tony was pleasantly surprised when the Duke embraced him. "Now we must have a drink," the Duke said, "a little ceremony." He was flattered that the Duke was treating him as an equal. He'd never thought of himself as his mentor's equal. The Duke lifted the glass. "To that rare accomplishment—the skill of a master mechanic," he said.

"And to the guy who made it possible," Tony said in return. They drank, and sat down.

"I have an apology to make," the Duke said.

"What for?"

"Miranda. It was a mistake. I wouldn't have exposed you to that danger if I'd known."

"Nobody knew. He seemed to be a stand-up guy, but he turned out to be a two-faced rat. Lombardo was entitled to get cut up about it." The Duke nodded. "What I don't like—this Schwarz character has guys out looking for me."

"That'll fade. You have to lie low for a while, until this blows over. Things are brewing there, in New York. Soon Schwarz will have bigger problems on his hands, bigger than finding a dice mechanic."

"Miranda blew my cover."

"It's not as bad as it looks. From what Lombardo tells me, only Cusik would recognize you. The people who work at the Acapulco don't know nothing about it. I'd make a guess that Cusik is too proud of his reputation as a dice player to broadcast that he got took by a mechanic. And Schwarz's hoods are working on description only—they don't know what happened."

"How you know all this?" Tony asked curiously.

"Lombardo has a friend on the other side."

"That still leaves Miranda, the asshole."

"Miranda won't be troubling nobody. He fell down an elevator shaft," the Duke said quietly.

Tony stared at him. The Duke's gray eyes were expressionless. "I think I need another drink," Tony said.

The Duke asked a lot of questions. He wanted to know about the New York gambling scene and seemed to enjoy hearing about the political chicanery that was the lifeblood of Miranda's. Tony described the Court Street game, and Skeeter's predicament, and was surprised at the Duke's concern that he had got into the action over in Brooklyn. "I told you never to get into a game like that. You don't have to prove anything, you know you can win—and what those jerks think doesn't matter a

186

damn. You must confine your talents to the right place at the right time. The hoods in those traps will burn you just because you're winning—nothing to do with making moves. They'll do it to any sucker thinks he can take their dough. They're just looking for trouble."

"My buddy was in a jam," Tony said.

"So you thought you'd teach those people a lesson? You fool—they'd have broken your back soon as look at you. You should have paid up and got out."

"The bastards got under my skin," Tony protested. "I'm only human."

"Not where the dice are concerned," the Duke came back sharply. "We both know it don't go like that. You're a machine—act not react. It's the only way if you want to survive."

The Duke was right, and he knew it. "I gotta have a little excitement now and then." He grinned ruefully.

"That's like teasing a hungry lion. Leave the excitement for the players—they're paying for it. If you want excitement, get it somewhere away from the felt. In bed—anywhere, but not at the table."

It was late. The excess of food and drink had become toxic in his stomach, and his head was beginning to feel thick. He got to his feet. "What do I do now? I don't aim to hang around Steubenville making myself a target for Schwarz's mob."

"You'll have to move on somewhere and lay low for a while."

"Question is, where?"

"Well, you don't want some two-bit hideaway, so I have a suggestion to make. I know of an interesting place. Somewhere you can move around freely."

"Sounds good."

"Cuba."

"You kidding—ain't that out in the Pacific somewhere?"

"No, it's hardly a hundred miles off the Florida Keys. There's a regular ferry service, it's that near."

"So what's special about Cuba?"

"It's a nice place to be. Tropical climate and plenty of tourists. But here's the interesting part: it's opening up for gambling in a big way. And Lombardo has friends out there."

He thought about it. "I don't wanna get locked into some fly-blown sandpit out in the middle of the ocean. I had enough of sawdust joints, too, for a while . . ."

"You're making a mistake. There's a lot of investment going into Cuba, to make the place a luxury resort. Big hotels and casinos are being built on the island."

"Carpet joints?" Tony queried. These days he was getting particular.

"Best you ever saw."

"Sounds like Cuba's just my style." He grinned.

187

CHAPTER FIFTEEN

The Cuba-bound Key West–Havana ferry, four hours from land to the north and the south, steamed purposefully on across the Florida Strait. A balmy breeze, warmed on its journey across the Gulf of Mexico, blew gently out of a clear, dry sky on the ship's starboard beam. To the east, as if totally unrelated to the pleasant weather on the other side of the Floridian promontory, a single, massive hammerhead cloud, silent, black and threatening, reached up for the stratosphere against a maritime backdrop of bright blue over the Atlantic. It was like being between two worlds.

"You're looking good, Skeets," Tony said.

"I'm feeling fine."

They sat on deck sunning themselves. The sea air had brought color back into Skeeter's cheeks and, for a change, the haunted look was gone from his eyes. "Yeah, you're gonna be a different guy, once we get settled down over at Cuba."

Skeeter said it for the tenth time: "You sure I'll make it as a crap dealer?"

"You can't miss," Tony said. "You been playing craps since we was kids, ain't you? You forgetting the game we used to operate down at The Meanspot? Boy, we sure made the corner of Sixth and Market hum, them days."

"Them was the days."

"You got a good head for figures and you know the game inside out, all the odds and all. I'm gonna train you myself how to operate on the felt. When I'm finished with you, you gonna be one of the best stickmen around. It's guaranteed."

Skeeter looked doubtful. "Maybe, when I get out there on my own I'll . . ."

"Listen, I'm gonna be right there with you. You'll be working the same place as me, the same shifts, all the time. No problem."

"I still ain't got the hang of that law-of-probabilities deal," he said anxiously.

"I told you before, you don't need to know all that. There's dealers working all over who don't understand that side of it. You're not aiming to be a mechanic, like me. That'd be different. All you'll have to do is service the table—see the players toe the line, and pay the winners. It'll all come natural, after a while."

"Maybe the house won't wanna employ an inexperienced guy like me—someone with my problems."

"Don't worry about that. They'll do as I say. If they don't want you, they don't get me. Any case, I got other ideas."

"What ideas?"

"I'm thinking of my own joint. Gambling's legal in Cuba. It's not like in the States where you need juice with local politicians and the police."

"That sounds great."

"First we gotta get the hang of the place."

"Didn't you say the Duke gave you an introduction?"

"Yeah, I got a job to go to at the Internacionale Hotel Casino if I want. I'm told it's quite a joint, best in Cuba. But I ain't in no hurry. I had it with them connected joints."

"So, where do we start?"

"We start right here, by relaxing. Boy, this is the life, ain't it? Know something, Skeets? I'd like to take a world cruise, on one of them big luxury liners. You know, spend six months doing nothing. Just cruising around, place to place."

"You gotta be rich to live like that."

"Nah—I could afford it right now."

Skeeter looked across. "So what's stopping you, if it's what you want?"

Tony closed his eyes and became limp. "I'm too busy," he said.

From the moment he set foot on the island, he was seduced by its charms, captivated by its superb climate, its palm trees, its beautiful girls. A quick run around Havana and he was dragging Skeeter off on sightseeing trips clear across the country. They visited Mantanzas and Gamaguay, traveling the main road the length of the island to Bayamo. There they stood on a hilltop outside town late one evening watching the lush magnificence of the Sierra Maestra mountains sink into the black pools of its night valleys. From there they took the rickety train, packed with sultry, smelly, chattering locals, down to the bay city of Guantanamo, from where they could look south, out over the clear blue waters of the Caribbean.

He liked the friendly, open, dirt-poor Cubanos, always curious about the two rich gringos in their midst, always willing and polite. He was appalled by the widespread poverty of the peasants, subsisting in shacks in the fields, hacking tall sugar cane the long day for a peso, or less; enduring their penury resignedly under the baleful eyes of the ever-watchful police. As time passed, he became distantly aware of the unseen but omnipresent Batista forces, barracked secretively at vantage points across the nation, ready to silence the slightest murmur of complaint; quell, with a jackboot, the first sign of an uprising. The army was a tool of Fulgencio Batista, the true sovereign master of a subject people, while a puppet President Frederico Bru, seventh in a succession of figurehead leaders since Batista's ascendancy in 1933, served the role of politico that Batista scorned.

Here and there, as they traveled the land, they caught glimpses of the other side of Cuban society. Heavily staffed, secluded haciendas peeped out of the lush foliage: landowner fortresses—the estates of those who'd long held sway over the wealth of the country, and would continue to do so, as long as their man, Batista, remained in power.

In Havana itself, they found the least contrast between rich and poor. The city held a cosmopolitan cross-section of people from different origins, catering to the multifarious trades of a busy metropolis. Prominent among these trades was tourism, for which Havana provided like no other recreational resort. The strictures of puritanical Roman Catholicism failed to confine excesses in this hungry society. Gambling was openly available everywhere. As was sex in all its varieties and forms, perversions and disciplines, and in such profusion that Havana had deservedly earned for itself the title: LIVE SEX CAPITAL OF THE WORLD. The Prado, and structural splendors like the Internacionale, contrasted with a seedier Havana where a variety of entertainments was offered from dirt-floor enclosures. These ranged from bestiality, through cockfights, to live sexshows, featuring as many as six women; or Superman, a huge Cuban boasting the biggest organ in the world, who gave a live performance at half-hourly intervals throughout the day. If that wasn't sufficient, brothels were provided for personal participation on every street in this area.

The spacious, high-roomed, rococo suite at the Sevilla Grande must have been among the best in town, all marble and onyx. "What we doing in a classy joint like this?" Skeeter asked.

"I'm finished with them dives, with the bugs and the roaches. We go first class from now on, you and me. Don't you like the place?"

"Sure I like it. But we ain't royalty, you know."

"I can hack it."

"You gonna be working at that casino, the Internacionale?"

"I didn't make up my mind yet."

"Looks like the best joint around."

"I don't mean that. Like I said before, maybe we can get a joint of our own together, here in Havana."

"Gee, that'd be something, wouldn't it?"

"You saw all them tourists in town. We'd clean up."

"You sure it's legal here?"

"That's what I hear."

"Won't it cost a lot of dough, setting up a joint and all?"

"I got eight, nine grand left over—enough to set up a decent crap game."

Skeeter rubbed his hands together. "When do we start?"

"Tomorrow we go looking for a place." Tony threw off his shirt. "What you say we take a bath and then go down to dinner in the restaurant?"

"Do we have to?" The frightened look returned to Skeeter's eyes. His bravado was short-lived. In each hotel where they'd stayed, Tony had ordered their meals in their rooms. It was time to break Skeeter in.

"Yeah. You have to get used to having people around."

"All right." He paused, delaying the moment. I'll have my bath when you're finished."

"You got another bathroom in there," Tony said.

"No point in getting both of them dirty."

"Don't let it bother you."

They ate a leisurely dinner in the fashionable, busy restaurant, enjoying the orchestra and the attentions of a multitude of waiters. By the time they'd eaten, Skeeter had accustomed himself to the bustle and was even beginning to take an active interest in what was happening around him.

They'd been sitting there long enough. "What you say we take in one of them sex shows downtown?" Tony said. He watched for Skeeter's reaction, which was uncertain. "Yeah, I think we'll do that," Tony said firmly. "Let's go back to the room—I want to change into some slacks."

They were walking along the lofty hotel corridor when Skeeter said suddenly, "Hey, Tony, how come the door's open?"

"Our door?"

"Yeah. I remember closing it. I got the key in my pocket—here it is."

They walked faster. Now they could both see clearly that the door to the suite yawned wide open. When they got inside, it was immediately obvious that their belongings had been ransacked. Tony rushed across to a wardrobe and dragged out a small suitcase. He stared at the empty interior in disgust before kicking the case across the room. "We got took for the dough," he said angrily.

Skeeter sat down on the bed. "What do we do now?"

"I dunno. I'm tapped out, I guess." He sat down on the bed next to Skeeter.

For a while they both stared into space.

Finally, Tony said, "O.K., if that's the way it's gonna be, we go back to square one and start all over again."

CHAPTER SIXTEEN

They walked dejectedly in the hot midday sun. Cuba could be a pleasant place, relaxing in the shade with a cool drink. Walking the streets at noon in 102 degrees, with the sweat running down their faces, was the flip side. "Where we walking to?" Skeeter asked damply, after a while.

"Just walking. I think better when I walk," Tony said. He needed a plan. The mothers who'd stolen his money had precipitated a condition he'd long ago forgotten about: being broke. True, there was still the hundred-dollar bill he kept in his wallet for emergencies, and a few dollars he had in his pants pocket. Hardly enough to open a gambling house.

"Ain't much we can do here in Cuba without dough," Skeeter said. "Maybe we oughta go back."

"Can't go back."

Skeeter was silent a moment. He'd forgotten it was necessary for Tony to lay low. "There's casinos here in Havana. You don't have to be short of dough, not you, not when there's a crap game around."

"That's out," Tony said. "I don't want to show my face around a crap game in Cuba. Not yet."

"So what we gonna do?"

They'd walked as far as the Caluxto Garcia hospital. On the grounds a fete was in progress, celebrating a saint's day. They stopped to watch the joyful play of the Cuban children. A clutch of colored balloons was released and everyone's eyes rose, following the progress of the balloons on the wind. By the time they were out of sight, Skeeter noticed the smile that had come to Tony's face. "What's funny?" he said.

"The balloons remind me of the Carny," Tony said.

"So?"

191

"I was forgetting something I learned when I was with them."

"What's that?"

"How to make money from nothing. How to hustle." He paused. "Ever hear of the flimflam game?"

"No," Skeeter said.

"Well, you're gonna learn about it. Let's get back to town." He quickened his pace, and Skeeter followed.

They began scouting downtown Havana, seeking a location frequented by tourists. They found what they wanted behind the Prado, in a shabby, but well-used street market. At one end of the street the dirt-floor enclosures jostling each other reminded him of the Carny stalls. Here he found a small, vacant booth that had been used for selling lottery tickets. It was little more than an oversized wooden crate made of planking, but it would serve their purpose. The owner turned out to be the proprietor of a shoe store down the street. He spoke reasonable English, was happy to quote them twenty dollars a week, and delighted to accept fifteen. They were in business.

They went back and studied the interior of the wooden structure. A couple of shelves had been nailed to the planks forming the walls. A split counter formed the entrance and was near enough to the sidewalk to give access to passers-by. "Next thing is to get the flimflam board made up," Tony said. "That won't be no trouble. The problem is, we need some prizes." He looked thoughtful. "Or at least one good one."

"You gonna buy something?"

"I'll need the dough I got, when the board's made, to operate the game."

"So what we do?"

"We gotta have something that looks worth at least a hundred bucks."

"Don't look at me." Skeeter gave one of his rare grins. "I got nothing."

Tony mentally sorted through his belongings. "Clothes are no good. We'll have to use my leather suitcase. It's tooled cowhide and it looks new. Cost me a couple of hundred bucks in New York. We'll get some cellophane and wrap it up."

When they'd made their plans, they returned to the store owner. He quickly found them a carpenter and translated Tony's instructions for making the flimflam board into Spanish. One board was to be drilled with sixty holes, each the size of a quarter, and fitted with a wooden rail at its edge. Another board, the same size, would be fixed beneath it, making a sandwich. The locations of the holes in the upper board would be numbered on the lower so that when the two boards were fixed together, the result was sixty numbered pockets. Tony carefully marked out the numbers to go on the lower board; they appeared to be random, following no set sequence. The carpenter promised the flimflam board for the following day, and they took off in search of some large glass marbles, suitable for quarter-size pockets. They found them in a toy store. Finally, Tony bought some cardboard and some marking ink and took Skeeter back to the hotel to prepare the card that was to be the key to the whole operation.

The next afternoon the board was ready for use. They took it to the booth and positioned it on the counter. They carefully placed the cowhide suitcase, in its transparent wrapping, in a prominent position and scattered some colored ribbon around the empty shelves. Then, to be sure people would understand that the business of the booth was gambling, he threw a few dice on the counter. They settled down to wait.

By dusk, when he switched on the single bare bulb swinging above their heads on an emaciated piece of cord, they'd taken exactly two quarters from curious passers-by. "How the hell we gonna make dough with this game?" Skeeter complained. Tony had made no attempt to explain the operation to him, and he'd been waiting patiently for a practical demonstration.

"We only need a couple of suckers. Just be patient. You'll see," Tony said, unconcerned.

The evening cooled and the tourists came out, their bellies full, to patrol within strolling distance of the nearby hotels. Now the street was busier than it had been during the day. Whenever anyone came near the booth, Tony rolled dice on the counter, calling out sevens and elevens to attract their attention. Eventually a fat guy in Bermuda shorts parted from his group and came across. "Say, what's that game you're running there, buddy?" he called in a southern accent.

Tony put the dice away. "Win a cowhide suitcase for a quarter, sir—last prize today." He offered a Bakelite cup that held ten glass marbles. "All you gotta do is get twenty points."

The fat guy peered into the pockets on the board. "That all I need, twenty?"

"Yes, sir, For twenty points you win this beautiful, hand-tooled, two-hundred-dollar suitcase. Last prize of the day," he repeated.

"O.K., I'll try it." The man paid his quarter, shook the cup, and poured the marbles over the board. Four of the marbles stuck at the rail and six went into holes. Tony picked the marbles out from the pockets and looked down into the holes for the numbers. He picked up his scorecard and made a rapid calculation. "You got ten points, sir." He smiled. "You need ten more to win the two-hundred-dollar prize."

"Hit me again." The player placed another quarter on the counter.

"Next shot's fifty cents, sir," Tony said encouragingly. "And this time, if you win, you get a crisp five-dollar bill to go with your prize." He smoothed a five-dollar bill and tucked it half into his breast pocket so it stuck out temptingly. A week's rent and twenty dollars for the flimflam board had left sixty-five dollars change from his hundred-dollar bill. After that, he would have to bluff it out. The player stared at the five-dollar bill and came up with another quarter. He threw the marbles. "Four and a half points," Tony calculated from his card. "You need another five and a half to win." He took a ten-dollar bill and added it to the five poking out of his pocket.

"How much this time?" the player asked.

"One dollar," Tony said.

"O.K., I'll play." He threw again.

"Oh, that's too bad, One half-point," Tony said sympathetically. "You still need five points." He took out a twenty-dollar bill and added it to the prize money.

The fat man eyed the bills. "I get all that if I win?"

"Yes, sir. And the suitcase, too. Next shot's five bucks. Remember, all you need to win is five points." The player tried again. "Wow, just missed the ten." Tony counted up the points. "One and a half. But you got the double."

"The double?"

"That's right—yessir, I can see you know about the double. You played this game before. Now you're on double money—everything in my pocket times two, that's the deal, plus that beautiful, hand-tooled cowhide suitcase worth two hundred dollars."

"Gimme the cup."

"It's ten dollars next go. Remember, all you need is three and one-half points." The player threw again. "Gee, I never see a guy miss so often," Tony said. "That's one and a half points."

"I still need two?"

"Now you're getting the hang of it. Tell you what, sir—because you're such a sport, this time I triple all I got here in my pocket. Not times two. Times three."

"Twenty dollars to throw?"

"You got it."

"I'm quitting if I don't get the two points this throw."

"How can you miss?"

The marbles bounced across the board. Tony flipped them out of the pockets and looked at his card. He shook his head. "That's a fault. I don't remember the last time anyone got a fault. Sir, that some kinda record you're making here tonight."

"Let me see that card."

"Of course—here you are, sir, your numbers added up to forty-seven. You see where forty-seven says fault?"

"You sure you counted right?"

"Don't never make a mistake. Ain't that true, Skeeter?" He turned.

Skeeter nodded glumly. "He's always right, sir," he said.

"Next time I'm counting up myself. Next time you leave the balls in the holes, you understand?"

"My pleasure, sir." Tony offered the cup. "Next shot's a hundred dollars."

"How come it's gone up to a hundred dollars? You've been doubling—it should be forty dollars this time."

"Not after a fault."

"How about the prize money?"

"Goes down to half. A fault's a penalty."

"That's not fair," the man complained.

"I don't make the rules," Tony said. "Rules been the same a hundred years."

"I got no chance to get my money back."

"You wanna play or not?"

"I'm not satisfied here."

"I can't change the rules on a hundred-year-old game, sir. If you ain't playing, move along please, you're blocking the entrance." He called out over the man's head: "Who's next?"

The player stood uncertain, frustration on his face. "I'm not moving from this spot," he said.

Tony turned on him. "Sir, if you wanna take a tip from me, you'll go off quiet. Them Cuban police, they get rough. The jails here, they ain't very nice, with the rats and the roaches and all. They throw you in soon as look at you if a businessman

194

like me makes a complaint. They don't take kindly to foreigners causing a disturbance."

The fat man's wife, who'd stood quietly by until now, took the hint. She dragged him off, complaining, down the street.

Skeeter came up to the counter to say, "I don't understand this game. I been watching. You counted up them numbers in the pockets all wrong."

Tony gave him a stare.

One more sucker turned up before the tourists disappeared from the street for the night.

Within a week the shelves bulged with attractive prizes and a row of colored electric bulbs lit up the front of the booth. Across the interior, dollar bills were strung out on lines, like bunting. Painting the booth in gaudy colors had given it a Carny air. Of the hundreds of tourists who strolled past in the warm, pleasant evenings, there were nearly always a couple of gamblers with nothing better to do, who found their way to the flimflam board.

Nearly always—but today was the exception. Today, nobody wanted to play the flimflam game, and it irritated him that the lightweight Japanese guy in the dishcloth suit had been hanging around the booth for so long. He called out to the Jap, who came across instantly and bowed courteously. It amused Tony to return the bow. "You wanna play?" Tony offered the cup. "Old Oriental game."

"No, sir, not like ball game."

"So what you hanging around here for?"

"Waiting for dice game to start." He eyed the handful of dice scattered at random on the counter. Tony knew the look.

"You play dice?"

"Oh, yes—like dice very much."

"You need lots of money to play dice." In his thin cotton suit the guy looked like a penniless peasant.

The Oriental eyes traveled to the dice and returned. He appeared to be debating with himself. Then he said, "I have money." The wad of bills he pulled from an inner pocket made Tony start. The Jap returned the money carefully to his pocket.

The temptation was strong, and things were so quiet. "Know how craps is played, fella?" Tony said, rattling a couple of dice in his hand.

"Craps?"

"What dice game you play back home in China?"

"Me Japanese. In Japan we play numbers. Bet on spots."

"Show me," Tony said. He offered a couple of dice, and didn't miss the sparkle in the Jap's eyes when he handled the cubes. All the more because the man's expression was proverbially inscrutable. He showed Tony a simple game, each player paying his opponent for the points thrown. "It's new to me," Tony said. "I hope I don't lose. How about a dollar a spot?"

"Dollar a spot O.K. with me."

He let the Jap win. They increased the value of the spots and he let the little fellow win again. When Tony was a couple of hundred dollars down, he said, "I think you too good for me—I better stop now."

"Please, not stop. Very enjoyable game. You win soon. Your turn come—you see."

"You think so?"

"Sure. Your turn to win soon."

"O.K., you talked me into it. First we gotta increase the value of the spots—it's the only chance I got of getting my money back."

"How much?"

"Ten dollars a spot."

The Jap reflected. studying his winnings. Tony picked up the dice and went to put them away. "Yes, we play," the Jap said hastily.

Tony pitched tens and twelves, calling out "Gee" and "Wow" until he'd soaked up the Jap's bankroll, until he had it all and the man was dry. At the end the Jap didn't have enough to pay his final bet. "That's O.K., I'll take what you got," Tony said magnanimously.

"You very lucky fellow, sir."

"That's the way it goes, pal."

Then, as if the man had been charged with electricity, he stood upright, rigid. Tony stared at this new development. The fixed facial expression hadn't changed, but Tony didn't like what he saw in the man's eyes. They were alight with sudden comprehension. ". . . All my money gone."

"Don't take it so bad, buddy," Tony said cautiously.

The man turned and walked out of the booth like an automaton. On the sidewalk he stood as if uncertain what to do next. Then, with no warning. He broke into a series of blood-curdling, anguished cries that made Tony stare in disbelief at the diminutive figure. Throwing himself down, the Jap started to bang his head violently on the ground.

Tony gawped, stupefied. He couldn't believe what he was seeing. It soon became apparent that the Jap intended to break his own head. Tony rushed out from the booth and grabbed him, trying to prevent the man's head from striking the sidewalk. He seemed to possess demonic strength and, despite Tony's holding on to him desperately, still managed to get in some hard hits. The blood was gushing from the Jap's head by the time Skeeter realized the seriousness of the situation and ran out to help. Together they managed to restrain him, lifting him off the ground, and they staggered back into the booth with the struggling figure. They sat on him to keep him down. Tony yelled into his face: "You'll kill yourself, doing a crazy thing like that."

The Jap was shaking violently. His teeth chattered when he got out, "I die now."

"Don't gotta kill yourself for a few lousy bucks." Tony tried reasoning with him.

"I dishonor my village—now I must die please."

It was difficult to understand his words. "You saying it wasn't your dough?"

They got it out of him in fits and starts. "The money—the people in my village—send me here to Cuba to study sugar cane. Village need work—grow sugar cane. No study, lost money—bring dishonor to village—to Emperor. Must die now."

Trying to understand his words, they'd loosened their grip. He struggled out of their hold, reached the partition of the booth, and was smashing his head again.

196

They jumped on him. "I'll give you your money back," Tony yelled in his ear. He had to keep repeating the words before he got through to him. "O.K., now stop it. Here's your dough."

Blood spouted from a vein at the Jap's temple. He stood there, his cotton suit stained red, his eyes staring and wild, as Tony forced the money into his hand. In disbelief the Jap fingered the bills. By now Skeeter had found a cloth and was bandaging the man's head. Slowly, bill by bill, the Jap counted the money. When he'd finished, the blood was running down his nose and dripping onto the money. Carefully he returned the bills to his inner pocket. When he turned to Tony, his eyes had calmed. Without a word he bowed formally, stepped out of the booth, and marched off down the street, a trail of red spots marking his path.

Standing with the jabbering group that had collected outside the booth, Tony and Skeeter watched him walk off into the distance.

"Jes-us Christ." Skeeter shook his head. "And I thought I was crazy."

CHAPTER SEVENTEEN

He heard the squeal of brakes in the street, but thought little of it. When he saw the locals scattering away from the front of the booth, fear on their faces, he began to take notice. By then it was too late. Six policemen came crowding into the booth and began clearing out everything that wasn't nailed down. One of them picked up the flimflam board, discussed it animatedly with his partner in voluble Spanish, then proceeded methodically to smash it to pieces on the edge of the counter. Justice served, he calmly collected the pieces to remove as evidence. Tony and Skeeter, watching the proceedings with stupefaction, were grabbed by two policemen. Without explanation, they were unceremoniously bundled outside and shoved into a meat wagon. The entire contents of the booth, from the prizes to their personal belongings, were thrown in after them. Then the police piled in and the van set off, howling turgidly, through the streets of Havana.

He'd heard distantly of the notorious El Macho prison, of the unspeakable torture that routinely went on there, but he hadn't expected to see it from the inside. The rumors said it was overflowing with political prisoners, opponents of Batista. It was well known whose iron fist waited to crush whatever muted, fearful resistance the peasantry could muster. A citizen was with Batista, or against him. A liberal attitude was good for nothing but an empty laugh, an empty belly, or a bullet. The urbane sophisticates loved Batista. Almost as much as the peasants hated his soul and reviled him—as they reviled the ever-watchful army that stood guard over their desolation.

What in hell all this had to do with the flimflam game, Tony couldn't imagine. And not a soul wanted to explain.

The first night in the rank, stinking cell, they each received a hunk of stale stone bread and a bowl of black beans in some indefinable liquid, shoved silently through the bars. They were glad to sleep, huddled together on the wooden shelf that served as a bunk and was supported from the wall by two rusting chains. At least, off the ground, they escaped the vermin-ridden earth floor—now they only had to deal with the *quasasas,* the tiny, all-pervading, biting insects. The second day they were given a rotting sack to share as a blanket. At night the moans of a new prisoner, out of their vision in a nearby cell, kept them awake. Tony's complaints were ignored by the leering cretin who was their guard, and they hadn't heard a word of English spoken since their arrest. On the third day, they were prodded out of the cell and taken before a police captain. He sat facing them over his desk. His uniform was no standard issue; these days Tony knew a hand-tailored suit when he saw one, and its subtleties were out of place in the bleak surroundings. "Good morning, gentlemen," he said. "I'm Captain Maceo. I understand you wish to complain about the facilities of the prison."

It was their first intimation that the mouthful of obscenities Tony habitually let rip at their guard hadn't fallen on deaf ears. He started to storm at the captain, then checked himself. "What in hell we doing in here?" he got out.

"You have been arrested, obviously."

"For what?"

"There have been complaints against you from tourists. Robbing visitors is not an occupation we encourage, gentlemen. In Cuba, it classifies as a crime against the state. No doubt you are aware that the tourist industry is an important part of our economy."

"How about *us* being robbed?" Tony retorted. "We got cleaned out, back at the hotel. We had plenty of dough when we came to Cuba. We were forced into doing something to make a buck."

"I see. I'll tell that to the examining magistrate at your trial. When did this robbery take place, and to which police station was it reported?" He took up a pencil and looked at them.

"We didn't report the robbery to the police."

"Oh—I presume you made a report to the hotel manager? It's his duty to make out a police report."

"What's the use—here in Cuba?" He was instantly sorry he'd said that.

Maceo's eyes narrowed angrily. He dropped his pencil, "I'd advise you to hold your tongue. You come here to rob, and now you insult the Cuban people with a tissue of lies."

"We being charged or not?" Tony said forcibly.

"I haven't got around to thinking about that yet."

"Look, we got rights. How much you fixing bail for?"

Captain Maceo laughed. "This isn't the United States, my friend," he said. "Bail here is a privilege, not a right."

"Oh, yeah? That's what you say. I want a lawyer," Tony said aggressively.

"Of course. You have resources, I presume? Lawyers don't work for nothing, you know."

198

Tony stared at him. "I got money—there was six hundred dollars in my pocket when we got dragged in here."

Maceo glanced at his papers. "There's no record here of six hundred dollars among your possessions." When his head lifted, he looked at them mockingly.

"You goddamn thieving bastard . . ." Tony was about to lunge at the captain, but the two guards had him by the arms before he could reach the desk. They dragged him back so that he almost lost his balance. "How long we gonna be stuck in this hole?" he yelled.

"If you're lucky you will appear before the magistrate in six months, a year, perhaps—who knows?" Maceo was enjoying their predicament. He took out a long, thin cigar and lit it unhurriedly.

While Tony fumed, he heard the low moan that escaped from Skeeter. During their time in the prison cell, Skeeter had deteriorated badly, and now all the warning signs were back. It was Skeeter's condition that brought Tony to his senses. He'd heard of the appalling corruption that riddled the Cuban administration; it was a way of life apparently. He was playing the game with the wrong dice. Worse, he'd lost his cool. The time had come to figure a way out of their predicament. He was almost too late. "Take them back to their cell," Maceo ordered suddenly. The guards reached out for them.

"Hold it," Tony said. The guards ignored him and began shoving them out through the doorway. "Captain Maceo, there is other money," he called back into the room. "Hey, I got money."

Maceo heard. "Bring them back," he said in Spanish.

When Tony faced the captain again, he said, "We been very foolish. But what I said before, it's true, so help me. Our money was stolen and we had to find a quick way to make a few bucks. I worked the flimflam at a carnival back in the States, but I'm not very experienced. I guess I overstepped the mark a little. My friend here, he's sick—he ain't strong enough to be locked up in no prison cell."

Maceo ignored Skeeter. "Are you confessing to the crime?"

"Oh, sure," Tony said immediately. "I didn't know them Carny games was a crime here in Cuba. And there was circumstances, like I explained . . ." he added.

"I'm glad to see you've decided to cooperate." Maceo made a note.

"Captain Maceo, what's the penalty for this crime?"

Maceo shrugged. "Perhaps a year or two in prison."

"Or a fine?" Tony suggested.

"The fine would be a very large one. This is, strictly speaking, a prison offense." His dark eyes looked up.

"How much will this fine be?"

Maceo touched the tips of his fingers together and leaned back in his chair. "You can pay a large fine?" he queried.

"I can arrange it," Tony said. "How much?" The captain was silent so long he began to think he'd made a mistake. Now he had to see it through—and five grand had saved him once before. "Would five thousand dollars pay the fine?" It should be a lot of money to a Cuban policeman, and he was in no mood for bartering.

"Yes. Five thousand dollars is an excellent sum." Maceo sat forward in his chair.

In his eyes was the look of avarice Tony knew so well.

For the first time he relaxed. "Captain, I presume five thousand dollars will get us bail. I mean, I'll leave the money in your care until the case comes up, if that's O.K. with you. You pay the fine for us, seeing as maybe we won't be around."

"That can be arranged."

"Gee, I sure appreciate your help, captain." He paused. "O.K., now I have to wire someone in Steubenville for the money."

"Steubenville?"

"My hometown."

The possibility that the Duke wouldn't send the money didn't even occur to him. The money was there, like the Bank of America. He ordered it by wire. He worded the cable in such a way that the Duke could alert someone in Cuba to his predicament. Maceo had to be made to keep his end of the deal. Once the cable was gone, he knew they were safe. Extraordinary how the Duke's influence, from a small gambling house in a dusty Ohio town, could extend down to this green and brown island in the Caribbean Sea. But it did, just as it had extended to New York, of that Tony was certain. He reminded himself that, one of these days, he would have to find out more about the Duke's background.

They were put in a cell with a cement floor, two wooden benches with strawfilled mattresses, and an electric light. Half an hour later a pot of hot, incredibly sweet coffee arrived.

Room service in the joint was expensive—but it was nice to have the option.

The gates of the forbidding jail clanged shut behind them and he blinked in the warm, bright sunlit morning. He glanced at Skeeter, pale at his side, and grinned. "That's it, old buddy. All over—everything's O.K., now."

"I want to get away from here," Skeeter said.

"Right. Let's hit the road."

"What we gonna do now?"

"I'll think of something," he said, with forced cheerfulness.

They moved off. At the end of the drive leading to the prison gates, a cab stood at the curb, its engine running. As they approached, the driver got out. "Señor Vitale?" he inquired.

"Yes." Tony looked at him in surprise.

"I am send to pick you up."

"Who by?"

The driver shrugged. "All I know is, I must take you to the Internacionale Hotel."

"Beats walking."

They settled back in the passenger seat. Before the building was out of sight, innocuous and white in the morning sun, he took a last glance through the rear window. He'd made a bad mistake and it wouldn't happen again. There was no room in his life for mistakes of that sort.

When they got to the Internacionale, the big hotel was overflowing with American tourists coming and going, ebullient and confident, sure of their rights and noisily demanding their comforts from a harried staff bending over backward to be of service. The contrast with the deprivations of El Macho was ludicrous, Tony thought, as they were led to an elevator between groups of gaily dressed vacationers. He guessed that few of the hotel's pampered guests were even remotely aware of the real Cuba lurking beneath the surface of Caribbean laissez-faire—of repression, torture, and political corruption. They knew the natives were poor, and that knowledge gave them a subconscious sense of superiority. Of the excruciating, grinding poverty that was the real Cuba they knew and understood nothing. And why should they? They were here on vacation. They came to Havana for its weather, its luxury hotels, its gambling; its *ballus*, catering to every whim and sexual perversion a whorehouse could satisfy. They saw little outside Havana. They might, perhaps, make a trip to the private beach resort of Veradero, but Havana and the white sands of Veradero weren't Cuba in its entirety, and few of the tourists wandered into the underdeveloped hinterland. In remote Cienfuegos-Trinidad they could have seen the hopes of a deprived people centered on the tilling of neglected land, a road through a mangrove swamp—on sanitation, sewerage that worked effectively, an electric light, perhaps. On the first stumbling steps from illiteracy. But they were unlikely to leave the tree-lined Prado, the fashionable stores of Havana's Fifth Avenue, to visit a sugar conglomerate's *latisfundia* in Las Villas Province, where they might see a brown child dying on the soft, loamy earth, dreaming of a simple *negrito atropello* to assuage its hunger. Nor would they see, on the death of that child, the tapeworms escaping from its mouth and nose, seeking a more hospitable refuge than a cooling, decomposing, stinking carcass.

When they got to the big, cool room they were surprised to find their clothes hanging in the wardrobes and their toilet articles carefully arranged in the bathroom. Tony wondered who'd sent across to the Sevilla Grande for their belongings. "How'd this happen?" Skeeter's eyes were rounded.

Tony didn't answer. "I need a hot bath. I'm gonna just soak and soak," he said.

"I don't understand." Skeeter stood there, looking around.

The telephone rang. Tony picked it up. "Señor Vitale?" a woman's voice said. "Yes."

"When you have rested, will you please come downstairs to see me? I am Juanita Ortiz."

"Of course, Madam Ortiz," he said without question. "Where will I find you?"

"My office is in the casino." She paused, as if surprised he didn't know. "I run the gambling here. You haven't heard of me?"

"No, I'm sorry," he said. "Should I have?"

She laughed. "Perhaps. It is because of me you're here in Cuba. I asked for you."

He frowned. "I didn't know I was so famous."

"Perhaps I should explain. I asked for the best man available. They said it was you—do you understand now?"

He was silent, the thoughts racing each other through his mind. "Yes, I understand," he said eventually.

"Good. I'm looking forward to meeting you."

"I'm gonna take a bath," Tony said. "Then I'm gonna eat."

"There's no hurry. Your room is comfortable, I hope?"

"It's fine. Thanks."

"Order anything you need," she said. "Charge it to the room. The house will take care of your bills."

"Thanks," he said again. He put the phone down, went into the bathroom, and started to run the water. For a few moments he leaned across the bath, as if mesmerized, watching the big tub fill. Then he shook his head and turned to call to Skeeter: "Get a bottle of bourbon from room service, willya, old buddy? I need a stiff drink."

She was at least forty, he decided, and she just had to be the most glamorous woman in the world. What the hell was it about Cuba, he found himself thinking—he'd never seen so many beautiful women. She had the figure of a young girl, and he couldn't take his eyes off her. She was white creole, the Spanish side of her dominant in her proud, almost regal bearing. Her gleaming black hair was tied back in a chignon. Her hair couldn't gleam that way naturally. It had to be brilliantined—did women do that sort of thing to their hair? She wore black velvet to accentuate the creamy texture of her skin and, even this early in the day, plenty of jewelry to counterpoint the monotone effect of black. At her throat a pearl necklace was complemented by a large, pear-shaped, blue-white diamond. Her earrings glistened, and she wore rocks on the fingers of both hands, as if she were running out of places to hang them. It was crazy, he thought, a woman running things in this business. "You don't like the idea of working for a woman?" She was smiling at him.

"I didn't say a thing," Tony said.

"You don't have to—it's in your face."

"I guess I'm just a little surprised."

"You're not the first one. I've seen that look before."

"What did you mean, you're the one responsible for bringing me to Cuba?"

"Haven't you spoken with Lombardo?"

"Not since I left New York."

"I asked him for a top mechanic."

"It wasn't mentioned. I came over here to drift around for a while."

"I don't understand." She looked puzzled, then shrugged. "Anyhow, you're here now."

"What you want me to do?" he asked.

"I need a casino manager. Someone who knows what he's doing. Someone I can trust completely."

"You can trust me," Tony said flatly.

"I know—I was told. On special occasions I'd like you to work the crap table yourself."

"What special occasions?"

". . . Selected clients."

For a moment he looked at her. What the hell—she was only a woman. "I'll want a percentage of the take," he said. "Only on the special deals, of course."

"I was going to offer an equal cut."

He didn't blink. He'd had in mind a ten-percent commission. "Down the middle?" he said blandly.

202

"Yes—half each, after a figure off the top for expenses."

"O.K., sounds fair. You got a deal."

"Good. When can you start?"

"Anytime." He paused. "I never worked for a lady before—O.K. if I call you Madam Ortiz?"

"It will be a closer relationship than that—please call me Juanita. Your name is Tony, isn't it?"

"That's right."

She sensed he had a question. "What's bothering you, Tony?" She smiled at him.

"A woman operating a big casino like this . . . Where'd you get that kind of experience? I never hear of a woman knew enough to run a joint."

"Oh, I don't know so much about the gambling operation. That's why I need someone like you—someone I can trust completely. Cuba isn't like other places. Over here, before you can operate, you need pull with the administration. The politicians. That's where I come in. I'm a valued member of Cuban high society. And Batista is a personal friend." She smiled again at him, confidentially.

"Seems that's the key to everything around here. It ain't as different as you think," he said, reflecting on the New York politicians he'd seen at Miranda's. "How you manage so far?"

"I had a guy for some years. A very close personal friend. Things went wrong."

"What happened to the guy?"

"He lost his usefulness. Permanently," she added, still with a smile.

"You oughta keep business and pleasure apart."

"I'm not afraid of personal relationships. I'm Cuban—we Cubans are a very warm people. We find it difficult to remain detached." She stood with one hand on her hip, her body arched sensuously.

He had to shake himself mentally. He cleared his throat. "There's something you can do for me, ah, boss. I lost my dice when I got arrested. I need some replacements."

"We have plenty, All types."

"No, I need my own specials. Can you let me have a check for five hundred bucks?"

"Yes. Certainly." She went to her desk and wrote it out.

"Thanks. You can deduct it."

He got as far as the door before she said, "I suppose you've already found out, Tony—there are plenty of available women in Cuba?"

"I been too busy," he said neutrally.

"What I mean is, there's not much point in playing hard to get, is there, when a guy can go around the corner and take his pick."

He stared again. "I guess not." He closed the door carefully behind him.

When he got back to the room he took some hotel stationery from a bureau drawer. On the envelope, he wrote: The Great Lakes Gambling Novelties Company, and he added the address in Cicero. He took a sheet of hotel notepaper and wrote his name and room number on it. Nothing else. He folded the check inside the notepaper, put it in the envelope, and sealed it. Now he needed a stamp.

He leaned back, debating whether or not to return to Juanita's office. In his mind's eye he explored that enticing body. He thought of the pleasures his delectable employer could offer. But he knew better than to mix business with pleasure, even if she didn't, he decided.

He picked up the telephone and called the front desk.

CHAPTER EIGHTEEN

"You got six dealers on the take," he announced to Juanita. "Here's my winnings—I took fourteen grand from the house, playing straight. I guess your dealers stole about the same, near as I can judge. They're using every trick in the book." He slapped the money down on the table. She stared at him in amazement, and he waited for her to digest the information.

"But that's a third of the staff," she gasped.

"At least. Two of them are professional artists, stealing from customers as well as the house. One guy, I know his face from when I worked at the Acapulco, over to New Jersey. If I remember right, they threw him out of the joint. He didn't recognize me—he wasn't around long enough to get to know me, them days."

He hadn't yet formally taken up his position in the casino. Instead, he'd spent a week posing as a freewheeling tourist, playing the tables, acclimatizing himself to the action at the Internacionale, and watching the dealers. It soon became clear to him that they were reaping a harvest. The rigid control called for in an efficient casino was entirely absent. The dealers were all Americans, as they were in most Cuban houses, and the easy pickings had attracted a class of dealer Tony liked least—the one with entrepreneurial leanings. He resolved to change the entire staff as quickly as possible. In the meantime, the operation cried out for reform. "This must have cost us a fortune." Juanita sat down. "Most of the dealers were taken on by Carlos."

"Who's Carlos?"

"The man—the one I told you about, who ran things for me."

"Some friend. Was he just an idiot—or on the take?"

"I'm beginning to think all sorts of things. At first I regretted what happened to him. Not anymore." She paused. "Tony, you have to promise me you won't say anything about this. Not to anyone outside, I mean." She turned her face to him, pleading.

"My job is to report to you. Nobody else's business I know of."

"They mustn't know."

"Who's *they*?"

"The partners. We have to clean this mess up quickly and quietly. Do whatever you find necessary. I give you a completely free hand."

"O.K., I know what to do. They need some discipline out there. The house is run so loose, they got the field to themselves."

204

Her anger flared suddenly. "Throw them out. Get rid of them at once—all of them."

"I'd like to do that, except that we'd have to close down if I did it that way."

"Not for long. There are plenty of dealers in Havana looking for work. We get some of the biggest players here at the Internacionale, and the tips are the best on the island. They'll come running when word gets out."

"Sure there are dealers—throw-outs from the States. Cuba's a good hideaway when there's nowhere else to go," he said.

"What do you intend to do?"

"Get rid of the thieves first, in one hit. The rest I'll move on slowly, when the chance comes along."

"Can you handle it? We'll be short-staffed."

"Oh, sure. I'll work a table myself, and I already got one replacement. My buddy's here with me in the hotel. He's a dealer."

"All right. Do it soon."

"O.K. This time, leave it to me to choose the dealers. I got the feeling we can generate a lot of new business here if we have the right class of person working on the floor. I wish I had a couple of Steubenville guys here . . ."

"A dealer's a dealer." She dismissed the notion.

"Oh, yeah? How about the charmers?"

"The what?"

"You sure got a lot to learn about the casino business, lady." He grinned.

She grinned back. "In Cuba I don't need to know the casino business—I know politicians," she said.

He was getting rich. Incredibly, in a country where the vast mass of people was abandoned to dire poverty, he was earning more money than he'd ever dreamed possible. Among the tourists was a bigger proportion of high rollers than he'd encountered before. People seemed desperate to speculate, and money appeared to be losing its value. They were fevered with gambling and a strange excitement that was founded in the flames of the conflict threatening to engulf Europe, and possibly the world. Rumors were rife, and every day brought a new crop. The contagious fear of war spread its poison slowly, an adrenaline that impelled people to grasp at another hour of pleasure, as if it were to be their last. The gamblers had found an excuse that justified whatever drove them to extremes in their search for greater thrills, bigger risks, and heavier bets. Who knew what tomorrow held in store? Excitement was in the air. The hell with tomorrow—double the hit with a sixie from Dixie.

The Cubans who came into the casino to gamble astounded him. They had money to burn. Landowners, sugar barons, politicians—especially the politicians. Any form of government agency was a license to print money. Any favor was possible, any accommodation feasible, at a price. And while the select, affluent society of Havana junketed, the peasantry groaned under the unceasing, unchanging burden of trying to provide for the simplest necessities of life.

Juanita lived in a private apartment on the top floor of the hotel. He hadn't been up there before. He rang the bell and a woman servant opened the door. As he went in, the servant immediately let herself out, closing the door behind her. He walked up and down on the thick carpets, admiring the décor, then sat down to wait. When she appeared from the bedroom she wore a French negligee in black. With Juanita it was always black. The negligee was just transparent enough for him to make out the outline of her body. She was freshly bathed and perfumed, and again it struck him how devastatingly beautiful she was. He didn't want to stare, so he looked away, but soon his gaze returned, tantalized by what he could distinguish behind the lace—the aureoles that surrounded the nipples of her full breasts and the dark triangle of pubic hair. "So you decided to come at last?" She couldn't keep the triumph out of her smile.

"Yes. You said it was important."

"I have said it is important before, but I have had to wait until I found you in the casino. You've always managed to sidestep meeting me in private—somewhere really private."

"Nothing deliberate," he said blandly.

"Now you are lying." She pouted petulantly.

In his mind, Tony couldn't reconcile the change from hard-boiled casino operator to siren. The body was a trap—he had to keep that in the forefront of his thoughts. "Am I?" He looked directly at her. "You're a very desirable woman, Juanita. Why should I avoid you?"

"That's the question that torments me. You make me feel . . . unwanted."

"I don't intend to. I guess I'm a little preoccupied these days." He was silent a moment, then, "Got a drink up here?"

"At the bar. Help yourself."

"Something for you?"

"No, thank you."

Now he knew he was distracted. He walked across to the mirrored bar that he somehow hadn't noticed, and poured himself a stiff bourbon. He turned. "Well, Juanita, what's so important?" he asked, without expression.

"Oh, Tony, you really are impossible. You're mocking me. You know very well why I asked you up here. Why don't you admit it?"

"All right, I admit it." He downed the bourbon and placed the glass carefully on the bar. This wasn't going to be easy.

"You're a cold fish, Tony, for a young man. Someone with red blood in his veins would have had me in bed by now." When he made no reply, she walked across and stood with her body touching him so that her every fragrance filled his nostrils. "Kiss me," she said. He leaned over her and tasted the nectar of her full, moist lips. With a cry of abandon she crushed herself to him. He could feel the heat of his own body blending into the soft form beneath the negligee. Between them its substance was nonexistent, as if she wore nothing. "You want me—I know you do, I can feel it." The words escaped her in a forceful, lustful rush of pleasure, anticipating triumph.

"Oh, yes, I want you." The urge poured into his loins as she pressed herself against his rising manhood, the urge he could hardly contain.

She loosened herself from him, slipped the cord that held the negligee at the waist, and it fell open. She took his hands and placed them on her full, velvet breasts. "There. Am I not beautifully made—enough to satisfy the most demanding? Do I not arouse your desire?"

"I desire you, Juanita. God knows, I desire you." His throat was dry again, and the words came out harshly.

Now her hand had dropped and her fingers were tracing delicately the outline of the protuberance in his pants. "Come. You are ready. Come with me."

She took him by the hand and led him into the bedroom. She kicked her shoes across the room, threw off her negligee, and rolled naked onto the bed. She lay there smiling in pleasurable anticipation as he slowly undressed, her fingers stroking herself absently. All this time Tony's expression hadn't changed. When he climbed onto the bed, she reached out eagerly for him, but he avoided the embrace. Instead, he kneeled over her, and she allowed him to part her thighs so that he was kneeling between her open legs. "You are in a hurry, my little one." She reached out and stroked him playfully. Still he made no reply, but just kneeled there, looking down at her. "What are you waiting for?"

"I want you to remember this moment."

"I will remember it, lover." Still the smile.

"I'm sure you will."

She sensed the change. "What's wrong?"

"You must know how much I want to make love to you, Juanita. Look at me—look at the size of me."

"Yes, I can see. You are ready. You want me as much as I want you."

"Then you understand the effort I'm having to make to control myself."

"Why control yourself—I don't understand?" The smile had gone. "I'm waiting for you, can't you see?"

"Because I have to teach you a lesson, beautiful Juanita, once and for all. You're a very desirable lady, nobody knows it better than me. It's all I can do to stop here, but it's something I gotta do. We won't be making love—not now or ever. You see, if I got no discipline, no personal control, then I'm nothing. I told you once I don't mix business with pleasure. I meant it. Now maybe you'll believe me."

The disbelief, the realization came over her. With an outraged cry, she tried to move, to escape him. Tony pinned her down, her legs held wide apart, her body twisting in tortuous anger beneath him. "Let me go," she screamed at him.

"No. I'll let you go when you got things under control."

"You swine—bastard gringo," she hissed. She got one hand free and, quicker than him, got in a resounding slap on his face. He calmly lifted his hand and slapped her back. In an instant her anger turned to tears.

"Do you understand me now, boss?" Tony said soberly. "Business is business."

"Yes, I understand." It was little more than a whimper. "Please let me go." He got off the bed and began dressing. She covered herself with the bedclothes and, when he turned to her, the look of venom had returned to her face. "You are finished here," she spat. "Get your things and get out of this hotel. I never want to see you in my casino again."

"Don't be naïve. You know what'll happen if I leave—it'll cost you a fortune."

"I don't care. I'll find someone else."

"Someone like Carlos?"

"That's not your affair."

"Maybe not. But I'm sure your partners gonna take an interest in how much dough you lost because of slack management now that I've shown the way." She stared at him intently, her eyes open wide. "How long you think you'll last, you go back to the old ways? I had some explaining to do already to get you off the hook—I'll tell you about that sometime."

He walked out of the bedroom and out of the apartment. The servant waited patiently in the hallway outside. He motioned for her to go in. Maybe now he'd get some peace. Juanita really should learn that business and pleasure don't mix.

CHAPTER NINETEEN

"Hey, Skeets, time to get up." He walked into Skeeter's darkened bedroom and opened the shades to let the midday sun pour in. The bright daylight revealed the usual pillow over the telephone. Once Skeeter closeted himself away in his room, he switched off the outside world, and it was a habit Tony couldn't break him of. He walked across the room, flicked the pillow off the telephone, and stood over the bed. "Come on, old buddy, shake a leg."

"What time is it?" Skeeter emerged from under the bedclothes. Looking like a creature arising from hibernation, he rubbed the sleep out of his eyes.

"About one-thirty. I ordered breakfast for us—bacon, eggs, toast, and coffee, O.K.?"

"Yeah, that's fine." He got out of bed and made for the bathroom. He yelled back through the open door. "That was some shindig last night, them Germans and all. What the fuck was that all about, Tony? I was too busy to ask. They almost took over the hotel, didn't they? Five o'clock in the morning, they was still coming into the casino."

"Some kind of political rally. They had a meeting in the banquet hall early in the evening—a couple of them crazy organizations they got here. The Cuban Nazi Party and the Fascist Party, I think. Some shit like that . . ." He stood looking out the wide window at the beautiful sweep of Havana harbor, the small boats busy on their business across the calm water, the wide vees of their wakes spreading out and being consumed in undercurrents. Out in the huge bay two cruise ships rode at anchor, perfectly symmetrical forms, their sizes deceptive in the distance. One ship flew the Stars and Stripes, the other the German swastika. He studied them for a moment, trying to detect activity on board, but the ships were too far away. He let his gaze wander to the ancient walls of El Morro, the fort guarding the harbor's entrance. It stood out sharply against the crystal-clear background of deep blue. It was all so calm and restful, from up here. He turned back into the room. "We took

208

in plenty of dough last night—plenty. Don't remember the last time we had so many high rollers in the joint all at once."

"Seemed like most of the socialites in Havana were in the place."

"Yeah, plenty of them politicians. That guy Benitez was there—the one made all the money selling fake immigration visas to German refugees. You remember—when the refugees got to Cuba, they weren't allowed in."

"He still around? How'd he get away with a thing like that?"

"How? He was licensed. The guy was Director of Immigration for the Cuban government."

"You saying it was the government sold them fake visas?"

"No, it was Benitez set up his own private bureau, charging the Jews five hundred bucks a head. The visas weren't worth the paper they were written on."

"And the Cuban government stood for it?"

"His story was they had a change in government policy, that they might be offending the Germans by taking in refugees. He said it happened to be legal because the visas were sold outside Cuba and didn't break any Cuban laws. It was up to the Germans to prosecute if they thought they had a case—he knew damn well the Germans didn't intend protecting no Jews."

"Even that ain't right. I hear they were selling them visas here."

"Sure they were. Who is the government anyway? President Bru? He's hiding out at Parrada, his country estate, because he maybe put a foot wrong with Batista. Any case, Benitez is a pal of Batista's, the way I hear it. He'd have to be to pick up a good number like Director of Immigration."

The sound of running water drowned out Skeeter's reply. There was a knock at the door, and Tony opened it to admit a couple of waiters with breakfast. When they'd gone, Tony sat down to eat. Skeeter emerged from the bathroom, wiping his hands. He threw the towel over the back of a chair and sat down. "Didn't you hear what I said?"

"No." Tony looked over the top of his Miami *Herald*. "What was that?"

"I said Juanita's probably one of them."

"One of what?"

"The Fascistas—she seems to be pretty close with all them local politicians."

"Nah, she's just a regular fuck for one or two top names in the government. She more or less told me so. I even get the idea she's been given a screwin' by old man Batista himself. She's certainly connected—but you can take it from me, politics' the last thing she's interested in."

"Seems you gotta be connected to survive here."

"Yeah, you don't know people here, you dead." He chewed for a minute. "I'm making a few connections myself these days," he said. "The Batistanos already think I'm one of them."

"You're not interested in politics, are you?" Skeeter gave him a sharp look.

"Me? I don't give two shits, except maybe for the Vitale party." He laughed. "The only people with juice around here are the Batistanos. Any move I make on casino business, I gotta grease the palm of a Batistano. They hold all the aces."

"Who's that guy I see around you a lot lately—the one with the silk suits and plenty of dough to burn?"

"Bernardo?"

"Yeah, that's him."

"You never believe me if I tell you."

"Try me."

"That's Bernardo Garcia. He's chief of police."

Skeeter stared at him. "He don't look the type. The police are assholes. Torturers and sadists. Everyone knows that—they use violence to keep control."

"Sure, in the police stations and the prisons. The Cuban's worst enemy is his own class. Bernardo's appointment is political. He's a playboy by vocation. If he stood in the street and tried to direct traffic, he'd get killed—that's how good a policeman he is."

"A handy guy to know," Skeeter suggested.

"You can say that again. I started collecting people who matter around here. Seems the only way to get ahead."

Tony took a last bite of toast. Still munching, he got to his feet. "I'm going down to the casino to check the balance on one of them roulette wheels. I got my suspicions there's too many numbers coming up in sequence. If the wheel is straight, I'm gonna be keeping a close watch on a certain dealer tonight. After I check out the wheel, I'll be practicing the dice for an hour in my room. You want me, I'll be there."

"O.K.," Skeeter said. When Tony had gone, he walked across the room to the open window. Just for a moment, his hand went up to the shade to close out the light. But his attention was taken by the beauty of the day and the sun over the bay. He left the shade open and returned to the breakfast table and sat down with the newspaper Tony had been reading. At his side was the latest in radio receivers, brought back from their last trip to the mainland. He flipped it on. The set was tuned to Miami.

Absently, he found himself listening to the announcer's voice. There was a sense of urgency in the speaker's words that made him put down the newspaper and pay attention. He frowned and turned to look at the radio. After a garbled, hurriedly prepared version of White House statements, the news reporter went on: "Information now coming in from London confirms without doubt the rumors that have been reaching Washington all morning. The Prime Minister of Great Britain, Mr. Neville Chamberlain, has issued an ultimatum to Adolf Hitler. If the British government has not received a satisfactory reply by 11 A.M. Greenwich mean time today to its demand for the immediate withdrawal of German troops from Polish soil, then a state of war exists between Great Britain and Germany." The announcer went on, "In the light of recent events, a satisfactory reply to Prime Minister Chamberlain's demand seems unlikely. Newsmen are gathering at the British Embassy in Washington for the announcement, expected later today, that Great Britain and Germany are officially at war . . ."

He felt a shiver go through him.

CHAPTER TWENTY

He was strolling along with Bernardo Garcia, and they could hear the noise in the distance. When they got closer, they were able to distinguish the sounds of steel bands from the voices of the thousands of revelers, some singing, some chanting slogans, some simply yelling in exhilaration. When they turned down the street that led to the Obispo, they could see, in the distance, the crowds that had gathered in Havana's main business street.

"Why have you brought me here?" Tony asked the police chief.

"I want you to see my people happy. There is no joy in the world to equal a Caribbean's when he abandons himself to happiness—it becomes a thing of wonder."

"Is it so special, this new constitution?"

"Perhaps the most important thing to happen to the Cuban nation since Christopher Columbus discovered the island in 1492."

Tony glanced across at him as they walked. He found it hard to associate the svelte, playboy public official, immaculate as ever, with anything so mundane as the declaration of a constitution. Monumental pronouncements were daily fare in Cuba. It was only a matter of time before they'd be back to the same old round of corruption and martyrdom, violence and suppression. Or perhaps he was a cynic. A man like Bernardo, he reasoned, didn't attain high public office without a fairly astute insight into what made the government tick. "Do you think it'll stick, Bernardo?" He said casually.

"Yes, I do," Bernardo said seriously. "Today Cuba takes her first step toward becoming a true democracy. The Constitution of 1940 will become a milestone in our history."

"How about the Batistanos—don't tell me they're gonna give up this easy."

"There will be changes, but at least they will be peaceful changes. We'll avoid the revolution and bloodshed that's traditional in Central American countries. The Batistanos will have to learn restraint; in return, the country will have the best solution to its political problems, a coalition of democratically elected parties—a Popular Front. What more can one ask? A combined voice representing all sections of the community."

It was all too pat. "How about Batista himself?" Tony said. "He gonna back this new deal with the army? We both know it won't work unless he gets behind it."

"That is correct. In a country of so many dissenting elements, there has to be a strong hand at the helm, or there would be chaos."

"So he remains the secret power behind the government—in other words, they gotta do what suits Batista. Don't change things much, does it?"

Bernardo looked at him thoughtfully for a moment as they approached the noisy crowds. He said, "I think you're a man who can be trusted with a secret, so I'll tell

211

you—it will become public knowledge soon, anyway: in a few weeks, Batista will be officially elected President of Cuba."

Tony stared back. It would be gauche to ask Bernardo how he could be so sure of the outcome of a democratic vote. "But Batista's never been a politico—he's always ruled through a nominee. Why should he come out into the limelight now?"

"Because the time is ripe, and it will take a man with authority to administer the new constitution. Batista is the only man in Cuba with that authority. We have to forget the past. For the sake of the Cuban nation he must be the one to preside over the new era."

Perhaps he'd been wrong, Tony thought. Perhaps, in a troubled land with a history of slavery, exploitation of the poor, graft, corruption, and violence, it took a man with an iron fist to finally put things right. Perhaps the leopard had changed his spots. "Well, whatever happens, this is an important day for you, so I'd like to wish you and your country good luck," he said.

"Thank you," Bernardo said formally, and gave a small bow of his head.

They entered the Obispo and the noise was deafening. They were jostled and shoved, pulled into dancing rings of people, and, willing or not, forced to join in the celebration. They took it in good spirit, even when they, along with the crowd, were crushed to one side to allow the passage of the carnival parade—flower-laden floats representing the history of the island, from the time of the original Siboney and Taino Indians, who were the first Cubans, through Velasquez's exploitation of the natives on behalf of Spain. There were floats representing the Spanish immigrant settlers, African slaves, others showing the intermingling of the races that produced the *mestizos,* half-white creoles who now constituted a good proportion of Cuba's population.

He was a lot wiser when it was time to return to the Internacionale to prepare for the evening's work. He was also poorer. In the crowd his pants had been neatly slit with a razor, and his wallet was gone from his hip pocket.

As Bernardo had predicted, Batista became president. Havana was in a good mood. The new constitution promised a bright future for everyone, right down to the most insignificant *quajiro.* On the night of the election, when the fish-eyed soldiers and the police had followed the last voters home, the socialites went out on the town to celebrate. Their man was in. To add to that, the war in Europe was bringing an unexpected bonus in extra trade to the most important port in the Caribbean. More important, sugar had suddenly become a strategic commodity for the warring nations desperate to maintain food supplies for their peoples. Deals could be made with both sides, and were. The world was beating a path to Havana's door. What was more, the number of Americans vacationing in Havana had increased dramatically. Suddenly the hotels were full again. The upturn in an American economy revitalized by the instant demand for unlimited quantities of war materials had begun to melt away the towering mass of American unemployed of earlier years. The nightclubs were crowded, champagne flowed, and morning light bathed the land before the gay pleasure-seekers spilled onto the streets.

The casino had been going flat-out all night, and money had been pouring across the tables. Tony was beginning to feel the effects of constantly monitoring the

212

action. He hadn't seen Juanita since yesterday, and he thought it strange for her to be absent on such a busy night. But the thought of her slipped from his mind by the time he'd consolidated the accounts in the cashier's cage and was making his way tiredly to his rooms. As he walked along the hallway he was surprised to see his door ajar. The only one with a key was Skeeter—but Skeeter had gone off to bed an hour earlier and would have closed off the world by now. Tony stepped carefully up to the door and listened. There was no sound from inside. He stepped back, put his foot to the door and kicked it open. This time he hoped the thieves were still inside.

On the other side of the door, Lombardo sat in a chair, smoking a cigarette and looking very surprised. The two bodyguards who'd been seated a respectful distance away were on their feet, their hands inside their coats. "Do you always come into a room this way?" Lombardo said.

"I'm sorry if I startled you," Tony said, grinning foolishly. "I been robbed once. I thought, this time, maybe they're still here."

"I see. Never mind. How are you?" Lombardo stood up and came across to him. Tony was pleasantly surprised at the warmth of the old-fashioned Mustache-Pete hug.

"I'm just fine, Mr. Lombardo. I wasn't expecting you."

"I don't like turning up without warning, but sometimes it's necessary. I know you'll forgive me being in your room—I don't want to be seen in the hotel, if I can avoid it."

"Sure, I understand," he said. Secretly, he enjoyed the courtesy Lombardo extended to him. "You know you're welcome here. I'm honored by your visit."

"Thank you." Lombardo sat down again solemnly. "I always notice about you that you maintain respect. That is important." He nodded again, as if satisfying an inner doubt, and studied Tony for a moment. "You're looking older than when we last met. How long ago was that—a year, eighteen months?" Tony nodded, and Lombardo seemed in no hurry to continue. "You like it here, in Cuba, Tony?" he said unexpectedly.

"Yes, I'm very happy here."

"Good. That's important too." He gave no explanation for his remark other than, "I have no hesitation in bringing you forward to the next step."

"The next step?" Tony repeated, puzzled.

"Yes. I'm putting the casino entirely in your care."

"How about Juanita Ortiz?"

"Juanita is no longer in charge. You are."

"But, the politicians—she always handles that side of it. She's the one with the connections, ain't she? I don't know who to grease," he said doubtfully.

"Things have changed," Lombardo said. "We no longer need her connections. Now that Batista is officially president, we carry the seal of government approval, so to speak."

"Batista's your man? In person?"

Lombardo didn't answer directly. "Let's just say you'll be free to operate without interference. There will be none of the usual problems with Cuban officialdom."

"So who were Juanita's connections?"

"Intermediaries. It was necessary to do it that way while Batista had no public

213

face. You'll find that many officials have lost their powers. They were useful as go-betweens, but, as I said, things have changed. It's just as well—Juanita was becoming a nuisance," he added.

A thought occurred to him. "She know about your decision? I haven't seen her around today."

"Don't concern yourself about Juanita. She won't cause either of us any more bother." It took a moment to sink in. Tony made no attempt to hide the look on his face. "Don't trouble yourself about people like that—they serve a purpose, that's all. It's not the same as our relationship—you've become a significant servant of the outfit, and your services are highly valued. You have our complete trust. We'd no more dream of harming you than you would of betraying us. I'm sure I don't have to tell you that . . ."

Lombardo's words brought home to Tony the truth of what he hadn't been able to admit to himself. For a while he stood there in silence, then he said slowly, "Mr. Lombardo, I thank you for your trust. But it's better you don't tell me any more. I'm happy to operate the casino for you—let's just leave it at that."

He caught the glimpse of disappointment in Lombardo's eyes, but the tone remained unchanged. "Your personal discipline is quite extraordinary. It will be of great value, as you develop."

"Value to who, Mr. Lombardo . . .?" He regretted immediately that he'd allowed the brittleness into his voice. He didn't wait for an answer. "Anyhow, I think I already developed as much as I'm gonna."

"No, you have a long way to go. One of these days your curiosity's gonna get the better of you. Or maybe you'll need us. When that day comes, I hope you won't hesitate to come to me personally, and we'll discuss your future."

"I don't think that day will come, Mr. Lombardo," Tony said bluntly.

Lombardo got up and prepared to go. "I presume you know the banking procedures here, Tony?" He nodded. "All you have to do is carry on as usual and make your own decisions. There will be small changes from time to time—someone'll come along. For you, I'm always on the end of a telephone," he added. He moved toward the door. One of the bodyguards got there first.

"How about the games I operate myself—the specials?" Tony said suddenly.

"The same arrangement you had with Juanita. I want you to make money. But I expect you to use a great deal of discretion now that you're moving up into a senior position. You must always put the interests and the reputation of the . . . the house before your own."

"I'll be careful," he said.

"It'll show up if you're not. Goodbye, Tony."

"Goodbye, Mr. Lombardo," he said formally.

When they'd gone, he closed the door and sank into a chair. The tiredness came over him swiftly, and he rubbed a hand across his forehead. Absently, he felt for the dice in his pocket and fingered them, like *cobuloi* beads, as if they gave him solace, a contact with his Deity. Now would come the real test, the real personal test—the test he'd been waiting for over the years. This would be the watershed of his entire career. And there were a thousand ways he could blow it.

His curiosity wouldn't get the better of him, he resolved. Once he allowed that to happen, he would cross the divide that protected him from the dangerous world beyond.

CHAPTER TWENTY-ONE

"Valparaiso. The Gulf of Mexico—what the fuck you talking about?" Tony said impatiently to the tall, thin guy standing before him. The man had slid into the casino office behind him, and at first Tony suspected a stick-up; clearly the guy had been waiting for an opportunity to get him on his own. But it soon became apparent that he presented no threat, and Tony allowed him to talk while he leafed through the daily reports, listening with half an ear. Crackpots were a regular feature of gambling life, especially when people lost their dough. The guy had been saying something that sounded like he worked for the U.S. government, but now he was talking nonsense, Tony decided.

The guy pushed his fedora back on his head and hesitated before he said quietly, "The Duke said I should tell you it's O.K. to help if you can."

"The Duke?" He sat back in his chair. "What you know about the Duke?"

"I had someone talk with him, back in that Ohio town, that Steubenville. We need to know all about you, you understand, before we can put a proposition to you. We took a rundown on your background."

"Oh, yeah?" Tony said cautiously. Now he was paying attention. "What for?"

"To find out if you have connections with foreign powers."

He laughed, and relaxed. "You got identification?"

"Sure . . ." The guy took out his wallet and slid it across the desk. "Bud Carlstrom. U.S. Army Intelligence. O.K. if I sit down?"

"Go ahead." Tony opened the wallet.

"I don't tell everyone what I do, you understand? I'm making an exception in your case because I hear you know how to keep your mouth shut." Tony glanced at him for a moment, then returned his gaze to the wallet. "I'd appreciate a drink." The man's eyes roved around the office and returned to a bottle-laden cart.

"Help yourself, Mr. Carlstrom."

"Bud. Thanks . . ." He got up and poured himself a generous shot. Tony waved off the offer. The man seated himself again and took a gulp. When the whiskey slid down his throat, he gave a small shudder. "That's good stuff."

"Fourteen-year-old Scotch," Tony said, returning the wallet. "What can I do for you, Bud?"

Carlstrom was silent a moment, his gaze intense. "You ever hear of something called Operation Sunbeam?" he said softly.

"No," Tony said promptly.

"You understand German?"

"No—well, maybe a few words. I hear quite a bit around here."

"Your friend Skeeter Froelich is of German extraction. He speaks German fluently." Tony couldn't help staring. These days, his own and Skeeter's youthful affiliations were receding into the mists of time. Life consisted of Cuba, the casino, the dice, his standards of propriety. "So what?" he said.

"I only mention it in passing. Do you have German sympathies?"

"No," Tony said.

"Are you a patriot?"

"I never thought about it."

"I want you to think about it now."

"I'm as patriotic as the next guy, I suppose," he said guardedly.

"I'll put it another way. Do you love America, Antonio Vitale?"

His mind went back to the cesspools he'd lived through, the gestation of philosophies that made him the person he was. Now that he was a man, he knew that his life could have been very different. The same application of personal discipline could have made him the doctor or the lawyer his father had hoped for, instead of a dice mechanic. An American Doctor Vitale—how it would have enobled his beloved papa. From the sun-seared, angry, hungry back streets of Salerno to the orderly, prosperous dignity of professional life in the New World, in one generation. He'd failed his father, he felt, despite the money. Honor had been his for the taking, honor for his family's name—and he'd blown it, rejected it in favor of immediate excitement. At least, in America, he'd had the choice. Cuba, its violent, martial dictatorship, its mortified poor had brought home to him the worth of the freedom he valued so lightly. Yes, for all its faults, he loved America. "Aw, come on, Bud . . ." he said uncomfortably.

"Comes a time you gotta stand up and be counted," Bud said simply. "It's time."

"You talking about war—we going to war with Germany?"

Bud shrugged. "Five'll get you ten."

He was silent before he said, "I'm an American citizen. I don't put no other foreign country before my own."

"How about your friend?"

"He's American as apple pie."

"Good. I have to be careful, you understand. His family background—."

"Every guy outa Steubenville got a family background somewhere from Europe. I'll vouch for Skeeter, all the way, even though his family is German."

"What's this strange dependence he seems to have on you?" Bud shot it at him.

The agent had been looking him over for some time, Tony realized. Funny that he hadn't noticed a thing; ordinarily he was very observant. Awareness was instinctive in him. "We been friends since we was kids together. Skeeter had a breakdown one time—you know, his mind. Mostly he's O.K. these days. When he's not, I look after him. He'd have done the same for me."

"I see." Bud chewed on this for a time.

"What's this thing—this Operation Sunbeam?"

"I'll start at the beginning: The Germans have organized an espionage ring in South America, operating out of Chile and Argentina—Valparaiso and Santiago. They want to extend their influence on this side of the Atlantic, for obvious reasons.

216

As you know, there are Nazi sympathizers here, too. They're building up an organization for smuggling defense secrets out of the States through Cuba—and for smuggling in spies. But that's only part of it. Take a look at the map and you'll see that Cuba's sitting on the gateway to the Gulf of Mexico—the underbelly of the United States. German U-boats operating out of Cuba, in the Florida Strait, for example, could slaughter shipping between our southern ports and Europe. You get the picture? We have to know which way Cuba's gonna jump."

"But Batista's pro-American," Tony said. "He'll never allow them Nazis to operate out of Cuba against the United States."

"You're probably right," Bud agreed. "But what happens if Batista is overthrown?"

"That's impossible. He's the most powerful guy in the country," Tony protested.

"Yeah, I know it looks that way. But twenty-four hours is a lifetime in Cuban politics. And the Cuban Nazi Party ain't exactly hayseed, y'know—its members represent powerful interests and they're all hard-line right-wingers. If Batista suddenly discovered the Humanities, they'd find a way to get rid of him. You have to remember, too, that outside money and influence can have a big effect on internal affairs in a country this size that's short on natural resources. I wouldn't even put assassination past the Nazis. Thing is, we gotta know what the Germans are up to. And we have to stop them from stealing our secrets."

"What's the proposition?"

"We want you to help. You're in a unique position. This here casino is something of a meeting place for Cuban socialites and politicians. It's places like this where the Germans make their contacts."

"Yeah, come to think of it, we're getting a lot of Germans in lately."

"Some of them are agents. The man who put the South American ring together is a regular customer of yours—Heinz Ludwig."

"I know him—a high roller."

"Nazi money. It's nothing but a front to make contact with Cuban politicians. I want you to let me know when he's around, who he keeps company with, or picks up."

"I understand. Sure, if the Duke says it's O.K., I'll be glad to help."

"Thanks," Bud said. "I appreciate that. So does Uncle Sam."

"If they talk German, I'll put Skeeter on it when I get the chance. He understands the lingo, like you say. Maybe we can pick up something that way."

"More than I expected . . ." Bud was pleased. He got to his feet. "Not often your organization and the U.S. Government get together on a deal, is it? As they say, strange bedfellows."

Tony thought about Bud's remark for a moment. He was about to challenge the agent on it, but by then the guy was on his feet and making for the door.

The German war machine ground onward, crushing the free nations of Europe beneath the Nazi jackboot. Uninformed Americans who favored isolationism could not conceive of a Nazi dream that encompassed world domination. Remote and safe in their New World sanctuary, academicians blithely debated their illusory options.

In the insignificant French port of Dunkirk, on the slate-gray English Channel, the Germans came to the end of mainland Europe and drove the remains of the British Expeditionary Force into the sea. On the green fields of an ill-prepared England, at the time of the summer harvest, a few diffident airmen shook off their prissy middle-class upbringing and prepared their Spitfires to do gladiatorial battle with Goering's aerial armada. It would prove to be a frenetic Hitler's first setback.

On the other side of the Pacific the Japanese warlords, in concert with their German partners, prepared plans for their share of the global assault. Soon Vice Admiral Nagumo would be briefed to prepare his flagship aircraft carrier *Akagi* for an attack of unremitting savagery on an American island outpost.

The stench of rampaging, gory death mounting over the world's battlefields was of little immediate consequence in distant Cuba, and almost unreal in the context of Havana's virulent nightlife. The crowds celebrating at the Sevilla Grande and the Internacionale grew more boisterous and demanding of their pleasures. For those who could afford it, it seemed the fun would go on forever.

She was somewhere down among the hair on his stomach, moving the point of her tongue on him in such a way as to cause the blood to tingle beneath the surface of his skin in a sudden delicious heat. He lay unmoving, enjoying the heightened sensation that ran through him, the thrills following one another in quick succession. What she didn't know about arousing a man wasn't worth knowing. His gaze was fixed sightlessly on the ceiling of the darkened bedroom, and he was oblivious to the sounds of music and laughter that filtered through from the living room of his suite. Her movements stopped and he knew, without having to see her, that she was looking up at him with those wide, shining brown eyes, eager to know if she was pleasing him. "Don't stop now, little Effe, go on . . ."

The erotic movement resumed. He reached out to touch her dusky, pliant skin. With the lightest of pressures he drew a sensitive finger gently and slowly along the inside of her moist thigh. When he lingered, he felt the shudder go through her. Suddenly the pace of her movements quickened. Then the climax was on him and, in the grip of its intensity, he grabbed handfuls of her silken flesh so that she moaned with pain. His passion spent, he expired into inertia.

A few minutes later, she was ready to start all over again. He stopped her. He sat up and held her out at arm's length, studying her shape in the dim light, his eyes finally coming to rest on the proud fullness of her firm, young breasts. "Kiss them," she whispered fiercely, thrusting her chest at him.

"Not now, Effe."

"Aren't I beautiful enough?"

"You're very beautiful," he said.

"Come, we make love properly now."

"No. Let's go join the others." He released her.

"Do we have to?" she complained.

"Sure we do. It's my party, ain't it? What sort of host is it leaves his guests, goes off and spends the night fucking?"

"They should do the same," she suggested.

"Come on, let's move."

The Latin-American rhythm group was beating out a scintillating number when

218

they stepped into the next room. It seemed they hadn't been missed after all, so they joined the other couples dancing in the middle of the floor. When the dance finished, he took a couple of glasses of champagne from a waiter circling the room with a tray. "Damn," he said suddenly, his eyes searching around.

"What's wrong?" Effe said.

"Joe Palooka—he's gone missing. Probably sneaked off to bed."

"Joe who?"

"Skeeter."

"My friend Carmen is missing, too," Effe said pointedly, her gaze sweeping the crowded room.

"I mean on his own—you don't know Skeeter."

"And you don't know Carmen," she retorted, with a secretive little smile.

"You mean it? I thought she'd given up trying." It was through Carmen he'd come to know Effe. Carmen was the one he'd brought in originally to break Skeeter out of his self-inflicted incarceration. But, as Tony had expected, Skeeter had shied away from the beautiful creole seductress. It had been going on for weeks now, and Tony had subconsciously accepted defeat.

"He's sort of got used to having Carmen around. Things are different now."

"If you're right, she gets a five-hundred-dollar bonus. You got my word on that." He paused. "There's a connecting door between my bedroom and Skeeter's. What you say we go take a peek?"

Effe nodded. Together they returned to his bedroom and crossed to the door on the other side. Carefully he took hold of the knob and turned it fully. He waited for a moment as the musical number came to an end in the living room. In the ensuing quiet, he pushed on the door with a carefully controlled pressure, and it opened slightly. The bed was located on the far side of the room, and a short projecting wall by the door put it out of their immediate sight. When they stepped softly into Skeeter's room it was to see that the bedcovers and pillows had been pulled to the floor. Carmen sat naked on them, her back supported by the bed. Skeeter's head, his eyes closed, was cradled in her arms and pressed to her full bosom. In a low voice she was singing a strange, sweet, timeless lullaby. From Skeeter's throat came a weird wail, something between a hum and a moan, as he followed the notes on some tuneless scale of his own. Every so often he broke off humming and his body was wracked by dry sobs. Recovering, he would pick up the tune once again—all with his eyes closed. For a few moments they watched, unobserved. Then they stepped back and Tony reached out to close the door in silence.

He was unaware that Bernardo Garcia had crept up on them quietly. Suddenly there was a raucous yell from behind, and Tony was shoved forward violently, stumbling into Skeeter's room. "Hey, hey, hey—what's going on in here? What's the big secret, eh?" Bernardo roared genially, his eyes bright with anticipation.

"You goddamn jerk." When Tony recovered his balance his gaze shot immediately to the bed. Skeeter was on his feet, ashamed in his nakedness. Far, far worse, the wild stare was again in his eyes, the look Tony had come to hate and fear. "Oh, sweet Jesus, here we go again . . ." He groaned in utter defeat.

"Whassamatter? What'd I do?" Bernardo muttered drunkenly.

"You stupid prick—know how long it took to bring him along this far? You got

219

any fucking *idea* how long it took?" Tony yelled angrily.

"Ah, I dunno—."

"Six years. That's how long. You busted the whole deal in one second flat."

"Six years . . ." Bernardo repeated dully.

He glared at Bernardo in frustration and disgust. The lines of self-indulgence etched into the other's face made his boozy expression of concern appear totally insincere. Suddenly he was thoroughly sick of his own self-discipline. Up to here. Something inside him snapped. He looked at his hands—the long, sensitive fingers. He made a fist of the right hand, lashed out with the fist, and knocked the Cuban playboy out cold.

CHAPTER TWENTY-TWO

It was Sunday. He knew it was Sunday because the raucous din of the Havana streets failed to reach up and hammer on the windows as it did on week-days. It also felt as if he'd awakened earlier than usual. He turned his head to the right, and sure enough the hands of the clock were coming together at midday. It had been six o'clock before he'd gone to bed. He decided he needed more sleep. He turned onto his left side, closed his eyes, and made himself comfortable. Then he realized what he'd seen. He opened his eyes again. Skeeter sat silently in an armchair staring across the room at him. "What you doing there, Skeets—you O.K.?"

"Yeah, sure."

"Been up long?" They'd gone to bed at the same time.

"Coupla hours. Lots of commotion in the hotel this morning. The Japs—they bombed Pearl Harbor."

"They *what*?" He scrambled to a sitting position.

"I heard it on the radio."

"You sure—maybe you got it wrong?"

"Bombers—hundreds of them. Sank a lot of our ships. The Americans in the hotel are panicking to get back Stateside."

"The real thing, then . . ."

"Yeah, now we really at war with Japan."

"Jes-us Christ . . ." A chill went through him.

"What we gonna do, Tony?"

"I dunno." He was at a loss for words. Who could have guessed that the war would be brought to them in the form of an impudent Japanese attack?

"How will it affect us?"

He shrugged. "America will mobilize. I'm twenty-two now—guys my age will get drafted."

220

"How about me? I'm twenty-three."

He looked at Skeeter. He'd always been square with his buddy—no sense trying to kid him now. "No, they ain't gonna take you, Skeets. You gotta admit, you're in no condition to be a fightin' man."

"That ain't for you to decide. It's up to a draft board doctor."

It was the first time he could remember, since they were in Cuba, that Skeeter had spoken angrily to him. He was pleased to see the flash of spirit; it was a good sign. But Skeeter would find out for himself soon enough. "Yeah, maybe you're right. Let's wait and see, huh?" He still found it difficult to assimilate the notion that the United States was formally at war. He threw off the bedcovers. "Order up some coffee, willya? We gotta get a few things organized." He headed for the bathroom. "And turn on the radio—let's get the latest news."

When he returned from the bathroom, he said, "I better get in touch with Lombardo. I have to make arrangements to hand over the casino."

"Where we going?"

"Back to Steubenville and get ready for the draft. Where else?"

"I won't like it back there."

He took a long, hard look at Skeeter, and he wondered whether his buddy would survive what was to come. It hadn't occurred to him before; when he was gone, his friend would be in deep trouble, on his own in Steubenville. "Listen, I got an idea. Just in case—that is, if things don't go good for you at the medical, maybe I can arrange for you to stay on here. You like it here in Cuba and—."

"I'll be O.K. at the medical," Skeeter cut in determinedly.

"Sure, 'course you will . . ." He said it immediately. This wasn't the time to argue. He hoped he was wrong, but he couldn't see beyond the cloud that hung over Skeeter's future.

Bud Carlstrom came into the office, sat down, and lit a cigarette. Tony had been clearing out his desk. The agent eyed the carefully stacked documents. "Going someplace?" he said laconically.

"You kidding?" He glanced over, annoyed.

"Your people closing down the casino?"

"What for? You know well as I do, a casino here in Cuba's gonna make a fortune in wartime."

"Yeah, that could happen. I didn't think of it that way."

"You government guys are all the same. You got no idea how to make money, but you're good at spending the taxpayer's dough."

"So, all right," Bud said, hurt.

Tony continued sorting out his personal belongings. "Listen, Bud, what you think—will Cuba stay neutral?" he said, after a while.

"I got no information on that," Carlstrom said noncommittally.

"Whatever way it goes, that Batista will score, you betcha. Now we need him more than he needs us, I guess . . ."

"I guess," Bud agreed.

"What will you be doing yourself?" Tony asked.

"Working harder, now it's official."

221

"You staying here?"

"Sure—I'm the Caribbean expert, right? Someone gotta do the dirty work."

"I'm gonna miss the place myself. It sure ain't gonna be no pleasure, being a buck private after what I got here." He grinned. "You ever hear of something called the blanket roll?"

"No."

"In the army, that'll be my best chance. In the last war, there was guys got rich in the army, using the blanket roll." In normal times he wouldn't have dreamed of talking to Bud this way. "On paydays," he added.

"I don't understand."

"I'm talking about dice," Tony said.

"I don't play dice. Not on my pay."

He savored his private little joke. "You think they need a mechanic in the army, Bud?"

"Sure. A modern army runs on wheels, don't it? What sort of mechanic—automobile? You a mechanic, Tony?"

"Sort of."

"I didn't know that." For a moment he worried over this gap in his knowledge of Tony's history. "Well, I guess they could use you, all right. But it'll be over my dead body."

"What you mean?"

"I want you to stay here in Cuba. And that's official."

"How can I do that? I have to register for the draft."

"You're more useful to Uncle Sam working here than carrying a rifle. It took me a long time to set up my little organization. I don't aim to get it busted by a formal declaration of war. That'd suit the other side just fine. I've been at war for years. You and your buddy have done a good job—better than you'll ever know. I'm in a hole if you walk out on me. It's too late for me to start over—not now that Heinz Ludwig's espionage ring is coming into its own. He's been preparing for this a long time. And so have I."

"Bud, you didn't hear what I said. What about the draft?"

"I heard. I'll take care of it."

He stared. "You can do that?"

"I don't hold the rank of colonel for nothing, you know. I have some authority." Tony found himself surprised that this casual, untidy character, whom he'd never taken completely seriously, was a ranking officer. Bud took some papers from an inside pocket. "I want you to sign these," he said.

"What are they?"

"This one's your draft application. The other one's your medical certificate. Let's see—you don't hear too good, you got incipient syphilis. Also flat feet. Guess you're gonna be graded 4F."

"Bud, this for real?"

"You sound disappointed."

"It don't seem right. Everyone else will be going . . ."

"Ain't you lucky?" Bud grinned, then said purposefully, "You can do your bit for your country right here. Now, don't go stupid on me, pal. You know the score."

222

"How about Skeeter? We need him, too."

"O.K. He stays."

"I guess you got a deal, Bud." He put out his hand and they shook.

When the agent had gone, he sat at his desk in silence for a while. Strangely, he felt cheated—the uniform, the drama of war, the patriotism, the hardships, perhaps the friendships, and maybe even the death would pass him by.

Goddamn idiot. He'd hit the jackpot and didn't recognize it. Who else could conduct his war from the comfort of home? He glanced at the documents piled on his desk, and they triggered off a new train of thought. He reached for the telephone. Lombardo would want to know of his good fortune. They could put it to worthwhile use.

CHAPTER TWENTY-THREE

The smart Central Park West apartment was somehow less daunting than he remembered it from his previous visit. That seemed so long ago now, as if it had all happened in another world. When he found himself subconsciously criticizing the décor, he realized suddenly that he'd come a long way.

Lombardo was waiting for him and he came across the room with open arms. "Tony, I'm glad to see you. Here, let me take your coat. I suppose you're feeling the cold here in New York after Havana?" he said in his husky voice.

"Sure am. That's a drop of fifty degrees—takes some getting used to."

As Tony slipped the topcoat from his shoulders, Lombardo stepped back in admiration. "Say, that's some suit you're wearing, Tony. Just look at that shoulder line."

"I got a good tailor back there."

"When I'm in Havana next time, you must arrange for him to make me some clothes."

"Be my pleasure," he said.

"I appreciate that." Then Lombardo stepped aside, and Tony recognized immediately the little guy sitting in the chair across the room. He gave no sign that he knew the man's identity, or thought he didn't. "I want you to meet Berman Levin," Lombardo said, with a smile.

The little guy didn't get up, and Tony moved forward to shake his hand. He became aware of the piercing, analytical gaze, and somehow felt glad he had nothing to hide. "I see you know me," Levin said. He spoke with a voice that had grown out of the Lower East Side.

"Only by reputation," Tony said.

"I try to keep my name out of the papers as much as possible."

"I'm not talking about your public face, Mr. Levin," he said.

There was a glint in Levin's eyes. "So, what are you talking about?"

"I think it was Miranda once told me: To run a gambling house well, you need a good intelligence service. I got one. Not much goes on in Havana that passes me by." Levin said nothing, but his eyes were riveted on Tony's face. He went on coolly, "You're a regular visitor to Cuba. In fact, you were there a couple of weeks ago. You got close connections with some top Cuban ministers—I don't know which. Since we're the only ones in the room . . ." He glanced around. "I'll say something else. It wouldn't surprise me if you own a piece of the joint I run."

Levin's head was nodding slightly in amusement. "I'm gonna tell you—that's a good intelligence service you got there."

"The best."

"U.S. Army trained, I understand?"

Tony shot an annoyed glance at Lombardo. "You promised you wouldn't talk," he said sharply. "That's secret government business."

"Don't worry, you're among friends," Levin said quietly. "It stops here. When you're talking to Lombardo, you're talking to me. You understand?" Tony still rankled at Lombardo's betrayal of confidence. "Lombardo, explain it to him," Levin said, and sat back in his chair.

"Tony, listen to me." Lombardo took over. "We been talking and we decided it's time we took you into our confidence. You have become a significant servant of the outfit. We like your conduct and your bearing—you're a stand-up guy. We like the way you proved you can be trusted. These are important matters to us. The council—that's Levin and me and a few others—has decided to make you an offer."

"Thanks, but I'm happy the way things are," he said woodenly.

"You should hear me out, Tony. The war changes everything. When this is all over, it's gonna be a different world."

"I'll find a way to live with it."

"I'm not making myself clear. Things are gonna explode. There will be opportunities we haven't dreamed of. It's a long way off, maybe, but we have to start preparing now."

"I don't see there's much we can do right now, with everyone involved in the war effort."

"Not inside the United States maybe. Outside, it's a different matter. In Cuba we can make a start now. After the war we're going to be big over there. We're gonna be building huge new hotels and casinos. We'll be helping build up the Cuban tourist industry. Just remember, that's important to the Cuban economy. Besides the sugar, they don't have much else."

"So now we're becoming public benefactors?" Tony allowed himself a wry grin.

"We're in it for the profit."

"Them Cuban politicians, they'll want their share . . ." he said.

"We got Batista in our pocket," Levin cut in from across the room. "For three million a year in a Swiss bank account, he kinda sees things our way."

"And after Batista?" Tony looked over at him.

"Batista stays," Levin said shortly. "Anything happens to him, we'll find a way. Over there everyone's got a price. Leave that side of it to me."

He was astounded at the little guy's confidence.

"What I was coming to—we'll be offering you points," Lombardo went on.

"Points?" Tony queried.

"A percentage. You'll own a percentage of the Cuban operation. There's no telling how much that'll be worth, in time. It's only a question of how big a fortune."

After a moment, he said, "And in return?"

"In return we expect you to take some responsibility."

"What does that mean?"

"It means you make sure everything runs smooth."

"Look, I'm a technician," Tony said. "Inside a house you can leave everything to me. But I got no stomach for dealing with them politicians. They make my skin crawl—."

"We know your talents," Lombardo cut in. "And we know your limitations. The politicians, discipline, and things like policy decisions will be handled by us—they'll be our problems, not yours. This is how it will work: The places, when they're built, will be shared out among our members. It'll be your job to get the casinos running smooth and then keep watch, on our behalf, on all casino operations on the island. We have to know the places are being run good and we're getting our share. It's an important job."

"I appreciate that," Tony said.

"Myself, I'm satisfied it's something you can handle. But there's one thing more, and in a way it's just as important. To do the job right, you'll have to become our man completely. Do you understand what that means?"

He couldn't decide if there was an implied threat in the husky words. He was silent a long time. Then he said simply, "Yes, I understand."

"Good. You don't have to decide right now. Take all the time you want to think it over."

"Yes, I'll need time." He said it softly.

Lombardo's voice took on a lighter note. So, Tony, what are your immediate plans while you're in New York? Some nights out on the town maybe? Things are a little restricted, with the war going on . . . I can arrange all the hospitality you'll need. You only gotta speak. You been working hard, you need a little recreation."

"I'll be moving on. Touching base. I ain't seen the family for some time."

"Of course. The family is important."

"And the Duke."

"The Duke's a good man." Levin said it, from the chair across the room.

"Yeah, he's the best," Tony said.

"Give him my regards."

"I'll remember to do that, Mr. Levin," Tony said correctly.

He sat in the Duke's office in the semidarkness. This time the Duke hadn't offered to open the shade and the only light in the room crept in around the edges from the late-afternoon sun. "It's a big step, if you decide to take it. I'm very proud of you, Tony, what you achieved," the Duke said. There was a warmth in the voice he hadn't heard before.

"I been thinking it over. I can't make up my mind. I keep telling myself, who the hell needs it? I'm doing O.K."

"Take all the time you want. Lombardo said there's no rush, didn't he?"

"Money ain't everything. I got money. As things are, if I make a mistake, I can correct it and no more is said—don't mean the end of the world. With them people, things go wrong and it ain't so easy."

"But you're the one doesn't make mistakes, Tony—isn't that right?"

Coming from anyone but the Duke, he'd have taken it as cynicism. "Nobody's perfect. It's only a matter of time." It was contrary to his usual attitude—which was when he realized he was making excuses.

"Making a genuine mistake is nothing to be afraid of. We're all human, everyone understands that."

"I ain't afraid—it's not that."

"Isn't this what you've been working toward, in a manner of speaking?"

"No. I wanted to be a master mechanic. I reckon I made good—ain't nobody ever come along I couldn't beat. And I been up against the best. Some was nearly as good as me, but I had the edge. For a simple reason," he added.

"What's that?"

"Them others—they weren't outa Steubenville."

He caught the Duke's smile in the half-light. "Maybe it's time to stop and think what being a mechanic's all about: If a man's a good technician, he's a useful guy in a short-season situation, where there's gonna be no comebacks. When he proves himself reliable, and can conduct himself well, he gets to take charge of an operation, some day. Now we come to the guy who can apply self-discipline, got a head on his shoulders, and learns to keep his mouth shut. That's a once-in-a-lifetime combination."

"That's a master mechanic, right?"

"He's more than that, this guy we're talking about. He has to cross the line and become a principal."

"A mechanic always works for the house, no matter how good he is—you taught me that. I find out that's the way it lays up."

"As a rule of thumb, it's true. You're the exception."

"You saying I should throw in with them?"

"I'm not speaking for or against that particular proposition. I'm only saying that you personally can be more than just a mechanic."

"But I am. I run the whole operation at the Internacionale."

"I know that. You reached the top in your profession—as an employee. To go on, you have to change direction, take on a different philosophy. The time has come and so has the opportunity. Now you have to decide for yourself the direction your future will take. Nobody can do it for you."

Tony stared at his feet for a while. "This proposition," he said, "you think I can handle it?"

"Yes, I do," the Duke said.

"Will it ruin me as a mechanic if it don't work out?"

"It could if you become well known. But the outfit doesn't work that way, so it's academic. I think you'll be all right."

226

"You think they can do what they say? Sounds as if they'll have a lock on all the Cuban hotel and gambling business if it comes off."

"Levin knows what he's talking about. If he says he can do it, consider it done. But there's something more important to you personally—something you haven't mentioned."

"What's that?" He looked up.

"Once you go in with them, there's no backing out."

"I know that."

"I mean for real—for good. When you become their man, it's a total commitment. There's no way out for you, ever. You have to consider it the price of opportunity."

"What happens if the deal folds?"

"There will be other deals. Always with them. You'll be one of them."

"I don't think I want that."

"It becomes a way of life. Sort of like a marriage—you learn to live with it."

"It's one hell of a price to pay, giving up freedom for opportunity."

"Yes, I agree."

"So you think I should?"

"No, I don't think it's for you," the Duke said slowly, and Tony thought he sounded unsure. "Maybe you can't take the responsibility. There's a lot of guys work well in harness—take them out, they can't make it."

Tony felt a slight resentment. He knew well enough, he could make it if he chose. "That's your advice, then?"

"My advice is not to accept. But, I repeat, don't make up your mind now. Think about it."

"Yeah, I'll do that." He rose from the chair. "Well, I gotta get back home. Ma's making a special dinner—you know, all the things I like. All that stuff."

"Your mother is a fine woman," the Duke said courteously. "When are you going back to Havana?"

"In the morning."

"Then I won't see you again before you go?"

"I don't think so," Tony said.

"Let me know your decision, when you make it. Let me know before you call the others. If you decide against, maybe there's things we should talk over."

"O.K., I'll remember," he said.

Standing outside The Club, looking at the dusty Steubenville Street, Tony knew he'd already made up his mind. For the first time he'd be going against the advice of his mentor. The opportunity was too big to ignore. The canvas too vast.

Hell, he'd always been a gambler. How could he turn his back on the biggest gamble of all—his soul against the prospect of riches and power? He made his commitment within the first few steps. It was almost with relief that he dismissed it from his thoughts and turned to contemplating the gastronomic delights of his mother's table.

BOOK THREE Inside Out

CHAPTER ONE

He walked purposefully along the hotel corridor toward the Caesar Suite. Although his footsteps were almost silent on the thick carpet, the two alert guards at the door glanced around sharply. They recognized him and relaxed. Before he reached them he could hear the sound of raised voices coming from behind the closed door. "Good morning, Mr. Vitale," one of the guards said deferentially. He reached for the knob as he spoke. At the same time an aggressive bellow came from inside the suite. The guard allowed himself a half-grin. "Lively meeting today."

Tony paused but didn't return the smile. "There are no strangers on this floor?" he asked.

"Nobody, Mr. Vitale. We took the whole sixth floor for ourselves. We got guys covering the stairs and the elevators. You won't be disturbed."

"You better make sure we're not."

The guard pushed open the door for him and he walked into the room. Including Lombardo and Levin, there were eleven men present. They'd come to Cuba from all parts of the United States to attend the meeting. Between them they represented more wealth than any commercial financial conglomerate in the country. Towers of money built on the foundation of the Volstead Act and its subsequent bootlegging. Golden cascades amassed from the days of dollar-a-day labor. Not a man in the room except Tony had received schooling beyond the ninth grade.

"Ah, Tony . . ." Lombardo reached out for him. "Maybe now we'll hear some common sense. These guys, they're driving me nuts."

"What's wrong?" he said.

"We're arguing about the Caprice. Some of these guys think we should pull out. I never hear anything so crazy. We step out at this stage of the game, we're gonna lose a lot of money."

"Sure we are. We can't back out now, we're in too deep," Tony agreed.

"So tell 'em . . ." His chin jutted, Italian style, and he glared at the group.

"Listen, it's not for me to say. My stake's the smallest in the deal. For myself, I go along with whatever Levin's worked out. What he says, it's O.K. with me."

"There you are . . ." Lombardo's voice rose above the hubbub. "Another voice says we stay in. When you people gonna start making some sense? We gotta give Abe Carroll a chance to make good."

"I didn't say that," Tony said.

Lombardo rounded on him. "Tony, we got four million dollars riding on this deal. We gotta back our investment."

"I know that. What I said, I'll go along with Levin's plans. He knows best."

"Oh, yeah—right." Lombardo yelled for silence. "Now, settle down, willya? Let's hear what Levin has to say. When he's said his piece, that's the time we'll have the debate."

The voices died away and all eyes in the room turned to the little man. He settled himself in his chair and began quietly. "You people seem to think you got a choice. Well, I'm telling you now, there's no options. Nobody steps out. We're in and we stay in—that's the way it's gonna be. If you want a democracy, go out and vote for a political party." He shook the ash off his cigar. They waited while he found a match and relit it. "So, you can see, I get rid of one headache for you right away. Now that we know we're going ahead, what we have to talk over is how best to handle the problem. As you all know, I took the position, right from the start, that the Las Vegas deal is one of the best ideas we ever come up with. I stick with that. We do it right and this Las Vegas will turn into a mint. That's my promise. Anyone here ever know me to welch on a promise?"

For a moment there was silence, then a voice said, "O.K., so we're in and we stay in. So I got a question. How much more? We got four million invested up to now—how much it gonna take to get this joint off its knees?"

"Martoni, you was always dumb and things don't change much," Levin said coolly. "You never learned to use your head instead of that blackjack you used to carry around in your pants pocket." A laugh went through the room. "You was the same over them slots down in Louisiana—remember when you was arguing about New Orleans? I told you it would work out O.K., and now you got a deal down there that don't stop paying off. You wanna take a couple million for your end of that business? I'll accommodate you. I'll make a deal with you right now, in front of these witnesses." There was silence from Martoni's end of the room. "What the fuck difference it make how much we pay out now?" Levin went on forcefully. "So it costs us a few hundred grand more—so what? The place is built now, ain't it? We bought into difficult deals before. It's not the first time. The Caprice is the finest joint in Nevada—in fact, it's the finest hotel-casino in the whole United States. For the first time ever we own a joint inside America where the gambling is legitimate."

"Any chance Nevada will change the law on that?" another voice said.

"None," Levin said confidently. "What else they got there—sand?"

Someone else spoke up. "I been with you all along, Levin, but now I gotta say something against: I was at the opening of the Caprice and, I'm telling you, it's some place—finest I seen anywhere, including the joints we own here in Cuba. But what in hell's Carroll built it eight miles out in the desert for? And that Las Vegas, it ain't much, just a fly-blown desert water hole with a few bust-out traps downtown. Why didn't he build in Reno, where the action is?"

"You don't get it, do you? It's remote where it is, and that's part of the attraction.

And there's room to expand. Other joints will open up around it. In time Las Vegas will become a self-contained gambling colony. We're in at the beginning and we'll be the biggest and strongest."

"If you ask me, Carroll's not the guy to handle this deal," the man said. "He's O.K. out there in Hollywood, banging heads together. He done a good job on them motion-picture unions—I'm the first to admit it, so I ain't sayin' nothin' against him. Also I know he's your partner from way back, when you two started together. What I'm saying is, maybe he's out of his league."

"Let's get one thing straight." Levin's voice stayed cool. "The fact that Carroll and me was partners has nothing to do with this issue. I'll do what's gotta be done, and you better know it."

"I told you, I ain't saying nothing against—."

Levin cut in, "Don't sell Carroll short. It's 1947 now and things are getting easier, but I wanna remind you that last year, when he built the place, you couldn't buy a rusty fucking nail to bang two bits of wood together. Everything was still geared to the war effort. We been paying double and triple for the equipment. If you ask me, it's some kinda miracle he got the joint together at all."

"O.K., so where do we go from here?" It was Martoni again.

"I'm going to Las Vegas to talk with Carroll. I'll find out what's gone wrong out there. If I can't find a way around the problem, then I got another idea—I'll set up a promotion. Nobody except us knows the figures. I already got inquiries from interested parties wanting to buy into the deal. You know what them jerks are: they think, if we're onto something, it's gotta be good. Also, there's still a lot of black-market money around looking for a home. I'll sell points in the casino, and later, when we release the news it's a flop, I'll do them a favor and buy back for twenty, thirty cents on the dollar. That way we get most of our dough back, and we still end up owning the joint. Leave that side of it to me."

He sat back and lit his cigar once again. Lombardo waited a moment to see if Levin had anything further to say, then he got to his feet. "Levin won't say it, but I will: There's been some ugly rumors here today about us soft-pedaling on Carroll because he was Levin's partner in the old days. Anyone wants to say that to my face, he knows where I can be found—my suite's two doors down." He paused. "The other thing is this: Casino losses at the Caprice have been heavy. It don't seem to occur to you guys maybe we're being taken at the tables—maybe Carroll, too. The games at the Caprice are straight, and it sometimes happens a new gambling house gotta take a few losses, as we all know and understand. But just in case, we're sending Tony Vitale in to check out the situation for us. Once we got a clear picture of what's happening, we'll call another meeting and decide what's gotta be done."

Tony sat, unmoving, conscious of all the eyes in the room on him.

The heat of discussion had died away, and they were the only ones left in the room. Tony sat waiting for Levin to speak. "I didn't tell them the whole story," he said. "Only because I'm not sure what's happening myself." Levin contemplated his cigar. "I think we got a serious problem with Abe Carroll."

"I can only speak for the casino figures," Tony said. "They're bad—real bad. Of course, I can do something about that myself, when I get there."

231

"I'm not talking about the Caprice. I'm talking about the man."

"Well, you better give me what information you got."

"I wish I knew more. I'll get the whole picture in time, but for the moment you have to take what I say as an educated guess. First, I must explain about Carroll. Seems to me he's getting delusions of grandeur. His feet ain't touched the ground since we started on this project, and he's acting like it's his own personal deal. He's forgetting the value of money. Incidentally—and this is something else I didn't tell the others—I estimate the cost of the Caprice a lot less than the amount that was actually spent."

"You think Carroll's stealing?"

"I dunno. He's gotta be crazy if he is, with what he's got to lose. I know the guy since we was kids, and it hurts me to say it, but I'm not sure. He's a principal, and there's no need for a principal to steal—there's plenty for all of us, we do it right." For a moment he sat with his thoughts. "A few years back, things were different. In them days, I could trust the guy with my life. Sometimes I had to." He grinned momentarily. "I treated him the way I treat you now. But the guy's changed since he went out to the Coast. At first things were fine, when he was getting them movie-picture unions together. He did a good job on that one. You know, the guy's got terrific personality—always did have, even in the old days. Good looks, too, and the broads are crazy for him. Got more guts than anyone else I know. He's in his element out there, mixing with them movie stars. I think he even took a screen test himself, one time. Can you imagine the gall? Them producers must wanna spit. He screws up their unions so they can't make a picture without his say-so, then he goes prancing around in front of the cameras. A guy who was on every police blotter in the country in the old days. I told you, he's got guts."

"So what happened to change him?"

"Maybe he's going soft in the head. He forgot what we sent him out there for, the prick. He bought a big fucking house in Bel Air and started entertaining movie producers, living it up with the stars—you can't pick up a newspaper without seeing his face plastered all over it. Carroll with Rita Hayworth. Carroll with Clark Gable. Or one of them big names."

"You gotta admit, the guy's no fool to get Hollywood eating out of his hand," Tony said.

"That social crap's not for us," Levin said suddenly. "We work best in the background. One of these days, along comes some smartass newspaperman, adds two and two to make five, and starts out to make a name for himself. Carroll gets crucified, and maybe we get hurt, too."

"If he's screwing up, somebody oughta straighten him out," Tony said.

"Yeah. That's what I'll be doing. It has to be me. Lately, I'm the only one getting through to the dumb fuck. There's something else: one broad too many. Her name's Barbara Strauss. I think maybe she's got him by the balls."

"He don't sound like the kinda guy lets a woman run his life."

"This Barbara, she's something else. I come up against her once before. Carroll stole her from another guy used to be a name in booze."

The suspicion of jealousy jumped into Tony's mind. "Who's that?" Maybe the previous owner was out to make trouble for Carroll.

"He ain't. He got too big for his boots. One of the New York mobs decided to change 'em for new ones. Made outa cement. He's wearing them now—in the East River."

"Oh."

"Yeah, I don't want something like that should happen to Carroll." He rose from his chair and stood for a moment thoughtfully. Tony stood, too. Despite the fact that he was six inches taller, it was Levin who radiated the power. "When you leaving for Las Vegas?"

"A couple of days," Tony said.

"Who you putting in charge of the Internacionale?"

"I brought in Kovack—made him manager."

"I heard some good reports. He shaping up well?" Levin said.

"I think he'll turn out to be one of the best casino managers we got. Had a good start—the guy comes from Steubenville." He couldn't suppress a small grin.

"Who's watching him?"

"My buddy, Skeeter Froelich."

"O.K. A guy will contact you in Las Vegas. He's familiar with the West Coast scene. Use him any way you want. He's reliable."

"Thanks."

"You never met Carroll face-to-face, did you?"

"Not yet. The guy never comes east."

"Give his gambling operation the once-over before you introduce yourself."

"If it goes wrong, and I'm spotted, it could create bad feelings," Tony said doubtfully. "I might lose his confidence."

"Don't worry. Whatever Carroll is, he's not a fool. He'll know you're under orders." Tony nodded.

When Levin had gone, he stood in silence in the middle of the room. He wasn't enraptured with the prospect of leaving the comforts of Cuba for some Godforsaken dust bowl in the Nevada desert. He consoled himself with the thought that it was a job he could wrap up quickly.

But somewhere, at the back of his neck, a sensation told him it wasn't going to be that easy.

CHAPTER TWO

After the cool air inside the airplane, the heat of dusty little McCarran Airport wrapped itself around him like a warm blanket. He found the hot breeze just bearable, having grown accustomed to the summer humidity of Havana. He glanced with concealed amusement as his fellow passengers started sweating and pulling at their clothes on the long walk to the primitive reception area. From among the twenty or so people hanging around inside the building, he picked on the guy with the

233

deadpan expression. He'd guessed right. "Mr. Vitale?" the man said as he approached.

"Yeah."

"I'm Tom Druccio."

"It always this hot here in Las Vegas, Tom?"

"Waal, it's June—next month's the hottest in the year. They tell me it's nice here in the winter, though, Mr. Vitale."

"Call me Tony."

"I didn't want to sound disrespectful, ah, Tony."

"That's all right."

"If you'd like to come to the car, I'll send the driver to get your bags."

When they sat waiting in the car, Tony said, "You know why I'm here?"

"I understand that we'll be looking into the profitability of the Caprice," Tom said cautiously.

Tony liked his subdued style. And the fact that he had Levin's trust. "Wrong," he said. "We'll be looking into Abe Carroll."

"That's putting it on the line."

"Right," Tony said. "How much you know about him?"

"Up to the time he built the joint, I guess I knew as much as anyone around these parts. I helped him get established on the West Coast. That's my specialty, by the way—the picture studios."

Tony nodded. "What's gone wrong?"

"Since he got this idea about building a casino-hotel in the desert out here, he's just not the same guy."

"He originated it? I understood it was Levin's idea."

"Carroll or the broad—I don't know which. I'm surprised the outfit went for it."

Dimly Tony perceived that Levin had been supporting Carroll's personal enterprise against the resistance of the other members. Even so, for Levin to sanction the idea in the first place, it must have had merit. Then something else occurred to him: Levin was devious beyond measure. It might be that Carroll was becoming a burden. There were already signs that Carroll had personal aspirations for empire building, and was threatening to go it alone if the others didn't support him. That was a situation never allowed to take root inside the outfit. It could very well be that Levin had found a way to break Carroll, and, being Levin, come out with a profit in the end. Tony put speculation out of his head. He wasn't a principal yet, and it wasn't for him to question motivation—just to get his job done. "Levin looked into it," Tony said eventually. "The proposition's got potential."

"You wouldn't think so. The joint's never been more than half-full since it opened."

"It's still early."

The driver returned with Tony's bags, loaded the trunk, and got behind the wheel. As they drove out of the airport, he studied the arid, vacuous landscape.

"If you ask me, they dropped a brick," Tom said suddenly. "If they're hoping to attract trade from the West Coast, it won't work. It didn't work too good in Reno—over there they get mostly hicks. No real dough."

234

"Not the West Coast. The East—New York."

"Oh, now, come on . . ." Tom said scornfully.

"Listen, nobody's asking you. Keep your opinions to yourself." He said it sharply, and Tom went quiet. A few minutes later, in the distance, the monolithic Caprice appeared, alone on the undeveloped, flat panorama. "That the place?"

"Yeah, that's it."

"Looks good."

"I reserved you one of the best suites," Tom said.

"In my own name?"

"No. I got an agency to hold it."

"I won't be staying there. Tell the driver to keep rolling. We'll find a hotel downtown."

"There's not much suitable."

"I'll make do," Tony said. He smiled to himself at Tom's concern for his comfort. To Tom he was an important guy in the outfit. "I'll be looking at the casino operation in my own way," he went on. "What I want you to do is concentrate on the broad—this Barbara Strauss. I want you to put a tail on her. I wanna know every move she makes. Especially in regard to money. Can you get into her bank—can you get some figures?"

"I'll try," Tom said.

"Trying ain't good enough. I want to know what she's worth. And if she's holding dough for Carroll. Pay what you gotta, but get me information."

"O.K. I know some people," Tom said.

"Report to me every day. When I'm ready, I'll let Carroll know I'm here. And that's when we'll find out if they're running scared—when we know the broad's pattern of behavior. Maybe she'll make some panic moves."

"Carroll ain't running scared, take it from me," Tom said quietly.

"Pull in here," Tony said suddenly to the driver. They were approaching an ugly, sprawling motel on the outskirts of the city, with the jazziest electric sign he'd ever seen. What the place lacked in charm, it made up in sign. The sign said RIO RANCHO MOTEL.

"You staying here?" Tom said disbelievingly. "You gotta be kidding."

"I'm here for business, not pleasure," Tony said purposefully.

He gave it an entire week, spending each evening in the Caprice casino, keeping to himself, before he made a serious attempt to analyze the situation. Surprisingly, in all this time he went unrecognized, and there was no sign, in the Caprice, of either Barbara Strauss or Abe Carroll. He'd expected to find the place echoing and empty, and was surprised at the steady flow of visitors. Evidently the fame of this new, luxurious resort hotel was spreading widely and quickly, and attracting an influx of the curious. He gambled little, confining his attentions, when he did play, to the slots, blackjack, and a little roulette, so he shouldn't stand out as a stiff. He avoided the crap tables, other than to watch the action at arm's length from the felt. High rollers were few and far between in the untried atmosphere of this new gambling house, and he speculated on what a few live staff members could do for the place—especially one or two of those smooth-talking, quick-fingered guys from his hometown.

Of one thing he was certain right from the start—the accounts he'd inspected back in Cuba bore little relation to the true income of the casino, even with its limited action. From experience, he could relate the volume of play to its turnover, and it didn't come out to the numbers he'd inspected. There was a skim, and a heavy one. To make matters worse, there was an exceptional number of predatory faces around the place—a sure sign that something was wrong. Still more disturbing, some of the faces were behind the tables. Supervision was farcical, and there were many signs of a loosely run gambling house. He stood and watched a couple of dealers blatantly stealing—one of them fearlessly paying out phony wins to his confederate, ostensibly gambling at a roulette wheel. Not a night had passed without a hustler getting away with moves so obvious that he felt like going over and belting the dealer in the mouth for incompetence. The height of incredulity was reached when he watched a game of craps where two dice cheats unknowingly countered each other's moves. He studied all aspects of the casino operation without comment, watching the outfit's money going down the drain.

Now that he had a clear picture of the action at the Caprice, he was ready to proceed to the next stage. But he had one small problem. There had been no sign of Tom Druccio for three days. Not a word. Made all the worse because, for the first few days of Tony's stay, Tom had appeared with unfailing regularity at four o'clock every afternoon. And it was quite certain that nobody given that degree of trust by Levin could be so unreliable. Tony began to get concerned, hoping Tom hadn't run afoul of Carroll's West Coast mob. If he had, and Carroll came to the conclusion that the fix was in, it could lead to a lot of trouble.

It was Monday, his eighth day in Las Vegas, and he'd seen enough of the Caprice. On his next visit he intended to confront Carroll in his formal capacity as casino expert, and so trigger off the reaction that would tell him what Carroll and the broad were really up to. At three o'clock in the afternoon the cheapo, rattling air conditioner, which replaced a pane of glass in the window of his room, was fighting a losing battle against the broiling heat outside. He undressed and lay naked on the bed. Then, feeling restless, he got up, fished in the pocket of his coat for his dice, sat at the table, and began practicing. In the heat his fingers were sticky. He became irritated by the feel of the dice and flipped them back into his pocket. He lay down on the bed again and waited. Four o'clock came and went with no sign of Tom Druccio. He got up and found the pair of swimming trunks he'd thrown into his case. He hadn't yet seen the pool, but he knew it lay somewhere in back of the line of bungalows forming this side of the motel complex. At this hour on Monday afternoon, with the commercial motel half-empty, he'd have the pool to himself, he decided. Maybe he'd feel better after a swim.

When he rounded the corner, he almost came to a stop in surprise. Perhaps twenty women lay sunbathing around the pool on loungers, or sitting at tables shaded by wide, colorful umbrellas. Apart from three or four kids splashing around in the water, he was the only male in sight. He sensed the ripple of interest that ran along the poolside, and saw, from the corner of his eye, the heads turning in his direction. For a moment he hesitated, but he was too hot to be self-conscious. He dropped his towel on a chair, stepped up to the pool, and dived in.

The temperature of the water was just right. He swam for ten minutes, then hauled himself out onto the tiles. His towel had gone. He stood there, dripping, looking around. Then he saw the kids playing tug of war with it across the pool. He was debating with himself whether to chase them or go back to his room for another, when the voice said, "There's a fresh towel here you can use."

"Thanks." He accepted the offer, wiped his face, and rubbed his hair. Then he grinned. "I don't suppose your kids are worse-behaved than anyone else's these days."

"They're not my kids."

"Oh, I'm sorry . . ."

"That's all right. There's some cold beer here, too, if you want it. I brought two along because it's so hot. But I really couldn't drink a second."

"Thanks, I can use it. O.K. if I sit down?"

"Please do." When he sat down under the umbrella, he caught the inquisitive movements among the female heads. It was strange, so many women in the motel on their own. Maybe it was some kind of convention, he thought. He opened the can and, as he drank, studied her over the rim. She had a good figure, and her skin was deeply bronzed all over from the sun. Her dark hair was tied back with a chiffon scarf, and he guessed from the shine of her face that she was smothered in suntan oil. He couldn't see the color of her eyes behind the dark shades, but he liked the way her mouth crinkled at the corners when she smiled. "You doing six, too?" she said suddenly.

"Six what?"

"Six weeks' residence for a divorce." She waved an arm. "That's what most of the girls are here for."

He smiled. "No—no, I'm not." After a moment, he added, "How come they all choose this joint?"

"I think the lawyers in my neck of the woods have a package deal with the owners. Quite a few of the girls are from the West Coast. I'm from San Diego myself."

"Nice," he said. "I hear it's nice down there."

"Where are you from?"

"Steubenville, Ohio."

"Steel mills," she said immediately.

"Right. You been there?"

"No. I was a geography teacher before I got married. I seem to have a memory for trivia," she said, almost apologetically.

"You ain't missed much," he said.

"Are you here on vacation?"

"No." He said it without thinking. She seemed to be waiting for him to explain. "I'm on the road—a salesman."

"What do you sell?"

"Dice." It was as good a reason as any to be in Las Vegas.

"I never imagined anyone sold just dice. I suppose it's a specialized field?" she said.

"Very." Suddenly the loneliness and the sadness of these women got through to him. At least a dozen of them had been watching them covertly from beneath their umbrellas or through slitted eyes as they lay on their loungers, their heads conveniently turned. Just as suddenly, his own loneliness hit him in the pit of his stomach. Sometimes it did that when he least expected it—the awful, yawning chasm of nothingness that lately epitomized his existence. "What's your name?" he said.

"Grace. Grace Ventmore."

"I'm Tony Vitale."

"Italian extraction?" she said politely.

"Yes." He paused. "Will you have dinner with me tonight, Grace?"

She hesitated only a second. "Yes, thank you." He thought he caught gratitude in her reply.

"I'll pick you up at seven."

"I'm in thirty-three."

He got to his feet. "I have to get back now—I'm expecting a call. Thanks for the beer; it was real good."

It was important to remember the small courtesies. Some people had little else.

Inwardly he was preparing himself for the loss of Tom Druccio, so when he turned the corner and saw the Studebaker parked outside his bungalow, he hurried forward. Tom stepped from the car. "What happened to you?" Tony asked.

"Let's go inside."

The air conditioner had stopped rattling and the room was stifling hot. He fiddled with the switch and it started up again. "I been waiting to hear from you," Tony said as he turned.

"I just got back from Switzerland. I came straight here."

"Back from where?" Tony stared.

"You said to stick to Barbara Strauss. I did."

"What the fuck she doing in Switzerland?" As if he couldn't guess.

"What you think?"

"You could have phoned."

"I didn't know whether they picked up on you or not. Spending every night at the Caprice, you could easily have been recognized. If they're watching you and you get a call from Switzerland—the same time Barbara Strauss is there—we blow the gaff."

"Yeah." It was good thinking. "So what happened?"

"She makes this regular trip to Geneva. Every eight, ten weeks, maybe. Tells people on the Coast she's going to visit her mother. She takes the train to San Francisco. Changes cabs a couple of times and winds up at the airport, where she gets on a plane for Paris. There she disappears overnight. She loses me. I'm at the airport next morning, waiting for a seat on a plane home, and who should walk in? Barbara Strauss. Sheer luck, nothing else. From Paris, she takes the plane for Geneva. This time I keep on her ass."

"She didn't spot you?"

"No way—I was a private dick one time. I know what I'm doing."

"What happened in Geneva?"

238

"She goes to the Crédit Suisse—to their safe-deposit section. It's a regular deal. They recognize her immediately—it's 'Good morning, Mrs. Van Damm, this way Mrs. Van Damm . . .' "

"Who in hell's Mrs. Van Damm?"

"That's the name she travels under."

"You think Carroll's in on this, or she working solo? I wouldn't put it past her, what I hear about the broad."

"They're working together. The plane tickets are booked by an agency in San Francisco—I managed to trace it through—and billed to Carroll's Los Angeles union office. In eleven months she makes the trip five times."

"So they're salting the dough away . . ."

"Looks that way. Maybe Carroll's planning to blow, one of these days—go and live abroad," Tom said.

"That's impossible. He wouldn't get away with that and he knows it."

"The dame's a powerful influence on him. Since he knows her he seems to be doing some crazy things, real crazy. Remember, I know him before and after, so you can take it from me—he ain't the same guy he used to be. There was a time he was satisfied with being a Hollywood big shot, but no more—now he wants to be Emperor of Nevada. If you ask me, Barbara's telling him he ain't getting his. And in case their plans don't work out, they got the dough over there in Geneva as backup."

"It don't look too good," Tony said.

"What happened at your end?"

"The casino's being run like Coney Island. Hustlers beating each other over the head to get at the tables. That's one thing. The other is the skim. It's a big one—people back east ain't gonna like that."

Tom whistled. "He's taking chances all the way down the line. Do we go in?"

"No, it's not our problem. Not yet, anyway. All we have to do is report. Carroll's a principal, and someone's gonna have to make a big decision."

"It never happened before—one of the bosses, I mean."

"No."

"You gonna see Carroll personally?"

"Levin's talking to him. Lombardo's out here, too."

"What do I do now?"

"The broad—keep watching her. I want to know every move she makes. They'll have to make a decision on her, too."

"There's something I didn't tell you. She's two-timing Carroll. The overnight stop in Geneva—she spent it at a ski lodge up in the mountains. With a guy."

"What guy?" Tony frowned at this new complication.

"I got a name. I'm having it checked out."

"Anyone we know of?"

"No. A Frenchman. I don't think there's any connection. If you ask me, she's just getting her rocks off."

He thought for a moment. "Keep tabs on that situation, it could develop into something. Maybe we can use it for a lever on Carroll. On the other hand, we may have to do a deal with the broad eventually. Yeah, it's important," he decided.

239

"O.K.," Tom said. "Anything else?"

"Just keep in touch." The air conditioner gave a convulsive hiccup, then picked up again. Tony wiped his brow with the back of his hand. "Jesus, it's fucking hot in this town."

"It's the desert."

"You don't say?" he said sardonically.

He wondered why it annoyed him when people kept repeating the same thing. Didn't cost him anything.

CHAPTER THREE

The Cadillac's tires sang on the hot, sticky, black pavement of the desert road as they drove toward McCarran Airport. The air in the back of the car was claustrophobic, but neither Tony nor Lombardo made a move to open a window. He was sweating gently all over his body. Although his years in the Caribbean had to some extent inured him to the heat, the fierce onslaught of the Nevada sun was something outside his experience. He glanced across at Lombardo, sitting silently in the corner, swaying gently with the motion of the car, his face impassive. Tony started to say something, then changed his mind. Inwardly he shrugged—he'd done his part, the rest was up to them.

He dismissed the Carroll affair from his mind and allowed his thoughts to wander back to the previous evening—and Grace Ventmore. "There's something I want to tell you," Tony had volunteered as they strolled back to the motel from a local restaurant, grateful for the cool of the evening.

"Yes?" She waited.

"You don't look like a woman who's getting a divorce."

"How's a woman who's getting divorced supposed to look?"

"I mean, you look kinda nice—soft and feminine, I guess."

"Thank you." He saw the blush start in her cheeks.

"Just then . . . you reminded me of a girl I used to know. A long time ago. Her name was Francesca."

"Francesca's a beautiful name. Was she beautiful? I hope she was."

"To me she was the most beautiful thing in the world."

"And you loved her?" He said nothing. "You still dream of her?"

"No. I saw her a couple of years back, matter of fact. She's fat and bad tempered now. Got three, four kids. You know them Italians." Grace giggled. There was an air of girlish innocence about her, at odd moments. "He's gotta be crazy," Tony said.

"Who?"

"Your old man—for letting you go."

240

She stopped smiling. For a while there was only the sound of their footsteps on the sidewalk, occasionally swallowed up by a late-night car hurrying along Las Vegas Boulevard. The thought faded from his mind by the time she finally spoke. "Ours was a wartime marriage. It seemed right at the time. I suppose it's an old story: the glamor of an officer's uniform, a whirlwind romance. Then the call to go overseas. You wait for two long years—long, long years. It seems forever. He comes back and you think you're one of the lucky ones. Then time passes and you begin to realize he's not the guy you thought you married. He's mean and hard—it was all a mistake, and the two of you have nothing in common. Not a damn thing. Two people can't go on living together, having nothing to say to each other. Life's too short for that, isn't it?" She looked at him uncertainly, as if he could reassure her that she was doing the right thing. He said nothing, and maintained an even expression. ". . . I'm sorry," she said. "I didn't mean to sound off about my husband."

"That's O.K.," Tony said. "But why you still questioning yourself? If you made up your mind to split, then do it—and no regrets. It's something I notice with all them women at the motel. It's in their eyes, as if they're not really sure they're doing what's right—as if it's all a big mistake, and after the divorce, when they taught the guy a lesson, everything's gonna go back to normal."

They turned into the motel entrance. "How about you, Tony?" she said. "You're not married?"

"No."

"I suppose all dice salesman say that when they're on the road."

"I suppose they do."

"I don't mind if you are. Married, I mean. Is that wicked of me?"

"Not as wicked as kidding yourself."

"I guess I found that out."

Outside the door to room 33 she stood uncertainly. "You gonna ask me in or not?" he said.

She hesitated a moment, then opened the door with her key and stepped into the dark interior. He followed her and closed the door quietly behind him . . .

Lombardo spoke up suddenly, and Tony turned to look at him. "Levin tells me he might as well have been talking to a fucking brick wall," he said fiercely, "for all the notice Carroll took of him. It's as if all them years they spent together don't mean a thing. He just don't understand what's got into the guy."

"The woman—what else?"

Lombardo snorted. "Carroll ain't no lovesick kid. You gonna tell me a guy who comes from the Lower East Side, who gets to be a top man in the outfit—a guy like that's a pushover for some smartass dame? A guy who gets into the pants of them Hollywood movie stars?"

"You got a better explanation?"

"Yeah. He's having his second childhood, that's what. He's soft in the head."

"She's some dame, if you ask me, this Barbara Strauss."

Lombardo had allowed his thoughts to move on. "What?"

"The dame—she got some backbone, screwing the Frenchman the same time she's leading Carroll around by the nose."

"Maybe we oughta be dealing with her instead of him," Lombardo said in disgust. "She sounds like our kind of people."

"What you say we blow the whistle on her to Carroll? Maybe that'll bring him to his senses," Tony said.

"We talked about that. Levin's got the feeling we could be making a mistake, we do that. It could backfire. If the dame's cute enough to talk her way out of trouble, and I wouldn't put it past her, it could set Carroll against us. He's in control of the entire operation in the West, remember, and he runs it like it's his own. Maybe it's our own fault for letting him get away with it all these years. Nothing we can do about it now—ever since I remember we concentrate on the East and we leave the West Coast like it's a foreign country or something. If Carroll takes it into his head to stand up to us, his mob's gonna follow his orders because it's *his* mob. Not more than a dozen guys out here even know who we are. Know what that means? It means, if we ain't careful, we could end up with a mob war on our hands. We have to move soldiers out west, where they're unfamiliar with the layout. We do that, the first thing we get is a lot of bad publicity. Can you imagine the headlines—New York, Chicago hoods take over West Coast? The pricks don't know—we already own it."

"We can't just let him go on stealing our dough," Tony said.

"Sure we can't. We don't intend to."

"Why not put it to him that we move in and run the Caprice? At least, that way, we could steer it into profit. It'd be a start—then we could go to work on taking over his outfit."

"You reckon we ain't thought of that? He's wise to them moves. He says he don't want no interference from our end. He wants things the way they always been—we gotta leave him to do things his way out here, he says. The way he sees it, he's as big a man in the outfit as any of us, and that's the way it's gonna stay."

"He's doing things his way now, the prick. It's costing us a fortune."

"According to Carroll, the Caprice got off to a bad start. It was one of them things goes wrong with a legit operation sometimes. We gotta give it time, he says. What he don't know—his own time is running out, the dumb fuck."

In their opposite corners, they lapsed into silence. Tony turned to the window, staring sightlessly, in silent anger, at the desert scrubland rolling past. Again, to cool off, he allowed his thoughts to wander . . .

"Can we keep the lights off?" Grace had said. He had reached out for the bedside lamp. They undressed in the semidarkness and climbed into bed. He said nothing. "Did you hear me?"

"Yes, I heard."

"You don't mind, do you, Tony?"

"Yes, I do mind." He touched the switch and a soft glow flooded the room. "We got nothing to be afraid of. We don't have to hide in the dark."

She lay with the bedclothes pulled up to her neck. He took hold of them. For an instant she held on, then her fingers relaxed. Slowly he drew the covers down until her body was revealed. He looked at her. She had a very good shape, now that he saw her without her bathing suit. Her breasts were firm and full, her waist slim, her hips not too wide. He studied her stomach, the puff of dark pubic hair, the shape of

242

her thighs. "Don't look at me that way," she said softly.

"Why not? You can look real hard at me if you want. I won't stop you." She turned her head away. "Say, you got it bad," he said.

"Got what?" She turned back.

"Hangups. You're ashamed of yourself—you're ashamed to be here with me, as if it's a crime or something."

"I'm not ashamed." She said it quickly.

He gave a small laugh. "I'd forgotten there was women like you existed. Where I been they . . ." He stopped.

She looked at him, puzzled. "Where have you been?"

"I mean to say, there's a lot of broads around can make a guy feel like he's been living on the moon. Know what I mean?"

"Maybe I'm a little old-fashioned. Is that so bad?"

"No."

"After all, we haven't even kissed yet," she said lamely. "Is that any way to treat a lady."

He was forgetting the proprieties. It made him realize how different his life had become—how far removed from the niceties of ordinary conduct. He gave her a grin and leaned across to plant his lips gently on hers. She returned the kiss, cautiously at first, then, after the second and the third, she allowed her lips to blend with his. He could feel, from the quickening of her movements, that the heat was rising in her. For a while he kept his arms by his side. Then, when he thought she was ready for him, he reached out, took her hand, and placed it on him. He could feel the pulse stirring in her arm. "Just hold it," he said quietly.

"Isn't the man supposed to do this sort of thing?" she whispered.

"Sure—I'm next. Right now it's your turn. Do as I say—hold it." He felt himself growing larger as her fingers closed timidly around him, hesitantly, as if it were some unfair imposition he'd burdened her with. In a flash of annoyance, he said, "Oh, for Chrissakes, you're the one wanted to fuck me, remember? You're the one gave me the come-on in the first place. What you think, I'm a fool or something? What you afraid of? If you wanna grab, then grab. You ain't kidding nobody with this ladylike act of yours. Nobody except yourself."

Her breasts were rising and falling as her breath came in fierce gasps. When he put his head down to caress the nipples with his tongue, he felt her fingers tighten on him. Her searching movement became more confident, more demanding. He explored the silky contours of her breasts with careful movements, then moved to the firm roundness of her stomach. Suddenly, unexpectedly, her thighs parted and she was pushing up, seeking the solace of his skillful fingers. He could contain himself no longer. He rolled quickly on top of her. Deftly he guided his tip into her magical moisture and then, with a gasp of gratification, eased himself into her willing crotch . . .

"How much longer to this flea-bitten airport?" Lombardo asked suddenly.

"What?" Tony said.

"The airport."

"We're almost there."

"Carroll's gotta be screwy, building a resort hotel in a Godforsaken part of the country like this," Lombardo complained. The heat was getting to him at last. "Can you imagine people coming out here in serious numbers? I mean real numbers?"

"Yes, I can," Tony said. "Levin thinks so, too. We both come to the conclusion it's right. Out here, there's a sense of getting away from it all. Some people like that; gamblers most of all. But the real strength of the proposition lies in Nevada's laws. People can do out here what they can't do at home—and they can do it legit. All we gotta do is make sure they can do it in comfort."

"There's no facilities out here. A person's gotta stay in the hotel. If he goes outside, he fries."

"Nothing wrong in that. He stays in the hotel and gambles."

"They'll want more."

"We'll give them everything they need, right there in the hotel. They won't have to go out for nothing." A windsock on a pole, out in the dry scrub, passed the corner of Tony's vision. He looked forward, out through the windshield of the car. In the distance he could see the outline of the airport buildings. "We're nearly there," he said.

Despite the heat, Lombardo fastened his collar and straightened his tie. "There's gonna be a meeting when I get back to New York," he said. "Now that we know the facts, we'll make a decision."

"What you want me to do?"

"Just wait. I'll be in touch."

"Is it O.K. if I move into the Caprice?" Tony said. "The joint I'm staying in—it ain't exactly the Ritz."

"No, don't do that. Not yet."

"What's the difference? We got the information we need. What we care what Carroll thinks? He knows well enough we're gonna be looking to protect our interests."

"Wait till after the meeting. If the others feel the same way I do, and we're all out of patience, there will be some action. You better stay where you are until the dust settles."

"That could take a long time," Tony protested.

"Not so long." The Cadillac came to a dusty stop at the airport terminal. In the midst of sweating, Tony felt a cold shiver run down his spine as he stared at the mask of Lombardo's features. For a moment Lombardo sat, immobile, impervious to the beads of sweat standing out on his forehead. Then he reached for the door handle. "Let me outa this oven," he grated. "Me, I had it with this goddamn hick town."

244

CHAPTER FOUR

He lay on the bed studying his hands, the fingers covered in the talcum powder he was using to keep them dry while practicing the dice. He brushed off the powder, let his hands fall to his sides, and gazed up at the ceiling. As he traced out the papered-over cracks, he wondered what was going on in New York. What decisions had been made and how they would affect him. The days were passing and he'd had no contact with anyone except Tom Druccio, who was keeping a constant watch over Barbara Strauss. Between them they knew more about the woman than Carroll ever would. The telephone rang. "How about lunch?" Grace's voice said.

"I'm not hungry."

"Me, neither. See you at the pool?"

He hesitated a moment. "Yeah, O.K.," he said eventually. "Ten, fifteen minutes." He was bored stiff with lying around the pool under the wistful gaze of twenty near-liberated, curiously passive women. He'd come to know several of them by name and found the most interesting part of the proceedings to be how the parade of faces and figures slowly changed as new divorcees replaced the old. But there was little excitement in it for him. He'd quickly been tagged "Grace's guy," and that was the way it stayed as, day after day, he waited for a message from Lombardo.

When he arrived at the pool Grace was frying in oil once again, her daily fifteen minutes, front and back. He flopped down under the umbrella. After a while he noticed that she was studying him obliquely, her head turned in his direction, from where she rested on her stomach. "I've been wondering," she said. "You sure you're a salesman—I never see you sell anything?"

"It bother you?"

"A little. When do you sell your dice?"

He smiled inwardly. "I do most of my deals on the phone, in the mornings," he said.

"Don't you have to show the merchandise?"

"People know what dice look like."

She seemed doubtful. "I don't believe you're a dice salesman."

"You don't?"

"No. I don't suppose you've anything more to do with dice than I have."

He stared at her for a long moment, without animosity. She didn't notice his hand creeping toward the pocket of the terry-cloth robe he'd flung down on the tiles. In the same movement he sat up and she found herself staring at the pair of transparent reds he held in his open palm. "What these look like to you—onion rings?"

"Where did they come from?" Her eyes widened. She rolled over and sat up.

He smiled at her. "They're magic dice. They'll do anything I say."

"Come on . . ." Grace said.

"Give me a number. Any number, two to twelve."

"I don't gamble." The puritan ethic stiffened her back.

"I'm not asking you to gamble. Just give me a number."

"What numbers do gamblers like?"

"Seven's a good number."

"How can you be sure you'll throw a seven?"

"I told you, they're magic. Look, just a small bet—if I throw a seven, you pay for dinner tonight, O.K.?"

"They're trick dice, aren't they?"

"No, they're straights, honest."

"All right, just to please you," she said half-heartedly.

He pitched the dice on the smooth tiles. They rolled up a six and an ace. "Dinner's on you, babe," he grinned.

"It wasn't a trick?"

"Not unless you want to call manipulation a trick."

"It didn't look difficult. Can you teach me to do that?"

He laughed. "Honey, there are guys in this town, if they could do what I just done, they'd get rich overnight."

"That's garbage. Gambler's talk. I've heard it all before. I'm not that naïve," Grace said firmly.

"It's true, honey." He wondered why he was arguing.

"If it's true, how come you're just a salesman?"

"I like the work," he said lamely.

She turned away, disbelief on her face, to pick up a newspaper and begin reading. A few minutes later, he heard her voice again: "Gee, guess who's appearing at the Caprice Supper Club?"

He looked up. "The Caprice?"

"That new place."

"Who's appearing?"

"Johnny Angel, in person. Can you believe it?" He looked across to see if the reverence in her voice was genuine.

She meant it. "You like him, this Johnny Angel?" Tony asked.

"Like him? I'm just wild about the guy—so is every other red-blooded American woman, if she'd admit the truth. He's so good looking, and when he sings it just does things to me . . ." She gave a sensual shudder. "Didn't you see him in *Jason's Blues*?"

"No. I don't see many movies these days."

"You sure missed something. I'd give almost anything if I could see that show. The Caprice Supper Club—I guess it must be hideously expensive."

"Maybe I can get us a table if it means that much to you." He was surprised to find his male chauvinism expressing itself.

"You mean it?" The excitement rose in her throat. "Wow, wouldn't that be something to tell the folks back home—I saw Johnny Angel sing, in person."

"Fact is, I know the guy. He comes from my hometown. We used to work together when we was kids."

"You know Johnny Angel *personally*?"

246

"Remember the girl I told you about—that Francesca? That's his sister." He laughed. At last he'd found something to raise his stock in Grace's eyes. "Maybe I'll introduce you to the bum."

When the lights went down and, to a fanfare of trumpets, Johnny Angel was announced, Tony was amazed at the wave of adulation that rose from the audience. Then the orchestra struck up and Angelo appeared, picked out on the darkened stage by a single spotlight, the smooth tones of his voice pouring over them from the speakers strategically placed about the room. The sighs that went up from the females in the audience were instantly replaced by a thunderous welcome in recognition of his current hit recording, and the sound of their applause reflected the joy in their eyes at the physical sight of their hero. Angelo had clearly come a long way since the Steubenville days, or even the early performance in Pittsburgh that Tony found himself suddenly remembering. Confidently the singer carried his listeners along with him on a roller coaster of subtly suggestive lyrics, caressing and enrapturing the women's sensibilities. It was abundantly clear now that Angelo had always had the talent, just as it was written on the squeaky-clean, shining, respectable middle-class American female faces that they were willing partners to the rhythmic seduction expressed in his song. And, for all that, Tony could still recognize in him, behind the professionalism, the buddy from his youth.

"Isn't he stupendous?" The awe in Grace's voice reached him across the table.

"He's a good singer. Always was," he agreed.

Grace shot him a disgusted glance. "He's more than just a good singer. He's the best—everyone knows that."

He shrugged helplessly at the emotion Angelo evoked in this usually sanguine lady. He couldn't explain to her that the singer's style, his whole demeanor, was just another variation on the old hometown theme that had originated at the gambling tables: *Charm 'em to death.* Bringing himself back to the present, he inched his chair back so that he merged with the shadows behind him. It had been a crazy thing to do, jeopardizing a sensitive, multimillion-dollar proposition with a surreptitious appearance at the casino theater for the sake of gratifying Grace's whim. He should have known better. So far he'd been lucky to avoid recognition at the Caprice. The sudden appearance of a representative of the outfit might be enough to upset the whole Carroll apple cart. He was grateful that they were seated unobtrusively at the rear of the room, at one of the worst tables, their vision partially obscured by a pillar. Nobody would look twice at him here. He'd deliberately refrained from tipping the captain so they wouldn't get a prominent spot. Then he grinned to himself, wondering why it was he still got a kick out of taking a gamble. He edged back even deeper in the shadows and settled down to listen to Angelo.

Now he was taking an even bigger risk by going backstage. "Is Mr. Angel expecting you?" A burly, cold-eyed guard barred their way to the star's dressing room.

"Tell him Tony wants to see him."

"Tony who?"

"Tony Rockefeller—just tell him Tony from Sixth Street. He'll know."

"Wise guy, huh? Well, Mr. Angel ain't seeing nobody right now. He's resting for the late show. Give me a number—if he wants to speak to you, he'll call," the guard said levelly.

"Get outa my way," Tony said impatiently, and stepped forward.

"I got my orders." The man spread a massive hand on Tony's chest.

"Take your paw off me, punk."

Patiently, the big guy said, "I ain't letting no fans bother Mr. Angel tonight. This morning they get in the hotel and tear the coat off his back. Last week they pull out a fistful of hair. Right now he's real sore about the fans, and it ain't gonna happen again while I'm around. Let me give you a little inside information: If the lady wants an autograph, she can write in and get a photo of Mr. Angel inscribed with a personal message. So be nice and push off—and take the dame with you."

He looked up at the blockhead and decided to try a different angle. "O.K.," he shrugged, "you take the responsibility. I said I'd get the dough here by tonight. If I can't deliver, I can't deliver, right?"

"What dough?" The big guy frowned.

"The thousand bucks." Tony dipped into his pocket and came up with his roll. "Tonight's the deadline."

"You owe Mr. Angel a thousand bucks?"

"Yeah. So let him chase me for it. Who cares anyway? Come on, Grace, let's go." He turned away.

"Just a minute. I'll take the money for you."

"No way—I ain't parting with this dough, except to Mr. Angel himself."

"All right. Wait here. I'll ask if he wants to see you. What you say your name was?"

"Tony Vitale."

A few minutes later, Angelo came roaring out of his dressing room. "Hey— hey—hey." They embraced like long-lost brothers. ". . . Tony, it's really you. I don't believe it—must be a thousand years."

"Sure has been a long time, old buddy." They both grinned from ear to ear.

"Come on in here. Boy, how you've changed . . ." The smell of whiskey on Angelo's breath instantly transported Tony back over the years. Nothing had really changed, including the glazed look in Angelo's eyes, despite the singer's success. "So how you been, *compare*—how's the old dice ace?"

"Just fine, Angelo, I'm fine. You still talk to poor people, now you're such a big celebrity?"

"Oho, listen to him—you ain't so poor, not from what I hear of Tony Vitale. I move in circles, these days. You know what I mean, circles? I hear big things about my old Steubenville buddy."

"This is Grace Ventmore, a friend . . ." Tony cut him short with a warning glance.

"Oh, I get it. The broad don't know nothing, huh? Hi, Grace . . ." She stood staring at Angelo as if he were unreal. She nodded dumbly in reply.

"Grace is a fan of yours. She wants to be able to go home and say she met the Great Johnny Angel," Tony said.

"Really, Tony . . ." She began.

"Honey, since you're a friend of Tony's, I'm gonna give you a photo of myself

248

signed by me personally." He took one from a pile and scribbled a few words on it, then handed it to her. "O.K., now we gotta have a drink to celebrate the reunion of two old friends." He poured out the remains of a whiskey bottle into three glasses. "To the good old days . . ." His went down first.

"You still boozing, Angelo? I read in the papers how you got a problem with the booze. Something in that?"

"That's horseshit, Tony. Sure, I take a snort now and then, same as the next guy. That's all hooey, what you read in them papers. Them publicity people, they gotta earn their dough. They'll say anything to keep their client in the public eye. Know what I mean?"

"Oh, sure," Tony said. "Say, that's some job on the nose . . ." He hadn't stopped looking at it since they entered the dressing room.

"You like it?" Angelo's gaze shot to a mirror. "Looks good on me, huh?"

"Looks terrific," Tony said. "You got a genuine Michelangelo there."

"Yeah, the guy who did it, he's the greatest—he's remodeled half of Hollywood. He took out the guinea hook like it was never there. And me, I never looked back since the day I got me a new hooter." He paused. "Know something, Tony, I was never so frightened in all my life like before the operation. Changing the shape of my nose could have changed my voice. It was the biggest decision I ever made."

"I'm glad it worked out for you, Angelo," Tony said.

"You wouldn't believe what happened. My voice came on even better. After that I couldn't do nothing wrong. That was when it all started, when my career really got off the ground." The telephone rang and Angelo answered it in a brief, short-tempered conversation. When he put it down, he said, "There's a crowd of people on their way over from the casino. Friends of that Carroll, the guy who owns the joint. The hotel management wants me to say hello to them, all that shit. Just hang around for a while, it won't take me long to get rid of 'em."

"No, I gotta go now," Tony said quickly.

"Hell, Tony, what's the rush? We ain't met in ten years—."

"I don't wanna be seen in the joint," Tony said, and, out of Grace's vision, gave Angelo the urgent *nix* sign they both knew from their youth. "Any other way out of here?"

Angelo understood immediately. "No. Tell you what, though, I'll go out and meet 'em in the hall, then I'll walk 'em back toward the casino. When we're gone you can slip out the way you came in."

Tony held out his hand. "Here's to the next ten years, old buddy."

"That's a hell of a lot of whiskey under the bridge, pal." Angelo's grasp was warm and strong. At the door he turned. "Tony, there's something I always wanted to ask you: The guy who went missing that time, back in Steubenville—you remember, the hustler. The time you crashed your car in the river and took it on the lam. You ever have anything to do with that? I always wanted to ask."

He stood stock-still before he said, "How you know about that guy?"

"His partner came looking for him. Didn't the Duke tell you?"

"The Duke said the guy wasn't missed."

"Hoyle was paid to keep his mouth shut, the way I heard it."

"So why didn't the Duke tell me?"

Angelo shrugged. They heard voices on the other side of the door and there was a knock. "I'll get rid of 'em," Angelo said.

"So long, *paisan*," Tony said softly.

Angelo opened the door halfway and carefully slipped out.

He awoke about ten o'clock and sensed the heat of the day beginning to build up outside. For a while he lay there, listening to the rattling, battling air conditioner. Then he got up, showered and shaved, pulled on some linen slacks, and picked up the telephone. There was no reply from Grace's bungalow. He made a cup of courtesy coffee from the machine on the wall. Outside his door the burgeoning, fierce sun hit him in the face so that he blinked. He strolled along to bungalow 33 and knocked. There was no response. He was surprised that Grace was out so early; it was unusual for her. He toured the grounds of the motel; she was nowhere around. The sweat was beginning to ooze out of him by the time he returned to the protection of the lobby. He picked up a newspaper and folded it under his arm. The guy on regular morning duty behind the desk was called Joseph, he'd discovered. Joseph had a permanent unfriendly look about him, although he tried to be pleasant. Joseph was rubbing his eyes. He stopped when he saw Tony watching him. "Good morning, sir," he said.

"Good morning. Another hot one today," Tony said.

Joseph glanced out through the glass. "Funny," he said. "I notice it's always easterners say that—about the weather, I mean."

"The heat don't bother you?" Tony said.

"Not in here. I don't go out, not unless I have to."

"That makes sense." He took a last glance at the pool area through the glass. When he looked back Joseph was rubbing his eyes again. He grinned self-consciously when he saw Tony watching him. "Late nights?" Tony said.

"Yeah, too many."

"You're a gambler, huh?"

"You kidding—on the dough I make here?"

"I didn't mean to get personal," Tony said.

"There's something more interesting than numbers to stay up for around here." There was a sly look on Joseph's face.

"What's that?"

"The broads. All the gay divorcees on the loose around here. And in the mood. You found that out, haven't you?"

". . . Oh, yeah, sure," Tony said.

"It wasn't for the broads, I don't stay around this place one day more'n I have to. I'm off to L.A. where a guy can make a decent living, right?"

"Got you," Tony said.

"The way I see it, I got the choice between getting tail and earning more dough. Guys I know who earn big dough, they spend it chasing tail. Me, I'm a realist. If I go to L.A. I earn more dough, but I don't get tail. I ain't the kind to kid myself—I know I'm not good looking and I got no magnetic personality, nothing like that, so I don't have much going for me with the broads. Seems to me I'm better off around here, picking up freebies. It's all a question of priorities, don't you agree?"

"Oh, sure," Tony said soberly.

"I know where I'm at. These broads, they're lonely and frightened. They need a shoulder to cry on, so I listen sympathetically, and eventually they come across. It's a fair trade. Some of 'em, it's their first time outside the box, and they don't know what to expect—so I kinda let 'em experiment with me."

"Joseph, I get the feeling you're performing a public service."

Joseph leaned across his desk. "Great thing is—and this is the important angle—none of them stays longer than six weeks. No involvement, right? When their six weeks is up, they scoot out of here faster'n a prairie wind."

"You got it made."

"Sure. Look at it this way—I eat well, get plenty of tail, and I don't work too hard. What more can a guy want?"

Tony found himself staring past Joseph's head to the key resting in slot 33. "Mrs. Ventmore gone out?" he asked.

"That's thirty-three—the lady checked out this morning."

"Checked out, you said?"

"Yes, sir. Just a minute . . ." He flipped through his ledger. "Right on time. Six weeks today, on the nose."

He looked up at Tony, who hadn't changed his expression, except that he'd spotted the note resting in his own slot. "Is that for me?"

"Oh, yes, sir, it is." Joseph had assumed his formal attitude and handed it over.

"Thanks for the talk, Joseph."

He lay on the bed and read Grace's letter:

My Very Dear Tony,

I hope you will forgive me for running away like this. I know it is the coward's way out, but I cannot help it. I find it difficult to define my feelings for you, but I do know that we are two very different people, in background and moral outlook, and the strangeness of your ways sometimes frightens me. I think you have not been entirely frank with me concerning your work, and (my luck) you probably have a wife and family somewhere waiting for you, if the truth is known. No salesman could possibly have the money you appear to have, wear the clothes you wear, and know people like Johnny Angel. So I think you are being devious with me, and I do not want to start another relationship that may bring me more unhappiness. I think we are both mature enough to leave out the word love, at least as we know it from the movies. I want to thank you for the wonderful experience of teaching me what my body is capable of, and I will remember you and Las Vegas for the rest of my life.

I hope you will forgive me for discovering how lonely you truly are, and I pray you find the happiness you seek.

Grace

P.S. Johnny Angel is one singer I don't want to see or hear again. The sound of his voice sickens me now that I know he's a drunkard and a boor.

For some time Tony lay in utter stillness, staring at the letter in his hand. Then, in a fit of rage, he threw it into a corner of the room. In that moment he dismissed

251

Grace Ventmore from his mind completely. Joseph was right. Screw 'em and forget 'em—he was a fool, for all his experience.

He reached across the bed and picked up the newspaper. He opened it and the headlines screamed back at him:

STARS' CONSORT SHOT TO DEATH BY MARAUDER

ABE CARROLL SLAIN IN BEL AIR MANSION

CHAPTER FIVE

Tony heard the car pull up outside the bungalow. He knew from the light sound of the engine that it was Tom Druccio's innocuous Studebaker. Tom stepped in and waited until Tony had closed the door and parted the drapes to glance outside. When he closed them again, Tom turned to him, and said briefly, "Well, that's the end of the Carroll problem."

"Everything go as planned?"

"Yes. Exactly. They made it look as if he interrupted a burglary. They took a few pieces of jewelry—it's the dame's house. And they blasted the safe outa the wall to make it look good. There was no dough, incidentally, but a lot of papers. I got them stashed away. When things cool off, I'll hand them over to you."

"Make copies. I don't wanna handle the originals," Tony said sharply.

"Right."

"I heard it on the radio—there's a lot of rumors flying around. Levin's name was mentioned several times."

"Nothing I can do about that. Lots of people know they were partners years back. The rumors will die down. Don't worry about it. And the law can't prove a thing. Believe me, Tony, there's no way they can trace the killing back to us."

"To you," Tony corrected. "Now it's all over, I'm gonna tell you again: You're on your own if they do—you understand?"

"Yes, I understand."

"It's a stinking job and nobody's happy about it—that dumb-fuck Carroll brought it on his own head. It's the first time a thing like this happens to a member of the council. It's gonna teach everyone a lesson." He paused. "Levin wants you to know he appreciates the way you handled everything. I think he's got his eye on you for boss of the West Coast team. Think you can handle it?"

"I can handle it." Tom's eyes brightened. It was his only show of emotion. "I know Carroll's operations so well, people won't even notice I stepped into his shoes."

Tony swung around on him. "Don't make that mistake," he said harshly. "Nobody steps into Carroll's shoes. Carroll was unique. One of the old school. He was right for his time and place. It's different today, and he couldn't adapt. We don't want characters—smart asses, anymore. This is big business. A business this size, it runs on teamwork."

"I'll handle it any way you want. You only gotta say."

Tony spoke quietly again. "I want you to know—I put in a good word for you."

"I really appreciate that, Tony."

"So you'll owe me one," he said laconically. Then added, "You got my recommendation because it's due. Nothing else."

Tom nodded respectfully. "Listen—to bring the Carroll situation up to date . . . I didn't think it was important, now that he's dead, but Barbara Strauss gave me the slip. She dumped me a few hours before Carroll got it, so there's no connection."

"Think she was wise you were on her tail?"

"Yeah, I think so, in the end."

"So where is she now, you think?"

"My San Francisco contact called me. She got on a Paris plane this morning. It's no routine trip to the bank in Switzerland, she was just there last week. If you ask me, when she heard about Carroll, she decided to make a run for it."

"We'll have to find her if we wanna get our dough back."

"When she gave me the slip, I didn't follow through. It would have meant hanging around the house in Bel Air to pick up her trail. That ain't wise. Especially now there's a million cops buzzing around the joint."

"I understand," Tony said. "But that was yesterday. This is today, and you better find a way to get back on her tail. You're wasting time here, so get moving."

"O.K." Tom accepted another Paris trip stoically. "By the way, there's something else I just found out. Carroll and Barbara Strauss were married in Mexico."

Tony whistled. "That cinches it. She was the boss, all right."

"Yeah. By the way, how does that affect her position now?"

He grinned slowly. "That's another monkey puzzle for the council. It's part of the deal, like they drew it up years ago—the family gets taken care of when it happens to a member, no matter what the reason."

"She classifies?" Tom scratched his chin.

"You betcha. No exceptions."

The telephone rang. Tony picked it up. "We're very pleased with the way you handled things," Lombardo's voice said.

"You can thank Tom Druccio, he's a clean worker."

"Yes. He deserves recognition. We have plans for him. When you seeing him next?"

"He's right here with me."

"Good. Tell him he's to move in and take over Carroll's union business immediately. We'll pass the word it's approved."

"That's gonna have to wait. I'm sending him to Paris. Barbara Strauss is over there—she took it on the lam."

"It's all right, we know."

Tony was surprised, but didn't say so. "If she disappears, we can say goodbye to our dough."

"Levin's gone over there to talk to her."

Again he was surprised. "How'd you find her so quick?"

Lombardo was silent a moment before he said, "Her Frenchman is one of our guys. He's a plant. We had our eye on her for some time."

He stared into the telephone. "You might have said so, instead of letting Tom and me make fools of ourselves chasing her halfway around the world—."

"It was a useful double-check," Lombardo cut in succinctly.

"I suppose you know they were married, too?"

"Yes. We heard about the Mexican wedding."

"Is there anything you don't know?" Atypically, Tony allowed acid to creep into his voice.

"Yes, we don't quite know how to handle the broad, now that Carroll's gone. She has rights."

He forgot his annoyance. "So she is family?"

"Naturally. She's Carroll's wife, we like it or not. She's a clever dame, that one. She bought herself protection." He was silent again, as if thinking it over. "We can't make exceptions, it could lead to some ugly situations. That's why Levin's gone over there to talk to her personally. He's putting a proposition to her—that she returns our money and we look after her as family in the usual way."

He grinned to himself. "She made suckers out of us."

Lombardo began again. "So here's your next move—."

"Hold it," Tony said. "Now the pressure's off, I got something to say." He paused. "So far, I make no complaints. So far, I cooperate to the best of my ability . . ."

"You're capable and reliable, Tony, we recognize that. What's the problem?"

"The problem is me. I ain't suited to this type work."

"I don't get you."

"This job, it sickened me," he said simply.

"Sure, I understand. It's no picnic, knocking over one of our own."

Lombardo didn't understand. "It just ain't my style—one of our own or not."

"So let's hope it don't happen again," Lombardo said coolly.

He thought he detected a sardonic note. "I'm telling you now. In the future you can count me out."

"Listen, you're a member. You take your responsibilities, same as everyone."

"I'll accept responsibility—in my own line. I'll handle any gambling proposition you care to put up. But I got no stomach for this kind of thing. There's guys around you can do the job without turning a hair. Why pick on me?"

"Because you were there, and you represent us. Because it's what the council decided." There was an uncomfortable silence before Lombardo went on in a calmer voice. "All right, maybe you got a point. In the future I'll remember you're a specialist. Is it O.K. if I go on now?" He waited, falsely patient.

"I'm listening," Tony said.

"I guess you're expecting to take over the Caprice, now that it's running wild. But it don't fall that way. The joint's going to Sy Mulhfield." Sy was one of the originals, like Levin and Lombardo, and one of the most powerful members, Tony knew.

He didn't question the decision. After a long minute, he said, "I'd just as soon go back to Cuba."

"You're not going back to Cuba. You're staying in Vegas."

"Doing what?"

"First thing is to organize the gambling at the Caprice for Sy. We want you to set it up with the best team in the country. It's going to be a showplace."

"Why a showplace?"

"People will want to invest when they see what we're doing. After the Caprice there will be others. Bigger and better."

"What happens to me when I've set up the Caprice?"

"You'll be taking over one of the downtown clubs in Las Vegas. A place called the Casablanca."

"That hick joint?" Tony's mind flew to the flashy, hysterically lit bunch of gambling houses huddled together down where the desert roads met. "What the fuck we want with that trap?"

"We own it."

"You're kidding."

"We own it some time, matter of fact."

The truth began to dawn. The extent of Levin's interest in Las Vegas poured over him. "We own it before Carroll builds the Caprice?" he asked.

"Long before he even thought of it," Lombardo said.

It all fell into place. Levin's incredibly long-term plans. The demise of Carroll. Of course—it would have been impractical to go ahead with development and massive investment in the West, with a puppet emperor crashing around like a bull in a china shop. Perhaps even Barbara Strauss was a Levin operative. Who knew with Levin? A man who could slip Cuba into his pocket wouldn't have much trouble developing a Nevada hick town. "We going ahead with other deals in Vegas?"

"Yes."

"I understand," Tony said simply.

"When the Caprice is pointing in the right direction, we'll start building new ones. That's why you gotta stay around. One of them will be yours to run. For you, the finest."

"I'd just as soon go back to Cuba," Tony repeated wearily. He really was very fond of the island, he found himself thinking.

"We'll see," Lombardo said. "Don't be impatient. In time, we'll see."

A thought struck him. "Why'd you give me that shit, that time, about Carroll being a jerk for building out here in the desert?"

"Sometimes," Lombardo said, "there are things Levin don't even tell *me* about."

He sounded sincere, Tony thought.

CHAPTER SIX

He secretly enjoyed the larger-than-life atmosphere of the crazy, jazzy little joint festooned with flashing lights. Down here they even had flashing lights in the john. The place was small only by the opulent standards to which he'd become accustomed, although the Casablanca still managed to employ a hundred people in its three daily shifts. It ran twenty-four hours, and the graveyard shift was the honky-tonkiest of the three, with incongruous flashing lights and tawdry slots in gaudy competition with the powerful Nevada morning. The joint was running live with broads, chiselers, and sharpers, all feeding off the seemingly endless supply of out-of-town suckers passing through the desert oasis. Of the hundred employees, he decided, at least fifty showed signs of honesty, and the rest followed a riotous course of stealing from everyone within reach, including the sloppy hired management. He initiated his old routine of hanging around the place for days in the guise of a sucker working at disposing of a windfall, making an easy target of himself. It soon became apparent where changes would need to be made. When he'd seen enough, he revealed his identity to a sore and stupefied staff, and, by the time the remaining employees had come to terms with the new-style management, he was running a tight ship, even if it was a little short-handed. In the meantime, he took the precaution of wiring east for crew and soon had things running smoothly.

Now that the club had taken on a businesslike air, he indulged himself occasionally by dipping into the crap games, acting as shill, to heighten the action. Guys staking the remains of their paychecks on penny-ante thrills at the crap table would find themselves witnessing a spectacular performance—Tony spinning up a five-dollar stake into a three-inch pile of checks. Or he'd blow a roll of bills on an apparently desperate attempt to chase an incredibly elusive win. It was all good, clean fun.

"There's a call for you, Mr. Vitale, sir." He was standing alone in the casino, watching the action at a distance.

He broke his concentration. "What was that?"

"The telephone, sir." The bellboy was new and had the soft, natural courtesy of local westerners. He led Tony to the telephone and handed him the receiver.

"Yeah, who's that?"

"Tony, it's me . . ."

He could recognize that rusty voice anywhere. He brightened. "Hey, Mokey, you finally discovered we got telephones here in Las Vegas," he yelled. "How's the folks?"

"They're fine, Tony. I ain't calling from home."

"So where are you, little brother?"

"I'm here in Los Angeles."

"You're where? What's the big idea, coming to the West Coast without calling me?"

"I got trouble, Tony," Mokey said hesitantly.

He stiffened. "What's wrong?"

"I'm on the run from the police."

"What you do?"

"That's just it. I ain't done nothing. Not against the law, that is."

"So you done nothing and you got the law on your ass for it—don't you think you better explain?" Tony said patiently.

"It's like this: You remember that girl, that Ginny Brandon from Sunset, over to Hilltop?"

"Mokey, I been away a lifetime . . ." Tony said wearily.

"Sure you remember. Hoyle's niece, the one he's fond of. Her face ain't much, but she got tits can bring tears to your eyes."

"Look, I don't remember, O.K.? So, what's the difference—go on, willya?"

"Hoyle's the Fix now."

"Yeah, I heard."

"Well, Ginny, she's gone and got herself knocked up and complained to Hoyle it was me."

"Was it you?"

"She screwing around with two or three other guys the same time. It could be anybody. Why should I take the blame?" Mokey protested.

"Calm down," Tony said. "Just tell me what happened."

"Hoyle came after me. Says I gotta marry the broad, he don't want no family scandal. I tell him to go to hell and we take it from there."

"What you mean?"

"I socked him. He fell down and split his head on a rock."

"He dead?" A cold feeling gripped him.

"Nah, he's O.K. Sore as hell, though. I make a run for it and he puts out an APB on me. So now I'm a fucking fugitive, would you believe?"

"So what you doing over there at Los Angeles?"

"A couple of Hoyle's boys cornered me. I stole a car to get away. I headed west and kept going, traveling at night. I go any further, I end up in the fucking ocean . . ."

"Why didn't you make for Las Vegas?"

"I ain't that dumb. I don't wanna lead them cops straight to you, do I? Any case, I figure maybe they watching you out there, waiting for me."

"Nothing happening around here I know of. I'll check. You better get out here right away."

"I'm stuck. I got no dough."

"Where are you? I'll send someone."

"I'm in this dump of a hotel—the Pueblo, in West Los Angeles. The car's down in the street. It's nearly out of gas, but I guess there's enough left to get me a few miles."

"Don't touch it," Tony snapped. "You're gonna stand out like a sore thumb, a car with Ohio plates and all. Some wise guy gets curious and you're in trouble. Stay in your room and I'll get someone over to you. What's your room number?"

When Mokey told him, he slammed down the receiver and, for a moment,

257

studied it thoughtfully. He picked it up again and called Tom Druccio at the Los Angeles union office.

There was something about the lean, fit, quietly dressed young guy that fascinated Tony. There was discipline in every line of his body, and Tony had been covertly watching him since he set foot in the club half an hour ago. Perhaps it was the alert awareness of the young gray eyes, or the confidence with which he held himself, but Tony knew from across the room that there was an affinity between them. Just what it was, he couldn't define. Then the young stranger was at the cage, buying a few rolls of quarters. He handed these to the gorgeous young blonde who'd entered on his arm, and she went off to attack a bank of slots. The young guy stood watching the girl until she settled into a rhythm, then left her to walk across to the busy center crap table. As if magnetized, Tony found himself, too, strolling toward the crap table. For a while the young guy stood outside the circle of players, his eyes coolly searching the scene, consuming every detail. Tony noticed the casual flexing of the fingers, the continuous, quiet stretching of the digits whenever the arms hung at his sides. When he saw the same fingers diligently brushing one or two strategic points on the jacket, examining the subtle swellings hardly discernible through the material, he knew for certain. The cubes were well concealed. He smiled to himself as the young man stepped forward to take his place at the rim of the table. Tony waited until the guy had bought some checks, then he moved in to take over from the dealer. For an instant the young guy's glance flew to him curiously, but Tony ignored him, dealing with his customary, sterile efficiency; after a few moments, the other appeared to have lost interest in the sudden change of dealers.

He was ultracautious, Tony soon discovered. The dice had gone around the table three times, and he was losing about fifty dollars before he made his first move. His bets weren't large and netted him only a little over four hundred dollars before he allowed the dice to pass to the next shooter. Tony was puzzled, and it was all he could do to stop himself from staring in the direction of the hustler; but he exercised self-control and continued to deal as if he'd noticed nothing. The dice came around and the young guy was shooter again. Tony stood at an angle from which he could see clearly when the hustler grabbed the dice from the table. He saw the switch. But only just, and the incredible speed with which the hustler's fingers worked was miraculously faster than anything he'd ever seen before, so much so he could hardly believe his own eyes. He was so intrigued by the guy's dexterity that he allowed a second switch and almost missed it because he chose to blink at the wrong moment.

Now the kid was building, and he couldn't allow that to happen. When Tony pulled in the dice, he switched them for a pair of house straights before feeding them back to the hustler. When he looked up, he saw instantly, by the look in the other's eyes, that he'd spotted Tony's switch. Tony was so surprised that, for the first time he could remember, he faltered. When their eyes met, the questions that flew silently between the two manipulators were legion. Then the hustler pitched the straights, using an exaggerated, open gesture, sevened-out immediately, and pulled out of the game.

258

Tony stepped back from the table, and the dealer waiting behind him took over wordlessly. As he walked away, he snapped his fingers, and, within seconds, two security men were at his side. He ordered them to pick up the hustler, then continued on his way to his office. He was seated behind his desk when they brought in the young man and his blonde companion. He dismissed the security men. "Please sit down." He gave the blonde a formal smile to put her at ease. He noticed that her sunburned face had gone white. She sat down without comment.

"You can't hold us." The young guy spoke up. His words were controlled and he spoke in an educated voice. But Tony could see the tension in the tightening of the corners of his mouth. He guessed it was the young guy's first brush with casino management.

God knows what the punk's got away with so far, he found himself thinking. "You can sit down, too," he said quietly. For a moment the hustler looked rebellious, then he thought better of it. He sat down next to his girl. "What's your name?" Tony asked.

"Joe Doakes," the other said promptly. He stared challengingly at Tony, who grimaced.

"Well, Joe Doakes, I got to tell you what you were doing out there at the crap table is illegal here in the State of Nevada. They call it cheating." The blonde grasped the hustler's arm, and Tony waited for a change of expression on his face. It didn't come. He found himself wondering if the kid had the nerve, too. If he had that, too, he had everything.

"You can't prove a thing."

"Don't need to. This joint pays a lot of taxes. If I hand you over to the authorities, who you think they're gonna believe—me or you?"

"There are lawyers. I'll fight you. And gambling houses are at a disadvantage in court. Specially if I can get the case pulled out of this place. In any case, you won't do something like that," he said.

"I won't?"

"You casino people are afraid of getting a bad name. I hear you don't prosecute. Anyway, how much we talking about—a lousy few hundred bucks? You make that in a few minutes," he said scornfully.

"That give you the right to steal?"

"I didn't steal much—I could have taken more."

"Oh, what was holding you back?" He was genuinely curious.

"I know I won't get into serious trouble if I don't get greedy," the young man said honestly.

"I see." Tony studied him in silence for a moment. Then he said slowly, "You know, it's true, what you say. There ain't much to be gained by calling in the law. It's easier just to break the hustler's fingers." The kid was halfway out of his chair, the girl clinging to his arm, whiter than ever. "Sit down," Tony said.

"We're getting out of here. If you want to make a charge, do it now, or we're leaving."

"I said sit down," Tony repeated forcefully. It had the desired effect, and they sat down again. "Who taught you the switcheroo?" he went on mildly.

"I dunno what you're talking about."

"Look, you wanna be treated with respect, or you wanna get thrown out on your butt?" he said, annoyed.

The hustler thought better of it. "An old guy called Marty McFadden," he said resignedly. "Used to work for my old man on his ranch in New Mexico. I was sick one time, and I was recuperating on the ranch. That was when he showed me how. I did nothing else for a year. He gave me the bones and everything. I've been fascinated ever since."

Tony's nod was barely perceptible. He remembered the name as someone Boston Bailey had mentioned when they'd been discussing the blanket roll. He'd often wondered if old mechanics survived—now he knew. And it seemed they never got over the compulsion to exercise the cubes. "You're good. You're one of the best I seen," he said simply to the hustler.

The young guy's eyes lit up as he understood. "You're good, too. Jesus, I never saw anything to match your switch—it's unbelievable. Old Marty used to tell me there were guys like you, in the old days. I never believed him. Not till now. Are you a real mechanic?"

"Yes, I am." He said it with dignity and felt a pride in saying it to someone who knew completely what it meant.

"Gee . . ." There was hero worship in the voice.

"Now, I come to the reason I bring you here," Tony said carefully. "I don't come across someone with your talent every day. I know people who could use you. You interested in going pro?"

"Me, a professional?" Joe Doakes looked startled.

"I got the contacts to train you properly and get you started. Of course, the mechanic works only for the house, not for himself, so you'll have to forget about freelancing—that don't work out. I think maybe you're good enough to become a top—."

"Hey, hold it—hold it . . ." The punk was laughing at him. "It's only a hobby with me. I don't take dice *that* seriously."

He stared. How could anyone so good treat his talent so lightly? Personally, he'd spent his entire adult life striving for perfection. Now along comes this young punk, nearly his equal, and almost without trying. Maybe even has the nerve, too. "You'll earn a lot of dough," Tony said temptingly.

The kid was laughing again. "I don't need dough," he said. "My old man owns half of Phoenix, I guess."

How can a person deal with a guy who don't need dough? In his mind's eye it all flashed before him—the poverty, the struggles of his youth, and those of his parents. The Steubenville amendment to the Ten Commandments: *"Get the money, honest if you can."* There'd been hardly a kid in town didn't know it by puberty. Wasn't the desire for money the driving force behind his search for perfection? And how does a guy get there if he's not driven by need? Yet this punk had made it the easy way. There was no justice.

Joe Doakes was speaking again. "I graduate from Berkeley in a few months," he said. "I'm going to be a mining engineer. The old man—he's got oil wells, too, you understand."

260

"Yeah, sure," Tony said. A Doctor Joe Doakes. He couldn't keep the sour note out of his voice.

"All that nonsense about how a mechanic has to work only for the house—that's all bullshit, according to old Marty. He says it took him fifty years to find out. By then it was too late. Marty says it's a story the old-time gambling-house operators thought up to stop freelancers from wiping them out, and to get the hustlers working for them."

He continued to stare at the irreverent jerk in disbelief. The words coming from the young mouth were sacrilege.

"Well, if that's all, we'll be going." Joe Doakes and his beautiful blonde companion were on their feet. He held out his hand. "Sir, it sure was a pleasure to meet a real live mechanic."

"Get outa here, you jerk." His voice was surly. They were through the door before he remembered. "Hey, punk, you owe the joint four hundred bucks," he yelled after them.

He was too late. They were gone.

CHAPTER SEVEN

"Are you telling me you can't handle some two-bit Ohio cop?" Tony roared at the man sitting livid, his briefcase open on his knees, on the other side of the desk. "What kind of lawyer are you anyhow? What the fuck we pay you a hundred-grand retainer for? Answer me the question, willya?"

Beniton, usually benign, was rigid with controlled rage. He forced himself to speak rationally. "There's nothing more I can do within the law," he said.

"Screw the law. A process server I can get for ten skins. Don't sit there giving me no lecture. I want results."

"Mr. Vitale, I assure you I've tried everything I know, right down to offering to compensate the man for his head injury if he'll cooperate and drop the charges. He won't listen to reason."

"Look, why you think they call Hoyle the Fix? Because he's a crooked cop, that's why." He couldn't keep the sneer off his face. "You telling me you can't do a deal with a crooked small-town cop—that he suddenly growed principles?"

"Apparently Hoyle considers this a personal matter. It's his view that the honor of his family is at stake, and he seems quite determined to see that your brother is arrested and charged with—."

"You believe all that garbage?" Tony howled. "The man's a dog. He always was a dog and he'll never be any different. He'd sell his own father down the river. Everyone knows what he is—there ain't a single operation in town he ain't stealing from. Everyone knows except you."

"I can't concern myself with the whole spectrum of the man's behavior, only the legal implications of his actions," Beniton said.

"*Up* his spectrum," Tony jeered, "and yours, too, if I don't get some action. Look, I'm gonna tell you once and for all what's in the guy's mind. He smells money, that's what. He knows Mokey's my brother and he knows I'm connected, so he thinks he found an open seam. Let me tell you your trouble, Beniton—you're not getting results because you're treating him like a human being. Hoyle just ain't used to that kind of treatment. The guy's an animal. Treat him like one, it's all he understands."

"I've tried every legal angle open to us to get the charges dropped . . ." Beniton was unimpressed with Tony's views on Hoyle.

"You ain't done nothing. They're still out looking for Mokey."

"My advice to you is not to harbor your brother here the way you're doing," Beniton went on doggedly. "It's what you're paying for, my advice. If he goes back to Steubenville and surrenders himself—in my charge, of course—then I can make an entirely different approach to the whole matter. We can bring in top counsel and fight it out in open court where Hoyle won't have the advantage of—."

"I just told you, prick, that Hoyle will try to implicate me. As things stand we're out of state and that's our best shot. If Hoyle gets his hands on Mokey, he'll throw the book at him, including pages you ain't read. I know that motherfucker. If Mokey comes outa jail in one piece, he'll be lucky. No dice—he stays here with me."

"You're tying my hands, Mr. Vitale. In law these things have to be handled a certain way."

"You deaf? I said no deal, didn't I? Find another way."

Beniton shook his head in defeat, closed his briefcase, and got to his feet. "I'll go through the whole case again from beginning to end and see if I can find some loophole. I can't hold out much hope," he added.

"If you can't handle it yourself, then find someone who can," Tony said coldly. "I'm giving you a free hand on the ticket—what more you want?"

"I'll do my best. Good day, Mr. Vitale."

Beniton had gone, and Tony sat in silence at his desk, staring angrily at the closed door. After a moment a door on the other side of the room opened, and Tom Druccio stepped in. "You heard?" Tony asked.

"Yeah, I heard it all," Tom said.

"That prick. How come we ain't got someone better'n that to handle our business?"

"He's good. Make no mistake."

"He ain't good enough. Start easing him out. Find someone better—someone with a little imagination."

"O.K., I'll make arrangements. But it doesn't help the present situation. We have to make a move on your brother's problem. There's no alternative."

"Yeah, I guess you're right. First I gotta make a call." He picked up the telephone and asked for a Steubenville number. When a voice came on the line, he said, "It's Tony. We're making no progress with the dumb cop. The fucking asshole's out to make us crawl. What happened your end?"

The soft voice came over the distant wire. "The same. He won't listen to reason," the Duke said. "The man's a fool."

"We gotta make a move. If we leave it any longer, maybe they'll grab Mokey. He can't stay in here forever."

"Yes, I agree. Do you want me to make the arrangements this end?"

"No. It's better we do it from here. Less chance of someone local putting two and two together."

"Call me if you need anything."

"Thanks, Duke."

"When will we see you again, Tony? You haven't touched base in a long time."

"One of these days, I guess. Maybe when this business has blown over."

"You're always welcome."

"I know." He held the telephone thoughtfully for a moment before he put it down.

"We go ahead?" Tom broke into his thoughts.

"Yes, we'll do it your way. We're gonna need a young broad, a hooker maybe sixteen, seventeen—there's always young broads hanging around River Street looking to start in the business." He paused. "You don't have to go far outside Steubenville, the state line's on the bridge. Over the river and you're in West Virginia. Go south on Route 2, then east on 27. The motel's near Wellsburg."

"You want him roughed up a little?"

"No. Just fill 'em both with booze. Make him drink until it comes out of his ears. Remember, it has to look like they had an orgy. When you leave the motel, call the number I gave you. They'll be waiting, and they'll do the rest."

"Can you rely on the West Virginia cops?"

"Sure. Over there we got juice. And they been waiting a long time to get even with Hoyle. They got an old score to settle: Hoyle used to have a racket, grabbing important guys from West Virginia when they came over to River Street, or to Cora's for a piece of tail. He'd pull them guys right off the broads, steal their dough, and turn 'em loose on the bridge to walk home without their pants. His idea of a joke. Some of them guys was cops, but it made no difference to him. They couldn't do much about it, but them West Virginia police, they got long memories."

"What will he be charged with?"

"For starters, transporting a minor across a state line for immoral purposes—something like that. And Hoyle's full of shit. When he opens his mouth he's gonna put his foot right in it. He'll get plenty of trouble from those West Virginia boys."

"Unless he cooperates."

"That's the general idea." Tony grinned for the first time.

"I better get started," Tom said.

He walked quickly to the door to greet Skeeter. "Hey, old buddy, you finally made it to Las Vegas. How you been—how are things back in Havana?"

"Fine, Tony, just fine." They hugged each other. The wide, natural smile on Skeeter's face was something Tony hadn't seen in years, and he knew immediately there was something new in his friend's life.

"Boy, am I glad to see you. Can't tell you how long it is since I see a friendly face

263

around these parts. A real friend, I mean."

"Tony . . ." He paused. "I got something to tell you. This is Selina . . ." He moved aside to reveal the slim, button-nosed girl who hardly reached to his shoulder. Bright eyes, full of fun, blinked out from her dusky features, the hybrid Spanish-Negro features typical of Cuba.

"So-ho, you brought a friend." Tony's grin broadened, although he knew instantly there was more than simple friendship involved. "Pleased to meet you, Selina." He showed none of the surprise he felt and put out his hand in welcome. She smiled, her red, moist mouth and full lips enhanced by two rows of perfect, pearl-white teeth.

"What I got to tell you—Selina and me, we're married." Skeeter blurted it out suddenly, at the same time searching Tony's face.

"You're what?" He didn't falter. "Well, I'll be damned. You sly old dog, Skeets. How come you keep all this good news to yourself?"

"We made up our minds on the spur of the moment, just before we left Havana."

"I guess congratulations are in order," he said easily. "Say, I'm gonna lay on some champagne. This is a big, big day, and we're gonna celebrate." He instilled wonder into his voice.

Relief flooded Skeeter's face. "Gee, I'm glad you're pleased, Tony—tell the truth, I was worried what you'd say."

"Pleased? I'm delighted." He smiled broadly at the girl and she smiled in return. "Why shouldn't I be? I been trying to hook you up with a broad for years, ain't I? It's what you need, someone to care for you, someone who'll—."

"You're not just saying that?"

"No, I mean it. I really do."

"You're not thinking, maybe, I shouldn't be marrying a colored girl?"

"I ain't thinking nothing, except what's good for you. You gotta do what you think is right, and the hell with everyone else. Mind you, I'm not saying it don't come as a surprise. But what the hell. I'm glad of one thing—right or wrong, you made the move."

"You mean it?"

"Sure do." He paused. "Say, don't you think it's a little embarrassing for Selina, talking this way in front of her. After all, she's your wife now, and you gotta have respect." He glanced toward the still-smiling girl.

"It's O.K." Skeeter grinned. "She don't understand what we're saying. She don't speak English. Maybe a few words. I'm teaching her, and she's teaching me Spanish. You know, the Cuban lingo."

Tony was glad he could speak freely. The smile plastered on his face didn't match his words. "Tell me, Skeets, what made you decide to go get married? Just curiosity on my part, you understand," he added.

"I was lonely." Skeeter shrugged. "Too goddamn lonely, with you gone and all . . ."

"I sent for you. You wouldn't come."

"I like it there in Cuba. It's so easygoing, I feel kinda safe—you know what I mean. I thought maybe I couldn't face up to the States again after what happened."

"You got nothing to worry. Not with me around, you know that."

"Sooner or later I have to stand on my own two feet." A flicker of torment crossed Skeeter's face, then was gone. "I just gotta."

"You been doing fine the last couple of years. Hey, look, buddy, I don't make just any chump a casino inspector, you know, even if the guy is a pal. No way—this is a business. A guy's gotta have ability and be reliable. He has to deliver."

"Can the bullshit, Tony. I know what you done for me, and I'm grateful. I owe you."

"That's all history now. Forget it."

"Yeah, maybe." Only Tony would have recognized the fleeting doubt that clouded Skeeter's eyes. "Anyway, like I was saying, I was feeling sorry for myself, as usual, and Selina—she was a new chambermaid at the hotel—she comes from Oriente, out there in the country. Well, she was so damn hot to get into my room and clean up—you know how I stay in the room by myself—she kept creeping in when I'm under the covers and tickling my feet to get me up. I was sore at first, but it got to be a joke in the end. Then, one day, when I was watching her, something clicked. She just crept in bed with me and we stayed there a whole day and a night, and I never been so happy in my whole life, even though we ain't got two words in common . . ." He stopped and looked up from his feet. "You don't wanna hear all this crap. I didn't mean to start running off at the mouth."

"That's just where you're wrong. You're telling me about a guy who's found himself, and I want to know everything that's happened," Tony said solemnly. "You're important to me—I put a lot of work into getting you back on your feet, and I'm interested in how my investment's paying off."

"You been a good friend. I won't never be able to repay you."

"Hey, listen, I'm gonna order the champagne now." He lifted the telephone. "Say, I got another idea. Lombardo's here, and tonight we promised to have dinner at a new Italian restaurant opening in town. A classy joint, and the owner's a friend. If we go, it sorta lends distinction to the opening, know what I mean? What we'll do, tonight we'll celebrate your marriage at the opening of the Casa Trevia—what you think of that, old buddy?"

"That sounds swell." Skeeter's eyes gleamed in gratitude, and he took his bride's hand.

Tony looked at them, standing there together. "Leave everything to me," he said.

"Some joint, huh?" Lombardo said admiringly, gazing around the resplendent interior of the brand-new restaurant.

"Coletti's nuts," Tony said briefly. "It's a bum investment."

"Why you say that?"

"Because every hotel in this town will have its own gourmet restaurant. Or more than one. Take the Caprice—a guest don't have to step outside, there's everything he needs. The same will apply to new hotels coming along, only more so. If people go anywhere, it'll be to another hotel. It's not New York, here—people won't go out to a straight restaurant to eat. They'll be too busy busting a gut at the gambling tables. Las Vegas don't need no *el grande* guinea dineries."

"If Coletti hears you say that, he'll blow his brains out." Lombardo grinned.

265

"He's into the mobs for real dough on account of this place."

"His hard luck. What's the favor we owe the faggot anyway?"

"I dunno. Apparently he did something for the outfit once—Levin says we owe him a trick."

"Hmm." Tony kept his thoughts to himself as the waiters bustled about, laying yard-long menus on them. On the other side of the table Mokey munched breadsticks, spraying crumbs on the crisp, white linen. Coletti, having welcomed them personally, removed himself a discreet distance away and watched them nervously, anxious that everything should be perfect. The champagne arrived in pewter buckets filled with crushed ice.

"Where's Skeeter?" Lombardo asked. "I'm starved."

"They'll be here any minute. I arranged for them to take the Cupid Suite at the Caprice. They're coming straight on here."

"Listen, if he wants to screw the ass off the broad, I don't care, but let him do it on his own time. I'm ordering—and if they're not here before the food arrives, I'm eating."

"Take it easy," Tony said. "They'll be here." Slowly the room was filling with new, curious clients and invited guests. Some who knew the difference threw sidelong glances in their direction, then looked away quickly when Lombardo or Tony turned their way. "This town," Tony said idly, "three or four years ago, the place was nothing but a battlefield for Texas cowboys. They came here for whoring, boozing, gambling, and fighting. Now they don't dare show their mugs. Soon as a big hat steps inside the city limits he gets arrested."

"We have to change the town's image. What you seen so far is nothing, it's all to come. The town will explode. The news is getting around and everyone wants a piece of the action, everyone wants to invest. We got propositions up to here."

"Screw the outsiders," Tony said. "What Levin says is right. As the casinos get built we gotta share them out among our own people. How else we gonna keep the politicians and the police in line? How we gonna keep 'em out of our pants if we don't do the same as we did in Cuba?"

"That's not the same as being open to investment," Lombardo said. "We'll need an awful lot of dough to turn Vegas into a big attraction."

"Just so long as we keep control. We ain't growing no plums for someone else to pick."

"There's plenty for everyone."

"I never seen anything like what's happening here. Joints are growing like mushrooms along the Strip."

"They don't hurt us. It all helps make our places look bigger and more glamorous." He paused, glanced at Tony quizzically, then grinned. "Have you seen it, the new site?"

"Yes," Tony admitted. "I couldn't resist. The place is gonna be huge—unbelievable."

"The foundations are in. Them contractors are breaking their necks to earn the bonus we promised. When it goes up it'll make the Caprice look like a chicken shack." Tony said nothing, but the excitement was there in his eyes. "It'll be the finest resort hotel-casino in the whole world," Lombardo went on. "And it'll be yours to run. The outfit honors you."

There was a small commotion on the other side of the room and heads were turning. They looked across to see a knot of waiters closing in on the restaurant entrance. A voice was raised, and Tony recognized it as Skeeter's. He got up and walked over.

Above the heads of the group, Tony could see that Coletti was barring the entrance to Skeeter and Selina. "We're full up," he was saying. "All the tables are taken."

"But I told you, we're invited as guests." Skeeter was growing red with anger.

"Guests or not, we can't take anymore. Can't you get that into your thick head?" Coletti said insultingly. "We got important people in here, and there ain't no more room."

"We're expected," Skeeter insisted. "It's a special occasion—there has to be room."

"Look, punk, do I gotta spell it out?" Coletti glared viciously. "This is a big night—we don't want it spoiled by no nigger fuck sitting down to eat with respectable people. Now get that douche bag out of here before I have you thrown out on your ear."

Tony watched, fascinated by the fight that came into Skeeter's expression.

"You guinea asshole, this woman is my wife . . ." Skeeter grated, and grabbed for Coletti's throat.

As the waiters lunged forward, Tony stepped in. "Hold it—hold it," he yelled, digging his way in to grab Skeeter. "These people are with us."

The waiters fell back, and Coletti blanched. "I didn't know—how was I to know?"

"Go on over to our table, Skeets," Tony ordered. Skeeter took Selina by the arm. As he passed Coletti, Tony saw the knuckles whiten on his hand. He grabbed his friend. "Forget it," he said. "It ain't worth the bother. Go and sit down, we're waiting to start dinner."

As the couple walked away, Coletti slid to his side. "How can I apologize?" His voice trembled in fear. "How was I to know they were your guests?"

"It was a bad mistake. Because of your stupidity, we lose face," Tony hissed icily. "The favor we owe you—it's been discharged."

"I'll do anything . . ."

Tony ignored him and walked slowly toward the table, where the waiters were jumping like beans. Despite the chill look on his face, an inner warmth was spreading through him at the realization that the long struggle was over at last. Skeeter was back to being his old self again, it seemed. Skeeter had found a cause. And the cause was his cure.

267

CHAPTER EIGHT

He was back in the Border Club in Calumet City and jazzing a high roller. The atmosphere was so oppressive he could hardly breathe, and he was surrounded by swarthy Sicilian faces above silk suits, all waiting for him to make a mistake. Clouds of cigar smoke rolled across the crap table as he switched dice, his fingers flying, the cubes disappearing into his hand with one identity and leaping away with another. He couldn't work fast enough and the high roller was winning, amassing a mountain of checks. Now the Sicilians became threatening, edging closer to him, nudging him with their shoulders, breaking his rhythm. Then his concentration went completely and the dice came tumbling out of his hands, straights and gaffs all mixed up. He wanted to cry out that he never made a mistake, that they should let him start over. But no sound came from his throat. He knew his time had come and he was about to do something he'd never done before—give up. With a deep sigh, he placed his hands flat on the green felt and spread his fingers. A Sicilian with a face like Willie Freschia's advanced, pulling a hammer from his pocket. Resignedly, sorrowfully, he waited for the first of the blows that would smash his fingers to pulp.

He awoke panting and sweating.

He snapped on the bedside light and was surprised to see four-fifty on the clock. He'd been asleep less than one hour. From down below, in the bowels of the Casablanca Club, distant night noises floated up to him. He reached out for a cigarette, lit it, and fell back on the pillows, strangely exhausted yet knowing it was useless trying to sleep. As the ash on the cigarette grew, a sense of despondency rolled over him like a chill fog. Lately it had become regular, and he found himself questioning the direction his life was taking—a direction over which he had no control. His commitment was total. He had become nothing but a puppet, never again to savor individuality, never to know the joy of liberty. He had prostituted his skill, debased his talent with voluntary servitude. And the joy, the self-esteem, the glory of being a master mechanic had become nothing but a sour taste in the back of his mouth. At odd moments he dreamed of walking away, of disappearing to parts where their interest and influence hadn't reached. And with cold fury he'd forced himself to face the truth—that if he made a run for it, sooner or later, somewhere, somehow, one day he would walk into a casino, drawn by the lure of the spinning cubes, the only life he knew and understood. That day would be the beginning of the end. He would be seen and they would come to claim their rightful dues, the soul he had so glibly traded to them for an illusory pot of gold.

The telephone rang suddenly and he jumped, spilling ash on the bedsheet. He brushed it off and picked up the receiver. "Mr. Vitale, sorry to wake you, but we have a problem. I thought you'd want to know." It was the manager on the graveyard shift.

"It better be good," Tony said gruffly.

268

"How about—your brother?"

"Mokey?" Tony sat up.

"Yes, sir. A guest playing in the casino lost his dough early, decided to go to bed. Mokey, ah, beat him to it."

"I don't get you."

"The guy's wife was there."

"Oh, no . . ." He groaned. "Who's the guy?"

"Maclellan. Big, red. Been out on the floor most nights this week. Plays till dawn—except tonight. Looks like Mokey's timing was off."

"Yeah, I know the guy. Hothead gambler. So what happened?"

"There was a fight."

"Mokey get hurt?"

"They're both a little bruised. Nothing serious."

"Where are they now?"

"The security guards are holding everyone in my office. Maclellan's hootin' and hollerin' and threatening to sue. I'm calling from your office."

He thought for a moment. "Anything we can slap Maclellan with?"

"Nothing I can think of."

"They married, him and the broad?"

"I'd say so, the way they hate each other. We don't have a leg to stand on."

He inhaled and let the air out slowly through his teeth. "O.K., I'm coming down," he said.

He took his time dressing, racking his brains for a move. Nothing came. When he left his room he ignored the elevator, and walked down the stairs to gain time, deep in thought. When he stepped into the night manager's office, Mokey stood sullenly in a corner, dabbing at the raw marks on his face. A puffy blonde sat in a chair, anger on her face, smoking nervously. The big, red-haired guy in the loud jacket was Maclellan. Three uniformed security guards stood in various postures, ready to part the two men.

"You the boss around here?" Maclellan roared at the sight of Tony. "What's the big idea holding us here? This is unlawful detention—boy, this is going to cost you guys plenty. I mean plenty. My lawyer's gonna sue the pants off your casino. I hear the punk's your brother. Don't think that's gonna do him any good—he's an employee and that leaves you wide open."

He wished for the old days, when he could have thrown the bum and his frumpy dame out on their ears. Now policy dictated a different approach. An idea was forming in his mind. A long shot, but he had nothing else left. "I agree with every word you say, Mr. Maclellan," he said respectfully.

"What's that you say?"

"Of course. We're responsible for the behavior of the staff on our premises. That's accepted. I can only extend our apologies."

"Screw your apologies. I got rights. A guy's family ain't safe in this joint. I'm gonna teach you people a lesson—I'm taking you to the cleaners, it's the only thing you understand." A gleam of triumph had come into Maclellan's eyes at Tony's acquiescence.

"I may be able to save you the trouble," Tony said.

"Oh, yeah?"

"I'm suggesting that we come to an amicable agreement."

"What sort of agreement?" He eyed Tony suspiciously.

"Well, look at it this way—after a lot of legal wrangling, your lawyer'd come up with damages of, maybe, fifty thousand dollars . . ."

"I, aah—I'm going for a hundred grand," Maclellan said arbitrarily.

"Mr. Maclellan, if you want to talk sense, we can maybe do some business. If you start spouting telephone numbers, there's nothing I can do for you, and I have to wash my hands of the whole affair. You can go to court and try your luck—maybe you'll come up with a big zero and costs. Your wife's not exactly blameless, you know. I put your damages at fifty K to settle the matter here and now. Make up your mind." He turned his back to Maclellan and missed the confusion that crossed the other's face.

"O.K., let's talk."

Tony swung back. "I gotta tell you, it's not that easy. I can't pass over fifty big ones of the joint's money just like that. What I can do is authorize a fifty-grand marker and put it in the books as uncollectable. That means you gotta play up the money. You interested?"

Maclellan stared. "Fifty-grand table money?" he said incredulously.

"That's what I'm saying. Craps—one heat. Right now, out on the table in public. I'll deal for you personally, so you'll know everything's on the up and up."

"I never played that much in my whole life." Maclellan's voice was hoarse and his forehead had become damp.

"You always wanted to be a high roller, didn't you? Here's your chance." He used his soft Steubenville voice.

"I dunno—." Maclellan's face was tortured.

"There's serious players'd give a year of their lives to roll for fifty g's," Tony went on quietly. "Ain't never gonna happen to you again, a chance like this."

The blonde screamed suddenly: "Don't listen to them. They're trying to cheat us out of our fifty grand, can't you see that?"

"Shaddap, whore." Maclellan turned on his wife savagely. "This could be the biggest night of my whole life. I don't want you spoiling it with your fat mouth."

"But, Bill, just think what we could do with the money. We could remodel the house and build a big swimming pool. We always wanted a big swimming pool, like the Newtons'. I could have that diamond ring you've been promising me all these years," she pleaded.

"Aw, screw the house *and* your diamond ring," Maclellan said thickly.

"How much you lose this trip, Maclellan? Tony spoke in the same level tone.

"Seven grand. I drop my pot, all seven grand."

"Give you a chance, sport. I'll add in the seven K for good will. You roll for fifty-seven big ones. What you say now, gambler?"

"Holy God . . ." The moisture on his forehead had turned to beads of sweat.

"O.K., forget it. Do it your way, the hard way." He changed his voice suddenly and turned away. "Mr. and Mrs. Maclellan are leaving," he announced loudly. "Pack their things and bring them down to the front desk."

"No, wait—."

270

"Yeah?" He turned back.

"I'll take the deal." Maclellan forced out the words.

"Good man." To the manager, he said, "Go get a marker." Maclellan scribbled his signature in a shaky hand, and the procession trooped into the casino.

As they made their way to the crap table, eyes followed them. Late-night hard-liners sensed excitement and came crowding around as Tony took his place on the stick and Maclellan positioned himself at the rim. "Fresh dice for Mr. Maclellan." Tony clapped his hands and the boxman produced them, breaking the seal in clear view of everybody. He slid the box across to Tony, who removed the top, then flipped it over on the table so that when he lifted it, a neat stack of twelve dice stood on the felt. With swift movements of the stick Tony scattered the dice, then gathered them neatly together and presented them to Maclellan for his choice. Maclellan reached out and chose a pair, the trembling of his fingers plain for all to see. Fifty-seven thousand dollars in checks stood at the pass line on the layout as Maclellan rattled the dice frantically in his damp right hand.

"Shooter coming out," Tony announced loudly.

Maclellan stopped rattling the dice, looking as if he couldn't go through with it. When he resumed, a tense silence hung over the table. Even the ubiquitous chatter of the slots around the large room had dulled, it seemed. Suddenly Maclellan made up his mind to pitch and threw the dice forcefully, following through with his shoulder and the line of his whole body in a subconscious desire to will the dice on. "Natural seven, baby," he yelled as the cubes flew from his fingers. "Hit me, dice, hit me with the big time." The red bones thudded against the backboard, spun in the air, and flopped down. The crowd strained forward to see the result.

"Little Joe from Kokomo—it's a four." At Tony's announcement, a hubbub of excited chatter ran around the table. A few hands grasping checks came forward over the rim of the table. "No outside bets. Mr. Maclellan has the table, his point is four." He slid a white chuck across the layout to box 4. The crowd pressed closer to the rim as Tony delivered the dice to Maclellan, who picked them up like they were hot coals. "Four's the point," he called pleasantly, and smiled at Maclellan.

"Two—snake eyes."

"A sixie from Dixie."

"Sevened-out—too bad."

"Oh, shiiit . . ." Maclellan said. The moan that rose from the crowd came from deep within the hard-liners' hearts. Maclellan reeled away from the table, his eyes glazed.

"Give that man a free whiskey," Tony said. He turned back to the table to gather in the dice.

Back in the manager's office, he cleared out everyone except his brother. He strode across the room and cracked his open hand hard across Mokey's bruised face. The slap echoed through the room as Mokey fell back, startled. "What was that for?"

"For giving me trouble. I had about as much as I'm gonna take from you."

"You ain't worried about that Maclellan creep, are you, Tony? He ain't coming back in no hurry, not after the way you shafted him out there."

"I just don't understand you, Mokey, honest to God. All the whores around here, all the available broads, and you gotta be found in a married man's bedroom. What's worse, when he's in the casino on serious business. Don't you know the rules by now? Don't you know it's not policy, interfering with a married couple?"

"She gave me the eye. If it wasn't me it would've been some other guy," Mokey protested. "What's the difference?"

"You never learn, do you? I wouldn't mind if she was so beautiful, so gorgeous that you couldn't resist her. Worth the risk, worth the scandal. The dame looks like yesterday's laundry. She got the mind and body of a knothole. Ain't you got no respect for yourself? Ain't you got no respect for me?"

"Sure I got respect. Why you so angry, Tony? What difference it make to you if I have a little fun now and then?"

"You call that fun, screwing every dame comes your way? Maybe I oughta put you out to stud—yeah, that's it, I'm gonna make a fortune. I'll start a stud farm— Mokey's Stud, women served three times a day, call us anytime. Our motto is service . . ." Tony finished hotly.

"Knock it off," Mokey scowled. "You know I don't like it when you make fun of me."

"What you want me to do, keep score? When am I gonna get through to you?"

"So what, I fuck a few horny broads? Would you rather see me live like a monk? You want me to live the way you do—what sort of life is that, for Chrissakes?"

"Don't judge me by your standards. I'm too busy to waste my time screwing around. We got big deals going down in this town."

"Yeah. Well, I got no high ambitions like you. No direction, I guess. I take life as it comes, day by day, and I squeeze out juice where and when I can. That's all there is to me, that's what makes me tick. Simple, ain't it?" They glared at each other. "If it's not good enough, maybe I better go. Maybe you're right, I been hanging around here too long. It's time I got out and hit the road."

"You don't have to leave," Tony said. "I'll find you a job that'll keep you so busy you won't have time for—."

"It wouldn't work," Mokey cut in. "Everyone in this town knows that my brother's a boss. Because of you I get away with murder." He paused, and a wry grin cut across his bruises. "That kind of thing don't help build a guy's character. Yeah, I guess it's time I was moving on."

Tony was shaken by his brother's determination and regretted his words. "Listen, I was just shooting off my mouth. You don't gotta take it so serious."

"I been thinking about it a lot lately." It was a new, resolute Mokey. "I was gonna tell you, sooner or later, so I guess now's a good a time as any."

He softened his voice. "Where will you go, little brother?"

"First I'll go back home to visit with Mama and Papa, then I'm thinking of going south to—."

"Hey, you can't go back home to Steubenville," Tony cut in sharply.

"I'll creep in at night, so nobody'll spot me. I'll stay in the house a couple of days, then leave quietly."

"Listen, bonehead, get it into your thick skull that you seen your hometown for the last time. How often I gotta tell you? We made a mistake there—knocking off Hoyle wasn't part of the plan. The guys were unreliable. Your name is still on the police blotter, and we don't want to give them the chance to bring it all up again. The case died a natural death, so let's leave it that way. Why you always want to put your head in a noose?"

"When do I get to see Mama and Papa?"

"I'll bring them out here for a vacation. You'll have to wait."

"You been saying that for a long time, Tony. The old man writes me that Mama's crying herself to sleep at night, she ain't seen us in so long."

"Yeah, I know." There was a troubled silence between them, then, "I got a better idea. You liked Havana, didn't you, Mokey?"

"Oh, sure, them Cuban broads . . ." He shut up.

"I'm sending you there. You'll stay with Skeeter. I'll send for Mama and Papa to come over for a vacation, and I'll come over, too, so we'll all be together for a few days. Before I come back here I'll fix you up with a job in one of the joints and you can stay there long as you want. How's that?"

"Sure. For a while, I guess I'd like that."

"I'll fix it up right away."

Walking back to his suite, he made no attempt to hide the frown that creased his face. He would miss his spirited brother. Lately Mokey had been his one contact with normality in an existence that moved farther and farther away from human qualities, and deeper into utterly callous material values.

He had long ago made his choice and there was no turning back. Sometimes he regretted that choice.

This was one of those times.

CHAPTER NINE

"Stop here," Lombardo ordered the driver. The car stopped on the Strip at the entrance to the imposing driveway that led to the Winter Palace, and they both stared out the window. It could have been an Eastern European castle, except that it sat incongruously on the edge of the Nevada desert, and no European castle ever had to withstand the heat that bore down from this relentless sun and belted off the coppered domes and soaring spires in translucent waves.

"Jes-us Christ," Tony breathed.

"You keep saying that," Lombardo said, a little annoyed.

"I never saw anything like it."

"Is that intended to be critical?" Lombardo was touchy today, Tony thought.

"Oh, no. I'm just thinking, it's one hell of a hoist up from Sixth Street."

"We didn't build it so you'd have somewhere to sleep."

"It's enormous. I hear we can park a coupla thousand cars out there."

"More," Lombardo said. "It takes an army to run the joint. The kitchens could feed a small town. What's more, we're gonna run the operation with class." He glanced at Tony, who had become impassive. "You losing your nerve?"

"No." Tony smiled. "I gotta admit, I get a little worried sometimes. But I know what I can do and what I can't. If things go wrong, it won't be on account of I didn't do my bit."

"So what's the problem?"

"You gotta admit, thirty million bucks is a hell of an investment for one guy to take responsibility for."

"Who told you the numbers?" Lombardo said sharply.

"Nobody. I been following the construction contracts. Pretty good guess, huh?"

"The final figures aren't in yet."

"So, a million here, a million there—all I know is, we'll need some pretty fancy business to turn a profit."

"We'll be getting it," Lombardo said confidently. "We're putting out the word right now. We'll be getting high rollers in from most big cities. Junkets will be flown in from all over the country."

Tony nodded. "That's only the icing on the cake. We're not depending on high rollers to pay the nut, are we?"

"No, of course not," Lombardo said impatiently. "We'd be crazy to use that strategy in a big place like this. One thing we know: It's volume that'll turn this town into a mint. The days of feeding off a few suckers are past. We been doing things all wrong. The Caprice showed us the way—lots of people, small players, guys with a couple of C-notes to leave behind at the table, that's where we'll make the dough. Table percentage—and the wives who feed them goddamn slots like they was starving children." He paused. "They'll come in thousands to Las Vegas. They'll come for the vacation of a lifetime, for the glamour, the excitement of letting loose for a week or two. For the broads, or maybe just to see their favorite moviestar in one of the shows. We got something to offer now. We got something to sell. What everybody's looking for—dreamland."

"Maybe you should keep your feet on the ground," Tony said cautiously. "I'm talking about me—maybe you're expecting too much from a lil' old crap dealer."

"We know what we're doing."

Tony nodded again. "I guess you do. Levin gonna show?"

"No. Why should he? He's done his work—he thought of it. He raised the dough. What you want—he should bring a spade and help with the digging?"

"I ain't seen him for a year or more. Last time we spoke, he promised me points in the new joint," Tony said quietly, "like I got in Cuba."

"Things have changed. We had to make a lot of commitments to get backers."

He frowned at this new twist. With Levin's genius, people had been falling all over each other to make their investments. Was he about to get a touch of frost? "We agreed. I'm holding him to his word. I'm part of this deal, same as you are. I can't walk away, even if I want to."

"None of us can," Lombardo said soberly.

"You gotta treat me on the same level as yourselves." He missed the look that Lombardo gave him, and it passed.

"We don't think of you any other way, Tony."

274

"It's time I moved up a notch."

"We don't appreciate threats. We'll decide what happens."

"I'm not threatening. I'm stating a fact."

"What you call this? We're putting you in charge of our most important project. A showplace. The whole outfit will be judged by what happens to the Winter Palace. And the running of it will be entirely in your hands. This isn't a convenient time to change your attitudes—not when we give you this honor."

"I'm not changing my attitudes," Tony protested.

"We ever been cheap with you?"

"No," he admitted.

"You know something? The President of the United States don't make more dough than you."

"I want recognition," he said stubbornly.

"I tell you, Tony, this is not the time for ultimatums. Not when the joint is ready to open." Lombardo's voice had cooled.

"You don't understand. I'll operate the joint either way. I just want what Levin promised me. And it's not for the money either. I'll take a cut in dough if I'm given points."

"I don't get it."

"Don't you see, I gotta belong somewhere? My life's going away, and I got nothing to show for it." He looked out the window again. "Maybe if I own a piece of the joint, I'll feel this is where I belong. That I've achieved something."

"You never gave any sign you're not happy with our arrangements." Lombardo's voice had crept back into its shell of caution. "I always thought there was complete understanding between us."

He was suddenly, unaccountably, desperately tired of all the deception—the posturing that was endemic to his way of life. "Let's cut the crap for a change. I never been nearer the council than the door, and that door will never open for me, I know that now—just as it never opens for any outsider. The day I'm no use to you is the day I better start looking out for myself. I want you to understand, I'm not complaining. You told me from the start it would mean total commitment, and I accepted the terms. Well, that's what you got, my side of the deal. It's what you're getting now. What I'm trying to do is cut myself a slice of the cake. Not for the dough, but to make my position more secure, so there's less chance I get a knife between the shoulder blades one of these days. Know what I mean?" He paused. "I'm within the rules—I'm always within the rules." For the first time he could remember, he'd let his tongue take control. Inwardly, he was amazed—it was like someone else was talking. "Levin made a promise, and I'm holding him to his word. I want points."

Lombardo had sunk back into his seat, and now his deep-set, black eyes were burning. After a long silence, he said, "You've become bitter, Tony. That isn't good. We've done a lot for you and you should understand it. If Levin gave his word, it will be honored, and there is nothing more to discuss. I'll remind him."

Suddenly, he felt better than he had for a long time.

Suddenly, he was almost his own man.

CHAPTER TEN

"Call for Mr. Vitale." The sexy voice crooned the message again, and the words drifted melodiously across the lobby above the voices of dozens of people. He was already on his way to his office, so he walked past the courtesy telephones. When he stepped through the door, his secretary said, "Mr. Druccio's on the line from Los Angeles. We've been paging you for twenty minutes. He says it's important."

"I'll take it inside." He shut the door to his inner office and picked up the telephone. "Tom?"

"Yeah, Tony. I found him at last."

"Where is he?"

"Here in L.A. The bum's hiding out in some cheap hotel, drowning slowly in the hard stuff."

"Give me the address, Tom." He scribbled it on a pad. "How bad is he?"

"Pretty bad. I mean, he's not the same guy he was. From what I see it's true, what they say. He's just never gonna dry out. He ain't headed nowhere but skid row, you ask me. Shame, the guy had a good voice."

"He ain't finished yet, Tom. I know the guy—he's got fiber."

"How come you're interested in a lush like that?"

"He's a buddy from way back. His old man called me to ask if I could help. I owe that family from the old days. We'd have starved, one time, if his old man hadn't given my father a job."

"You sure got a long memory, Tony." He sensed, rather than heard, the sardonic note in Tom's voice.

"A person shouldn't forget things like that."

"I'll remember you're a soft touch," Tom joked.

"You do it your way, I'll do it mine," he said softly.

"Look, you want me to try and get this guy dried out? I can take a doctor along and—."

"No, that won't work. He's been a hard drinker since we was kids. It's best I talk to him myself. Maybe I can talk him out of it."

"You coming in to L.A.?"

"Yes, tonight."

"I'll lay on a limousine to meet you at the airport. Where you wanna stay—the Beverly Hills O.K.? I'll call and book you a—."

"No. Thanks all the same, Tom. I don't want the brass-band treatment this time. I'm just slipping into town to see an old pal. Nobody will know I'm there."

"Hey, man, you're a big shot now," Tom said, pained. "You rate the full treatment. I don't want it said I didn't treat you right."

"That big I ain't," Tony said, amused. "But I'll remember you offered."

"If you need anything, call me."

276

"Yeah—thanks again, Tom."

"Any time."

He sat in a window seat, impatient to go, oblivious to the chatter of weekenders around him, the crowd returning to the Coast. As the plane climbed out of McCarran Airport and turned in the night sky toward California, he found himself remembering another night nearly twenty years ago. He remembered vividly the remote house outside Steubenville where Skeeter had taken his bride, and how the mission to rescue Angelo had taken him there. Ironic that Angelo, the original cause of Skeeter's disturbed mind, was in need of rescue again. Then the lights in the aircraft were dimmed, headrests went back, and the chatter became a subdued murmur as passengers tried to grab an hour's sleep before their final transition from the tinsel fantasies of Las Vegas to the harsher realities of regular life.

He must have slept because now they were descending and, through the window, he could distinguish individual lights in the Santa Monica Mountains; beyond that, the fairyland carpet of illumination stretched south from the Hollywood Hills into the valley. Soon they were low enough to make out traffic moving along the freeways. Then everything below went black as the aircraft swung out over the ocean to turn onto its final approach for Los Angeles. He got a glimpse of the bright approach lights of the airport reaching up for them through the night before the aircraft took up its final heading for the field, then he transferred his gaze to the acres of electric suburbia expanding beneath them. He heard, rather than felt, the landing, then was straining against his seat belt as reverse thrust bit into the airplane's momentum.

At first there was no reply to his knocking, but he persisted, and eventually a bearded, red-eyed Angelo cracked open the door a couple of inches. "Let me in, Angelo, I want to talk to you," he said.

"Just go away, fella, willya?"

"It's me, Tony, your old buddy."

"Who'd you say?" Angelo squinted out through vein-ridden eyeballs. "Oh, yeah, Tony—what you want?"

"Let me in."

"Sure. Come on in."

The shabby room with the cheap furniture stank of booze and sweat, and was littered with the debris of days of mindless living. Angelo looked thinner and more haggard than when Tony had last seen him. Lines bit deeply into his face, and the usual bags under his eyes were puffed up like small balloons. He sagged onto the bed. "When'd you last eat?" Tony asked.

"I'm on a liquid diet."

"How long you been stewed?"

"Whomee?"

He sighed. "If you're trying to knock yourself off, no point in doing it in a stinking rat hole like this."

"The booze won't kill me. I'd have been dead a long time ago if—drink never . . . I ain't . . . aaw, shit . . ." Angelo's tongue refused to obey him.

He'd always admired Angelo's ability to remain coherent when smashed. But this time the prolonged binge had knocked him over. Tony started to count the empty bottles around the room, but gave up. "I'll order some coffee," he said. "You're sobering up, you like it or not."

"What for?"

"Cause I gotta talk to you. No sense even trying, the way you are."

"Don' wanna talk to nobody . . ."

"You're talking to me, buddy, believe me."

"Screw you," Angelo said. "Why don't you piss off and leave a guy be."

"You stink like a polecat, you know that? First you have some coffee, then you take a shower." He picked up the telephone.

"You're wasting your time—no room service here," Angelo said, with a leer of triumph.

"Oh, no?" A voice came on the line. It was the weedy clerk at the straight-jacket desk in the untidy lobby below. "This is room three forty-nine," Tony said.

"Yeah, I know," the voice said drily. "The drunk. When you gone let the maid in to clean up in there?"

"I'm his uncle. I'm paying twenty bucks for a large pot of hot, sweet, black coffee," he said.

There was a moment's silence. When the voice spoke again, it had brightened. "I have to send out. Make it twennyfive, you got a deal."

Tony liked enterprise. In the right place. "I'll pay thirty if it's quick."

"Yes, sir. Right away, sir."

He poured coffee into Angelo until it almost came out of the singer's ears. When Angelo came out of the shower and returned to the room, rubbing himself briskly, he was a different guy. "What you want here, guinea?" he said roughly.

"Your old man called me. He said things been going wrong for you."

"So?"

"Why you run away and hide?" There was no reply. "I come to help."

"You don't owe me nothin'."

"I owe your old man. He called the debt."

"Not a thing you can do, smartass."

"Look, your family don't know where you are—you got a wife and two kids ain't seen you in three months. Your agent's scouring the West Coast for you. You blow your recording dates. Everybody's saying you gone to pieces—."

"I had enough, that's all. Simple as that. All my life I try to make it into the big time. I work my butt off. Then, when I finally make it, this happens . . ." He stopped, then added, "I had enough. I'm finished."

"I don't get it. The last I heard, you were doing fine. A national singing star—radio, a couple of pictures. What went wrong? It can't be dough, you still got good record sales."

"It's not dough."

"So what else is there?"

He took his time answering. Tony had guessed right, Angelo was happy for the chance to talk it out. Once he got started, the words poured from him: "It was the last picture—they crucified me. Said I couldn't sing. Me. I shouldn't have done the picture, with all that crazy, way-out music, them twanging guitars. They oughta send all them fucking guitars back to Patagonia and burn 'em. People like to hear the old standards—the saxes, the clarinets, not all this modern trash. That's the trouble with music today—kids coming into the business wanna make funny sounds, wanna be different. Got no real talent. Just wanna make sounds. They don't understand what it is people like to hear—the old stuff. That fucking faggot of a producer, he told the papers the movie was a flop because of me. Said my stuff's going out of style, and I oughta be put out to pasture. Spread the word I'm unreliable, too—that I'm always smashed. That the picture came in over budget because of me. He owes everyone, that fruit. Now he's trying to put the blame on me."

"You telling me you're quitting because of a little criticism, and one big-mouth producer?"

"That punk, he got juice all over Hollywood and now he's gunning for me. You know what's so funny? He really thinks I ruined his picture—I guess he really does. But he got no right to spread the word around I'm on the skids. People been canceling out offers. I make calls and get funny answers—like, fr'instance, the guy's in Oshkosh, Wisconsin, on heavy business. Know what I mean?"

"That's no reason to roll over and die. You gotta fight your way out of the hole, like we always did, remember?"

"You don't understand. I can't start again, not after all this time, all the effort . . ." Angelo groaned, and the pain of the years came through in his voice. His eyes roved the room and stopped hungrily at a half-empty whiskey bottle. "Something else I found out. I guess I knew it all along, but I wouldn't admit it to myself. I'm hooked. I can't live without the stuff."

Something of Angelo's sudden, massive loss of confidence came through to Tony. "It never stopped you working before. Not from what I knew," he said. "What's so different now?" A spark of response came into Angelo's eyes, then faded. Tony had heard before of performers going to pieces, but it was inconceivable that a tough old bird of Angelo's caliber should succumb to criticism. And yet, he recalled, there was a time when even Skeeter had been the toughest guy in town . . . "Well, if you made up your mind you're finished, there's nothing I can do to help, I guess."

"Yeah, piss off and leave me alone."

"I was gonna ask a favor, but I guess you're in no condition to help me out."

"Ask me a favor?"

"Yeah. I'm no philanthropist. I'm admitting I had an ulterior motive in coming here."

"It's a sweet world. What you want?"

"I need top entertainers for our new trap, the Winter Palace. I thought maybe you fill a spot. Kinda help out."

". . . Uhuh. Don't bullshit me."

"I mean it."

"Word's out, it's some wild place." Angelo said it mildly.

"The best. I need names. Big names, Like Johnny Angel."

"A one-, two-week spot. It won't prove anything—you got a captive audience."

"I'm thinking of a whole season. Resident entertainer. We'll ration your appearances to avoid overexposure."

"Nah, it wouldn't work."

"Give you time to recover. All this will blow over in time."

"Forget it."

"O.K." Tony got to his feet. "I had another idea. But I don't suppose you wanna hear it?"

"No, I don't."

"To get back at that punk film producer."

"What you say?"

"My outfit's strong in the movie unions. We give the word, he don't make another movie. Not never."

Angelo was on his feet, his eyes blazing. "Yeah—yeah . . ." he yelled. "Bury the fuckin' prick. In cement."

"I can arrange to give him a lot of trouble," Tony said calmly. "If you agree to do a season at the Winter Palace."

"I'd sing for nothin' to get back at that faggot." Angelo breathed pure venom.

"Not for nothin'. You'll get the biggest fee ever paid to a performer for a regular date. We'll give that fact plenty of publicity. We have a deal, singer?"

"Let's drink to it." Angelo licked his lips.

"No, let's shake on it," Tony said. A revitalized Angelo shook hands. "O.K., now let's get out of this rattrap. We got work to do."

CHAPTER ELEVEN

"This is the most important junket ever," Lombardo was saying. "You sure everything's taken care of—we have enough suites? Nothin's too good and everything's gotta be perfect." They were waiting in the lobby for a fleet of limousines to arrive from the airport.

"Relax," Tony said, "everything's under control. I handled big junkets before, you know that. It's not the first time."

"Not like this one. Umberto Verdi spent months putting this one together. Some of the most influential people we know—politicians, industrialists, important businessmen—top people. *Crème de la crème*. It wasn't easy, talking them into coming out here. We have to see they want for nothing. They're gonna leave Las Vegas very impressed."

"I been looking at the list. Comps are one thing, freebies are another. A lot of 'em are bringing guests."

"We allowed two free guests to each junket member."

"Give me a regular crowd of dissipated high rollers any time," Tony said. "People who know the grind, guys who pay their own way and don't expect something for nothing all the time—."

"It's not like that," Lombardo said briefly.

"I know—we don't expect to make a profit this trip," he said resignedly.

"That's right. The idea is for these people to go back home and influence some very heavy investments—in our direction. *Capiche?*"

"Of course. I was at the meeting, wasn't I?"

"We play the expansion theme for all it's worth. Let the dumb fucks think we're gonna build joints like this on every street corner in Vegas. Then when we got their dough—zap, doomsville. We keep things depressed for a while, and when these people are sick, we buy out their investments for forty, fifty cents on the dollar. Later we pull out our own dough and what we find? We own Las Vegas and we got it for peanuts."

"Don't Levin never get tired of that old move?"

"It still works, don't it? When guys stop getting greedy, we'll find something else." Lombardo allowed himself a rare grin.

Tony, staring into the distance, shaded his eyes. He'd caught sight of the lead limousines moving sedately along the Strip. "Here they come." He snapped his fingers and the bell captain began marshaling his staff.

Distances in the bright, clear air were deceptive. At this pace it would be several minutes before the limos arrived. He left Lombardo's side to take a last look around the wide, glittering Winter Palace lobby, busy at midday. No clocks or windows disturbed the concentration of the gambler by reminding him of reality outside the walls of the casino. Past the lobby, a couple of steps running the full width of the interior led down into the great central well of the building that was the casino proper, the minefield that patrons always had to cross to gain access to the elevators and their rooms. The action at this hour of the day was slow, with many tables out of use. Countless slots, row after row, guarded the periphery of the room. Mirrors on the walls multiplied them so that they seemed to march off endlessly in every direction, filling the visible world with chrome fruit machines. Tony's attention was taken by a lone roulette player, who, tired of picking wrong numbers, had allowed his gaze to wander up into the roof of the building. He sat, head back and mouth hanging open, gazing past the soft hanging lights and the trunking that held the spy-in-the-sky stations to where a simulated Milky Way, a galaxy of stars, blinked high in the distant, soaring blackness of simulated night, as seen in the southern hemisphere.

He brought himself back to the present and strode out through the curtain of cold air blasting down over the entrance to where Lombardo still waited. The first of the limos was just turning off the Strip into the drive. "Verdi traveling with the junket himself?" Tony asked.

"Yes, as escort. We're giving them the blue-ribbon treatment all the way."

"Maybe it's just as well they don't know how privileged they are to have a council member handling them personally." It was his turn to grin.

"I told you, this is no ordinary junket. Verdi's been cultivating these people a long time. He wants to see the deal through himself—make sure nothing goes wrong."

A sudden, blinding thought occurred to Tony. "Hey, where in hell's the credit list? I asked you a dozen times. How we gonna write markers, we don't know a man's limit? I told you, I want that list in the cage before the first player steps up to a table."

"We decided, no limits. All referrals go to Verdi himself, by word of mouth. If Verdi authorizes one of them dumb fucks a hundred-thou credit line, it's to be O.K.'d immediately. No questions. You got it?"

"Oh, my God," Tony groaned. "We're leaving ourselves wide open. What happens when Verdi's not around? It's bound to happen."

"I dunno. We'll work it out. Meantime, you better memorize very carefully every face on the junket."

"*Now* he tells me."

The lead limousine had stopped and a bellboy jumped forward to open the door. Smiling in welcome, they moved out to greet the first guests.

He couldn't take his eyes off her. Whenever the opportunity allowed, when he could spare the time, he found himself going in search of her, their paths apparently crossing at random in the casino restaurants, the entertainment lounges, or out at the pool where everybody gathered in the early afternoons. When the serious business of the day began, she rarely accompanied Verdi into the casino proper, he noticed, which meant she had a lot of time on her hands. He sought her out surreptitiously, just for a passing smile, or to get a glimpse of her small, even teeth when her lips parted in frequent humor; to watch, from the corner of his eye, her svelte, subtle body movements. Her name was Nancy Powers and she'd been Umberto Verdi's broad for about a year, as near as he could discover. Verdi, old enough to be her father, had a reputation from the old days as a collector of beautiful dames, when it was the style to be seen out on the town with a gorgeous piece on your arm. He hadn't lost the touch, it seemed.

Tony couldn't remember such desire for a woman since his youthful lusting after the fulsome Francesca Boccardi. He told himself it was a reaction to overwork. Dames. In his time he'd had a choice most guys wouldn't even dream about to the day they turned up their toes.

They met unexpectedly, in the corridor outside the Verdi suite. He was taken by surprise, but didn't show it. He nodded courteously, and started to pass. "Mr. Vitale." She stood at the door.

"Yes?" He stopped, surprised again that she remembered his name. They'd been introduced only briefly in the hectic first moments of the junket's arrival.

"It's Tony, isn't it?"

"Yes, it is," he said, puzzled.

"I've heard them speak about you, in there. That's how I come to know your name." She smiled, pointing at the door.

"Well, as we're on the same team, I hope you liked what you heard," he said.

"For a guy who's been looking me over for four days, you're awfully formal," she said.

He didn't show the excitement that surged through him. "You're a very attractive lady. And I'm only human." He shrugged. "Mr. Verdi's a lucky man."

"You take in all the broads that way?"

"No, I don't. I didn't realize I'd made it so obvious. I'm sorry if I offended you. It won't happen again," he said coolly, and went to move off.

"Hey—you're touchy. You didn't offend me." She gave him another smile, the half-haunting smile that intrigued him so much. "When the guys stop looking, that's the time for a girl to get worried."

After a moment, he said, "I guess I'm a looker, not a buyer. Nice to have spoken to you, Miss Powers."

"You afraid of him?"

"What?"

"The big shot. Umberto Verdi."

"No, I'm not afraid of him. I'm not exactly small fry around here myself, you know." He realized, incredulously, that he was boasting.

"You act like you're afraid of him."

"Verdi's the last thing on my mind right now."

"Then why don't you ask me for a date? You want to, don't you?"

"This is an important junket. It would be irresponsible of me to jeopardize its success by doing something so foolish. It just ain't my style."

Her eyes were wide. "Screw the junket," she said. "What's important is us."

The heat started in him again. He stared at her. Slowly, disbelievingly, he heard his own voice saying, "Around ten, when the tables get busy, I take a break. We could have a drink. The Princess Bar, by the pool."

"I can't wait." She slipped through the door and was gone.

As the day passed, he found it increasingly difficult to concentrate on his work. His behavior was entirely out of character—good old dependable Tony rutting after a council member's woman. But it was happening, it was real, and he knew within himself, that there wasn't a damn thing he intended to do to stop it. It was crazy; he tried to balance in his mind the worth of his career, his reputation for judgment and sagacity, against the value of a woman's smile, the small light in her eyes. Around twenty-five bucks in any of a dozen Nevada brothels. Hell, he'd been dead long enough, he decided—repressed and disciplined since he could remember in an environment that existed to serve, and profit from, the abandonment of inhibition. He shook his head. He was taking himself too seriously. For once he would let things take their course and rely on his natural caution.

But he was throwing caution to the winds, and he knew it.

At ten the Princess Bar was quiet. Most of the action at this hour was in the casino, the theater where patrons stood in line to hear Johnny Angel sing, and the entertainment lounges. She walked in, her gown clinging to her breasts, its front a deep, revealing vee. A bare back showed her skin pleasantly tanned. The sight of her as she came through the entrance sent a thrill through him, and her sheer beauty brought a dryness to his throat. He watched her moving toward him and devoured every footstep. He took her arm and guided her to a booth. The waiter was at his side instantly. Tony lifted an eyebrow at her. "I'll have the same as yours," she said.

"Scotch on the rocks twice," he told the waiter.

When they were alone, she said, "Please don't look at me that way, you give me goose pimples."

"I don't know what it is you do to me. You look . . . very beautiful."

"Took me hours to get this way," she said frankly.

"It was worth it."

"Only if you think so."

"I think so." He watched her superb mouth.

"Then it was worth it."

"You smell good, too."

"Chanel will be pleased." She laughed at him, but he didn't mind.

"Here's the booze." The cool drink eased his parched throat. He emptied the glass and, when the liquor hit his stomach, he realized suddenly he hadn't eaten. "You hungry? Oh, I suppose you've had dinner."

"Couldn't eat a thing," she said.

"Me neither." They looked again into each other's eyes. "I think I need another drink," Tony said. He caught the waiter's attention.

"Let's get one thing straight," she said. "I'm not a whore. I don't want you thinking that. I'm a one-man woman."

He held up his hand. "You don't owe me any explanations, Nancy."

"I just want you to know. If it's what you're thinking, we have nothing more to say to each other."

"Knock it off. I know all I need to know. You're not the first woman I met either."

"Are you married, Tony?"

"No."

"I was married. Before I met Bertie. Oh, he didn't steal me from my husband. I was divorced before we met."

"Do you love him?"

"Bertie?" She gave a laugh. "No. I was alone and afraid. He represented security, power, and money—all the things I never had. The things everybody wants. It's all a crock, really, you know that? But it's such a long time before you find out." She was silent a moment. "He's an old man and not demanding. A sort of father figure, I suppose. Bertie's always been known for his beautiful women, so I guess I'm just decoration."

"You satisfied with that?"

"I didn't say I'm satisfied. I'm a realist. Life's hard, out there in the cold."

"A beautiful woman like you could have the world at her feet."

"I don't want the world. I found that out. I want . . ." She stopped. "I guess I'm just hard to please."

"Maybe I can please you."

"Maybe I'll let you try."

He had an almost unbearable desire to reach out and touch her, but he refrained. Their relationship was so new, so tender, and he knew so little about her.

"I've heard you mentioned often," she said suddenly.

"You have?"

"Yes. Mostly they talk in secret, but there are times—well, a person just can't help overhearing."

"I understand."

284

"They think a lot of you, the council. They say you're a top operator, and very reliable."

"Good old reliable, that's me."

"They're using you." She said it suddenly. "They can't do it without someone like you to handle it for them. I heard Lombardo say it was you who straightened out the Caprice—that they owe its success to you. And that your systems made the Winter Palace pay off right from the start. Now all the Las Vegas houses are using them."

"That's what I'm paid for. I'm a sort of . . . consultant."

"You're a mechanic, big boy," she said briefly. "The best there is."

He looked at her keenly. "You know too much for your own good."

"I also know how to keep my mouth shut." She paused. "And I know something else: They need you, but you don't need them. Why'd you let them boss you around?"

He frowned. "It keeps 'em happy. Why should that concern you? A mechanic works only for the house—."

"I'm sorry. I shouldn't have said that." Her tone softened. "Let me hold your hand." She reached out. "Your hands are so beautiful."

Her touch electrified him, and again the heat surged through his body. The contact had affected her, too. They stared deep into each other's eyes and knew they shared the same deep hunger. "Let's get out of here," he said hoarsely.

"Where shall we go?"

"I have a suite here in the hotel, on the top floor."

She nodded, and they got quickly to their feet.

He let her get a couple of minutes ahead of him; then, looking to the front and, praying nobody would call him as he crossed the busy casino floor, he made for the elevators. A pair of aluminum doors slid open conveniently as he reached the elevator lobby. He stepped quickly inside and punched the button that would take it to the penthouse level. She was waiting for him at his door. He let her in, and, as he kicked the door shut behind him, in a swift, mutual movement, they were in each other's arms. They sucked hungrily at each other's lips, the desperation of their shared need so fierce and the fire of their suppressed yearning so strong, that it seemed, in that moment, the flames of their tormented passion raged up and engulfed them. A wordless agreement had been reached, and they tore at each other, gasping and breathless, reveling in sheer primeval desire. It was insane, and, just for a moment, he was afraid for both of them. The sensation was smothered by her pervading presence, and he cast it aside to crush her to him. When the tidal wave of first emotion had passed, the infinitely soft blending of their embrace was everything he'd hoped for. He opened his eyes to find her smiling into his, and he knew there had been nothing to fear. Their sudden, crazy abandon had evoked nothing but spontaneous joy. "Oh, Tony, I want you. I want you so much." Her words came from deep in her throat, almost a low moan.

"Nancy." He could say nothing but her name.

Together they tripped and stumbled toward the bedroom, leaving a trail of clothes behind where they'd been pulled or simply ripped off. Locked again in an embrace, they fell together on the bed. The touch of her flesh on his own set him on fire. It was a thousand times the sensation he'd felt when they held hands, and he could hardly endure the delicious torment. There was no time for initial touching and stroking, the gentle prelude to heightened sensuality. They were already way up there. Their need was immediate and frantic. Desperately he slid his hand down to part her legs and find the vibrant, soaking petals of flesh that awaited him. She gave herself eagerly, her legs coming up to entwine him. He fought to enter her as quickly as he could and thrust himself forward with a movement that was almost brutal, penetrating her with a great, gusting sigh of gratification. For an instant she shuddered, then quickly recovered, and bore up to consume him. In a very few strokes he was ready to explode. She cried out in her joy when she, too, began her orgasm; she seemed to go on endlessly, drawing from him the last vestige of the seed he sought to place in her. Damp and deliciously exhausted, they collapsed together.

Some time later, her voice full of wonder, she said, "That was the most marvelous thing I've ever known."

He struggled up on to his elbows and smiled at her. "They say it can happen this way, sometimes. To lucky people."

"Will it always be like this for us?"

He smiled again. "Naturally."

"I just love your smile," she said. "and your blue eyes. I think I love everything about you."

"You don't know everything about me."

"I will." She reached up for him. "Hold me close. I don't want this moment to end, my darling."

He lay his cheek against hers, and she closed her eyes. After a while he opened his eyes again and stared into the distance. Slowly he allowed his thoughts to return to reality.

And reality, unfortunately, was Umberto Verdi.

CHAPTER TWELVE

They were six days into a seven-day junket. Around the hotel, Umberto Verdi's party was preparing to depart. More and more Tony found his thoughts occupied with Nancy, until the image of her consumed his waking hours. He'd found a joy that never existed before. Not for him. He was desperate not to lose her, and the desperation welled up inside him.

It was their last few hours together, snatched surreptitiously in his suite high above the gambling house. It burst out of her, the subject they had assiduously avoided: "We have to come to a decision, Tony, before it's too late. I told you there

286

can only be one man in my life. I meant it."

He took her in his arms and touched the tear that sprang to her cheek. "There's no need for tears, baby," he said gently.

"I can't live this way. I won't—hiding around corners. I can't split myself in two. Bertie's so busy with the junket, he's hardly had time to notice where I am. When we get back to New York, it'll be different."

"I been thinking about it." His tone made no commitment.

Her eyes were enormous. "This is it, then? It was fun while it lasted, thanks and goodbye, hon?"

"I been trying to tell myself it's crazy—that I can't be in love with someone I know just a few days. But I gotta admit it, I'm hooked. I'm in love with you, Nancy. You better believe it. I never said that to a dame in my whole life." He found it difficult to get the words out.

"Oh, my sweet darling." She buried her head in his shoulder, and he could feel the sobs of relief racking her body. When she looked up again, her face radiated joy. "I was hoping and praying . . . I was so afraid we'd never meet again." Safe now in his arms, his strength comforted her. "What can we do? I can't go back to New York with Bertie. Not now that we've found each other. I would die."

"The hell with Bertie. And the rest of them," he said.

"I agree, but it's not much of a plan of action, is it?"

"I'll give you a plan of action. We're getting out of here right now."

"Where to?"

"Reno."

"Why Reno?"

"I hear that's where folks go to get married."

She screamed in delight. It was some minutes before they were speaking coherently again. "What happens when they find out we've run off together?" she asked fearfully.

"We ain't running," Tony said. "And we ain't hiding from nobody. No way."

"Tony, they're dangerous . . ."

"Honey, there's nothing to be afraid of from the outfit. I'm just taking a vacation to get married. Ain't nothing they can object to in that."

"And Bertie? He'll be sore as hell."

"We'll take our chances with him. It's my guess he'll bite the bullet. He's got more sense than to go complaining to the council that I stole his woman. They'd tell him to go piss up a rope. Anyhow, the sooner they get to know about it, the better. We'll have something going for us then."

"What's that?"

"They'll realize I'm a lot more use to them alive than dead."

He grinned cheerfully. He hoped he was right.

By late evening that day they were in Reno. The Marryin' Sam Chapel they chose was characteristic of several on the main drag. Outlined in neon to represent an edifice to the worship of God, it was the epitome of commercial bad taste. A running electric arrow descended from the roof of the shack to point baldly at the door, easing the burden for those incapable of finding the entrance. Twenty-five bucks bought the ceremony, the bride's corsage, a canned wedding march, a photograph (to be forwarded when processed, postage extra), and free parking space for the duration of the nuptials.

They found it hilarious, and quite beautiful.

That night, totally freed from inhibition for the first time, they surrendered to each other. They made love fiercely, blending their flesh, melding their hearts and souls, fiber and spirit, to become as one. In those magical moments the marriage was made complete, the partnership secured, and each gave selflessly. He was filled with wonder that he could give so completely, that he could abandon a lifetime's careful conditioning and pass into the loving care of someone who, until a few days ago, had been a total stranger. Yet, somehow, it seemed right. For her part, Nancy's happiness was boundless: fate had preserved for her lover her beauty of form, her grace, her wit, the deep joy of totally sincere love, the fleeting treasure of her womanly dowry. For both it had been a rocky path to the green pastures of their contentment, and they were deeply grateful.

They made a commitment. They vowed that their love would last forever, or as long as they both would live.

The days went quickly, and the nights were pleasantly slow. For four days they went no further from their downtown hotel than they could walk. In the afternoons they strolled through the busy stores, sometimes buying articles they had no particular use for, just for the pleasure of finding they had a mutual liking for them, then leaving a trail of discarded artifacts in the most unlikely places. They ate long, leisurely meals, or just sat smiling foolishly at each other over cold coffee, occasionally holding hands. From their hotel room they could see Harrah's Casino, so one day they strolled over there to admire the decorative motifs inlaid on the sidewalk outside. Inside, the familiar rattle of the slots momentarily shook Tony out of his lethargy, like a hunting dog reacting to the scent. At first he found himself smiling at the naïve, sterile action at the tables in this sidewalk gambling house, the hick players with their handfuls of dollar checks. He pulled himself up short when he realized that Reno had already captured, in miniature, the market they were aiming for with their vast, expensive Las Vegas operations. The mass-market—Joe Soap. Here it was on a smaller scale, unlike the outfit's vision of volume and turnover that was far in excess of anything Reno had dreamed of. After a few minutes, they walked out. There were other things to think about besides casino business.

Or so he thought. When they got back to the hotel, they found Tom Druccio waiting for them in the lobby. "What kept you?" Tony said sourly, at the sight of him.

"Don't blame me, Tony. You know I'm only following orders," Tom said uncomfortably.

"Well, what they want?"

"They wanna know what the fuck you're playing at," Tom said in a quiet voice, turning his head from Nancy.

"I left Lombardo a message. I'm taking a vacation."

"This ain't like you, Tony, walking out on the job. They got nobody to take over the Winter Palace on such short notice. Lombardo had to stay on himself."

"So?"

"Verdi blew his top. You walk off with his broad—that ain't polite." Tom still averted his gaze from Nancy.

"Any other messages?"

"They want you to come back and straighten things out. Explain yourself."

"You explain for me."

Tom looked at him. "Sure. What you want me to say?"

"Tell them—Nancy and me, we seen enough of Reno. Tomorrow we're going up to Lake Tahoe for a few days. You got any more messages, we'll be up there. Now, piss off, Tom."

Tom was silent a moment. "You lost your marbles, pal?" he said stiffly. "You wanna be another Abe Carroll."

"Yeah, tell 'em that," Tony said rebelliously.

Tom stood uncertainly for another moment. He turned and walked toward the hotel entrance. They hadn't moved when he wheeled about and came back. His grim expression had changed to one of real concern. "Listen, Tony," he said. "I don't wanna go back there and cause trouble for you, you know that. You been a good friend to me. Just give me something to say that makes sense—any old bullshit, I don't care. Whatever it is you want me to say, I'll tell 'em. You wanna take a vacation? That's O.K. with me. I'll go back and say your grandmother died. I'll say I checked it out and it's true—."

"No, don't do that, you'll walk straight into trouble. You're not dealing with fools . . ." Tony interrupted him.

"Then give me something to say, for Chrissakes," Tom pleaded.

He thought for a moment. "Just tell the truth."

"What's the truth?"

"Just say we fell in love and went away to get married."

". . . You and Nancy?"

"Yeah, me and Nancy, wise guy."

"Well, I'll be . . ." A grin spread slowly across Tom's face. "Why didn't you say so, schmuck? The outfit'll be tickled pink—that is, apart from the fact you left 'em in the lurch. You know how sentimental they get over family matters."

"Tell them we just wanted a quiet wedding. Apologize for me that it's inconvenient, but we couldn't wait."

"Sure—."

"And be polite." Tony's sense of equilibrium was reasserting itself.

"I get it. Leave it to me."

"When you get back, go see Verdi first. Tell him to his face I said he missed the boat with Nancy. Say I said he'll know what I mean, and no hard feelings. Watch his reaction. If you think he's gonna make trouble, put me wise."

"O.K., Tony, I'll sound him out."

"Thanks, Tom."

Druccio stood for a moment, an amused smile on his face, watching the look of understanding that passed between Tony and Nancy. He put out his hand. "Well, I guess I should offer my congratulations."

"Appreciate that, old pal." He took the proffered hand.

"And to you, ah, Mrs. Vitale," he added respectfully.

Lake Tahoe was beautiful. The hotel was built out from a rock cliff above the cool, clear water so that, from the wide balcony running the width of their room, they could look down and see the small, mottled fish feeding on plankton. The glass side of the room slid back completely, and they could sit inside looking at the panorama of the steely water of the lake against a backdrop of distant mountains soaring to the sky and capped with small, fluffy white clouds. It was a view they didn't tire of. They were gazing out idly when the telephone rang. Tony picked it up. "Sorry to disturb you," Tom Druccio said.

"Where are you?"

"Here, downstairs in the hotel. I brought someone along to see you."

"Who?"

"You'll see. He's on his way up."

"Thanks a million, pal, whoever he is," Tony said caustically. Tom had put down the telephone and hadn't heard.

When the knock came at the door, he opened it and found Levin standing there, a gift-wrapped package under his arm. He wouldn't have been more surprised to receive a visit from Santa Claus. "How are you, Tony?" Levin was smiling pleasantly. "And how's your lovely new wife?" He looked past Tony to where Nancy had got to her feet.

"We're fine, thanks, Mr. Levin. Come on in."

"Thank you." He walked into the room and placed the package on a side table. "A small gift for the newlyweds. I'm disappointed in you, Tony. You don't give me the chance to come to your wedding. It's a big event when one of our people gets married, don't you know that? It brings us all together. Things like that are important."

Despite himself, he felt a surge of gratitude that Levin made a point of including him in the exclusive group. "We decided in a hurry," he said quietly.

"So I understand." Levin stepped forward to take Tony, then Nancy, by the hand so that the warmth flowed between them. "Well, my children, now that you've chosen one another, I want you to know you have my blessing. I don't doubt for a minute that you chose wisely, so let me wish you many years of happiness."

"Thank you." They said it together. This was a side of Levin he hadn't seen before. The three of them were facing out through the open side of the room, across the terrace.

"What a wonderful view," Levin said. "I envy you the peace and quiet. I could do with a little myself." He let go of their hands and turned, and something of his businesslike manner returned. "We have to talk, Tony," he said apologetically. "But only after I've drunk a toast to your marriage. What can you offer me to drink?"

"There's some Scotch here," he said, surprised.

"That'll be fine. Straight, no ice." Tony had never before seen Levin take a drink. He poured out three whiskeys. Levin lifted the glass and swallowed the contents at a gulp, like medicine. They sat down. "Tony, I'm not going to ask you to excuse your behavior. I'm human enough to understand there are moments in a

290

man's life . . ." He stopped, and shrugged. "To me, it's enough you show serious intent by getting married. If you'd run off for some irresponsible reason, it might have been a different matter." He paused again. "I regard what happened as a symptom, nothing more. If something's troubling you, this is the time to tell me. Otherwise, we put this episode behind us and look to the future. We have big plans, and there's a place for you in those plans. You're important to us, and we got many years effort invested in you. Don't forget that. We don't want that investment to go to waste. That's why I come out here myself, because I think we understand each other, and so you can tell me face to face if we got a problem."

Tony was silent for some time. It was his big opportunity to say that he wanted out. Inside him a voice cried out that he wanted back the individuality, the freedom they'd stolen from him. That he wanted to become a person in his own right once again, before it was too late. A man instead of a cog, a digit, an investment. Yet he knew in his heart there was no release from the irrefutable bargain he'd struck those many years ago. They'd made him part of them and, in return, had taught him to be wealthy and wise. But he was a limb, an appendage, and there was no salvation. At least he understood it—at least he knew better than Carroll. He turned to gaze out at the mountains soaring free into the blue Nevada sky. When he turned back, the opportunity was gone. "I think I just got tired, Mr. Levin," he said slowly. "Too many years doing the same thing. A guy gets jaded—needs a change."

"Yes, I agree," Levin said, and the intensity went out of his gaze. "You've earned a vacation. Stay here and enjoy. And your marriage will give you a new lease on life when you're ready to come back to work, I'm sure. Now you got reason to seek success. Maybe, later, a family comes along and—."

"There's something else. Vegas. I had it with that Vegas. The place just ain't for real." He blurted it out.

"I see." Levin drummed his fingers on the arm of his chair. "That's a pity. Vegas is where a big part of our future is."

"Maybe later." Tony recovered himself. "For now I need a change of air."

"What you suggest?"

"Cuba. I'd like to go back. I was happy there in Havana. I guess I just like the atmosphere of the place—it's free and easy."

"Things have changed. We got problems in Cuba—big problems. Batista is losing his grip, and the revolutionaries are giving him trouble."

"Yeah, I know. That prick Castro. A few months—nothing's gonna happen in a few months. Look, Kovack's still running the Internacionale. Bring him over to Vegas to operate the Winter Palace, and I'll take his place for a while. Make a change for him, too," Tony said persuasively. "I'll pick up the reigns in no time with my brother Mokey and my pal Skeeter working out there. Maybe I can even tune up the operation a little. What you say—just a few months?"

"I suppose . . ." Levin looked at Nancy thoughtfully. "It'd give Verdi time to cool off, too. Maybe it's not such a bad idea. O.K., I'll fix it," he decided.

"Terrific. I feel better already." Tony was smiling all over his face as Levin got to his feet. "Mr. Levin, I want you to know I appreciate your coming out here to see me."

"It's a token of the esteem I have for you, Tony," Levin said diplomatically.

291

When Levin had gone, he swung around to Nancy. "Baby, we're off on a long holiday in the Caribbean," he said enthusiastically. "You'll love it."

"Hey, I'm not flying. No more flying for me. I'm terrified of those damn airplanes," she said instantly. "That trip out to Vegas, I nearly died up there."

"For you, honey, I'd swim all the way to Cuba," he said happily.

CHAPTER THIRTEEN

When the Key West ferry had docked, and Nancy had finished admiring the colorful scene that made up a Caribbean marine vista, Tony quickly became aware of an electric atmosphere he hadn't experienced in Cuba before. When they were disembarking, he noticed the squads of soldiers guarding strategic locations at the docks, a military presence in evidence everywhere he looked. From the streets of Havana, in the distance, came the frequent, urgent howl of police sirens racing through the city. There were none of the usual crowds of gay or indolent Cubans on the dockside or the streets, and those people they saw moved quickly and purposefully, as if they didn't want to remain in the open longer than necessary.

Mokey was there to greet them, grinning from ear to ear. He hugged Tony, then Nancy, and gave her a cautious, sibling kiss. When she was getting into the car, Tony noticed him discreetly appraising her shape in a professional manner. It was no less than he'd expected from such an expert in the female form. They piled the baggage into the trunk of the car and moved out of the docks. "Well, little brother, what's the good word?" He smiled at the healthy tan on Mokey's face. His brother's cheeks had filled out and lost their midnight Vegas pallor, and he looked better than Tony had ever seen him. "Cuba agrees with you, huh?"

"I'll say," Mokey said enthusiastically. "Swimming, the beach, fishing . . ."

"You fish?" Tony was surprised.

"Sure. Love it. Some nights we take out a boat, fix a light, and the fish come and wait in line to grab the hook. It ain't fishing—they committing suicide. Yeah, this is the place for me. Never had it so good my whole life. Best move you ever make, sending me out here."

"I'm glad."

"And the broads. Here they got broads—."

"I expected Skeeter to be here." Tony shut him up. He felt a twinge of disappointment that Skeeter hadn't been at the dock to meet him and his new bride. "He O.K.?"

"Oh, sure, he's fine. Looking forward to seeing you both. He can't leave the joint just now, though. Kovack left for Vegas yesterday like you arranged. Someone gotta stay and mind the store. The police, they're in and out like they're on springs or sump'n. We got police and the military everywhere in this town."

292

"Yeah, I noticed." Tony had been watching bands of soldiers on street corners eyeing them suspiciously as they drove past. "What in hell's going on around here?"

"A few days ago them revolutionaries attacked. They ambushed some soldiers over at La Plata. That Castro, he's been hiding out in the mountains biding his time, I guess. They ain't released all the news yet, but it looks like the army took a beating. The way Batista's reacting, I guess Castro's got him worried. He's locking up thousands of political prisoners."

"That's ridiculous. Batista's never gonna let a handful of revolutionaries get on top of him. They got no chance."

"That's what we all thought. Seems Castro has a lot of support among the peasants. They hide him out there in the hills where the army can't get at him. Nobody can find the guy. He makes a hit, then disappears like a phantom."

"How long this been going on?"

"Year or so. Seems he trained some rebels in Mexico and landed back here with eighty-five men. They all got wiped out except fifteen, but he's built up an army since then. He's recruiting from the peasants all the time. This is the first time he had any big success though."

"It won't last. Not if I know Batista."

"Sure. He's gonna give them Castro guys hell before he's finished."

They were approaching the cosmopolitan center of Havana, where the seedy streets gave way to wide thoroughfares with expensive shops. Here the city took on a more normal appearance, except for the occasional police vehicle howling suicidally across their path, its banshee siren wailing. Here people moved more naturally, more confidently, safer in the hub of Havana's prosperity. Here the soldiers who were in evidence stood more circumspectly, like whores in a children's playground.

At the Internacionale, the welcoming committee, headed by Skeeter and Selina, soon included many of Tony's previous staff. When they'd killed a couple of bottles of champagne, Tony noticed they had been joined by Bernardo Garcia. As the excitement died down, he took the playboy police chief to one side. "Hey, Bernardo, I sure appreciate your coming in to welcome me. I know how busy you must be."

"Oh, it's all over now. What you see out there, it's just a publicity exercise. Makes the people happy to see the police earning their keep."

"Didn't look that way to me, old pal. Them paddy wagons, they full of people got themselves arrested for breathing, seems to me."

"We're pulling in anyone suspected of sympathizing with the terrorists. We just question them and let them go if we find nothing suspicious. It teaches them to be cautious and reminds them we're watching them."

"That include tourists?"

"We don't bother tourists, you know that. Not unless they break our laws, of course, and then we're very lenient. But then, tourists are unlikely to be interested in our sordid little domestic squabbles."

"You better watch that heavy hand, Bernardo. Word's out on the mainland things ain't right over here. I don't want you scaring off my customers."

"I assure you, Tony, it's all rumors and exaggeration. If it's your investments here in Cuba you're worried about, you have nothing to fear. We'll protect your property, just as we always have. The Cuban government has great respect for law and order."

"I know you'll protect us, Bernardo, because it's in your own interest. Cuba needs the tourist business we bring in. That wasn't what I meant. I meant you're not exactly encouraging people to come to Cuba by putting the frighteners into every poor bastard steps in your way. Out there in the streets they're all running like scared rabbits."

He knew he'd gone too far when he saw the glitter in Bernardo's eyes. He seemed to have forgotten how to step lightly. "You must allow us to conduct our affairs as we see fit," Bernardo said stiffly. "You should bear in mind your presence here is entirely at the pleasure and convenience of the Cuban government."

It came tumbling out of him, this new-found articulation. "Our presence here is because we got that greedy bastard Batista in our fucking pocket. Three million skins in the bank in Switzerland every annum—that's why our presence here, señor." He said it sharply, and knew at once it was a foolish remark to make, except that he'd become desperately tired of deception. And what the hell—*they* had the juice with Batista, not the police chief.

Bernardo stared at him icily for a moment, then turned and walked out without another word.

He sat down. He'd decided he no longer wanted Bernardo for a friend, because he didn't speak the truth. And because Bernardo took him for a prick.

He rang the number he knew so well, the one he'd used during the war. "Call Washington," a voice told him in accented English. He called Washington and quoted his old cypher code. A wise guy asked him if he was Buck Rogers; they'd stopped using the codes that long ago. The wise guy found someone who traced the old records. He was given a number to call. In Havana. It was the same old number. He called and this time asked for Bud Carlstrom by name.

The following evening Bud strolled into his office. The agent was lean and fit, just as Tony remembered him. But the years between had etched lines into the sparse flesh on his face, and there were crow's-feet at the corners of his eyes, under the graying hair. Just for an instant, when Tony first saw him, he was transported back in time. He found himself thinking: Everyone's getting older all at once. "You're one guy I never expected to see again. I thought you'd be good'n dead by now," Tony greeted him cheerfully. "Either there's an awful lot of inefficient foreign agents around, or you got a charmed life."

They shook hands warmly. "Not so easy for a guy to get himself knocked off these days. Too busy filling in forms in triplicate. We got a new weapon—confuse the enemy with paperwork."

"What you now, a general?"

"Nope. Got no rank, now. Things changed."

"Need a drink?"

"Yeah." Tony poured out the Scotch. Big ones; somehow he always enjoyed drinking with Bud. "Funny you should call me. I been retired three years. A few weeks ago they haul me back on special assignment."

"What for?"

"I guess because I know this theater of operations better'n most." Tony waited. "Problems—we got problems here in Cuba."

"Tell me."

Bud looked at him. "You're not cleared for security these days."

"Oh, come on, nothing's changed—I'm still the same guy. I ain't forgot how to keep my mouth shut." Bud swilled down some whiskey. "If it makes any difference, I told that mother Garcia to go screw himself," Tony added.

The humor came back into Bud's steel-gray eyes. "You got nerve doing that right now."

"Why—because he big police chief and talk with forked tongue? Balls to that jerk. He'll do like he's told. We own his boss."

Bud nodded. "Your people's relationship with Batista may turn out more significant than you expect. It's important to the United States that Batista stays in power." He grinned. "Looks as if we're on the same team again, don't it?"

"I don't get you."

"Commies. I'm talking about a threat to American security directly through Cuba."

"Fidel Castro's a communist?"

Bud shrugged. "He's a revolutionary. Communism's the easy path for an ambitious rebel."

"Castro's pure nowhere. We both know it. What you talking about?"

"Don't be too sure. Things aren't quite what they appear in Cuba these days." Tony frowned and waited for him to continue. If anyone knew what he was talking about, it was Bud. "Castro's been working away quietly out there in the bush, winning the peasant farmers over to his side. The peasants hate and fear the landowners and the army. They're hardly more than slaves, and if they open their mouths to complain, the army rams a jackboot down their throats. The country feeds on a diet of violence and corruption . . ." He looked up.

Tony moved uncomfortably in his seat. "We didn't invent the corruption here, you know," he said. "We just learned to live with it."

"I'm not passing judgment, I'm stating facts," Bud said. "Here in Havana we don't see the degree of oppression that takes place in the provinces. Maybe it'd be better if we did. The prisons are overflowing, and torture and killing's routine."

"Garcia told me they're only pulling 'em in over at El Macho for questioning. The lyin' shit."

"A lot more walk in than walk out."

"Fine partners we got. Maybe we should do a deal with that guy Castro instead. Put him in to run the country."

"Between ourselves, it could be better for the Cuban people. Unfortunately, we suspect that his communist sympathies pose a danger to the U.S. *That's* the problem."

"What you intend to do about it?"

"We have to stick with Batista for our own good." He smiled weakly.

They sat in silence for a moment. "Look, you certain Castro's a communist?"

"Aah . . ." Bud cleared his throat. "That's our information. What confirms it is the guy he has along with him."

"Who's he?"

"A man named Che Guevara, one of his field commanders. He trained as a doctor. He also trained in Mexico as a Marxist-Leninist revolutionary. Where he goes, communism goes. They got nothing else to sell."

"Maybe we're taking all this too seriously . . ." Tony took a cigarette and threw it to Bud. He lit one for himself. "These countries down here, they breed revolutionaries like rabbits. What makes you think Castro'll be any more successful than the rest?"

"He already is."

"That little number over at La Plata? They tell me it was nothing but a street fight. You know how these people exaggerate."

"On the contrary, it was a serious military victory for Castro's *Barbudos.*"

"His what?"

"The Bearded Ones. Batista suppressed the facts because the truth would throw his supporters into a panic. With only three hundred men, Castro managed to kick the shit out of Batista's army—and they have reserves of ten thousand men. He staged an ambush and surrounded Batista's troops for ten days, until they were starving. He grabbed their radios and fooled the air force into bombing the government side. The troops genuinely thought they were facing a large force, but at no time did they have less than ten men to Castro's one."

"Jes-us Christ," Tony said.

"All over the country, outside Havana, Radio Rebelde is blaring out for the people to come and join Castro's glorious Twenty-Sixth of July Revolutionary Movement. To free themselves from the yoke of slavery. And, you know something? They're joining him—slowly he's getting the support he needs."

Again they were silent. Then Tony said, "Where does that leave us?"

"We can only wait and see." Bud got to his feet. "Little revolutionary cells are springing up all over. It remains to be seen whether or not Castro can put them together."

He rose, too. "I suppose we gotta be grateful we don't have much of this garbage going on right here in Havana," he said.

"But we do. There's a revolutionary cell right here, recruiting in the Internacionale."

He stared. "You're kidding?"

"Carlos Lopez, the man who runs your kitchens."

"Right—that's one guy needn't bother to turn up for work in the morning," Tony said angrily.

"I wouldn't do that if I were you," Bud said blandly.

"Why not?"

"Just in case the revolution succeeds."

"So, for that I gotta cultivate the jerk?"

"Let me put it this way: You're personally classified a Batistano by the revolutionaries. Lopez is probably dreaming of the day he can slit your throat."

"You're kidding." He said it again.

"Don't encourage him," Bud said.

CHAPTER FOURTEEN

The Cuba he'd returned to had become a very different place from the indolent, unhurried, pleasurable, palm-tree island he'd left behind ten years before. Its principal city had escalated into a gambling and pleasure resort that threatened to transcend a burgeoning Las Vegas. Downtown Havana was now a large, neon-lit haven of establishments offering aspects of vice that went beyond imaginable permutations—through erotic to the pornographic, on to revolting, bestial, and sometimes simply stupefying in their diversion from the mundane. For gamblers, the city now offered the glittering temptations of nineteen major casinos. From the Tropicana, the Riviera, and the Montmartre through to the piquant Sans Souci. At the Casino de Capri, an elegant George Raft, in knife-edged pants, hosted gregarious patrons. Massive bets were going down nightly at the recently opened Habana Hilton Casino in what were the biggest crap games seen anywhere, any time. In the early days of the Hilton, a crap layout, often frequented by Cuban and American casino owners themselves, could sometimes be found bearing half a million dollars as the players awaited the stickman's call: "Shooter coming out."

Cuba had become a phenomenon of its time. And beneath it all the rumble of the revolution, the anguished cry of the oppressed, the flames of rebellion fanned by Fidel Castro grew stronger, unheeded by those in the grip of the hypnotic miasma of gay Havana. The overbearing presence of police and the military was becoming more difficult to conceal as anti-insurgency measures increased. Which was about the time the oppressors, accustomed to flexing their muscles before a supine native population, began lusting after a greater share of the spoils.

"Tony, you better come down here quick. We got problems." It was Beppo Mendez, his Cuban house manager, on the phone.

"What's up? I'm having breakfast." He glanced at the clock; it was midday. "I'll be down there in a few minutes, anyway, to check yesterday's take."

"Come now. I'm about to have the slots emptied."

"You're late. That should have been done by now."

"We got delayed."

"By what?"

"The army. They want a share."

"Hold everything. I'm coming down."

When he entered the casino, the first thing he saw was the soldiers, machine guns ready, guarding every exit. The only other people in the big room were a group of three standing in the middle of the floor. On one side of Beppo Mendez stood the police chief, Bernardo Garcia. On the other side stood an army officer, bemedaled and jackbooted.

Tony walked up to them. "This is Captain Bayamo," Bernardo said coldly. "He is here as the representative of Madame Batista."

"*Madame* Batista?" Tony repeated.

"Yes. Our first lady has decided she wishes to help various Cuban charities. Captain Bayamo has been honored with the task of assisting her."

"Very commendable." Tony nodded. "What's that got to do with me?"

"Captain Bayamo and I have decided you may wish to cooperate."

He studied Bernardo's mocking expression, wondering how he could ever have been friends with this hyena. "If you're looking for a handout, the casino will be happy to make a contribution," he said dryly.

"Ah, that simplifies things considerably." Bernardo was playing with him.

"Come into the office, I'll give you a check," Tony said.

"That won't be necessary. We've already decided on the form your contribution will take."

"Oh, yeah?"

"We'll be sharing the take on the slots with you."

"Like hell you will."

"Whatever comes out of the slot machines will be divided equally, half to the casino and half to Madame Batista's deserving causes."

"You crazy? You're not getting away with that."

"What's to stop us?" Bernardo said, grinning.

"Me—I'm fuckin' stopping you right now," Tony yelled. He shut up when, from the corner of his eye, he saw a soldier stiffen and raise his gun.

"I told you before, gringo, you do not make the rules here. We do. If you don't like them, I'm sure you'll be able to find your way back to the United States."

"We invested a fortune down here," Tony hissed. "We built this town up from nothing to a big tourist number. If you think we did it for you, then you better think again. You ain't walking in and taking over just when it's beginning to pay off—no way. I'm reminding you we have an agreement with Batista. Let me tell you something else, wise guy: If we walk out of this town, there'll be grass growing up through this floor in a couple of years. On your own, you people couldn't run a peanut cart. Without us, Havana's just one big bordello. And you know it."

Anger in his eyes Bernardo began to reply. He was interrupted by Captain Bayamo, who spoke impatiently in Spanish. Bernardo replied and turned to Tony. "As the captain says, we're wasting time. Have your man open the slot machines," he ordered.

"I'm checking this out first," Tony said stubbornly.

"If you don't open them now, we shoot them open," Bernardo said. He murmured a few words to Captain Bayamo. The captain lifted his hand and a soldier stepped forward, gun raised.

"Hold it," Tony said. It was pointless to allow the destruction of the machines. Better get Levin to handle the situation.

"In the future, these machines may only be opened in the presence of Captain Bayamo." Or myself, of course," Bernardo added.

298

"Bernardo, seems to me you ain't thinking clear. Do you realize that putting this casino out of business is gonna cost your president a bundle?"

"*This* casino? What makes you think we're making an example of you? From today, every casino in Havana will contribute to Madame Batista's charities."

"In a pig's eye, they will. The dough goes straight in your pockets—you and your greasy pals." He was tempting fate.

"Are you going to open these machines or not? I won't ask again." Bernardo's voice became harsh.

Tony nodded to Beppo, who took a bunch of keys from his pocket and walked toward the machines, followed by Captain Bayamo. A soldier jumped forward with a large canvas bag, and the shareout began.

When the soldiers had gone, Beppo came back to stand forlornly with Tony in the middle of the room. "I think maybe this is only the start of our problems, amigo," he said.

"Yeah. That Garcia, he wouldn't have the gall to start something like this on his own—not unless he knew it was O.K. with Batista," Tony said.

"I think maybe it's time for me to join the revolution," Beppo said half-jokingly. Then he looked around sharply to see if anyone had overheard him.

"Maybe I'll join, too," Tony said. "The first one I shoot, it's gonna be that bastard Bernardo Garcia."

"Sweetheart, tonight we're eating out."

"Sounds crazy when we have one of the best restaurants in Havana right here in the hotel."

"I'm tired of eating in this joint. We need a change of scenery," he said to Nancy.

"Oh, I see . . ." she said. "The Habana Hilton."

"Yeah," He looked at her. "How'd you guess?"

"I heard Skeeter telling Mokey there's a bang-up crap game over there tonight."

He grinned. "Well, you know how it is—gotta see what the competition's up to. Gotta keep sharp."

"I'm not complaining, honey. It's great going out once in a while. With you working most evenings, we don't get out enough together."

"Yeah, that's the trouble. Everything we need's right here in the joint, so there's not much temptation to go out on the town."

"In this town, maybe that's just as well." She said it quietly.

He looked at her again. Her beauty never failed to thrill him, no matter how long they were together. "Say, the crap game won't get started till late. If we eat early and see the first show, we'll have time for a few dances, too. Call Skeets and tell him to bring along Selina—let's make it a foursome. We'll have a swell time." As Nancy crossed the floor, he said, "Hey, we'll have a laugh—watch me cut a rug with that Selina. You see her dance last time? She got rubber bones, that broad— she's a riot. I couldn't stop laughing."

"How about me, honey?" Nancy said, pouting. "Don't you like dancing with me?"

"I just love dancing with you, sweetheart. You know that."

"As much as you like dancing with that lil' colored gal?"

He stared at her, then roared with laughter at her tease. He crossed to where she stood holding the telephone and took her in his arms. "Whoever it is, baby, they ain't got nothing on you. You're tops. You're dy-na-mite."

He did not know then that his wording was prophetic.

They got out of the car outside the Habana Hilton, a gay party of four, tuxed and gowned, and moved toward the entrance, when Nancy said suddenly, "Oh, gee, I left my purse in the car."

They turned to look. Tony had instructed the driver to pick them up later, and the car was already moving off to return to the Internacionale. Traffic blocked the exit to the hotel drive, and the car had traveled only fifty feet. "I'll get it," Skeeter said. They stood waiting while he trotted after the car, to see if he could catch it. A couple of minutes later, he was back with the purse in his hand. "O.K., let's go," he said cheerfully.

They turned toward the busy hotel entrance. It was at that instant that the revolutionary bomb went off in the lobby. The blast flew outward, carrying with it a lethal cloud of shattered plate glass and masonry. Fortunately for them, they were in direct line with the wide, open entrance, and the blast only knocked them off their feet, while debris flew around them. As they crashed to the ground, bewildered and bruised, the fallout from the explosion smashed down around them like rain. Dazed, they lay there while the deafening sound echoed and re-echoed, and a choking cloud of black, dusty smoke drifted over them. An awful, stunned silence followed, then the screams and moans of agony began. Tony got to his feet and shook himself to see if he was in one piece. Fearfully, his heart pounding, he looked around for the others. By some miracle, in the midst of death and injuries, not one of the four had been seriously hurt. The three others, equally incredulous of their preservation, scrambled to their feet. Then the impact of it struck them, and they were all talking at once, not knowing whether to laugh or cry. The shock appeared to hit Nancy suddenly; she flew into Tony's arms and began sobbing hysterically.

Skeeter, blanched, dusted off Selina. There was awe in his voice when he said, "Do you realize, if hadn't been for that goddamn purse, we'd have been in that? Right there, in the middle of the lobby, where the bomb went off . . ." Their gaze followed his to the body-strewn, blood-bespattered scene.

"Oh, Tony, hold me, hold me . . ." Nancy began shivering uncontrollably, and he drew her into his arms again.

"It's all over now, baby," he said soothingly. "That was it—nothing more will happen." He brushed the hair out of her eyes.

She lifted a white, pinched face to him. "Tony, let's get out of here now." She was choking on her words. "Let's leave Cuba before we all get killed. It's their fight, not ours. Let them have it." The tears ran freely down her cheeks.

"Calm down, baby," he said soothingly. "Take it easy. You're upset now. We'll talk it over later."

"Please, Tony, let's go home . . ." she repeated.

"Nancy, honey, it's just an isolated incident. Don't mean a thing. The authorities are getting things under control now. This was a chance in a million. Believe me, it won't happen again. Not to us."

"Let's go home to America." She dropped her head to his chest, speaking the words damply into his jacket. "Dear God. Please. Before it's too late."

As if to reinforce Nancy's warning, he was subjected to another violent incident within a few days. Bud Carlstrom called to say it would be safer for Tony if they met somewhere away from the hotel. Which was how he found himself walking down the Malecón one evening at dusk. The car slid to the curb beside him; he'd hardly stepped through the door when Bud had it rolling again, and they were moving out into the stream of traffic. Tony lit a cigarette. "Ain't this a little melodramatic, Bud?" he said, amused.

"It's necessary," Bud said cryptically.

"What's all the excitement?"

"No excitement. I got a job for you."

Tony drew on his cigarette and blew out the smoke. "Nancy and me, we nearly got hit by that bomb over at the Habana Hilton."

"Yeah, I heard. You got lucky."

He glanced across. It seemed Bud knew everything that happened in Havana. "That Castro, he's becoming a pain in the ass."

"You don't know half of it. Out in Oriente Province he's giving it to Batista's men but good. Got 'em running around in circles, chasing their tails."

"That ain't what we hear this end."

"You wanna hear the news, listen to Radio Rebelde. Everyone else does."

"I don't speak the lingo." They drove on in silence for a while. "What's the job?" Tony said.

"Carlos Lopez, your head chef . . ."

"I keep away from that guy since you told me he's a revolutionary. I don't have any direct involvement with him. The hotel manager, Beppo Mendez, he handles all business outside the casino operation."

"I want you to cultivate Lopez. Find out his contacts. He's head of the local branch of the Gastronomic Federation of Cuba, so he has a lot of influence inside the union. He's using his position to make converts for Castro. There's someone directing him, and that's the guy I'm after. Lopez's boss is Castro's top man in Havana." Tony remained silent. "Give Lopez the impression you're sympathetic to the cause—that you want to help," Bud added. "He'll flip to think he's got one of the bosses on his side."

"You nuts? What makes you think he'll go for a line like that?"

"It's not as improbable as you think. It's been getting around that you hate the sight of Bernardo Garcia and Captain Bayamo."

"I told you about Garcia myself—how you know about the captain?"

"You've been shooting off your mouth," Bud said. "Things like that get back to me."

He pondered quietly who was Bud's contact inside the Internacionale. He also knew it would be pointless to ask. "Listen, if you wanna bury Lopez and his pals, why don't you just call in Garcia and give him the information?"

"It's more important to get the top guy. If *I* can't find him, what chance does Garcia have?"

"I'm not going out on a limb so you can grab some Cuban rebel," Tony decided firmly. "I got better things to do."

"I'm thinking of your welfare, too. It could come around in your favor, if a revolution succeeds, that you helped Lopez. Help to make your position safer."

"What if word gets back to Garcia I'm a rebel sympathizer?"

"I'll cover you on that if there's any trouble. I'll tell him you're working for me. You're in a good position to play both sides against the middle. And you have insurance—me."

"No, fuck it, I ain't gonna do it," Tony said angrily. "Why should I? It's their fight, not mine."

"Wrong. You'll be doing it for Uncle Sam," Bud said quietly.

"Like hell I will. Listen, if you wanna work on the guy, fine. I won't tell a soul. Me, I'm just a plain old crap dealer. Nothing else. Count me out." It was then he noticed that Bud had been staring intently in the rearview mirror for some time. "What's up?"

"I think we got ourselves a tail. The blue pickup. It's been following us for some time, hanging back in the traffic." He stared out through the windshield. "That next street to the left—any idea where it goes?"

"No," Tony said. "I never been in this quarter before."

"Me either. Hold on." Bud swung the wheel and they cut sharply into the next street. Too late he discovered it was one-way. Two cars traveling abreast ground to a halt before him, hooting angrily as their path was blocked. The blue pickup raced toward them from the rear. "Get down," Bud screamed, and threw himself under the steering wheel.

Tony had a glimpse of the bearded, intent faces in the pickup before he hit the floor of the car himself. The chatter of a machine gun was followed by bullets chewing into the metal around them and the crash of glass above their heads. The aim of the *barbudos* wasn't good, and by now Bud had stuck his hand up over the door and was firing a pistol wildly in their general direction. It was all over in a couple of seconds. The pickup howled off in reverse, demolished a car at the intersection, then screamed away down the main street in a cloud of blue smoke.

Carefully, Tony and Bud picked their way out of the broken glass. They stood in the street staring at the bullet-ridden car. "They after you or me?" Tony's voice was husky.

"Oh, me. It's the second time this month," Bud said blandly.

"And you want me to get involved in this?" Tony found it difficult to light another cigarette. He looked at his hands. They were shaking. He said, "I'm gonna let you in on a secret, Bud: They say I got nerve." He finally managed to light the cigarette. "Boy, I'm telling you—for this work I ain't got nerve enough."

CHAPTER FIFTEEN

For him it had been the New Year's Eve party of all time. The hotel was crowded with revelers, Cuban and American, all apparently determined on a celebration to match the new-found political stability. It seemed that Batista's strong-arm men had at last got the upper hand. In Havana, at least, there had been little in the last weeks to match the violent disturbances of the summer.

At one minute to midnight the lights went out, and several hundred jubilant people throughout the room hushed as they awaited the magical moment heralding the new year. At the first toll of the bell, a spotlight flicked on, picking out two contrasting figures, standing in the entrance, dressed in simple white half-wraps. One was an aging man with withering flesh and a flowing white beard, bearing a sickle and a lamp that flickered with a low, yellow light. The other was a small, cherubic child whose wand suddenly burst into white, sparkling light. Its mirrored stem reflected the spotlight with sharp brilliance. As they stood hand in hand, the old and the new, the crowd went wild with applause.

Then the celebration really got under way with true Caribbean exuberance, and they saw the new year in with style. Tony and Nancy danced often; and as the night wore on, he never tired of looking into her deep blue eyes. The celebration became a personal thing, secret to them. Her happiness was his happiness, and he couldn't remember a time when things had been so good. Between dances they cooled off with countless glasses of champagne which left them both light-headed when the party broke up at dawn. They had outstayed Skeeter and Selina, and Mokey had long since disappeared in pursuit of a snappy redhead from Savannah, Georgia. Arm in arm they sang their way up to the suite, and the hell with the paying customers.

While Havana celebrated, few who had heard took seriously the claims of Radio Rebelde that Che Guevara's forces had taken the city of Sancti Spiritus, in Las Villas Province. And the news that the troops of Fidel and Raúl Castro were marching on Santiago de Cuba out in Oriente was received with a yawn in the cosmopolitan capital. They'd heard it all before.

Except for one man. President Fulgencio Batista y Zaldívar, dictator of Cuba, former army sergeant who had himself led a successful coup against superior officers in the thirties, knew the difference. At two-thirty that morning, while the revelers at the Internacionale were whooping it up, Batista and his entourage had arrived at Camp Columbia air base after the drive from his extensive estate at Kuguine. A Douglas DC4, fueled and warmed up, awaited him on the ramp. As soon as the party was aboard, the DC4 taxied out, lined up, and took off. It was followed without delay by four transport aircraft containing the spoils of a quarter-century of office. In the black night above the island the five airplanes, one after the other, turned east. In that direction lay the refuge of the Dominican Republic.

Nancy's voice woke him out of a deep, mindless, wine-besotted sleep. It took a conscious effort to force his eyelids open on the small, thin light creeping into the bedroom around the edges of the drapes. His vision began to focus. "What'd you say?" he croaked.

"Did you hear that bang?"

"What bang?"

"I thought I heard an explosion."

He pondered how she managed to be so wide-awake when he felt like he was buried under three feet of molasses. "What time is it?" he asked.

She turned to look at the clock. Squinting, she said, "Eleven."

"I need more sleep." He closed his eyes and luxuriated in the sensation of his head sinking deeper into the pillow.

"What about the bang?"

"Didn't hear a thing, honey—go back to sleep," he muttered.

He felt Nancy settling back into the bed, and waited for the mantle of slumber to roll over him again. But it didn't come, and he realized he was absently listening to distant shouts, the yelling of slogans, and the sounds of running feet. Peculiarly, there was no traffic. He was puzzling over this when the next explosion came. This time it was much nearer, and the dull, ominous *crump* rattled the windows. They sat up in bed and stared at each other. "What the hell was that?" he said sharply. Together they dived from the bed and rushed to open the drapes. He pushed open the tall windows and they stepped out onto the balcony in the hot, bright sun, to see a dozen columns of black smoke rising at locations all over the city. From the last explosion, only a few streets from the hotel, flames were leaping into the air above the surrounding buildings. Not a vehicle moved in the streets, but here and there groups of people were gathered on corners, some carrying rifles, and Tony could make out the revolutionary flag of the Twenty-Sixth of July Movement beside the Cuban national flag. He watched as a crowd along 23rd Street smashed in a store window, their wild yells coming distantly on the still air, and disappeared through the storefront in an orgy of looting.

Something was missing. The skin crawled on his flesh when he realized he could hear no police sirens. It meant only one thing: there were no police.

They jumped at the sudden hammering on the door. He ran across to open it, then stopped to call, "Who is it?"

"Beppo Mendez."

He opened the door and his hotel manager slipped through, looking back down the corridor to see if he'd been followed, before closing it. "The revolution?" Tony said succinctly.

Beppo nodded. "Batista made a run for it during the night. He's left Cuba to Castro. There's still some resistance from government forces out in the provinces—it seems Batista forgot to tell them he was leaving. It won't last. They say Castro's already on the march to Havana."

"So it's all over for us, too." He said it as much for his own benefit as for Beppo's.

"There's a lot of violence in the streets. Vandalism, looting, people getting their own back on Batista's supporters and the police. Out in the country the peasants are

304

taking over the landowners' estates, according to the radio. There will be mob rule and chaos for some time, I'm afraid, until a new administration is organized."

"How about the Americans here in the hotel?"

"The revolutionaries have no interest in them, as far as I can see. They seem quite happy to allow the tourists to go peacefully."

He breathed a sigh of relief. "We better organize transportation for them back to the States as quickly as possible."

"That's what I've been trying to do."

"Good," Tony said. "I'll get dressed and come along to give you a hand."

"No." Beppo said it sharply.

"What's wrong?"

"Not you. Carlos Lopez has come out into the open. He classifies you a rank Batistano, one of the gringos responsible for Cuba's predicament. A couple of Batistanos have already died here in the hotel this morning. I think he intends to kill you in the name of the revolution. Lopez is a wicked bastard, given his head, and a fanatic. He worked with knives all his life in that damn kitchen—I think he'd have no hesitation about sticking one in you."

Nancy gave a strangulated cry, and Tony put an arm around her shoulders before turning back to Beppo. "I heard about Lopez. He's moved quickly. I thought, if it came to it, we'd have plenty of warning before the revolution reached this stage. Looks like I was mistaken. And this guy Castro—I guess we're gonna be hearing from him, too."

"Lopez is telling everyone he's instructed by Castro to take control of the Internacionale on behalf of the revolutionary movement. Nobody's arguing, in case it's true. Already he has squads out front on the driveway, drilling like soldiers—with broomsticks."

"What for? The fighting must be nearly over."

"Lopez is no fool. He's telling them they'll form the nucleus of the Revolutionary People's Army." Beppo shrugged. "Cuban peasants are easily impressed."

"There's something I don't get, Beppo," Tony said slowly.

"Yes?"

"You—Lopez classifies you along with me and the rest of us. We both know he considers you a Batistano, too, because you take your orders from my outfit."

"That is correct—he does."

"Then how come you walking around free and clear?"

"Simple—you still don't understand the Cuban mentality, my friend. There's plenty of time to deal with me. My time will come. In the meantime, the hotel is in chaos—it's overflowing with foreigners, and I'm probably the only one can handle it at present. Right now Lopez has his hands full, running down his list of political activists. He thinks he'll get around to me later. I'm safe enough for the moment— in a day or two it may be a very different matter. But you are a target. You're on his list. So you have to disappear before he comes looking for you."

"How we gonna manage that?"

"It would be dangerous for you to leave the hotel just now, with Lopez and his men running riot all over the place. Leave it until things cool down a little. You must hide. Later on I'll figure a way to get you out."

"Thanks, Beppo. I appreciate your help," Tony said gratefully.

"You'd have done as much for me. We have a relationship, do we not?" He smiled wanly. "Besides, who knows with these crazy rebels? Next month there could be another revolution and I'll want my job back. It took me a lifetime of work to get to my position—educated in America, trained in France . . . sometimes I regret I'm a Cuban. Perhaps, who knows, the day will come I'll be proud?"

"You got my word, buddy. If we get out of this O.K., you'll be managing a fine hotel again. If not here, in the States." Beppo nodded, pleased. "Now, you got any ideas how to get us out of this rattrap?"

"I've been thinking. A good place to hide would be the new staff quarters we're building in the roof of the hotel. It's a little rough up there, but several rooms are completed, at least the structure, and the new service elevator from there runs down to the rear of the building. Nobody will think of going up there for a while, not unless they intend to search the hotel room by room. And they're too busy for that."

"Right." He turned to Nancy. "Get packing. One suitcase each."

"No time for that," Beppo said immediately. "Just grab a few things and come with me now."

When they stood at the door, arms loaded, Tony said, "Beppo, Nancy and me, we're not the only ones. There's my brother Mokey, and Skeeter and his wife. If I'm missing, maybe they'll be grabbed instead."

Beppo screwed up his face. "It will lessen our chances of escape if there's a crowd of us."

"That's how it's got to be," Tony said. "We can't walk out on them."

For a moment, Beppo stood with his hand on the door knob. "Very well." He sighed. "You first, then I'll go get the others and bring them up to you."

"My friend, you just earned yourself a pension," Tony said soberly.

"Let's hope I live to enjoy it."

"It's six o'clock. One hour to go." Mokey was peering at his watch.

"Yeah. Keep your voice down," Tony reminded him quietly. He stood leaning on the wall just inside the frameless, glassless window so that he couldn't be seen from the outside. A section of roof, jutting out below, obstructed his view straight down. He couldn't see the hotel entrance, only further out, where the driveway met the road, and beyond. In the early dusk of January, it was strange to see Havana without its usual halo of colored neon and fluorescence. Now that it was fully dark, it was obvious that much of the city's lighting was out of action, although he could still make out the main thoroughfares.

"Hey, Tony, what are our chances of pulling this thing off?" It was Skeeter's voice, subdued in the near-blackness of the bare, cement-walled room behind him.

"Good—very good. Take it from me, we'll be O.K.," he said reassuringly.

"It ain't for me so much—I'm worried for Selina."

"She's the last one you need to worry about. She's Cuban, ain't she? They won't bother her."

"Them damn rebels . . ."

"You blame 'em?"

Skeeter didn't reply for a moment. "She's pregnant," he said suddenly.

"Selina? Hey, good news—you hear that, Nancy?" he called in a loud whisper. "I'm happy for you, old buddy. First chance I get, I'm gonna buy you a big, fat cigar." He punched Skeeter's arm.

"Here in Cuba, it would have been O.K. Over there—I'm not so sure."

"What's eating you?"

"A half-breed kid, a *pardo*. He . . . or she gets the worst of both worlds. I don't want that for a kid of mine."

Tony half-turned to look into the darkness, and his voice hardened. "Listen, turkey, you had to make your own way in the world, didn't you? Same applies to everyone else. A kid's just a kid anywhere, his parents either got or they ain't got. When you grow up, you take what God gave you, pick up the ball and run with it. Know what I mean? That's what life's all about, old buddy." Skeeter remained silent, and Tony added, "It's my guess, a few months and this cockeyed revolution will be forgotten. There will be another administration, we'll do a deal, and you'll come right back and pick up where you left off."

"You think so?" Skeeter said hopefully.

"Sure. That Castro, he won't be no match for Levin."

Later, Skeeter's voice said, "I hope that airplane is O.K. out there at the field."

"The revolutionaries ain't organized to that extent yet. They won't have got around to a couple of light planes parked at the airfield. They're too busy chasing Batistanos."

"I hope you're right." Skeeter's dim outline disappeared into the gloom, back to Selina's side.

Beppo's plan of escape was simple. His car was parked behind unlocked doors in an abandoned garage on the other side of the street, at the rear of the hotel. At seven o'clock they were to go down in the service elevator, which would deliver them near the rear entrance, quiet at this hour. They were to cross the street to the garage where Beppo would be waiting. For the drive out of Havana, the car would fly the revolutionary flag. Their destination was Rancho Boyeros Airport, where Beppo kept his Beech Bonanza. A short flight across the Florida Straight to a brightly lit Miami Airport and they could put the troubles of Cuba behind them.

The light airplane had started off as something of a joke between them. Beppo had learned to fly some years back, when he was training for hotel management at a college in Kansas. He boarded with a farmer who used a tattered yellow Piper Cub for dusting his crops. To Beppo private flying represented *the* elitist recreation. He persuaded the farmer to teach him to fly, and spent his vacations buzzing headily through vaporized clouds of DDT, a hundred feet above rolling Kansas fields. Bitten by the flying bug, he'd never forgotten how. The story came out one night in the casino when they were watching a wild gambler blow his dough, then try to hock his airplane for gambling money. Beppo had pleaded with Tony to grab it. "Who the hell needs an airplane?" Tony had said.

"But it's a Beech Bonanza. Fully equipped. The guy told me."

"You making a deal?"

"I'd jump at it if I had the dough."

"What's a Beech Bonanza, something special?"

"It's always been my dream to own one." Tony was amused at the usually conservative Beppo coming apart at the seams. "Do it for me, Tony, please. I'd give my right arm for that airplane, honest. You should see it, a vee tail, God, it's so beautiful . . ." He knew of Tony's skill with the dice. "I'll pay you back if it takes me ten years."

It would be so easy to fulfill the guy's heart's desire. Tony thought a lot of Beppo, and the prick at the crap table was asking for it. What the hell . . . He found himself moving toward the table.

At the end of the game he owned a Beech Bonanza. He gave it to Beppo, just to see the light in his eyes.

They'd got into the habit of using the six-seater airplane for quick trips across to the mainland. On a couple of occasions they'd even carried Levin, when he wanted to avoid the scheduled route. Recently, Beppo was allowing Tony to handle the controls and was teaching him the rudiments of flying. Tony had grown to like it, because to fly well was a matter of personal discipline. He was beginning to enjoy droning around up there at 2,000 feet, lording it over the lush green islands and the blue Caribbean.

Now the airplane was to be their salvation.

The racket coming from the street leading to the hotel became louder, and he strained his eyes into the darkness. When his vision adjusted, he saw the small column of revolutionary soldiers, led by a couple of officers, *barbudos* to a man. The column was surrounded by a couple of hundred excited people, cheering and singing, yelling slogans, waving flags, and generally pouring adulation over their heroes. The soldiers turned into the driveway of the hotel and disappeared from view beneath the projecting roof. The civilians were apparently not allowed into the hotel, and they remained below, circulating in the driveway, their exuberant chatter reaching up to him. "This gonna make a difference to our chances?" Mokey's voice came from the darkness behind him.

"Dunno. What's the time?"

"Six forty-five."

"Get the others ready."

"They're ready."

Exactly at seven, they slipped into the unlit service elevator. Tony struck a match and pressed the button. The match went out as soon as the elevator started moving down, and he didn't light another. When the doors slid open, they held their breath. They were at ground level, and there wasn't a soul to be seen at the service entrance. They slipped out of the rear of the hotel, listening to the uproar coming from the front as the soldiers were feted. They crossed the quiet, commercial street quickly and slipped through the unlocked wooden gates of the garage. The Dodge stood there open, a revolutionary flag on a stick poking from a window. There was no key in the ignition. And no Beppo. Tony ordered the others into the car and returned to keep watch at the crack formed by the badly fitting gates.

At seven-thirty they were desperate, and ready to break into the Dodge's ignition wiring, when there was a sudden commotion at the rear of the hotel. As Tony watched, drapes were torn back on the fourth floor and light from the room spilled out over a balcony. Soldiers came crowding out, there was a flurry of movement, then a cheer went up as a body flew into the air. The body released a scream as it described an arc, then dropped to the road with a sickening thud, directly in Tony's line of vision. Now it was still and silent.

He stared and could not contain the nausea that rose in his throat. He realized with disbelief that he recognized the mangled, crushed form. It was Beppo. He stumbled to the flaking garage wall and retched helplessly.

In the couple of minutes it took him to recover, nobody passed in the street outside, or came down to view the corpse, and the balcony had almost emptied. Act, not react. Now. He stepped out through the gates and walked unhurriedly toward the body. In a quick movement, he bent over and went through Beppo's pockets, forcing himself not to look at the mashed head of his friend. His fingers closed over the keys. He straightened and walked back to the garage at the same steady pace. He'd been seen, and voices were calling out angrily from the balcony, but he didn't look around.

The Dodge started immediately. He rammed the garage gates, and they flew off their hinges. He spun the wheel, and, with tires screaming, the Dodge roared off down the road. From behind them they could hear the crackle of rifle fire, but they were soon out of range; no bullets reached them, and they weren't chased. Twice before they reached the outskirts of the city they were challenged by mobs obstructing the road. Tony responded to the rifles pointed ominously in their direction by driving at the crowd, blasting jubilantly on the horn, while Mokey waved the flag vigorously from the window. By the time the marauders made up their minds, they were through and gone.

The road to Rancho Boyeros Airport was deserted. When the main airport building came into sight, he slowed down and switched off the headlights. As they got nearer, they could make out a few people moving around inside the lighted building, and the rest of the airport was in total darkness. A partial moon gave sufficient light, and, before they reached the main building, he turned down a narrow road running parallel to the perimeter track of the airfield. Tall, dark hangars slipped by mysteriously. It had been an inconvenience—the airport's bossy management insisting that light aircraft tie-downs be located out in the boondocks. Now he was grateful. He stopped the car. On the other side of a frail, chicken-wire fence stood the diminutive line-up. Three Cessnas, a Piper Tripacer, and the distinctive vee-tail of the Beech Bonanza. He turned off the narrow road and maneuvered the car so that it was concealed behind some shrubbery.

He hadn't answered their questions on the drive out to the airport. Mokey waited for the motor to die before he said, "Tony, back at the garage, you took one helluva chance to get them keys. We could've started the car by jumping the ignition wires. And you know it."

"Yes, I know," he said.

"Why'd you do it?"

"For a simple reason. The airplane keys are on the same ring."

"So what we gonna do, with Beppo dead?"

"We're flying back to Florida, as planned."

"Now?"

"In the morning, when it's light."

"Where we gonna get a pilot?"

"We got a pilot. Me."

"You can't fly an airplane," Skeeter said, startled.

"Beppo was teaching me. We did the Florida trip dozens of times."

"You sure you know how?" Mokey said doubtfully.

"Yeah . . ." Then he added. "We got any other options?"

"We could always give ourselves up to the revolutionaries. I dunno which is the bigger risk."

"Don't worry, little brother." Tony smiled at him for the first time. "I don't aim to kill myself, or anyone else. It's a breeze, this flying. Beppo says you can teach a monkey. First light of dawn, up we go. Up and away."

It was a good thing, in the dark, that Mokey couldn't see Tony's hands, resting on his legs beneath the wheel. He rubbed them gently on his pants to dry his moist palms.

CHAPTER SIXTEEN

The interior of the car was quiet, except for the sound of breathing. At one end of the back seat Nancy and Selina, huddled together, slept in utter stillness. At the other end Mokey, twisted awkwardly into the corner, snored gently with a sonorous rhythm. In the front seat Tony and Skeeter sat smoking, each with an elbow out of his open window, staring at the still darkness on the other side of the windshield. Outside, the night-chatter of undergrowth fauna had long since ended, in recognition of the strange, suspenseful gap between night and day. Suddenly, in a nearby tree, like dawn's first herald, a bird let rip with a strident, staccato chirrup so loud on the silent night that they both jumped, and Skeeter dropped his cigarette in his lap. Both heads swiveled to the east to see a faint, thin gray line on the horizon. "That's it," Skeeter said gratefully, finding the cigarette.

"We'll give it a few more minutes before we make a move," Tony said. "I need more light for a visual reference. Once we're in that plane, we don't hang around—we go."

It took another fifteen minutes before there was enough diffused light in the distance to give him a horizon. "O.K., that's good enough." He started the car and drove slowly out of the shrubbery, across the road, and aimed squarely for the fence. "Get your heads down," he said. He floored the accelerator, and the car leaped forward, hitting the fence with a tinny crash. The fence hardly slowed the Dodge. The car charged through, pulling down a long section on each side. He stopped the car and they got out, extricating themselves from the chicken-wire wrapping. They stood staring in the direction of the airport building where a single light still burned in the distance. Nothing moved—apparently the sound hadn't carried that far. Their luck was holding. They padded across the macadam to the aircraft. Tony opened it and installed the girls and Mokey in the rear seats. Skeeter climbed into the right-hand seat, and Tony got behind the wheel and shut the door. "Watch out for signs of movement over at the building," he told Skeeter.

"Nothing's happening. It looks quiet over there."

"Just as well. I can't see a damn thing in here." He said it nonchalantly, but his mouth was dry. He thought of turning on the interior light, but decided not to risk it. He was familiar with the cabin in the light of bright, sun-drenched day. Here, in near-dark, it all looked strange and complex. He lit a match down low and reminded himself where the switches and controls were located. He went through three more matches reading the pre-takeoff checks posted on the panel before him. When he straightened, he said, "O.K.—seat belts on and tight." Usually it was the final check, but this was no usual flight. He made sure the flashing beacon was switched off and flipped the master switch. The gyros on the panel began winding up.

"There's some movement over at the building," Skeeter reported.

They all looked across. A door had opened, spilling out light. It closed again. "What's happening over there?" Tony said.

"Nothing. It's nothing," Mokey said from the back.

"Keep looking." Now he had to give his full attention to the panel. He tried all the controls in turn, checked that the fuel was turned on, and cracked the throttle. He hit the starter and the propeller began to spin. The starter ground on and on, but the engine gave no indication of firing. "Come on, you mother, go . . ." he urged desperately. Another moment and he released the starter switch.

"What's wrong?" Skeeter said.

"The engine's cold." He frowned to himself. The damn thing should have started by now. It never gave Beppo trouble. Two or three runs like that on the starter and they'd have no battery.

"There's some movement over at the building," Skeeter said. The door of the airport building had opened again, and, in the distance, a couple of figures walked out to stare in their direction. "You think they heard?"

"Probably. That starter makes one hell of a racket."

"Yeah. They started to walk this way."

He reached for the starter switch again.

"Ain't this thing got some sort of choke, like a car?" Mokey murmured.

He could have kissed his brother. Of course—he'd forgotten to prime the engine. Even in the heat of midday, Beppo would always give the throttle a few strokes before starting up. There was no time to unlock the fuel primer—he pumped the throttle furiously a half-dozen times, then hit the starter again. The engine caught immediately. As the propeller began to beat the air, he felt the machine come to life, the movement of air over the control surfaces vibrating the column before him.

"They're running," Skeeter said urgently.

"They ain't running fast enough," Tony said. He released the parking brake and added five hundred revs with the throttle. Steering the airplane on the rudder, he ignored the semicircular taxiway and rode straight across the dividing grass strip. The bump as they hit the cement of the runway shook the aircraft. He jammed on full right rudder and, hardly waiting to line up on the wide cement strip reaching into the distance before them, he fire-walled the throttle.

"One of them guys is kneeling—I think he's got a rifle," Mokey was saying.

He was far too busy. As the airplane began gathering speed, he took his hands off the wheel, one at a time, to wipe his moist palms on his pants.

In the dim light he watched the airspeed indicator come to life and go through fifty, sixty, seventy, and creep past eighty before the machine seemed to want to fly. Usually they were in the air at this speed. He held it down for a few seconds to make sure, then gave a gentle pull on the wheel. The noise leveled as the hammering of the wheels on the runway ceased, and they were up. He was surprised to find it perfectly smooth, unlike the turbulence they generally hit on takeoff, when the heat of the day bounced off the runway.

"Hey, we're flying," Mokey yelled from the back.

"Whaddayou know . . ." Skeeter said, awe replacing some of the shakiness in his voice.

He was familiar with this part of the routine. He let the speed build, then pulled back firmly on the column for the climb, trimming to take the effort out of the operation. As they rose above the landscape, the light in the eastern sky increased with their height, making it easy to keep the wings level with the horizon. He watched the altimeter go through five hundred feet and climb toward one thousand. With a start he realized he'd forgotten the after-takeoff checks. He was reaching for the flap lever when it dawned on him that he'd made a flapless takeoff. He shrugged to himself—no wonder the airplane had been slow to get off the ground. Good thing it was a long runway, with this load. Also, Beppo would have had the gear up long before now. He'd never operated the gear himself. He wondered if it would cause any harm to leave the wheels down, and decided to risk it. At least he knew for sure they had wheels underneath the airplane. If he pulled them up, he might not get them down again—he was looking for safety, not speed. He'd never operated the propeller pitch control either. Beppo had always seen to the refinements, while he'd simply handled the flying controls. He decided to leave that alone, too, and fly in fine pitch. It was something like driving a car in low gear, Beppo had explained. Who cared—the airplane was flying, wasn't it? The healthy roar of the engine was music to his ears. He scanned the panel. All the engine instruments looked good, and they had plenty of fuel. That was another thing he'd forgotten, the auxiliary fuel pump. Fortunately it was only a backup for the primary fuel system. His gaze stopped at the engine tachometer—engine revs were moving up toward redline. When he reached two thousand feet he would throttle back to twenty-four hundred revs, the setting they normally used for cruise. With the propeller in fine pitch, there'd be some loss in airspeed. He chuckled to himself: so they'd be ten minutes late at Miami. .

During the climb, he'd been concentrating on the airspeed, so when he looked up he was amazed to see thick, unbroken cloud directly above him. If he went up to two thousand feet he'd be in it. At fifteen hundred feet he put the nose down level, reduced power to cruise, and trimmed the airplane to fly straight. He hadn't flown on anything but a clear day before and was amazed at the ceiling stretching in all directions before him. He looked toward the sunrise for the usual ball of fire rising over the rim of the earth. Instead, there was a gray, congealed mass on the horizon, seemingly in no hurry to brighten, and a vista that was obscure, threatening, and

312

oppressive in a way he'd never seen it from the ground. "Hey, ah, Skeets, what does that compass read?" he said.

"Where's a compass?"

"That thing in the middle of the windshield."

"I can't read it—yeah, it says N. That North?"

"Yeah, that's O.K." He looked down at the gyro direction indicator. At least he'd remembered to set that before they took off, and it, too, read North. Beppo had told him several times: "From Havana head North, add ten degrees East, give or take a few for wind—you'll see the Florida Keys in thirty minutes." There was no wind this calm morning. He turned right to add a few degrees and straightened the wheel. He checked the time on the panel clock.

"Hey, there's the coast down there—we're leaving Cuba," Mokey yelled. "Let's give the captain a cheer . . ."

"Cut it out, Mokey," Tony said, more sharply than he intended. He looked down. Way below the ocean had a gray, speckled appearance, nothing like the deep blue he was used to seeing when he flew with Beppo. It came to him now—they only flew in fine weather.

It felt like they were flying along between the clouds and the ocean in an endlessly wide, shallow slice of sky devoid of all other forms of life, as if they had the whole world to themselves. He looked down again, scanning the ocean in all directions. There wasn't a boat to be seen. When he looked up again, it was to see cotton-wool wisps at the ends of the wings and a wall-like solid mass of gray directly in front. He froze as he realized he was about to lose all visual reference. He pushed the column forward sharply. The airplane nosed over and began to pick up speed in the descent. Then they were swallowed by the grey mass, and Tony, his heart hammering wildly, held the controls rigidly where they'd been when they entered the cloud. The few seconds seemed an eternity. When they burst out the other side, the wings were still level.

He felt the tension in the small cabin. "What happened there?" Mokey asked.

"Oh, nothing, just some cloud. I'm going down—don't wanna get mixed up with that stuff." He leveled off at one thousand feet.

"Everything O.K., Tony?" Skeeter was staring at him anxiously.

"Sure. We're doing fine. Tell me when you spot them Florida Keys. They should come up on the nose, or maybe a little to the right." Skeeter peered forward. "Not yet—be ten, fifteen minutes more. Gimme a cigarette," he said.

"There's a sign here says no smoking."

"Fuck the sign. Gimme the cigarette."

He lit it and drew the smoke deep into his lungs. When he blew the smoke out, he felt better. What the hell was he worried about—everything was going fine, wasn't it?

This time it came as no surprise. More cloud, directly in his path. He dropped to seven hundred feet and passed beneath the ominous, threatening mass. It happened again, a few minutes later, and he found himself at five hundred feet. The ocean was beginning to seem uncomfortably close. Southern Florida terrain was flat enough, he knew, but there would be plenty of obstructions reaching up to five hundred feet. A trickle of sweat from his brow rolled down his nose. He flicked it away. It was hellish hot in this airplane—or was it his imagination? "Any sign of them Keys yet?" he asked Skeeter.

"No, I don't see them."

"Maybe five minutes. If we were flying higher, we'd have seen 'em by now. This damn cloud . . ."

"Hey, there's a boat . . . and another . . . and another," Mokey yelled.

They were passing over a fishing fleet inbound to the Keys, or perhaps the mainland. At the speed they flew over, the boats appeared stationary in the water. Tony felt a strange gratitude for this first, small contact with humanity. "Yeah, I see 'em—the Keys. Dead ahead. Boy, no mistake about that," Skeeter sang out.

"Right on time. How's that for navigation, old buddy?" Tony's confidence grew by the minute. Shortly, Key West and the string of islands reaching off to the right were clearly visible. U.S.1, linking them together, ran in a thin line to the horizon and disappeared beyond their vision in the direction of Key Largo and the Florida mainland. When they passed over Key West Naval Station, the girls suddenly came to life, pointing out the different islands to each other and the boats in the harbors. He aimed the Bonanza across Florida Bay, keeping the islands on his right. It was an easy run from here—when they hit the coast he'd simply follow it up to Miami Beach, from where he'd be able to locate Miami Airport over on his left. He began to think about using the radio, the way Beppo did when he was inbound, although he had no idea of how to operate it. There'd be airliners flying in the vicinity of a major airport, and it was probably dangerous to make an approach unannounced. He looked around the cabin. There was a list of frequencies somewhere in the airplane—he'd found it once for Beppo. Maybe, if he couldn't work the radio, he should look for a smaller airfield. If he could find one. Suddenly the landing didn't seem so simple.

It was then he saw it. The rolling fog obscuring the entire coastline, reaching up to the low clouds, forming a solid wall before him. He stared in astonishment. It was as if he were flying in a box—as if the open space that was sky ended at the mainland. He turned right a few degrees and continued along the coast, trying to decide on a course of action. For a wild moment he considered ditching the airplane in the ocean alongside the Keys. It looked so easy from up here. It was something he'd discussed with Beppo as they flew over the water to and from Cuba. Apparently ditching was far more dangerous than it appeared, with every prospect of the airplane's diving under the water on contact, even in the hands of an experienced pilot. He decided against it. Key Largo passed beneath them, and now they were over Biscayne Bay. He remembered having seen, on the map, a military airfield at Homestead, a couple of miles inland at this point. He looked toward the coast yearningly. Without the fog, the airfield would be clearly visible to them at this point.

Disbelievingly, he spotted the gap in the coastal fog, and beyond it he could see dimly the flat mangrove swamps of the Everglades stretching away across the Florida peninsula. He yelled with delight and swung the aircraft left toward the open patch. But the distance to the coastline was deceptive, and the airplane seemed to move interminably slowly in the direction of the gap. It felt like a giant hand held them suspended in space, while the low cloud and the fog rolled toward each other

314

and began to intermingle. The realization came to him that he was in a race to arrive over the coast before the gap closed. He knew within himself he should turn back if there was any prospect he couldn't make it. Yet the gap seemed so near, and so tempting. The cloud finally obscured his view of the ground beyond as the airplane arrived at the point where he aimed. He plunged determinedly into the gray, swirling mass. At the last moment, as the world darkened instantly about him, he reminded himself that he'd been a gambler all his life. And that he'd always been a winner.

Within seconds of being swallowed up by the deepening gloom, he knew he was in trouble. He should have passed out the other side by now; instead, the sensation overcame him that the airplane was turning left. He swung the wheel right to correct the turn, but now the forces on his body were wrong, and he felt himself leaning to the right. He found himself rising out of his seat, as if suspended from the roof. He tried to scan the instruments, but couldn't interpret what they told him. Two things registered—the turn-and-slip indicator showed the ball over to the left, and the airspeed needle was moving rapidly up into the red arc. Yet he felt the nose was high, and the airplane was climbing. He pushed hard on the left rudder to center the ball. For a moment nothing happened, then the ball shot to the other side. The airspeed dilemma defeated him.

Panic in his heart, he knew the airplane was out of control.

The Bonanza came howling out of the clouds in a spiral dive four hundred feet above Homestead Air Force Base. The terrified screams of Nancy and Selina behind him weren't registering, and he didn't feel the viselike grip of Mokey's hand on his shoulder. The big airfield was spinning clockwise, horrifyingly near, beneath the airplane. He saw clearly the long runways and the military aircraft parked neatly in rows. With a massive effort of will, he moved to regain control. He quickly decided he had to stop the spiral dive to the left. He pushed the rudder with his right foot and leveled the wings with the wheel. The rate of descent was suicidal. He eased the column back with an iron grip, ignoring the gravitational forces that drove him down into the seat. The airplane was responding—the speed bled off and the nose began to rise toward the horizon. But the ground was desperately close, and he needed to climb. He jammed the throttle forward for full climb power, and slowly the airplane overcame its downward momentum.

It nearly succeeded.

The Bonanza struck the ground almost flat, with the landing gear taking the shock before it collapsed. The airplane slid on its belly across the rough surface, shaking them like rag dolls, but their belts held them in their seats. As it slid, it turned so that it was traveling sideways.

It was stopped by a tall iron post at a disused entrance to the air base. The post cleaved into the fuselage of the Bonanza, cutting it in two. The collapsing aluminum of the fuselage decapitated Nancy and crushed Selina and Mokey to death on impact.

CHAPTER SEVENTEEN

He awoke to the serenity of the hospital room and the sterile white of his surroundings. Slowly it all stopped swimming around, and shapes began to solidify. He became conscious of a sickly sweet, antiseptic smell in his nostrils. He tried to move and found it painful, so he stayed in the same position on his back. It hit him suddenly—the flight, the nightmare of the crash. The memory of it all, up to the point of impact, flooded back into his mind. With it came the horror, the mortifying fear that made his blood run cold, of what he'd done to the others in the airplane. And to himself. His heart was pounding when he lifted his hand to his head to feel the swath of bandages around it. His chest felt tight, as if it were held by a steel hoop. He took a lungful of air, and the searing pain that went through him produced a long, low groan when he exhaled. He put his hand down to find his chest tightly wrapped in a medical support. Cautiously he tried moving his hands and legs and was surprised to find they seemed to work well.

The others—what had happened to them? He swiveled his head urgently. The sudden movement blurred his vision, so he had to close his eyes and wait. When he opened them again, he saw the switch hanging on a cord above his head. He reached up, pressed it, and kept his finger on the button.

She came through the door in quick, businesslike movements, her back stiff as a ramrod. She was short, dressed in spotless white linen, had a stern look on her face, and spoke with a Scots brogue. "Ah, you're awake at last, are you, mister? Well, now, how are you feeling?" She leaned over him to stare into his eyes. He hardly felt her nimble fingers testing his pulse, checking his temperature.

"Where am I?" he croaked.

"You're in the hospital, of course. You can count yourself a verrry lucky man indeed. You might easily have been killed, an accident like that. I don't hold with flying around in aeroplanes myself—nasty, dangerous things." She fussed over his bedclothes. "Now that you're awake, I'll get the doctor to come along and have a look at you."

"My wife—the others. What happened to the others?"

She ignored his question. "Verrry lucky indeed," she repeated, "to escape an aircraft accident with minor injuries. A couple of cracked ribs, a nasty gash on the head . . . and concussion, of course. They always get concussion. We'll have you on your feet in no time at all."

"The others . . ." He said it again, more forcefully.

She stopped to look at him, and her stern gaze was replaced by an expression betraying a lifetime's compassion. "Perrrhaps you'd like to speak to your friend? He's been waiting outside."

"Skeeter—he's O.K.?"

"Mr. Froelich. Yes, he's fine, except for a few scratches and a sprained wrist. I'll call him in."

316

The moment Skeeter came into his vision, he knew something was very seriously wrong. Skeeter's left wrist was bandaged, and he moved as if he were unaware of it. But mostly it was the cloud he brought into the room with him, the invisible, vapid cloud hanging over his head. The one Tony had fought so long to vanquish. *Had* vanquished, or so he thought. Now it was all there again—the old fear in the eyes, the way he hung his head, as if the years between had never been. He walked to the edge of the bed and stood there, staring without expression. "They tell me you'll be out in a few days," he said. "Ain't nothing serious."

"How about you?"

"Just a cut hand. Guess the wrist got a little twisted, too." He lifted the bandaged hand and allowed it to fall to his side again. "How much she tell you?"

"The nurse? Not a thing."

"Oh. I'm glad. I wanted to tell you myself."

There was that crawling feeling at the back of his neck. "What happened to the others?" He heard his own voice shaking.

"They're dead—all three, they're dead." Skeeter sighed deeply.

His brain refused to accept what he'd heard. "Nancy—?"

"All dead. I told you. Nancy, Selina, and Mokey." He spoke mechanically, without emotion.

Tony felt he was choking. When he could bring himself to speak, he said, "Were they injured? Did any of them suffer?"

"No—nothing like that. They were killed instantly. The pole cut through the plane right where they were sitting."

Then he was burning with rage. That he'd lived and the one he loved more than life itself had died. That his brother had died. That he had gambled and again won. That the price of winning was almost more than he could bear. "If God was good, I'd have died out there, too. I wish I'd died along with them." He was ashen, and the grief tore at his voice.

"Yes, I wish you had." The words penetrated, as cutting as the pain. He looked at Skeeter. "You had no right flying that plane. You're no pilot. Maybe, if we'd gave ourselves up to the Cubans, Selina would have lived. They had nothing against her, poor kid. Maybe, when the revolution's over, we could have gone on living in Cuba. Anything but that goddamn crazy airplane . . ." He spoke in a flat, even tone, like a person intoning a prayer. He no longer looked at Tony, but gazed at the far wall with a glassy stare.

He found himself pleading: "Skeets, I took a chance. I had to take the chance to get us out of there. You know I did."

"Sure. You spent your life taking chances. Someone up there called: "Shooter coming out," and you had to make your pitch, same as always. I understand. But there's something you forgot—this time the dice weren't loaded."

"If it wasn't for that stupid, fucking pole . . ." he began viciously. Then his tone faltered. A gambler's life was built on a million *ifs*. And all the *ifs* in the world never won a single crap game. The pole had nothing to do with it. *He'd* killed Selina, just as he'd killed Nancy and Mokey. Not the pole.

"Makes no difference now. I just wanted to say it—tell you to your face, what I felt. It was a rotten thing to do, murdering a sweet kid like that."

"Help me. Please, Skeets, help me—." He cried out in anguish.

"Ain't nothing I can do to help you."

"Skeeter. Old buddy—please." He was helpless to stop the flood of tears down his cheeks.

"I'm going now. Goodbye, Tony."

He heard the soft swishing of the silencer on the door, then the click of the catch. Painfully he turned his head, but the room was empty.

Nancy and Mokey were cremated. He sent Mokey's ashes back to his parents so that they could give his brother a proper funeral and bury him in a dignified manner, if they wished. He explained in a letter how he'd killed his wife and apologized deeply for killing their beloved younger son. He promised to visit them when they got over their grief. He took a short lease on an apartment in Miami Beach, so he wouldn't have to face people he might meet daily in a hotel. There he took Nancy's ashes. He spent his days on the public beach, rarely speaking to anyone, swimming in the Atlantic swells that rolled up onto the sands, letting the sun and the salt air dry the wound on his forehead and the grief in his heart. In the evenings, after he'd eaten at a small Italian restaurant nearby, he sat alone in the apartment. Sometimes he practiced the dice with some straights he'd bought locally, and it had a soothing effect on him to exercise his skill. At other times he read the newspapers, or watched television, for news of Cuba and the progress of Castro's revolution. At other times he sat by Nancy's ashes, remembering the good times, regretful for the times that were lost forever.

Slowly his strength and his will returned. With it came the determination to break with the outfit—to regain the freedom and the individuality he'd bargained away so long ago.

The day he scattered Nancy's ashes on the sea in a lonesome, wistful ceremony was the day he knew he was fully recovered. It was time, he knew, to touch base.

The valley, torn and gashed by diggings around its mines and mills, was much the same, superficially, as he remembered it. But Steubenville had taken on an air of quiet domestication, as if having come of age and burned off the fever of its youth, it now looked, in maturity, to the outward trappings of civic pride for substance. Few signs remained of the bordellos and gambling houses of old, and, if they were there at all, they operated behind façades of commercial respectability. The Club was one of the few such establishments remaining. To the stranger, there was no apparent sign of its presence behind the plain doors of its frontage. These days it existed only to serve the recreational interests of a selected roster of members. The dim office at the rear had altered little, and it came as a shock to Tony to realize that the Duke was aging fast. He sat in the same chair, at the same roll-top desk, but now he was a white-haired old man, with withered shoulders, and only his eyes radiated the power Tony remembered so well.

The Duke reached out and touched the scar that ran across his forehead. "That looks bad," he said. "Maybe you should consider plastic surgery. It's not such a big deal these days—not like in my time."

"I'll think about it," he said. "Maybe later."

"A crazy thing to do, trying to fly an airplane."

"We had to get out of the place."

"I sent your mother and father a very nice wreath, with my condolences on the death of your brother," the Duke said carefully.

"Thank you," Tony said. "The old man's real cut up over Mokey. I don't think he's ever gonna get over losing him . . ." The tears welled up in his eyes and he swallowed hard.

"You need a drink." The Duke poured out two glasses from the bottle on his desk. Tony gulped the whiskey down and cleared his throat. "It's time for you to get back into harness again," the Duke went on. Tony started to speak, but the Duke held up his hand. "The Chairman's expecting you. Now that Cuba's gone, there's a lot of reorganizing to be done. There's been no deal with that guy Castro. Levin can't get to first base with him. He stole everything and there's not a goddamn thing we can do about it, other than start another revolution over there. The way Levin's feeling, maybe that's not so remote."

"We lost an important part of the organization," Tony said.

"Yeah, it hurts. There's no way of insuring against a revolution. But I suppose we'll take it in our stride; there's plenty of other opportunities around the Caribbean and different places. We're looking at other propositions right now. For the time being, it looks like Las Vegas is our ace in the hole."

Something in the Duke's words was puzzling him. He couldn't put his finger on it because he wasn't concentrating on what the Duke was saying. His mind was full of what he wanted to say himself. He needed the Duke's advice urgently. "Look, I gotta know what you think: I had it in my mind for some time, and now I'm sure. I want to break with the outfit. I'm stale—there's nothing there for me anymore."

The Duke's expression didn't alter. "It's only natural for a guy to get restless from time to time. You'll get over it. Maybe you need a complete change of scenery. Why don't you make a trip somewhere? Europe, maybe. You'll come back a new man, glad of what you got."

"I don't need a vacation. My mind's made up."

"Give it time, Tony."

"No—I want out."

The Duke was silent a long time before he turned to face him. For all the appearance of age, the intensity in his dark eyes hadn't dimmed. "Tony, you must know by now as well as anyone—there's no way out. No matter what. There's only a way in."

"Listen, I'm no Abe Carroll. I'll just fade outa sight. I won't be no great loss to the outfit."

"Lombardo reminded you when you talked this way before, the time the Winter Palace was being built—."

"How'd you get to know about that?" Tony cut in curiously.

"You were reminded that you once made a total commitment. I told you myself, at the beginning. There's no going back on that commitment."

"What the hell they want—my soul, too?" He couldn't keep his voice level.

"Yes. We own it. We bought it and we own it. Get that straight once and for all.

We own everything about you. If you got illusions about that, it's time you learned to forget 'em. You're no kid any longer."

We.

It burst over his head like a thunderclap: the notion that had been irritating him since their conversation began. Now that he'd got things off his chest, he could think more clearly. For the first time since he'd known him, in all these years, the Duke was openly admitting to being one of them. Not simply one of them, but a *we*. Which meant he was a member of the council. Tony had always guessed there were more members than those he knew of, and this instant, blinding revelation explained how the Duke was always aware of what was going down. It explained how the Duke was always able to guide him through the minefields of the council hierarchy so that he'd become a key man. How he'd known his exact motivation, and to what extent he could carry responsibility. His capabilities, down to the smallest degree.

In horror, he realized that it meant, in a lifetime of seeking the Duke's counsel, he'd always been guided in the direction that suited their purpose. That his career had been shaped quite deliberately by the Duke. That he'd been coldly trained—a neuter, a digit, a performing dog. And how long had this been going on? He thought back, and his blood ran to water as the reality of it all poured over him—the realization that he'd been procured as an adolescent, a mill-town kid with a talent for the dice.

His mentor.

The shriveled, despicable, white-haired old man sitting in the chair before him. The man to whom he'd entrusted his faith. Even, perhaps, his love. This man had taken his entire adult life and consumed it in deception—priming him, testing him, playing him as a fisherman plays a catch on the line.

In his blind rage, he was unaware that he was on his feet, screaming obscenities. He reached for the neck of the whiskey bottle and stood over that pitful figure in the chair. He raised the bottle over his head and prepared to bring it down with all the force he could muster.

The dark, liquid eyes he knew so well were staring back at him calmly, unblinking, *and utterly without fear*. Through the enormity of his anger, he found himself listening to the words formed by the Duke's thin, white lips: "I taught you to act, not react." The words scythed through the hate boiling in his heart. Still he held the bottle high, trembling, pouring silent vilification over the Duke's frail shoulders. "Tony, you always listened to me. Listen to me now. Don't do it—if you do, it will cost you your life."

After an eternity, slowly, and still trembling in every muscle, he lowered the bottle. His mind began to clear and he knew, through his terrible anger, his raging thirst for revenge, that a phenomenon had reached out to him from the man who had been his mentor throughout his adult consciousness. He knew now that the Duke had the nerve. The eyes told him. The quality that set Tony apart and had enabled him to use his skill with the dice to become a master mechanic. The old man had it, too.

He hadn't realized. It was what they had in common, and it was the quality the Duke had recognized in him right from the start.

320

The bottle fell from his trembling fingers to crash and splinter on the floor. Without another word, he turned and walked out of The Club.

If oblivion was to be found, then somewhere, somehow, he would find it.

EPILOGUE

The travel-stained Plymouth turned off Highway 50 into the parking area of The Waggoners Roadhouse, a few miles outside Kansas City, Missouri. It creaked wearily to a stop. The driver killed the motor, then sat perfectly still for five minutes, seemingly staring at nothing in particular. An astute observer might have noticed that his eyes strayed occasionally to the rearview mirror. After five minutes, he got out of the car, entered the roadhouse, and walked up to the bar. He sat on a stool and ordered a beer.

The barman, an aware sort of guy, noticed that the man was a stranger, that he was correct in his mannerisms and gave an impression of neatness, although his box-fresh white shirt was casually open at the neck. He also surmised that the strange mark on the traveler's forehead, transparently whiter than the surrounding pink flesh, probably concealed what had once been an ugly scar. The stranger finished his beer, gave the barman a five-dollar bill, and told him to keep the change. He then intimated he'd heard there was sometimes a crap game in the back, and he was feeling lucky tonight. The barman, who was experienced in these things, and could smell a cop a mile off, felt quite safe in inclining his head toward the back of the room. As the stranger approached the blue door, the barman pressed a button beneath his counter that operated a buzzer in the back room. Behind the blue door a crap game was in progress over a professional East Coast layout. The stranger's eyes flicked across it, taking in everything about the stickman in a single glance. He produced four hundred dollars and joined the game. His bets were unambitious, and he lost consistently until half his stake was gone. Then, when he was shooter, in apparent disgust at his poor luck, he put his entire remaining roll down on a turkey hard-way bet that came up roses, doubling his original stake. Happy now with this change in his fortune, he confined the rest of his gambling to a few unsuccessful ten-dollar bets. He appeared about ready to leave, taking with him a three-hundred-dollar profit, when a second stranger came in through the blue door. He walked across to the crap table and stood by the first man. After a few minutes it was clear that, although the first man had not turned to glance directly at the newcomer, he was aware of his presence. The first man straightened his shoulders slowly, as if a weight were lifted from them.

"You're a hard guy to find, Tony," Tom Druccio said quietly.

"Yeah . . ."

"How's things?"

"Ah, O.K., I guess."

"You had me chasing through every goddamn tank town in the Midwest."

"I did a little mileage," Tony admitted.

"I nearly caught up with you, that time over in Canada."

"I didn't know that."

"I was ten minutes behind you. Blew a tire."

"Too bad."

"We can't talk here."

"Let's go outside. I'll buy you a beer."

They sat on stools at one end of the bar, out of earshot of the barman. "It's time to make up your mind, Tony. It's your last chance to decide if you're in or out," Tom said.

"Gonna be you who knocks me off, Tom?"

"Nah, not me. I don't handle that work anymore. I moved up." He gave a small grin.

"So what you doing here?"

"I volunteered to find you. The way I see it—they send out the dogs, there's only one way it's gonna end up." He was silent a moment. "I figure maybe you need a friend to talk to."

"You still a friend, Tom?"

"Oh, sure. I got nothing personal against you, you know that. You always treated me with respect. I don't forget."

"Thanks."

"Ain't you tired of running, Tony?"

He was desperately tired. Of looking back over his shoulder. Of hiding away in sleazy hotels. Of skinning dumb fucks in backwoods crap joints. He'd been careful each time to take no more money than he needed to see him through to the next hideout. The bush telegraph was very efficient, he knew—a high roller with a permanent sign on his forehead would rapidly become a marked man. And he missed the power—the glamour, the excitement of the carpet joints.

Tom was speaking again. "I told 'em back there, maybe by now you got over the death of your wife and your brother."

"I'm feeling a lot better these days."

"You ready to come back, now?"

"Yes, I'm ready to come back."

He must have shaken a dozen hands on his way through the Winter Palace. In the elevator, as it rose toward the Czarina Suite, he examined his reflection critically in the mirrors. He looked older, a little thinner perhaps. But the bearing was still there; the power radiating from his position as a senior member of the outfit was written all over him. He felt fit, and crisp and fresh in the dark, finely cut business suit.

Levin waited for him, alone. He came forward and embraced Tony in the style he usually reserved for members of the council. "Good to have you back, Tony," he said simply.

"It's good to be back," Tony said sincerely. "I can't tell you how good." He added, as an afterthought, "I have to apologize for wasting so much of your time."

322

"Growing pains." Levin shrugged it off. "Are you ready to go to work, now? I need you badly."

"Just name it."

"There's a lot going on. I'm not going to discuss Vegas with you right now—just take a look around, it speaks for itself."

"I saw, on the way in."

"I got other plans. We need to expand."

"Here?"

"No, Vegas is off and running. I'm talking about Europe. England. London is opening up for gambling."

Tony gave a low whistle. "That's news."

"Do you understand what I'm implying?"

"I think so."

"We set up in London, then we use it as a base to move out into Europe. There's a lot of potential. It could be the biggest deal yet."

Tony nodded. "It's an important step forward for us."

"Exactly. That's why I'm putting one of my most trusted people in there to handle it."

"Who's that?"

"You. I'm putting our expansion into Europe in your hands. You'll be answerable only to me personally."

Thinking about Levin's immense faith in him, the tears stung his eyes. He cleared his throat. "I don't know what to say."

"This is what we brought you along for, Tony. Something big as this."

He was too choked up to reply.

"There's something else."

"Yes?"

"From now on, you're on your own. It's no longer necessary for you to, ah, touch base."

He smiled his enigmatic half-smile, and Tony understood.

I. G. Broat was born into the poverty of London's East End between World Wars I and II. He remembers wanting to write from the age of eight. Subsequently educated at London University, he has since always been his own employer, but found irksome any business activity that left him little time to write. He has now accepted the inevitable and writes full time.